Zara Stoneley is the *USA To*  *Wedding Date*.

She lives in a Cheshire villa[...] cockapoo called Harry, and a very bossy (and slightly evil) cat called Saffron.

Zara's bestselling novels include *The First Date*, *Four Christmases and a Secret*, *No One Cancels Christmas*, *The Wedding Date*, *The Holiday Swap*, *Summer with the Country Village Vet* and the popular Tippermere series.

www.zarastoneley.com

twitter.com/ZaraStoneley
facebook.com/ZaraStoneley
instagram.com/zarastoneley

Also by Zara Stoneley

Standalones

Summer of Surrender

Love is a 4 Letter Word

The Holiday Swap

The Wedding Date

No One Cancels Christmas

Bridesmaids

Four Christmases and a Secret

The First Date

The Dog Sitter

The Tippermere Series

Stable Mates

Country Affairs

Country Rivals

The Little Village on the Green Series

Summer with the Country Village Vet

Blackberry Picking at Jasmine Cottage

HOT DESK

ZARA STONELEY

One More Chapter
a division of HarperCollins*Publishers*
1 London Bridge Street
London SE1 9GF

www.harpercollins.co.uk

HarperCollins*Publishers*
1st Floor, Watermarque Building, Ringsend Road
Dublin 4, Ireland

This paperback edition 2021
1
First published in Great Britain in ebook format
by HarperCollins*Publishers* 2021

A catalogue record of this book is available from the British Library

ISBN: 978-0-00-843627-8

Printed and bound in the UK using 100% Renewable Electricity
by CPI Group (UK) Ltd

MIX
Paper from
responsible sources
FSC™ C007454

FSC
www.fsc.org

This book is produced from independently certified FSC™ paper
to ensure responsible forest management.

For more information visit: www.harpercollins.co.uk/green

For Alice, my wonderful niece

Chapter One

This could be the worst day of my life ever. And I mean *ever*. Worse than the day I gave up my seat to a 'pregnant lady' who was on her way to slimming club, worse than the day I battered a guy with my oversize tote bag for shouting 'love your puppies' in my ear, when he was actually talking to a woman with two cute dogs walking behind me, even worse than the school prom when I walked the entire length of the hall dressed in my posh frock, with a *very long trail* of toilet paper stuck to my heel. Or the time I went up what has to be the steepest escalator on the London Underground with my skirt stuck in my knickers and laughed when some bright spark shouted out 'mind the thigh gap' because I still didn't realize. Oh my God that one was bad.

But I didn't feel sick then, I just felt embarrassed and a bit (okay, a lot) stupid. Right now, I feel slightly sick, and very sweaty.

Never read emails on your way to work, especially if you are running late. My mobile beeps, and I fumble, nearly dropping it from my clammy hands.

Where the F are you, Al??? Haven't you seen the email?!! Lou x

On the bus, running late. Yep, seen it. What do you think? Alice x

Disaster. Must be serious. Room is too small for everybody, we don't all f*g fit! We need to talk – hurry up!

How can I be late to the meeting that could ruin my life? Lou is not a doom and gloom kind of person. She normally looks on the bright side, finds positives. Before I get a chance to type a reply, there's another message. *This effing downturn in the economy has lost me 3 of my clients in the last month, any of yours gone tits up?* Some of Lou's messages are abbreviated and take some working out – this one doesn't.

My heart starts to hammer harder as I type. *A few are on hold.*

Perma-hold? Get your arse in here, quick!

Trying!!! Shit they can't shut the company down, can they?

Gah. This is so unfair; this can't be happening. Not now. Living in lockdown hell is finally supposed to be over.

I need my job; I need to be back in the office. I need normal. They promised us normal!

It was fun to be able to work at home for a few weeks. I didn't even mind balancing my laptop on my knee and wearing noise-cancelling headphones to block out my housemates and joking about the commute to the kitchen. Hilarious. Because we'd all be back to normal after a few weeks, wouldn't we?

Then coronavirus didn't go away and the weeks stretched to months, and even more months, and it started to wear a bit thin. Okay, it got bloody depressing, impossible to concentrate, and, well, frustrating. There was nobody to bounce ideas off. Just interruptions. Constant interruptions. People wandering in and out, borrowing stuff, asking questions. Arghhh.

I wanted my desk back soooo desperately. My own little space. My lovely work area, being surrounded by all the bits and bobs that make me feel good and inspire me. Instead of a cramped room in a noisy house, where the most exciting feature was a damp patch in the corner, which I swear has grown.

It was really doing my head in. The nothingness, not the damp patch.

I would have gone into the office and collected some of my stuff, except people would have messed with it at home and wound me up even more.

What's that about? Why can't people leave things alone?

Oh my God, the day I got the email confirming we'd be back in the office two weeks later was a-ma-zing! I couldn't stop grinning.

It wasn't just my tiny room that was the problem. I missed the buzz of the office; I missed my colleagues. Even the annoying ones.

I even missed sitting on this bus. Weird, eh? I glance around self-consciously. Very weird.

It was so good to be back that I kind of dismissed the emails that started on practically day one of the office reopening. The ones highlighting the reduction in business. The ones asking for voluntary redundancies, mentioning streamlining, slimming, working more effectively and efficiently; all of those things that you try and ignore. We all did it. *Pah, they can't mean me.* Delete, delete, delete.

We're back! Everything is going to be normal again.

I glance at the time on my mobile. OMG I am *SO* going to be late. Being late to the meeting could also be a sackable offence. Unless we're all going to be sacked anyway.

I gaze out of the window, trying to enjoy the scenery. Not happening. The bus is going so slowly that the people scurrying along the pavement are moving faster than I am, dodging puddles and hanging on to umbrellas and their coat hoods. It's drizzling with rain. A steady, depressing, soaking drizzle.

I might still be on the dry bus, but I've come out in a cold sweat, the back of my neck clammy. The palms of my hands, now pressed together, sticky.

This not knowing, this sense of dread is worse than working for months on end at home. Well maybe not. That really was the pits.

It's not normal, is it? Having to work on your own and only see colleagues over a dodgy internet connection, with their faces green or blue-tinged, depending on the type of lighting they've got.

The thing I missed most of all was my desk though, all the little knick-knacks I've collected somehow spark off ideas in my head. I didn't realize how important they were, until I had to spend months away from the office, and I know it sounds crazy, but when I'm sitting at my desk, I feel like I can breathe. It's mine. A space I can escape to.

At work, nobody moves or borrows my stuff. The stuff crammed full of memories that make me happy. And when I'm happy I'm creative. I can touch the smooth cool surface of the special pebble I picked up on a beach and remember that moment, that feeling of freedom, I can remember the perfect blue of the sky and know that it will work magically on the website I'm designing. Be confident that it will lift people's spirits and make them want to buy the candles that are being advertised.

Yeah, I'd found the perfect colour scheme for that one, and then it was one of the accounts that was put on hold.

I try and relax my face, chase away the frown that I know is forming. But the candle company went, are we next?

I can't go back to homeworking. I just can't face it. Not again. Even worse, I can't lose my job.

Somebody plonks themselves down on the seat next to me. Their arm jammed against mine. Dampness seeps through my sleeve.

Just how bad is this day going to get?

I always used to love my journey in on the bus. But when we returned to the office it seemed slightly strange to sit on public transport every day, squashed up against a load of strangers. The first day I'd felt nervous, twitchy, but the anticipation and excitement had faded the moment I'd taken my seat. It soon started to feel normal again. By the end of that first week I'd started to chill, I'd gone back to enjoying the journey.

That first day has nothing on today though. Today the fluttering in my stomach is worse than when I've been going for an interview.

This meeting could change everything. *Everything*. I could be jobless and homeless. Well, back to living with Mum and Dad, and sharing a room with my sister Sophie. OMG I can't do that, I just can't. But people are firing, not hiring, aren't they?

'Sorry, love.'

I blink at the woman sitting next to me and force myself to stop thinking the worse. 'No probs.' I smile, then wish I hadn't when she takes off her hat and gives it a good shake.

Why do things like this happen to me? If I hadn't checked Insta just as I was leaving home, I wouldn't have seen the photo my sister Soph put up last night, and I wouldn't have seen my favourite dress looking better on her than it does me. I had to message her. Like you do.

Have you got something you need to tell me, Soph? A x

I've been looking for that bloody dress for ages. I'd started to think I must have accidentally sent it to the charity shop. When you've got as little cupboard space as me you can't afford to keep excess clothes. This dress isn't excess though. It is essential. Every girl needs at least one dress that disguises their stomach and manages not to make their calves look fat. It is *exactly* the right length. Hiding my knees but sitting just above the bulge of my calves.

No, why? What? Sxxx

Dress? Last night? Insta?

My phone rang just as I was grabbing my coat and keys. 'Shit, Alice. I asked, didn't I? I meant to, but, oh yeah, I know, you were late back from work.' It was bound to be my fault. 'So I reckoned it would be okay to have a quick look through your stuff while I was waiting, cos I knew you wouldn't mind. Zoe said she thought it looked fantastic on me, she even curled my hair for me so I could get a proper idea. She's ace, you're so lucky sharing a place with a hairdresser; she's awesome, much better than the girls at the place where I normally go.' Sophie is always like this, lots and lots of words, and energy, and fun. It's totally impossible to stay cross with her. Which is why she gets away with so much. It's always been the same – the baby of the family, the one who had new not hand-me-downs because by the time they'd been worn by number three (me) they were too shabby.

'Any chance you can wash it before you put it back this time, Soph?' I tried not to sigh. Soph takes the attitude 'what's yours is mine, and what's mine is my own'. She went absolutely ballistic when one of our other sisters, Darcie, borrowed her hair straighteners without asking and didn't put them back. Apparently, they were 'special'. Hmmm. Maybe I need to go ballistic as well from time to time, although that would upset her, and I hate upset and arguments, and is it really worth it?

'Sure, no probs. Shouldn't you be at work, big sis?'

'I'm on my way.' That was when I'd glanced at my phone and nearly panicked. 'I'm late, oh shit, I'm really late.'

'You? Late? Never.' She had laughed.

Which meant I missed the train, and there wasn't one another for ages, so I jumped on the bus instead.

Mistake. Even on a good day I'd be cutting it fine catching this bus. On a rainy day, when the traffic is slow and everybody who normally walks has decided to drive, or catch the bus, there's no chance.

I actually don't like being late. Even when there isn't a very important meeting. I love going into work. I loved it even before our home-working stint, but I love it even more now.

I mean, it isn't the perfect job, and I know I'm not doing anything world-shatteringly important or will ever become a billionaire, and there are days when I'm jealous as hell that somebody has got a promotion and I haven't, and some of my co-workers do get on my tits if I'm honest, and some days the work is dull and nothing goes right and it's pretty shite. But Monday to Friday at work can still be better than Saturday and Sunday at home when I'm stuck in the tiniest room in our shared house, trying to ignore calls from my ex (who I'm trying really hard to resist, because it would be too easy to just fall back into our old bad-for-me relationship) and trying to find out who borrowed (and spilt something sticky down) my fav black top and who has scoffed the last slice of leftover pizza that I'd put in the fridge and was really looking forward to.

Those bits were a hundred times worse when I was there 24/7. Oh my God, resisting the urge to phone Dave when I was feeling down was a nightmare – but I've managed. So far. My fingers are twitching to call him now and ask him what he thinks about the email. I'm sure he'll reassure me. But I can't. I must not.

And don't get me started on the subject of the last Hobnob in the packet, or the half a bar of chocolate I'd struggled to resist as it was going to be my reward for sticking to one glass of wine.

See? It's not just a dress, or Hobnob, that's the issue here. People are always borrowing my stuff, nothing is my own. Nothing has changed from when I was a kid.

I grew up in a crowded, noisy house. I mean it was nice, but with four kids and two adults, plus various pets and friends constantly dropping round, it was hard to make yourself heard – let alone actually listened to. And I didn't

9

even have a bedroom of my own to escape to. I shared it with Sophie, my sister. You see, I was *born* having to share.

When we were kids, Soph never quite got the hang of hers and mine. It was brilliant when I moved into my own place. Until she started dropping by and I realized nothing had changed. In fact, it had got worse, because my boyfriend and all my housemates decided that I didn't mind sharing. Everything.

But my desk at work is different. My desk is my own personal space. My *only* private space. The only thing in the world that is really mine and nobody messes with. What am I going to do if I lose that?

At work I am a different person to the Alice I am at home. Not in a schizophrenic way, just in a personal space and boundaries way. I say home, but, I have to admit, my place doesn't feel like home. It's just a place to be when I'm not at work.

Even this commute, when I can daydream in peace, or people-watch feels even more precious now.

Well, obviously I'm not enjoying the commute today, because two minutes after running to catch the bus and collapsing onto my seat I'd opened my emails and found out that my lovely resurrected Monday to Friday life is about to be shattered. Again.

I just know it is.

I open up Insta again, to try and distract myself from *that* email (I mean, *all staff*, are we *all* going to be sacked?), and the snail pace of the bus and the fact that I really, really want to rub at my damp coat sleeve and check whether the water has seeped through, but it would be rude and the woman sitting next to me seems quite nice. Just very soggy.

Insta might not be a good idea right now. There's another photo of Soph. This time in my favourite jumpsuit.

The woman next to me shifts about and nearly knocks my mobile phone out of my hand. Okay, so looking at emails is a bad idea, looking at Insta is a bad idea.

I text Soph. *Do you want to buy that dress off me? I think I'm about to be sacked, so I'll need the money.*

Her reply pings back almost instantly. *What do you mean you're about to be sacked? You don't get sacked for being late! S xxx*

I might not be, it's just a daft email. We've got a meeting at 9, ignore me. A x

Don't worry, it'll be fine! S xxx Soph never worries, she thrives on chaos.

Yeah, sure you're right. A x. Okay, so Soph can be annoying, but she's good at knowing the right thing to say to me.

You are kidding though, aren't you? S xxx She can also tell when I'm worried. We're close (and not just because she wears my clothes); we grew up sharing secrets as well as a room – well the secrets bit happened after I found her reading my diary and realized that it was impossible to keep things from her.

If I kept a diary now, which I don't, I'd keep it at work. My Sophie-free zone.

I slip the phone into my pocket, lean my head against the damp, condensation-ridden window and try and be calm about this.

I can't make the bus go faster, and I can't do anything about the email. This meeting is going to happen. What can I do? I think I'll just close my eyes and rehearse my leaving speech.

And I can't stop the flutter of anticipation in my chest.

Is this what a heart attack feels like?

Why are they doing this on a Thursday? Is it so they've got Friday to clean up the office and burn our desks?

Chapter Two

I am a hot, sweaty, soggy mess, and I'm pretty sure my hair is plastered against my head from leaning against the damp window of the bus.

If my career is about to end, this is not the final impression I want to make. I want to look professional, cool and calm. Not like some disorganised mess that nobody would have ever wanted to employ in the first place.

I glance at my watch – aha, things aren't as bad as I thought! I'm not actually late, I've got nine minutes, plenty of time to go to the ladies and sort myself out. If the stupid idiot in front of me will hurry up and swipe his pass so that I can get out of reception and into the lifts.

He searches through his pockets again. Then balances his bag on the barrier and opens it up, oh so carefully.

It's too late to say, 'Excuse me, shift out of my way, I'm in a hurry!' I mean, why aren't people organized, why don't they have their pass in their hand? They do this every day!

He clicks the case shut, mis-swipes, swipes again and

finally plods through. I resist the urge to give him a shove, and instead reach up for *my* pass, which is dangling round my neck.

'Oh shit.' Why is my office pass not hanging around my neck? 'Shit!' I clutch lower down, as though it might have dived between my boobs. I open the neck of my jacket wider and peer inside.

Somebody behind me coughs. *So rude! Can't they wait? Why is everybody so bloody impatient these days?*

'Do you mind if…' A woman in ridiculously high heels and hair that is far too sleek to be real waves her pass in the air in a very pointed, rude way.

Oh my God, I can't step aside. I'm going to be late! 'I've got to get to the ladies!'

She raises an eyebrow.

'My hair, my coat,' I wave an all-encompassing hand. 'I need to sort my make-up, I might get sacked!'

A mini-queue forms as I shove my hand into my stupidly big tote bag and delve around blindly as though it's a game of hunt the prize in a box full of shredded paper.

Oh no! This is *so* not fair. I stare at the solid barrier. When I started work here it was one of those turnstile affairs that you could climb over the top of in an emergency. Now it is stupid glass sliding doors that aren't sliding. The gap between them is way too narrow even for a stick insect type of girl – which I am not.

It's never done this before. It has never refused my entry. I've never forgotten my pass before.

This is because I was talking to Soph about stupid, stupid clothes that don't matter at all. When I grab my keys,

I always pick up my pass at the same time. The keys go in my bag, the pass round my neck. I have a routine. Or I did.

Feeling like an idiot I slope over to the main reception desk.

'Can you let me in please?'

The receptionist smiles in that professional way that means it is not a smile at all. Where do they learn to do that? 'You need a pass.'

Don't sigh, do not sigh, you'll make it worse. Smile. I smile and talk through gritted teeth. 'I know I need a pass, but I think I've left it at home and…'

'You need your pass. I can't just let you in or what would be the point of having a barrier?'

Normally this wouldn't matter. Normally I would humour her. Today is different. 'But can't you give me a visitor pass?'

'I can't just hand out passes to *everybody*, can I? Doesn't that kind of defeat the whole object of the barriers?' She rolls her eyes.

'But you know me,' I hesitate, 'Melissa!' At least I think that's what her name badge says. Melissa hasn't been here long; they have a big turnover on reception, but I'm sure she *must* recognise me. I've said hello to her, I shared a sympathy eye-roll when she was being verbally abused by somebody she wouldn't let in the building. Ha. Last time I do that.

'I need to get in quick, please.' I have my hands together, I am begging. Melissa is filing her nails. 'It's urgent. I'm going to be late for an important meeting. Just this once, please.'

'You can't just *have* a visitor pass; you need to be signed in.'

'Fine.' It is not fine. It is humiliating. I never forget my pass. I never have to be signed in. But I am desperate.

She taps her nails on the keyboard. 'Company?'

'We Got Designs,' I say glumly, peering into my bag again. Maybe I dropped my pass in there with my keys.

'Name?'

I glance up at her and frown. 'We Got...oh, you mean me, Alice. Alice Dixon.'

I cannot believe this is happening to me.

She sighs heavily as though I am a massive inconvenience. 'I'll call your office and get somebody to come down and sign you in.'

'It's okay, I'll call.' I'm clicking on Lou's name in my phone as I speak.

Mel glares. 'It's my job. Take a seat.'

Oh pur-lease, as though I've got time to sit down. 'I'll stand, I'm sure they won't be long.' I try not to jiggle on the spot. I've already wasted two whole minutes, well three now. Why can't she call them faster? Why wouldn't she let me? I glance at my watch. Four. Nearly four minutes.

'Problem, Mel?'

I freeze at the sound of a deep voice, stare fixedly ahead at the sign behind Mel's head. The only part of me that is moving is the nervous flutter in the base of the stomach, and I really wish it would stop. Great. This is all I need. This day has just got even worse, if that is possible.

I'd know that voice anywhere. Why does it have to be Jamie, who has been sent down to sign me in?

I force myself to relax and smile. It's probably more of a grimace. Not that Melissa would notice. She's too busy grinning and batting her supersized eyelashes.

'Not anymore, Jamie!' Yep, Jamie Lowe. She sighs and rests her chin on her hand. 'You're such a hero.'

'Causing trouble again, Alice?' His warm hand comes down on my shoulder and I can't help it. I jump. Even though I know he's there, even though it's like I can feel the warmth of his body. The flutter inside me spreads. The back of my neck prickles. I feel all shaky.

'Nope!' I squeak out. 'Just forgot my pass.'

I daren't turn around and look at him until I've got my face in order, which isn't going to happen while he's touching me, while I've got palpitations and am wishing the ground would swallow me up.

Dealing with the humiliation of forgetting my pass and having to grovel to Mel is nothing compared to this.

Jamie is the one who will tease me about this, he is the most annoying person who works for We Got Designs.

Oh yeah, and he is also the one I snogged on some wild drunken impulse in my first year of uni and didn't even swap names with, and never thought I'd see again.

It was at the Reading Festival. The one and only time I've been, and it was a-ma-zing. I went with a couple of mates. We were high on the whole buzz of the place, magnified by the lager we'd been knocking back from plastic pint glasses all day. It was crazy, exhilarating, the freedom, the music, the singing and swaying to any act that came on whether they were out of this world or a bit crap. It didn't matter. We were elated – adrenalin, alcohol and burgers keeping us going until the early hours.

Thinking about it now still sends a shiver through me. The roar as they announced the headline act on the main stage. We'd been waiting all day for this moment. The whole crowd surged forward, people colliding good-naturedly, jostling for position, and before I could react, we were body-slammed together. Me and this gorgeous guy I'd never seen before.

Our gazes locked, and something bubbled up inside me as I stared into those blue-grey eyes. He grinned and I found myself grinning back, and the world around us stopped moving. My whole body tingled at the touch of his hand on the bare skin at my waist and our lips met as though it was meant to be.

Then the band hit the opening note of the track, and the crowd surged again, tearing us apart.

He was gone. Swallowed up by the swaying bodies. Lost for ever.

I danced with my mates until way beyond when the band packed up, we danced round the tents, sat by fires, talked to strangers, made new friends. But I never found the stranger I'd snogged.

Until I started my new job at We Got Designs. The same day that Jamie did.

I walked into the meeting room for our introductory chat, jittery as hell, and my eyes were kind of drawn to this one guy. There were four of us, but he was the one with this quiet confidence, and his genuine smile as I sat down kind of reassured me. I had this instant slight crush on him – because he was dishy. And nice.

And I had this instant feeling that we'd met before.

He was gorgeous in a casual, laid-back, cheeky kind of way, so I couldn't help myself – I kept glancing his way. Taking in the cute dimples, the way his mouth lifted at the corner, the mussed-up hair that was strangely familiar. He was, is, everything my boyfriend at the time, Dave, wasn't. You'd never have called Dave devil-may-care, or fun-loving.

I didn't recognize him that first day. I guess part of the reason was that he was dressed in a smart first-day-at-work suit, that his hair was shorter, neater. I'd never heard that deep voice of his before, and I was full of first-day nerves, trying to impress, and another part of the reason was that there was absolutely no sign of recognition on his side. Not even a flicker.

When it did finally dawn on me where I thought I'd seen him before I decided I must have got it wrong. He must just *look like* that other guy (okay, I admit, I only looked at him fleetingly before the kiss and in my inebriated state my memory might not match reality). It was a bit disappointing, to be honest. A doppelganger. But, hey, I was rather proud of the fact that although I'd been drunk, that guy must actually have been quite dishy if Jamie reminds me of him.

So I reckoned it couldn't be my festival guy, I didn't think I was being snubbed – or at least I convinced myself it wasn't true.

I was wrong. It was true, Jamie had been my drunken snog.

Snogging a complete stranger is not the type of thing I normally do; I had never, ever done it in my life before, or since. So that bit is mortifying, but what is worse is that he was so drunk HE DOESN'T REMEMBER ME.

Which I realized at about the time things got even worse.

Not long after we started working together, two years ago, there was a staff party and we came into very close contact and IT NEARLY HAPPENED AGAIN!

I was tipsy again but, hey, don't judge.

That was when the first time really came flooding back, to me, though obviously not to him.

Second time round wasn't much different to first time, if I'm honest, so you'd think that would bloody jog his memory! I was a bit merry, he was definitely at least two pints down, and we crossed paths when I was weaving my way back from the ladies, and he was staggering to the gents. We did that silly excuse-me dance trying to get past each other in the narrow corridor and ended up both going for it at the same time, and our bodies collided. And he touched me. And his gorgeous blue-grey eyes stared straight into mine. And I knew IT WAS HIM. I was also sure he recognized me. I was sure he remembered. It was as if we both knew this would happen one day. He tilted his head and his mouth was so bloody close to mine, that it was like the first time all over again. Oh my God, it was déjà vu.

We were going to kiss, and this time there was no crowd to drag us apart.

'Hey, you.' The hairs on my arms prickled as the deep, soft tone sent a shiver through my body.

'Hey.' It came out all breathless. My breath quickened; my pulse practically jumped out of my wrist. Wow, he smelled good. Even better than the first time. I leaned in even closer. His fingers danced on my waist and sent a very indecent tremor right to my knickers.

But it felt so right. So natural. So meant to be. This was it. This was the moment I'd been waiting for.

I wanted that kiss so much my whole body was aching for it. Even though it was wrong for so many reasons. Like, for one I had a boyfriend, two, I've always thought dating people you work with has to be the worst idea ever (what happens when you split up? Or you feel all hot and randy for each other while you're at the water cooler, or somebody notices, or you both just feel smug because you've had the most romantic weekend ever, or you hate each other because you've argued over something stupid. Awkward with a capital A, hey?), and, three, I had absolutely no idea if Jamie was single or not. Oh, and I should have also been pissed about the fact that he hadn't remembered me until now. But hey, you can forgive some things. I hadn't been a hundred per cent sure myself until now.

I was going to kiss him even if there were a zillion reasons why I shouldn't, because he was so bloody hot, this whole situation was so bloody sexy. I wanted him. I couldn't help myself as that first time came flooding back to me.

Even now, just remembering, I am gooey inside and

want to close my eyes to help me taste it, and I'm pretty sure I've got a silly grin on my face.

Anyway, we were millimetres away from some serious lip-mashing, in fact our mouths might have touched – it's a bit hazy – and some drunken idiot barged into us shouting, 'Hey, Jamie, waddya fucking about at? It's your round, dipshit!' and sent him staggering away.

What is *wrong* with people?

He wasn't exactly swallowed up by the crowd this time, but he did lurch off into the gents, with the other guy draped all over him, which amounted to pretty much the same thing.

I went back to the people I'd been chatting to but watched out for him coming back from the gents. My heart was pounding in anticipation, a smile ready to break across my face. He would come over. We'd do this. This time it would happen.

I'd find out if that amazing kiss was just my imagination, or for real.

But he didn't even glance my way, just headed straight across the bar and was waylaid by some girl who I vaguely recognised.

Git.

It was horrible. Gutting. Even worse because I'd had a few drinks. I felt a total idiot and torn between tearful and wanting to go and tip a pint over his head. But even as my stomach twisted, I told myself I was being stupid.

I'd got a boyfriend now. That first time was just a drunken snog, and this time it was just a drunken nearly snog. We'd just bumped into each other and I'd thought about doing it without thinking. Obviously, a bad habit on both our sides.

Gah, what was wrong with me?

The first time was only a two-second lip mash, not some romantic, full-on 'I fancy the fuck out of you' kiss and this was even less. I should be glad he didn't come back looking for me. That would have been wrong, stupid.

Next time I saw him he was in a corner with the girl – Claire from HR, so I turned my back and tuned back into Lou and one of her outrageous stories, and was very, very careful not to look over there again.

He'd left the bar by the time I plucked up the courage to casually glance his way again – so I spent the rest of the evening imagining him and *Claire* in a lip-clinch. Or worse: a leg-lock.

I shouldn't have looked; I know I shouldn't. But I couldn't help it.

I shouldn't have hated him either. But I did.

———

The next time I saw him at work the anger had gone. Instead I was burning up with awkwardness and nervous as hell about what to say. I did toy with 'remember Reading Festival?' Then I'd considered an 'is that what they call speed dating' approach, then I decided he might think I was having a go at him for talking to another girl after me. So I moved on to a 'that could have been a hot snog' yuk, that sounded leery and like it should be accompanied by a wink. *So* not me. I even thought about an apology, adding that I didn't normally do that kind of thing, and I had a boyfriend, and I didn't think you should date workmates, but I know he wasn't suggesting we date or anything. Obviously. It all got pretty complicated in my head, so who knows how bad it would have sounded out loud.

So, I just plucked up enough courage to look him in the eye and say a breezy 'morning' when I walked in. And had to sit down opposite him.

You have no idea how hard that was. I'd spent the whole journey in trying to work out what to say when I saw him, rehearsing my lines.

I got a casual 'hi' back as though I was just anybody. Well, nobody.

He hardly even looked at me, just treated me like the girl at the next desk (which I am), or an annoying sister (which I am most definitely not). No flicker of recognition or attraction, no apologies or demands for a follow up. Nothing.

Absolutely nothing. What can be worse than that?

I mean, hey, why would he remember kissing a drunken girl in wellies, T-shirts and denim shorts in a muddy field? The place was full of them.

But how can you nearly kiss somebody twice and not remember?

And I was so sure I saw recognition in his eyes. So sure.

Half an hour later the girl I'd seen him talking to in the bar sauntered up to his desk and got the full-on charm.

I felt sick.

After that it got worse. I couldn't stop thinking about the fleeting pressure of his lips on mine, and how a proper kiss would feel. He didn't know I existed and was probably thinking about how his night of passion (yeah, I'm sure it went to that) with Claire went.

I was all worked up. Fizzing and fuming as I logged on to my computer and hammered away at the keyboard.

It didn't get any better. I saw him talking to her a few times. But with me he just upped the teasing and winding me up. Our kiss and nearly-kiss had obviously never existed as far as he was concerned. He'd been drunk. He'd forgotten. He hadn't forgotten Claire though.

Claire left the company a *looong* couple of months later, which meant at least I didn't have to watch them together, and I was just the girl at the next desk that he liked to take the piss out of.

The worst part about all of this though, is that *I* can't forget it. Not the embarrassment, but the fact that those brief moments when he touched me were so bloody *hot*. It wasn't just the warmth of his mouth, the heat of his fingers that burned through my clothes so that the touch felt like we were naked – it was the way my whole body kind of jumped to attention and said *hello* in a way that has never, ever, happened before. Or since. With Dave.

It was scary. But nice. I couldn't stop grinning, and bringing my finger up to my lips (weird, to check they were still there?) and grinning (yeah I know I already said that), and feeling all quivery inside.

It also made me feel guilty. Dave and I had always had a bit of an on-off relationship. He's always there at the end of the phone if I need him, but he's not always there for a hug. It's like he holds back, dates are on his terms, and the promise in that clinch with Jamie kind of made me see what I really want. I want that, not what I've had with Dave.

Except it isn't real. And Dave is.

But if I could feel that way about just being touched by Jamie, was it right to carry on? Was I being unfaithful?

Anyhow, after the clinch I decided I wasn't being faithful, so we split up. And then some shit happened, and I rang him, and he said exactly the right thing, and he came round, and this *was* real life and nice and safe, so we got back together again for a bit.

Until I started to feel like somebody he took for granted again.

But then he'll do something sweet when I'm feeling down, and it's hard to walk away.

We're not together right now. After he more or less said I wasn't important enough to be in his Covid bubble of six so we couldn't have sex for the foreseeable, I decided enough was enough. Not because of the no-sex, just because I don't think he's good for me. Even if he does know how to cheer me up or say the right thing when I'm feeling lonely or fed-up.

Whatever, he doesn't make me feel like Jamie did, and he doesn't make me feel like I really matter.

The past few months without Dave (a record length of time) or seeing Jamie (probably for the best) has been weird.

In a way it was a relief when we were sent home to work. I didn't have to see Jamie every day – the avoiding eye contact thing had started to get a bit painful and totally embarrassing. It had been nearly twelve months since the corridor-bump, how ridiculous is that? I was pretty sure though that by the time the office doors reopened I'd have gotten over him, or he'd have left, or something.

Didn't happen.

He even showered me with a party popper on the first day back, just to make sure I didn't miss the fact he was there. Ha, no chance of that.

The moment I walked back into the office and sat down opposite him it was as though I'd never been away. He grinned his boyish grin and the same old flutter started up in my stupid body. The memory of that kiss was in my head the second his gaze met mine, my stomach was full of butterflies and I was aching to feel the touch of his hand on my waist again.

I have had dreams of pressing my body against his like some sex-starved loony and begging for more. It is so flaming embarrassing. I've never begged for more! I really need to work out how to regain control of my body when he's in the vicinity.

I haven't had a similar problem over not seeing Dave.

I suddenly realize that my fingers are on my lips. This is ridiculous. So is the fact that I've not wanted to look him in the eye, in case he can see how I feel – which is difficult when he sits opposite me. He probably thinks I'm rude and stuck up.

And *that* is why I'm not happy he's the one that has been sent down to sign me in.

I'm also not that happy about the way Mel is gushing and practically fawning over him. Eurgh.

I also haven't got time for this.

'I'm sure you've got lots to do,' I croak, needing to get

away. From her, from him. And, we're going to be late for this bloody meeting. 'Sign me in, please, quick. We've got a meeting!'

He grins. 'I know. You're in a bit late today, aren't you?'

'Yes!' I screech and scurry over to the barrier, hopping about from foot to foot as though that will speed things up. He doesn't follow. 'Jamie!' I rush back, grab his sleeve and tug.

He chuckles. 'I never knew you cared!'

I drop his sleeve as though he's on fire. 'I care about my job!' I say through gritted teeth as he dangles the pass before me. 'Thank you!' I grab it, practically vault through the barrier and leap into the lift the moment the doors open. Well, just before actually. I think I'm going to have a nasty bruise on my arm.

I know he is looking at me. It's unnerving. I stare straight ahead. Being trapped in a lift with Jamie is not how I wanted this day to start. This is even worse than getting the slow bus, being soaked by a woman and discovering I have forgotten my pass.

I am now a hot mess as well as a wet mess.

I look sideways at him under my eyelashes. He's half smiling, he's probably working out how to get the most out of this situation.

At least if we all get sacked, I won't ever see him again.

He is so dishy. My stomach flips.

'I didn't think you ever did things like this.' He breaks the awkward silence.

'What?' I squeak. Bloody hell, he saw me peep, he thinks I'm flirting in the elevator! I straighten up and stare ahead.

'Forget your pass?'

Oh that. Phew. 'I don't normally.' I can't help but glance his way at the sound of his deep chuckle. He winks.

He's not sexy. I do not fancy him. He is annoying. He's always taking the mickey, just, well, just being like a pesky younger brother.

I have three sisters; I don't need a brother as well.

Especially a shaggable one, that would be like mental incest, wouldn't it?

He grins. 'Glad to know you're as human as the rest of us. Here we go.' He puts his hand out to stop the doors closing. I open and close my mouth, goldfish style, trying to think of the right response. Of course I'm human, what does he mean by that? 'After you. Aren't you in a hurry?'

Shit, yes. I have less than four minutes left!

Chapter Three

'You're a bit late! Hurry up, meeting in five!' shouts Jade as I scurry past her reception desk, peeling off my damp jacket as I go and trying to smooth down my frizzed-up hair. 'Everybody is already in there!'

'Shit, they've not started early?' The office looks deserted. Nobody is sitting at their desk. My stomach lurches. Bugger, I really am late.

'No, don't panic. Here, give me your jacket, I can put it on your chair for you?'

'Thanks, you're a star!' She isn't, but it always pays to keep somebody like Jade on your side. 'I was just going to…' I point in the direction of the ladies.

'Don't worry about that, you look fine!' She gives me the thumbs up, so I pat my hair down again, give my top a tug to straighten it, try to ignore the damp patch on my shoulder where the rain leaked in, force my shoulders back and march down the corridor towards the meeting room.

This is it. This is the moment I find out that I am jobless, and potentially homeless – because, after all, does anybody have more than just-enough money to see them through to the next pay cheque in their bank account?

Oh God, what am I going to do if they do close down the company and sack all of us? Or just sack some of us. Or just sack me.

I can feel the prickle of damp sweat between my shoulder blades, and suddenly realize I'm clenching my fists so hard my fingernails are digging into the palms of my hands.

I flex my fingers. Chill, Alice. Chill. It will be fine. You're good at your job, you're competent, they're not going to just sack you.

The door is propped open and my heart drops even lower. It thuds to the bottom of my stomach, making me feel very unwell.

Heck, this meeting room really is small, and everybody is packed in without any thought of health and safety. Well, apart from the fact they've left the door open so that we don't all go into a carbon dioxide-induced coma.

I look around wildly, trying to spot a space to squeeze into.

Yay, there's an empty chair! I sprint towards it and nearly collide with somebody. We both stare at the chair with longing. Sometimes you covet a chair, like when you're expecting a long meeting that has a message of doom.

'It's okay, you have it,' I say with resignation when I realize who I've just bounced off. Mollie is tiny and quite well built. Only a heartless moron would push her out of the way.

'Are you sure, Alice?' she says breathlessly.

I nod and she shoots me a grateful glance before sinking down and I am left standing in the middle looking a bit of a lemon.

There is a hiss. It is Lou, waving at me and pointing at something by her side. Something big, bright yellow and round. I have been left with the option of a gym ball or standing room only.

I've always thought sitting down is supposed to be the best option when it comes to bad news. On the TV when the police knock on the door to tell somebody they've just found a dead body, they always say 'I think you better sit down,' don't they?

And before you start to think I work for a trendy, progressive company which likes their employees to keep fit as they work, We Got Designs (and Management) isn't. It's a bit like musical chairs when we have a 'big' meeting. Well actually no, to be totally honest, it's more like a scrum. You don't want to be late.

We have stand-up meetings, not standing desks. Well, unless somebody donates one.

The company works on a shoestring, and any other freebie which comes its way. You've no idea how many clients are so overwhelmed by the quality of website we create for them that they feel the need to offload their excess products on us. I'm all in favour of handmade chocolates, food hampers and specialist gin, but sex toys and exercise balls?

Whoever came up with the idea of sitting on an exercise ball to work is not in their right mind. I suppose I should be thankful it's not a sex swing (yep, we have a client who sells them). I mean, can you imagine doing this suspended in the air with your legs akimbo as though you're expecting a kinky gynaecologist, not the sack?

Anyway, this is bad enough, and whichever bright spark decided to put it in the meeting room has the type of evil streak you don't want to find in a co-worker.

I also reckon Jamie is sitting right behind us. I can't see him, I can just sense him, and the hairs on the back of my neck are prickling. I refuse to give him the satisfaction of turning around to check though. I will pretend I need to pick something up from the floor and sneak a peek under my armpit on the way back up.

This sets off a dangerous mini-wobble, so I stop and sit very still. How did he get in here and get a proper seat before me? He must have snuck past while I was fannying about texting Soph back to say, *I'm not kidding, it is actually happening, we are ALL about to be sacked*. I was the last person into the 'big meeting'. Even more last minute than I'd thought I'd be.

'Everybody here?' Diane the dragon lady stands up. Dragon Lady is not a compliment, and in no way alludes to *Dragon's Den*, it's more to do with her spiky hair, red face and the way she likes to leave you feeling singed at the edges. The fact that she's leading the meeting is bad news, it is basically an announcement that we are doomed.

It is not going to be fine.

They send her in when they don't want anybody to answer back, because she is truly scary. And she has *all the power*.

She once overheard somebody making a sexist comment about her and gave him the 'Backpacking Women Wee on Their Feet' account. He was basically in charge of designing a website to sell a female urination device that lets you pee standing up, *without* weeing on your feet, if you get what I mean. He had to spend weeks locked in a room with a development team who knew everything about full flow, weak flow and how it affects projection, and the pros and cons of durable cardboard and latex, and what will go in a backpack without sanitation or smell issues. After a week of that he went off long-term sick.

Couldn't have happened to a nicer male chauvinist twat.

Like I say, don't mess with the dragon lady. I think I am scared of, and admire her, in equal measures.

'We're fucked,' whispers Lou in my ear, sending a trickle of fear into my stomach and the rest of me nearly onto the floor. She grabs my elbow just in time. Sitting on this exercise ball, instead of propping myself up against the wall, was definitely a mistake.

Particularly when I seem to be slowly liquifying.

Who in their right mind wants to be holding their stomach in, pressing their knees together and have their feet splayed out, trying to stop their buttocks wobbling about, when they're facing redundancy? I probably look like a constipated chicken, and if anybody sneezes unexpectedly there's a good chance I'll end in a heap and the ball will take out the whole of the back row. A sex swing would actually have been safer. I'd have been roped in.

'Right, we'll keep this brief. But,' Diane turns slowly, glaring at each of us individually, working out who to fry first. This sets off another mini wobble, but this one is inside me. 'If you didn't get personal notification of this meeting, and just decided to follow the herd and come in anyway, please leave now.' There's a long pause. 'Darren.'

Darren who has just got engaged and has a (very) pregnant girlfriend flinches. 'I thought maybe I'd missed the email, and...' Diane shakes her head, he stands up reluctantly looking like I feel (about to burst into tears that is), then edges out. I'm tempted to go and grab his chair, but it would involve clambering over people. Unprofessional. And in these heels, possibly scarring for life or impaling bodily parts I shouldn't.

'You have mail now though, Darren,' Diane says with an evil glint in her eye. She opens her mouth again, but two more people stand up guiltily before she has chance to name and shame.

So 'all staff' didn't actually mean 'all'.

I'm not sure if they are the lucky ones who are keeping their jobs, or they don't even warrant the explanation. Knowing Darren, and the fact that he takes regular 'planned' sick leave on a Monday, and last week he accidentally published the test version of a website that sent you to a page saying 'LOSER' if you clicked on 'more information', I suspect the latter.

The door clicks shut and Diane strides over to make sure nobody is lurking by the keyhole. 'Right. Steven.'

Steven, the MD, does not scurry out – though he does look like he wants to. He stands up. Coughs awkwardly, then stares down at the sheet of paper he is clutching.

'Well, well, welcome.' This is not a speech impediment,

he starts off most conversations with 'well, well'. I think it gives him time to gather his thoughts. He pushes his glasses further up his nose. Steven is an internet geek, not a man-manager. I don't think he really knows how to deal with other (less intelligent forms of) human beings. He started up this company from his home, with only a cat for company, and I think he would have been quite happy to keep it that way. Employees complicate things. 'As you, er, know, times are difficult for, er, everybody in this er, economic downturn. We've always been able to er, soldier on, but some of our clients have been, er, experiencing problems and had to cut back, or, er, close down.' He coughs again as though it was painful to say the words. Diane twitches, I can tell she's dying to grab his sheet of paper off him and read it out herself. I can't blame her, so am I. I'm developing a nervous twitch. 'The first major loss for us was of course Lurve Toys.' Lurve Toys are (or were) a major client; they regularly asked for re-designs of their website, created new offshoot companies, asked for updates and generally paid us a ton of money to manage the IT side of their business. 'They have gone to the wall.' A nervous ripple of sniggers goes around the room like a Mexican wave, which falters when it gets to Diane.

'I thought shagging increased in a recession?' hisses Lou.

'Mine hasn't,' I hiss back, out of the side of my mouth, trying not to move my lips.

'When our clients are up against the wall, we're the first hole they plug.' Steven drones on in a monotone.

'Are we still talking about Lurve Toys?' Lou seems to have decided to bluff this out and not panic. I don't know how much more of this I can stand though. She nudges me with her elbow when I don't immediately reply. But I'm not at all stable, and if I as much as snigger, let alone start laughing, there is no way I'm going to keep my balance. The best approach is to stare straight ahead and work out how long the tins of soup I've got in my cupboard will last if I only have half of one each day. Presuming nobody has nicked them.

'Sadly, we must acknowledge that we are the end of the, er, chain. When a retailer starts to fail, we are the first choking point.'

'Like Lurve Toys who allegedly nearly strangled a client,' Jamie, who is just behind me as I suspected, mutters. He is grinning when I glance his way. He's definitely got that naughty-boy look about him today.

Not my type at all, I don't know what I was thinking, and very annoying at times. I mean, just because you're compatible on the kissing front, doesn't mean you're compatible in any other way, does it?

'Wow, really?' Lou leans across me. She fancies him. I wonder if I should try and roll out of their way. If he went out with my best work friend, then he'd definitely be out of bounds. And out of my head forever.

'Got sued when a sex swing failed. Dangerous things.'

See, I knew it.

'And you'd know, would you?' Lou is going into full flirt mode.

He raises an eyebrow. 'I bet Alice would.'

'Will you two shush.' My cheeks are burning. Why has he brought sex swings up now? Can he read my mind? I can also see Diane preparing to go into battle to silence the masses for her boss. 'If we get sacked for insubordination, we won't get redundancy money, will we?'

'So, there are, er, cuts to be made, so that we can see this through, and come out the other side all, er, guns blazing.'

See this through? I perk up a bit. That sounds promising. Maybe life as I know it is not about to end.

'We are expecting things to pick up again soon, but er, in the meantime, I hope you will all throw yourselves into our new way of working. Right, er, I'll leave you with Diane, who can er, answer any queries you might…' He's already tapping away on his mobile phone as he walks out of the room, head down so that he doesn't accidentally make eye-contact with anybody and have to answer a question.

New way of working? Did I miss something? I glance around, confused. Am I not being made redundant?

People are blinking and turning heads, owl-style, and frowning. I don't think I'm the only one who feels like part of that announcement was missing.

Diane looks around. Daring us to say anything.

'You will all receive an email with full details. If you aren't happy to continue under the proposed new conditions, let HR know ASAP,' she hisses the letters out. 'Although under the present climate…' She doesn't have to finish her sentence. We all know she's got us by the short and curlies.

She sweeps past us just as I try and stand up again on my wobbly legs, and I nearly take her out.

My mobile vibrates as I'm walking back to my desk.

Well? S x

My sister Soph likes to be the first to know the news. When you've got three sisters it can get quite competitive. To be fair though, I am closer to her than the others. We share the same sense of humour, shitty salary, hairdresser and taste in clothes...

Was that my jumpsuit you were wearing on your Insta photo? A x

Maybe. But WHAT ABOUT YOUR JOB? S xx

Yes, why am I stressing about flipping clothes right now?

Not sure yet. All the deets are going to be in an email. You'll be the first to know! A x ASK NEXT TIME, you know it's my fav outfit.

Sometimes I wish we were nowhere near the same size. What makes it worse is that she usually looks better than I do, in my clothes.

I had thought moving out of the family home would help on the sharing front. Give me some privacy, but Soph seems to spend more time at my place than she does at her own. She says it's cool.

I mean, I can't blame her. I wouldn't want to still be in my childhood bedroom, but she's not got much choice at the moment.

You'd say no S xxx

Exactly! x It's bad enough sharing a house with people who adopt the 'what's yours is mine' philosophy, without having your sister come and go as she wishes as well. Touching, but annoying. My dream of a house, or even a room, of my own still seems to be just that. A dream. At least I've got my desk back though.

A loud bang makes me jump and look up from my mobile phone. Darren is slamming his stuff into a box with undue force. He is swearing under his breath. There are a lot of F words. I have a bad feeling about this email; just thinking about it is making me queasy with anticipation.

I need the loo. Not only did I not have time to go to the toilet when I got into work and am absolutely bursting, I also need a splash of cold water and to give myself a pep talk in front of the mirror before I go back to my desk.

Why didn't they send it last thing, so that we could go home and weep over it in the comfort of our own homes? This seems a pretty sadistic way to kick the day off if I'm honest, I bet it was Diane's idea.

Chapter Four

'What are those?' After a quick diversion to the ladies' loos, I got to my desk to find Jade, our receptionist, sitting on my chair.

Why is she there? Can't she stand up like anybody else would do? I need to sit down.

My whole body is still trembling from the effects of the exercise ball and having to tense muscles that aren't used to demands like that. And from the whole being-late-for-work and being petrified I'm about to be sacked, then not knowing what is about to happen. The whole thing is *so* stressful. It feels like I've been at work for hours already, and it's not even ten o'clock. I am exhausted.

'Flowers?' She tweaks the foliage on both sides, then twists round to face me. She lifts her already very arched eyebrow slightly and looks at me as though I'm mentally deficient.

'I know they're flowers, I meant what are they doing on my desk?' There is not enough room on my desk for flowers, especially ones that have obviously been delivered to the wrong person.

'They're for you?' I've never known anybody manage to answer every single question with another one. She smiles as though she is personally responsible for the bouquet.

Jade is lovely, but a bit of a gossip. I reckon the question thing is a strategy to find out as much as possible as quickly as possible.

'Me?' I frown. I'm confused. Sitting down might help, I straighten my jacket on the back of the chair as obviously as I can. She doesn't take the hint. I consider wheeling her to one side.

'Don't you think they're gorgeous?' She sounds a bit put out. Then it dawns on me.

'Oh.' My legs are boneless, and I've come out in a sweat. She *is* personally responsible; she has arranged a collection – this is my leaving present. 'Yes. Do you mind if I?' I wave a hand at the desk.

'Somebody loves you!'

I'm confused. Somebody, as in not the whole office?

They're not my leaving present! How stupid am I? No way would she have had time to have a collection, plus if I've been sacked I can't be the only one who gets a leaving present. Darren definitely hasn't got one. And nobody else has Jade and an OTT bouquet on their desk.

I don't think she is going to get off my chair until she gets some answers. I could just wheel her and the chair out of the way and power up my computer. I mean, standing up while you work is supposed to be good for you, isn't it? But I'd still have the issue of no working space.

'Loves *me*?' It's not that I feel completely unloved, it is just that I wasn't expecting any extravagant floral arrangements. It's not my birthday, I've not been ill, and I do not have a new, hot admirer.

She leans forward, resting her forearms on my desk. She's here for the duration. '*Always in my heart*, it says on the card?'

Unless somebody thinks I have died. Don't 'always in my heart' and 'never forgotten' often accompany a coffin?

'And on the other side it says, "*Happy first date Anniversary*". Look.' She scoots the chair over a few inches and ushers me in closer, so that I can see the card that is hanging in a prominent position at the front.

To be fair, the bouquet is pretty impressive, but my desk has a lot of stuff on it, so the space is easily filled.

'Oh my God, how sweet is that?' She sighs dreamily, stroking a rose petal. 'How many years?'

I look at her blankly. 'Years?' How can I not know it's my anniversary? Maybe we're talking months here, or weeks. Surely that guy from Tech, who I accidentally made bodily contact with over a coffee a week ago when he recovered all my work that had disappeared doesn't think it's a date worth celebrating? It wasn't even a deliberate thing, more of an accidental peck on the cheek when I leaped in for an impulsive (and possibly sackable-offence) hug, and he spun round in shock, and well, our faces kind of clashed instead of went cheek to cheek. He definitely didn't look like the sort of guy who sends flowers. Shit, have I somehow started something without knowing it? 'Are you sure they're for me?'

'Yeah definitely for you, Alice, and it says, *"Time for a get back together to celebrate? Dave"* with kisses.'

Phew, not tech guy. But shit. Celebrate? Grrr, this is typical Dave. He just ignores the fact we've finished when it suits him. I got so bloody fed up waiting for any sort of commitment from him because it was always on his terms, when it was convenient.

And why does he have to do this to me now? It's almost like he's got this sixth sense for when I'm vulnerable, when I might need him. This is the longest period of time I've ever managed to stick to my guns and not get in touch with him. And now he's going to ruin it. I'll message to thank him; he'll message back and, before I know it, we'll be back to the easy-come-easy-go relationship that I know isn't good for me. Easy, but not good. He's got bored, needs a date, or needs a shag, or is just wondering how I've stayed away this long. He's good at finding reasons to see each other, when it suits him. If we'd been 'on', no way would he have remembered this.

Dave was a bad habit; I'd relied on him for far too long and I'm not going to start again.

'Why didn't you mention that bit first?' I don't need this right now; I am *not* going to cave in and run to him for reassurance about our office changes. Whatever they are.

Although he is quite good on employment law and… No! I must not call him.

'I've only just seen it; I haven't been reading your personal notes!' Jade says slightly huffily – letting go of my personal note. 'Aww, it's so romantic.'

'It's not romantic, we split.'

'It's still so cute that he remembers!' She sounds all dreamy.

'We split up ages ago.' This is ridiculous. Dave is no longer in my life, and that's final.

Why are so many men like that? They never send flowers when you'd really like them to, then, all of a sudden, decide to when you're so over them. When it doesn't matter anymore. You only get them when you don't want them.

'Awww, sweet. My boyfriend doesn't remember stuff like that and we're still together.'

She's missing the point. To be honest – and I didn't realize it at the time – Dave can be a bit controlling. It seemed sweet and made me feel safe at first. Then I realized that I don't want somebody to run my life, I don't need it. Dave is another reason for so much of the stuff I really value being here, on my desk. The fact I've more or less moved in, minus a bed. He used to throw away any of my stuff that *he* thought was rubbish. Then deny it was him when I found it in the trash. He also meddled and tried to make decisions for me.

He wasn't that keen on me staying over at his place, but he was more than keen to stay at mine when it suited him. I guess it's easier to walk away when you feel like it, than chuck somebody out when you've had enough.

One of my housemates even let him in when I wasn't there, because he *looked sad*. For fuck's sake, he's a guy, not a puppy. It might sound wrong, because he was my boyfriend, but it made me feel like my space was being invaded. That it wasn't just mine anymore. He'd actually do things like rearrange my toiletries into a neater order and bin the old receipts and bus tickets that were on my dressing table while he was waiting for me – for something to do. I wouldn't dream of doing that if I was at his place.

I can't stop staring at the flowers. I don't want them here, on my desk. It will tempt me to call him if the email is really bad news.

'You have them, Jade.'

'Gosh, what? You're being serious? Oh no, I couldn't!' She sneezes, hard, straight into the bouquet. 'Oops. Sorry, hayfever!'

'Of course you can! Anyway, there's just not enough room for them unless I move something else.' Which I am not going to do. This is my desk we're talking about. *My* space. 'Is that the phone ringing, Jade?'

'Oh, bugger.' She stands up, but kind of slumps. I think Jade finds her actual work a bit of a nuisance, it interrupts her day. 'Suppose I better answer it.'

'Take the flowers. Honestly.'

'Really?'

'Really, you'd be doing me a favour, you know, bad memories.' That one always works.

She beams and picks them up. Then holds them out at arm's length in my direction. 'You sure?'

'Positive.'

'Aww, I know what you mean. It's horrible, isn't it, when it ends and all you can think of is what it was like, and what they might be doing, and…' I nod in agreement, it's easier. I resist the urge to push her away. 'I'll put them on reception, so if you change your mind?' I won't. 'Don't forget, check your emails, chick!'

I won't forget to do that either.

I plonk myself down with a sigh and pull my keyboard back to its normal spot. So far this day has been stressful with a capital S; I need some soothing work to do.

My computer takes an absolute age to power up, it's worse than waiting for somebody to turn up at the pub. When you're starting to think you've got the wrong time, or day. Or they hate you. Or nobody told you that the plan has been changed.

I furtively glance over the top of my monitor at everybody else. To see if they're reading *the* email. Nobody is crying. Good sign. Nobody is talking. Bad sign.

Jamie catches my eye, so I look down. 'Stop panicking.' His tone is mild, reassuring.

'I'm not.' I suddenly realize I'm tapping my fingers on the desk, so stop.

He's leaning back in his chair, hands behind his head. Nothing panics Jamie. Life is too much of a joke for him. This is the other annoying thing about him – if you ignore the fact that he didn't even notice our snog – he sails through life, treating it as fun, and yet *still* manages to get the same promotions as I do. And sometimes he gets even better client accounts than I do. And he's not better at this than me, he's really not.

We started here on the same day and I know I shouldn't let myself be drawn in, but the dragon lady made sure that we both knew we were head to head when it came to impressing clients. So it is a teeny-weeny bit competitive.

Particularly when she started to remind us about our annual review, and possible promotion openings, and then he started to talk in that sexy jokey way of his over the phone and got clients begging for his services (yeah, I know how that sounds – it is how it feels) before they have even seen his work. Unfair, totally unfair. I mean, when I'm nervous and pitching I sound more cat on a hot tin roof than purring kitten. Not that I want to sound like a kitten, but he's just got this infuriating, laid back, I-think-you're-fascinating charm that I can't compete with.

It is annoying, so is he, and I'm not going to let him bloody well get that pay rise before I do.

Okay, I can obviously see why Lou flirts with him, but it isn't all about looks, is it? Or kissing prowess. Well it isn't at all. About looks. I can testify to this after dating the incredibly suave, nicely toned, slightly-obsessively-groomed Dave. When I say 'slightly-obsessively' this just about sums up his whole character. He is the type of person who would pick stray hairs off your jacket, and wipe smudges off your cheek, and rearrange the food on your plate before you were allowed to eat it. Not always. That would be weird. But he didn't like misplaced salad leaves, or drips of gravy. I liked it at first, being taken care of, it was cute, then it got annoying. Who wants their lettuce manhandling? Eurgh. Why did I date him for so long?

Shit, why am I thinking about him again? This is what happens when I'm stressed.

Jamie is totally different to Dave in every way. He's not suave, he's more a dimples and cheeky grin kind of guy, and when he leans in to listen to you, he looks like he's interested. Unlike Dave, who more often or not was studying me during a conversation because he'd spotted sleep in the corner of my eye, or a potential spot on my chin – not because he had an irresistible urge to kiss me.

But he is a good listener, when he's got time. Although we quite often had to 'circle back later', or he'd 'ping me when he had five'. I didn't want 'pinging', I wanted a relationship.

And relationships are supposed to be about emotional connections and support, not just practical advice and sex now and again, aren't they?

Not that Jamie is interested in even pinging me, he's even less interested than Dave. On the attraction scale he obviously rates me sub-zero. But he still has to talk to me and tease me. I reckon he's doing what my gran used to tell me to do 'keep your friends close and your enemies closer'. And wind them up and irritate them if you can.

'I thought people liked getting flowers.'

I jump guiltily, at least Jamie can't read my mind. 'Not from people they don't want them from.' I raise a finger to tap again, realize and stop myself just in time.

'You and Dave aren't an item anymore?'

'Uh-uh.' I shake my head.

'But he's still keen.' It's a statement rather than a question.

Yeah, when it suits him. I'm like an Amazon Prime subscription; he wants to be able to start me up when he needs me, then mute me for a bit.

'Not your birthday?'

'Nope. Do you mind, I…' I gesture at my screen and

wish he'd shut up. There are no new emails; my screen is still annoyingly blank.

'Wouldn't like to miss it.' He's doing his boyish-grin thing.

'I haven't died either,' I say, thinking about 'always in my heart'.

'I'd be giving you the kiss of life if I thought you were about to.' His voice drops to a more intimate level, he leans forward slightly.

I swallow, my mouth suddenly dry. I hate the way he flirts like this. It might be fun if I didn't still have a crush, or if he was interested in me. But he's not, and I do, and it's awkward.

'Oh yay! Email!' He glances down, his attention abruptly diverted.

'What?' I stare at my monitor, which has finally sprung into life, and click on my emails. *You have no new mail*. My stomach dives. Has he got an email and I haven't?

'Kidding!'

'Hilarious.' Why does he have to be like this? One minute the guy I lust after, the next Mr Jokerman taking the mickey. I refresh the emails, just in case. It's probably a good thing we've moved on from talking about mouth-to-mouth resuscitation. 'I thought they were sending it straight away?'

'Maybe they're sending them out in waves, in some kind of order? Most important people first?'

'Oh well, I'm surprised you haven't got one yet!' I say as sweetly as I can.

'Dragon Lady is probably testing us out, seeing who cracks first.'

'Shut up, Jamie.' I stand up, deciding I can risk going to the coffee machine. Anything has to be better than staring at my inbox and listening to Jamie.

———————

Predictably, the email arrives just as the coffee starts to trickle into my cup. I can sense it from the indrawn breaths and sudden tapping away on keyboards. I stare at the cup. Glance towards my desk. Torn. I can't leave my coffee, I can't. I need caffeine for this.

It drips in so slowwwwwly.

'Well, fuck me.' I try to ignore the temptation to rush over to Lou and ask her what it says. I have to read my own email. I mean, what if we've all got different ones?

I can't wait any longer, I dither for a moment, then grab the half-full cup out of the machine and dash back to my desk.

Thank you for your time and patience, this has not been written by Diane, blah, blah, *main overheads are of course staff and premises,* blah, blah, *major reduction in cost achievable by reducing our office space by half,* reducing it by half? Shit! Does this mean half of us are going, not just Darren and the other two? Will they draw a random boundary line and everybody on one side is out? Or will we be jamming our desks together in primary school fashion? *We have luckily been able to secure shared tenancy with another company* blah blah, *and so will be introducing a work-at-home policy…*

What? My throat tightens painfully. I feel sick. Work at home? Oh my God, no. This can't be happening. Not again.

I used to dream, no *fantasize*, about coming back to the office. I had every step of Boris's roadmap set as a notification on my mobile and would have (if he'd stopped public transport) walked all the way to Downing Street if he'd veered off course.

I don't have enough space at home; I have a tiny room. The smallest one in the house. I was the only person who had to prop a big umbrella behind me during zoom calls so that nobody could see my unmade bed and undies that hadn't made it to the wash basket.

I also don't have a decent internet connection. I've got noisy housemates. I've got (sorry, had) Dave. When I was stuck at home, I couldn't help myself. I'd end up ringing him in despair, needing somebody to talk it through with.

My palms are beginning to sweat.

Every time somebody decided to unmute me on zoom calls, so I could contribute to the meeting, I had to race with them to the mute button so they didn't hear Dave telling me that I really had to get a grip on putting the coffee back in its new place, and wiping down the shower with his new special squeegee thing. I mean, who has time for that in the morning? I count it a win if I get enough time to dry all the water off myself, let alone the cubicle glass.

That flaming mute button was on-off-on-off so fast it left me a jittery mess.

I love my work, but it was just impossible to concentrate, to be my best. I was surrounded by chaos, not my lovely bits and bobs that inspire me. I hated getting up in the morning because I felt like I couldn't breathe, I couldn't think, I couldn't come up with the ideas that would turn my client's websites from ordinary to attention-grabbing.

Kat saved me. Kat, one of my housemates had made the decision to go out to Spain. She hadn't been able to see her mum for months. And she saved my life by letting me borrow the desk in her room. Her locked room. Even though it wasn't my room and the decor was frankly a bit weird, it was still better. It was quiet, there was space. I could hide in there and work even if it wasn't like having a room of my own.

Kat is back though now. And I can't afford to rent an extra room, or office.

And this sounds worse, this sounds permanent.

I must not panic. I breathe in and out slowly, and blink to bring the email back into focus.

'and hot-desking.'

What the fuck? I sit back, my heart pounding even faster than it was a moment ago. Hot-desking? I blink and try to be calm. Must not panic. Must not.

Even the term sounds horrible. Hot. Desks shouldn't be hot, they should be warm, and comfortable, and homely. Working at home will be bad enough, but not having my own desk on the days when I am in the office? I realize I'm clutching the edge of mine. My one private space in life.

A percentage of your working hours will be conducted at home, and a desk-share arrangement will be introduced throughout to cater for the remainder.

I stop reading, close my eyes and lean back in my seat feeling queasy. Gutted is not the word.

'Wow, result! How good is that? Seemed a bit OTT to make us come in every day when we'd been fine at home for well over a year!' Jamie's deep voice breaks through my panic. 'I need a coffee to celebrate, want one?'

Been fine at home? Is he mad?

'No thanks.' I hold up my own cup, then watch his broad back as he heads for the coffee machine, humming. He is happy. In fact, quite a few people are smiling and look relieved. Am I the only one that is horrified by this news? Did some people actually *like* working at home?

I straighten up in my seat and glance over the barrier between us at Jamie's practically bare desk, then lean back and look at my own. Talk about yin and yang, the only common meeting point for us is our lips. Those fit perfectly. From my point of view anyway.

To some people, like Jamie, I guess my desk is covered in clutter, mess, and would do their head in. But I guess my desk is the space that I'd create if I had my own (as in proper, all to myself – or with somebody I trusted) home, if I could surround myself with things that I love and know they'd be there when I got back.

I let my finger touch the feather that reminds me of Gran and inspired the design of the 'Everything Apple' website. Gran loved baking; when I think of her I smell her apple pies, chutneys and freshly baked bread. I think of her colourful apron, of her floury hands…all things that we fed into the website. 'You've turned home-baking into a hug, I never want to leave this website!' the client had said. She'd been right. I'd been proud of that, and Gran would have been as well. It was good.

Where do I put Gran if this isn't my desk any longer? I can't carry all these things, all the memories and inspiration with me, can I? And if they're in my room they'll be picked up, touched, borrowed, moved. Trampled on. Gahhhh.

This isn't just a desk, it's my breathing space, my thinking space. My escape.

It was bloody lucky that when I was working at home there wasn't much demand for inspiration and blue-sky thinking – it was more about bug fixing and maintenance. Without my lovely things around me, my creativity was at an all-time low.

I'm being pathetic. This is not a big deal. It's not. I am a professional and this is just a chunk of fake wood that I sit in front of. It's not supposed to be a bloody home! I can deal with this; I can come up with a solution. That is what I'm good at. Solutions. Thinking outside the box.

It's to my benefit that today is announcement day, and tomorrow, Friday, is judgement day. We get the weekend to recover. To plan. Neat.

My mobile phone vibrates noisily, and I jump, grabbing it guiltily. I think people are still trying to take it in, just starting to mutter and huddle by the water cooler, but it's still very quiet.

Wassup? News??? S xxx

I *will* put a positive spin on this.

I've still got a job! A x

Great!

Hot-desking and working at home. Best of both worlds! A x

See? I've got this.

Wow! Cool! S xx

Soph is definitely a work-to-live person. She's worked in call-centres, shops, libraries, any casual job that will take her. She doesn't claim her territory at work, all she is bothered about is somewhere to park her bum and put her handbag.

You still up for lunch tomoz? Popped into yours but couldn't find your blue scarf, have you still got it? S xxxx

Ahh, so that's why she's texted. The scarf, not my mental (or financial) wellbeing.

Yep I've got the scarf, it's in the top drawer of my desk. Safe.

This is my space, and now I'm losing it. Maybe I need a lock on my door, like Kat's got?

Sure. See you at 12.30?

Fuck, gotta go, just served something big and meaty to a vegan! Sxxx

She adds three crying-with-laughter faces, and a big sausage. Another text comes in just as I go to put my phone away.

Don't forget the scarf! Luv ya!!!xxx

'What do you think? Better than the big heave-ho, I suppose?' The weight of Lou's hand on my shoulder, and her voice in my ear makes me jump. She squeezes. 'You okay about it?'

'Sure. I mean it'll take a bit of getting used to because it was so good to be back.' There's an understatement if there ever was one.

'God yeah, you're telling me. I was desperate to get out

of the house and see you lot again, it was so frigging boring.'

'It was chaos at ours.' I sigh, I'm always truthful with Lou, and she knows all about my housemates. 'A bit gutted I'll have to try and work at home again, to be honest.'

'I bet. No chance of working at your folks' place or anything?'

I shake my head. The thought had briefly crossed my mind, but with Dad retired and pottering about, and Soph often between jobs, I'm not convinced it would work. And I am supposed to have moved out. I'm an independent working woman. I will not run home.

'Can they do this without some kind of consultation process?' Mollie pauses by my desk, a frown on her normally smiling face. 'It's hell with two dogs, three kids and my mother, and even worse if Si takes a day off.'

We smile sympathetically. 'Not a clue,' says Lou, 'but to be honest I reckon if we said no, they'd shut the whole lot down. What do you think, Jamie?'

Can they do this? Maybe I *should* ring Dave, he knows all about employment law – my hand closes over my mobile. Then I snatch it away. I will not call Dave. I don't need him.

'Extra hour in bed, extra hour on the PlayStation before tea. What's to not like?' Jamie grins.

'Unless you've got a two year old,' says Mollie.

He stops grinning. 'Tough to concentrate?'

'You bet. Si will see it as an excuse to stop paying for a childminder.'

A slight air of gloominess descends.

'Maybe they'll have some flexibility? You know, let some people come in more if they want?' It won't solve my problem, but it might help Mollie. 'I'd ask if I was you. I mean it doesn't make any difference as long as they can fit people in?' I smile at her, and she smiles back. We're all in this together. 'We can support each other and make this work.' I must sound convincing, because she grins.

'For sure!' she says, then wanders back over to her desk.

'I guess I better get some work done.' Lou takes a step back.

'See you later?' She nods, and I pull up the spec for the new website I'm supposed to be working on. I have zero ideas, nothing original. Zilch. I might have reassured Mollie, but what if losing my workspace means I lose my inspiration?

How do I work without the things that inspire me? Maybe I need to take photos of all of them, pin them up like a police incident board. Or a mood board. But that's not the same as holding them, touching them, is it?

But I need to work this out. Where do I put my stuff? If it doesn't belong here, then where does it?

I glance under my eyelashes at Jamie's desk again. All his stuff must be at home.

And then it hits me. That is where I guess mine should be as well. I can bring some things in and leave them in a box, or pedestal, but most of it can't be here.

This isn't a problem; this is an opportunity (as my Gran would say – she was way before her time). I have to stop making work my substitute home.

I need to make my home, my home.

Jamie winks at me. 'Happy? All sorted?'

I suddenly realize that he's responding to my smile. I'm actually smiling, possibly for the first time today. 'For sure.' Then I pick up the golden-brown conker and roll it between my thumb and forefinger, before clasping it in my hand. I know exactly what the colour theme of the website I'm designing should be. What the heart of it is.

I've missed the obvious all along. We need warmth. Autumn.

Chapter Five

I didn't pick my house because of its fabulous views, spacious dining area or amazingly well-equipped kitchen. I picked it for convenience, and cost. Mainly cost.

When I was at university, I dreamed that once I graduated, I would waltz effortlessly into a job that would mean I could rent my own lovely flat or share a place with a boyfriend. My fantasy did not involve communal living with a random selection of strangers.

I had it in my head that it would be a world away from life as a student. I wouldn't have to hide my coffee, or hold my nose in the bathroom, or spend twenty minutes trying to find my mug, or have to use noise-cancelling headphones to block out the sound of the guy in the next room shagging (it wasn't just the headboard banging, or the grunts of satisfaction, it was the way he announced his coming as though he was some kind of Messiah. For a few months I actually thought he was shouting 'Hallelujah', then realized it was actually *I'm going to Yabba dabba doo-ya!*

Yuk. How is anybody supposed to revise with that going on?).

Anyway, seems I was wrong about my new fancy working life. The reality check came about the same time as the job offer. I'd misjudged the job market, and starting salaries, and rental costs.

I also discovered that the moment any vaguely nice and affordable place came on the market, it was snapped up within hours.

Unless it was a house share in the middle of nowhere with a bunch of welly-wearing eccentrics.

Okay, I'm exaggerating. Only one guy, Harry, wears wellies, and he's a gardener. Not necessarily an eccentric. But he never seems to take them off, I don't think he can be bothered. I strongly suspect he even wears them in the shower. He does wipe them on the mat, says 'how do' if there's anybody in the communal lounge or kitchen, grabs a beer from the fridge and goes for a smoke in the garden. The only other time I see him is when he's making a bacon sandwich in the morning. I have never ever seen him eat anything other than bacon sandwiches, which are always accompanied by a massive mug of coffee.

The nearest equivalent to Yabba-guy from my student days, is Della. I think she's a sex addict. She never bloody stops. The first few days I was here, I did honestly worry that I'd moved into a brothel by mistake, and 'shared communal areas' was a euphemism for something I'd rather not dwell on. But it turned out Della is a sex therapist, who likes to keep her hand in on the practical side and says experience counts for everything. There's also Kat the actress, who likes to practise her lines by wandering round semi-naked at all times of the day and night, Jack who likes to hog the lounge and play Xbox games, and Zoe who is a mobile hairdresser.

The only thing we all have in common is that we're broke. Even if some of them would prefer to pretend they're not and they're here for 'the community vibe'. Yeah, sure.

When I first saw the place advertised, I thought it was a steal. It was a bit more remote than I'd intended, but being surrounded by fields has to be better than roads, yes? And there's a bus stop at the bottom of the lane, a railway station within walking distance, and a pub that's staggering distance away (if you're wearing flats). And the convenience store up the road does stock all the essentials you need. Even if they are twice the price of the supermarket near work – so it's not for convenience at all, it's for emergencies only.

But, hey, I thought, all the walking will do me good. Fresh air is ace. Lugging shopping bags on and off the bus and carrying them for miles is a good workout. Better than the gym, which I can't afford.

It's also not remote-remote. Our place is a barn conversion, and there's another one next to it. Then, where I guess the original farmhouse used to be, there's a new housing estate in the making. I think 'new town' was in the developers' minds when they started this (along with big bucks) and then there was that 'economic downturn' that has given Steven nightmares. 'Town' is currently a show house, two 'affordable' homes and a lot of concrete foundations.

Anyhow, when I'd seen this place on the estate agent's website, I'd convinced myself that rural was fine. Commuting was fine. That was before I saw 'house share' in the small print. But then I thought, why not? It had to be better than a studio flat where the sofa was under the bunk bed, and you could boil the kettle, answer the door and open the window without having to stand up.

I'd also kind of thought that it was going to be very short term. Twelve months in I'd get a review and salary raise, two years in I'd have built up the kind of experience that would set me up nicely for promotion, a big fat hike in my wages, or the chance of a more senior position with a different company.

Didn't happen. Instead there was a global downturn. Nobody saw that one coming, well, I'm sure somebody will say they did. But I certainly didn't when I started work full of optimism and plans. And the prospect of an economic downturn, a mega one, was definitely not something that had occurred to me.

No way did I expect being home 24/7 when I signed the lease. Nor did I expect to have that scary feeling that there was always the chance the company could close down and there would be no other job for me out there. Nobody is recruiting right now; they're laying people off. Or downsizing.

So, no surprise then that my annual review, marking two years which should have been last month, was moved back to later in the year. Much later. And nobody is talking about pay rises.

I do actually like my job, I don't want to move, but the

money is pretty shit. Okay, I saved some money when I was working at home – no train or bus tickets to buy, no mega meal deal to buy at lunch time, no after-work drink (or three) with Lou. But it was pennies really, and now we're back in the office I'm paying out again.

I could be here for another twelve years, not twelve months.

But a frozen salary has to be better than a cut, or the sack, doesn't it?

To be honest, my housemates are all okay. They're cleaner than the students I used to live with, and there's less hard partying. But people have an annoying habit of borrowing without asking and I do have the smallest room in the place.

'Hey, Alice.' The confident twang hits my ears just before the rap on the open door and makes me jump. Zoe has a habit of bowling in before knocking if something needs immediate attention. Most things do with her. She's a do-it-now kind of person. 'You couldn't look at my laptop, could you? It's doing that thing again, where my emails go weird?'

In this place sharing is caring, there is no concept of personal space.

She drove me nuts the first time she was furloughed and bored. Second time round I could lock the door of Kat's room and I was harder to find – she'd stop off and chat to somebody else instead. 'Sure. Can you just give me five minutes, Zoe?'

'It's like urgent? They're on like my phone, but not my laptop?'

I do need to install a lock on my door. Or buy a shed.

Or learn how to say 'go away' politely.

I think actually I've just hit the nail on the head; if I'm going to live how I need to live in my home – I need to work out how to erect boundaries. At work, the divider between me and Jamie is pretty low, so my plants and stuff actually worked really well at putting some distance between us. I could hide behind things. It didn't actually stop me knowing he was there, lusting after him and what might have been though, did it?

I sigh inwardly. Putting a lock on the door here would be just the same. More of a sticking plaster than an actual solution.

'Have you tried just turning it off and back on? Honestly, I know it sounds naff, but it nearly always works.'

'Really?' She is standing in the doorway of my room, arms folded, her head tipped to one side. She doesn't look, or sound, convinced. She also doesn't look like she's going to go away.

I'll help her. Just this once because right now I can't think straight. But then I need a plan. How do other people do it? Stop people walking all over them, stop people invading their privacy? Hmmm.

'Hang on. I'll come.' If I don't, she'll just wait for me, peering over my shoulder and then I'll feel awkward and not get anything done anyway.

Five minutes later, after hitting the refresh button and checking the internet, I hit the 'flight mode' button on her laptop and everything pings back into life. Bloody hell, how many emails does this girl get?

'Oh wow! Thanks, jeez what the fuck is Elsa moaning about now?' She's already loading up emails with one hand, applying mascara with the other, and has forgotten I exist.

'It's the flight mode button, you must have hit it by mistake.'

'Not been on a flight, girl. Don't like all the germs and stuff. I did not turn her hair green! What the fuck's she on about?' She peers at her reflection in the mirror, then picks up her lipstick and waves it about. 'What are people like? She's always got an angle for money off, stupid cow.' Our gazes meet briefly. Then she smiles, a big broad smile that makes her look stunning. Girls like Zoe always make me feel conflicted. I should be madly jealous of their casual beauty, but instead I want to just beg them to value it while it's still there, but not too much. Sometimes it just makes me a little bit sad when I watch Zoe putting her make-up on (which she spends a *lot* of time doing).

My sister Darcie was born pretty, more than pretty. She's always been gorgeous, even when she was screaming blue murder because Mum wouldn't let her have the latest designer jeans. I just looked ugly-angry if I was upset.

As a teenager, Darcie had long legs, silky hair, a perfect English rose complexion. It was all so effortless; as though she'd been given the best genes and what was left had been shared out amongst the rest of us. None of us were jealous, because she was just Darcie. Our sister, and, if that was her thing, then hey, why not?

She was scouted by a modelling agency when she was thirteen and all of a sudden changed from a girl who *liked* make-up and clothes, into a girl who *obsessed* about them. Her looks became everything. The most important thing. And suddenly they mattered so much that she lost her confidence in them.

The thing that had been her blessing became her curse. She was always checking that we thought she looked okay.

And then, when she was sixteen, she had acid thrown in her face by the boyfriend of some girl who was jealous of her.

One quick, nasty confrontation about something that wasn't even important, and Darcie's life changed. How can it be fair that standing up for yourself, denying rumours can change your life in such a bad way?

She was lucky that there was a woman there who knew what to do, she was lucky that not much hit her – just splashes. She was lucky that the ugly streak down her cheek and one arm soon healed and the scarring wasn't deep on the outside. She was unlucky that it was on the inside.

Darcie didn't feel lucky, and she didn't feel pretty. She didn't feel anything. She didn't want to hear that beauty came from within. She'd completely forgotten that she was clever, funny, kind, that we all loved the girl we knew – not the image.

My heart ached so hard for her, I wished it had been me it had happened to. It wouldn't matter for me, because I wasn't the beautiful one. I could have coped, I'm sure I could.

She flunked her exams, lost her friends because she didn't have the confidence to go out, withdrew even from us.

Then one day my sister marched into the lounge, announced that she had been accepted on a beauty course and was going to teach people how to cover their scars and feel beautiful on the outside as well as the inside.

That was it. Darcie was back. Bigger and stronger than ever. My God, I love my sister. She's amazing.

'You okay, Al? You look kinda thoughtful.' Zoe has stopped applying mascara and is watching me through narrowed eyes.

'I'm fine, glad we got it working! See you later.'

'I'll do some highlights for you, if you like? You know, like caramel? Your hair's so gorgeous and shiny, and with your big brown eyes you'd really rock a cute Audrey Hepburn fringe, you could really work the look! I could cut into it a bit; you know, give you a modern take? You should do more with it, it could be gorge!'

'Brill, thanks! I did have a fringe when I was a student, but you know...' I shrug and try not to stare at her room. It is twice the size of mine. It has space for a desk and a chair, and it's the furthest room from the top of the stairs. There is no passing traffic. 'I better get back.'

I tug my shiny hair tighter through my ponytail band self-consciously and head back to my box room. Bumping into Harry, who is heading for the bathroom. It's hard not to bump into him, he's quite broad – which the corridor isn't.

'Okay?' He nods, not waiting for an answer as we squeeze past each other. We're practically grinding hip bones, but it's fine. Why couldn't bumping into Jamie have felt like this? Like nothing. Normal.

It's one thing to realize I have to not use my desk as a second home, but turning my home into a second office? Permanently? That's going to be a hell of a lot trickier.

I roll my sleeves up. This is just like any project. Totally doable.

It feels like only hours ago that office life resumed and I'd been able to pull the boxes out from under my bed and the bottom of my wardrobe, and put most of the stuff back on my dressing table/desk/general dumping ground. Honestly it had been like living out of a suitcase on holiday. Now it looks like it's all going back.

I grab my laptop. This needs Amazon, eBay and, very possibly, Ikea-type solutions for small spaces. I must be able to find some kind of drawers or shelves that occupy inches but store tons of stuff. Tardis style. Cheap.

Where's an office supplies client handing out freebies when you need one?

Chapter Six

Friday

'Shit, no! This can't, I can't...'
    Yesterday was not the worst day of my life. Today is.

Oh My God NO. I'm having palpitations; my heart is pounding so hard I feel faint.

After making a good start on sorting my room last night, I have arrived at work knowing I can make this work.

It's not like I've lost my job or anything really drastic like that. I just need to make some minor adjustments to my life. Simple.

Then I powered up my computer and opened the email. Like you do.

I need a drink. A double gin.

'What?' Lou must have heard my gasp and detoured on the way to her own desk.

She rests her chin on my shoulder, but I hardly notice.

I'm rooted. Staring at the list they've sent out with the 'new arrangements'. If I stare at it hard enough, it might change.

'I, I...' I can't get the words out, so just wave wildly at my monitor.

'Oh shit, the list! I've not seen that yet!' She is peeling her jacket off as she speaks. Lou works to the 'just in time' principle and tries to arrive at her desk on the dot of nine o'clock. 'Oh hell, no, you're working different days to me. Oh God.' She leans in closer. 'And you've got Friday afternoon.'

Have I? I hadn't noticed that bit.

'That is SO shit. Oh, I'm sorry. But I've got Monday, and that's pretty shit as well. At least you can have a lie-in, hun.'

I hadn't noticed the days, or the fact that her days were different to mine. I am all hot and clammy despite the air con. I peel my top away from my chest and try and let some air in. 'It's not that, it's...' I point.

I will be sharing my life, my desk with...Jamie. This is far too intimate, far too much. Shit. I will be sitting on the same office chair. My buttocks will be resting on the exact same spot that his toned bum has. I will be wriggling on the spot... Oh God, no, it doesn't bear thinking about.

I take a few of those short breaths that are supposed to make popping babies out less painful. It doesn't work, I feel dizzy. I must take slow, long yoga breaths.

'Are you okay?' Lou gives me a strange look. 'You're blowing down my neck.'

I clamp my mouth shut.

I can't breathe. Partly because my nostrils can't cope. Lou doesn't seem to notice. I could pass out on the spot and nobody would realize, because they are all looking at *the list*.

'Haha, you're sharing with Jamie fucking Lowe! You lucky cow.' She finally voices the thing I have spent the last few minutes obsessing in my head about.

Luckily 'Jamie fucking Lowe' is not at his desk to witness my meltdown, or Lou's loud voice. 'Are you okay, Alice? You've gone pale.'

I don't feel pale. I am burning up. 'Fine,' I squeak out and let out all the air that couldn't exit via my nostrils.

Calm, Alice, calm. There is an upside to this. You won't have him sitting opposite you every day of the week. You will be able to expunge him from your life, your vivid imagination. Okay, that didn't happen last time you worked from home, but that was different. You knew you were coming back.

And then you did come back, and the moment you saw him he reverted to 'Mr Perfect Gig-kiss'.

I take a deep, steadying breath. Yoga, not birthing style. OMG, how can I forget him when I'll know he has touched everything I am touching?

'I'd love to delve in his drawers to see what's in 'em.' Lou chuckles. 'He's hot, admit it!'

I am admitting no such thing. Nobody knows about what happened. Nobody ever will. Lou doesn't know about 'the kiss', or the corridor crush, nobody does, and nobody needs to because it is embarrassing and stupid, and meaningless. 'He's okay, I suppose.' I shrug. 'But I won't be the one seeing him, so it doesn't matter.' I. Will. Just. Be. Sitting. On. His. Chair.

'You'll be able to run your fingers over his keyboard.'

'Lou!' I don't know whether to laugh or cry. 'Shut up, you idiot!' Talk about conflicted feelings.

'Stroke his mouse...' Her voice has taken on a sultry tone as she strokes the back of my hand to illustrate.

'Stop it!' I flick her away. 'That's freaky!'

'Not sexy?' Her grin mega-wide, she sniggers.

'Shh!' I glance around to check he's still not in the vicinity. I'm worried she might start stroking him as well.

I've got it! I can ask if we can swap days, desks, anything! If Lou wants him, she is welcome.

'Result, though. That means I'm in the same days as him; more time to try and get my wicked way!' Well at least Lou is thrilled.

She winks suggestively, then her eyes widen as she looks at the list again, and her grin broadens. 'Oh yay, I'm sharing a desk with Sal. That's so ace, means I don't have to see her judgy face looking at me every day, and I can keep my Chris Hemsworth calendar on display cos she's got a crush on him too.'

She's just reminded me that it is worse than the 'touching his stuff and sitting on his chair' thing. I feel sick. Jamie and I couldn't be more different.

Jamie is Mr Neat and Tidy. His desk is completely clear apart from the stuff he's using. He'll want a clean desk policy, and I wouldn't trust him with my stuff anyway. I don't trust him enough to share anything. I really am screwed, no way can I keep things here.

'Oh shit, look! Forget Hemsworth. I'm going to be sitting at Jamie's old desk, opposite you! Get that! I'll be able to keep an eye on him for you.' She winks, then sobers. 'Oh come on, don't look so mis, Alice. How about going out at lunchtime? Last chance we'll get.'

'Brill, yes, fantastic. Oh bugger, I said I'd meet Soph, but I can ask her to—'

'No worries, she's funny. I like your little sis, the more the merrier! But shit, I can't believe we're working different days. Who am I going to moan about the dragon to now?' She gives me a quick hug.

I snap out of my Jamie-mist and process what she's been saying.

I'm not just losing my desk; the more important thing is that I'm losing the only real friend I've got here. And I had actually overlooked that point, because I'd been too busy worrying about the prospect of sitting on Jamie's still-warm chair and panicking about a load of 'student tat' as Dave called my stuff. I'm an idiot.

'Oh shit, no. Oh, Lou, I'll miss you.' Tears prick at my eyelids. I will. Lou is funny. She's the type of person without a filter, who says the most outrageous things. But she also says kind things. She spreads niceness around without a thought. Lou is the person who will instantly spot that you've had your hair done (even if it was a 2mm trim), or lost a couple of pounds in weight, or look like you need cheering up. She circulates the office in a way that the dragon lady would love to call time-wasting, but in fact makes people happy and more productive.

All offices need a Lou.

In fact, all people need a Lou in their lives. Even if she

does sometimes lead you astray because she loves a good party so much.

I scan the list again. I'd been really, really looking forward to being back in the office surrounded by my colleagues. I'd even missed the annoying ones. And now half the people I really like aren't even in on the same days that I am. I can change my attitude to the hot-desking, but this is something I can't change.

Who will I gossip with if Lou isn't here? And who will annoy me, if Jamie isn't there to do it? This is going to be *so* strange.

'Come on, Al, better get our arses into gear. There are some boxes over there for any stuff we might want to take home! Lunch at 1pm?'

'Sure!' Actually, there's a very odd atmosphere in the office today. Some people are laughing and joking as though it's the last day at school before the summer holidays, other people are quietly packing their work lives away with trepidation, unsure of what's coming next.

———

Right, let's do this. I grab a bankers box from the stack by the water cooler and bang it down decisively on the corner of my desk.

My desk, which according to the office plan, is going to be 'our' desk.

I have to admit, it scares me. We all need one place in the world we can call our own, don't we? Our safe space. And this was mine.

So I'll just have to create another one, won't I?

But I know in my heart that wiping this completely clean isn't really an option. It's part of me, my work, I can't operate in a vacuum. I'm not that person.

It all started when throw-it-in-the-bin-Dave decided to help me declutter. He doesn't like mess, and he doesn't understand why things are important to me. Why they're more than just useless objects, random junk. Anyway, I rescued some stuff he'd mentally assigned to the bin – and brought it to work. It's just mine here. Safe. And then I realized that when I looked at my personal bits and bobs, the office faded out a bit and I could think beyond the boring client specifications. I mean, when you've had a horrible meeting, how can you not feel better when you look up and see the wonky-donkey that you spotted when you were in Greece, and it was so bad it was good? Before I knew it, I was bringing more stuff in, all the things that I didn't want marauding sisters, boyfriends and housemates to touch – and looking at it made me feel good.

One of the guys jokingly labelled me 'ideas Alice' and it stuck; he started a trend of people arriving at my desk, saying a word and asking what the first thing that popped into my head was.

They're not really ideas, they're feelings.

Luckily the dragon lady started to huff and puff and ask what was going on, because I was started to feel as hassled as I am at home. The space I called my own wasn't any longer. Which was flattering for about two days, then just intrusive. Anyway, they went away. Or emailed.

I do need to sort through properly. Decide what I can

hide in my one tiny pedestal and what I might get away with leaving on the desk.

This would have been so much easier if I'd been sharing with somebody like Lou. We would have agreed to leave at least some stuff. Or would we? Would even Lou really want Rodney, my rampaging plant? I bought him on impulse to celebrate my first day at work. I guess I'd wanted something to brighten up my desk and make it more 'me'. He's a spider plant and if I'm totally honest he has got a bit (okay, a lot) wild and out of control, and spawned loads of babies who are reaching out triffid style – which is not 'me'. I hope. But it was the first step in making my workplace more homely, making my mark on the big, empty, sterile space.

Rampant Rodney also helped block out Jamie.

I sneak a look under my eyelashes in his direction. Now I know some people say, 'tidy desk, tidy mind', but I tend to think more along the lines of 'empty desk, empty head'.

Our desks look so different it's unbelievable.

So actually, the fact that he does not remember our kiss is a bonus. We would never have been compatible, it would have been disastrous. Two dates in we would have realized, and it would have been so much worse, because people would *know*.

I try to make my face soften, because I know I'm frowning. On Jamie's desk there is *nothing*.

Although no, that's wrong, there is *some* non-essential stuff on Jamie's desk. A football coaster, and a…well, I'm not sure what it is. A thing. Like a bobblehead. I narrow my eyes, what exactly is it?

I suddenly realize I'm starting to lean his way. Any second now, he'll catch me looking and I don't need banter, I need to sort my desk and do some work. I haven't done anything yet. And I need to clear my desk. Now.

I put the box on the floor, then put one hand on the edge of my (for now) desk and scoot my chair back a bit so I can lean down and toss my handbag under my desk decisively, and come eye to eye with…

Shit! I grab my hand back to the safety of my chest at double-quick speed. My heart is literally pounding, so I drop both my trembling hands into my lap because the frantic beat is making me even more queasy than just the sight of the spider.

Oh my God, how did I sit down without seeing it?

I was so obsessed with the email I'd been oblivious to anything else. But, really?

It is nestled between the Spanish Beanie Bull that my eldest sister, Lucy, bought me when we were on our first family trip abroad (to keep me quiet while she sneaked a snog with a waiter whose dodgy Spanish accent seemed to be tinged with a Brummie one), a rather raggedy Christmas reindeer that Darcie's daughter Tilly made at school for me, and a pop-up birthday card with cats on it that my first proper boyfriend gave me. We were still at school and he was sweet; he bought me cuddly toys and hid love heart sweets in my pockets when I wasn't looking. Whenever I need to create a webpage that will give people that first-love feeling, I look at that card.

But how could I miss something so *gross*? Right next to my feel-good card? Making my pulse race for all the wrong reasons. My heart still has the jitters, my skin is crawling, and a scream is bubbling up in my throat.

Okay, I know a fear of spiders is totally irrational. Especially when they're clearly not alive, or even real, and are encased in clear plastic. It is a computer mouse, with a spider in it. I know that.

'Everything okay, Alice?' Jamie is staring straight ahead at his monitor and I know he is laughing at me inside. I can see it in his eyes. Hilarious.

How can I have even thought we could compromise? Work out an arrangement. How can I dare leave my stuff out on my desk if he's going to be sitting here when I'm at home?

I can't trust him not to ruin everything.

'I suppose you think this is funny?'

He shrugs and grins. 'First there was Spiderman, now there's Spidermouse! He can take care of our desk when we're not here.' He puts an emphasis on the 'our'. Ahh, so he's seen the list. I swallow to try and lubricate my dry throat.

I glance back up. Jamie meets my eye. It's a challenge and it flicks something inside me.

This isn't just about a stupid spider and a stupid desk. This is about me, and my frigging life. Nothing is safe at home, I've hardly got room to breathe with all the comings and goings in my room, I'm being squeezed on all sides and this is the last straw. It's a horrible thing on my lovely desk. He's invading my space before I've even cleared it.

I've rearranged my life to accommodate everybody else, my whole work life is supposed to now be crammed into a stupid little office pedestal which is about as inspirational as a squashed slug. Enough is enough, why should it be me that makes all the allowances? Why can't people listen to what I want?

I cross my arms and glare. 'Move it.'

'What?' He had been leaning forward, his forearms resting on his desk, his head tilted to one side as he smiled. The smile fades.

'You think you're so bloody funny, well, you're not. It's immature, it's stupid, it's...' Inside I'm so angry I'm shaking, I can't think straight. 'It's pathetic. I don't leave crap on your desk, so don't do it on mine,' I snap.

He frowns, looks shocked. 'Sorry, Alice. I didn't mean to...' The normal confident, smooth tone has a hesitant edge.

Shit. What am I doing, shouting at a colleague? Shouting at the person I'm going to be sharing a desk with? It's not professional. It's not me – I've always been the negotiator, the appeaser, the one in our family who keeps the peace.

'Alice? Do we need to talk about this?'

I don't want to look into his eyes. So instead I look at his arms. His skin is a pale golden brown, the lightest shadow of hair brushing over them like down all soft and touchable and...

'We do. But I've got to go and get something off the printer first.' I walk off stiffly, heading for the ladies' toilets first so that I can stick my head under the cold tap.

I've fucked this up. I've overstepped the mark. We're supposed to be sharing and I've upset him. But how can we share if I can't trust him? Argghhh!

Chapter Seven

Jamie isn't sitting opposite me when I get back. He is sitting at the desk next to mine and, before I get a chance to say anything, he has scooted his wheelie chair closer and his hand is on the arm of mine. Moving away would be a good idea at this point, but I can't.

I am stuck. Partly by my inability to do anything but twitch, partly because he has a pretty firm hold. With his firm, strong hand. 'Are you okay, Alice? You seem really wound up.'

'Well it's a bit worrying, if the company is having to make cutbacks like this and—'

'I meant about sharing a desk.' I know he did. But I'm not going to say so. 'With me.'

'Well can you blame me?' I try and move away. Being this close to him is making me all hot and bothered. I take a closer look at the desk. The spider has gone.

'Sorry about that.' He must have seen where I was looking. 'I didn't mean to upset you.'

It's on the tip of my tongue to say sorry for shouting. But I stop myself. Yesterday, I resolved to be better at putting up boundaries, learning how to say no to people, and 'go away'. Today, with Jamie, I need to make a start on that. I need to stand firm.

'Fine. Anyway, sharing is better than being sacked and not having a desk at all, eh?'

I'm sounding a bit forced and jolly hockey sticks. Partly because my teeth are gritted – he won't let go of my bloody chair! I'm paddling away like a duck and not moving.

'But is it? I mean, you love your desk, don't you? All this, er c…' He falters. I wait. Staring hard at him. If he calls it clutter or, even worse, crap, I really will lose it. An image of me kicking his wheelie chair and him shooting past his desk and out of the office door flashes through my head. It is scarily realistic.

'Cute stuff.'

Oh. Didn't expect that. It stops me (and my killer stare) in my tracks. Is he being funny? I frown at him. Is there a follow-up killer line to take the piss?

'It's like seeing inside your home!' There's the hint of a smile, but he's not all twinkly-eyed. He leans in slightly. 'Or your head,' he says softly. This is weird, and strangely intimate. It's a good job the office is pretty empty.

I laugh nervously. 'You wouldn't want to see inside my head.'

'You reckon?'

Shit. I gulp and try to act normal. And not like I want to touch him so much my fingers are twitching. If I sit there with clenched fists, he'll really think I'm bonkers though, and probably go back to his normal jokey self. I'd like to hang on to the nice Jamie for just a few more minutes. After all, it could be the last time I see him.

Which is good, definitely good. Seeing him day in day out is not healthy. It's like having a box of Maltesers open on your desk with one left in and being expected to resist it. That kind of torture is stressful.

'I can see you in some sweet cottage, with lots of stuff.'

Uh-oh, hang on, he thinks I'm like some old spinster in a dilapidated cottage surrounded by stuff. A hoarding old woman. Great.

'My home doesn't have spiders!' I say pointedly.

He chuckles. 'How do you manage that, then? Some kind of magic?' His eyes are twinkling, but in a strangely intimate way.

No, not intimate. He is not being intimate.

Christ, Alice, when will you ever learn? Fancying Jamie is like fancying the last bottle of Baileys in the supermarket at Christmas. You know the moment you make a move, a hundred other people will make a lunge for it and you will be left empty-handed and disappointed. Or you will grab it first then get home and find it is five years past its sell-by date and rancid.

You will be broken-hearted.

Christmas can be like that. Cruel.

Must not think about stuff like that. Or being attracted to Jamie. 'Conkers,' I say decisively. 'That is how I do it.'

'Conkers?' His tone is disbelieving. 'Are you winding me up?'

'Nope. I put them in the corners of windowsills and

rooms. Spiders don't like them.' I give him a stern look. 'I must remember to bring more in,' I add, trying to soften the words. Wondering again if I should apologize. It's hard breaking a lifelong habit.

He grins before I can, deep dimples forming at the corners of his mouth. Why have I never noticed them before? They're making me feel warm and funny inside.

'I don't think you've got room for anything else.'

'No.' I pause and remember. 'Everything has to go!' I sound like some kind of mad sales lady. Last day! Everything must go! Grab your bargain buy now before it's all binned! Gone for ever!

'Does it?' He finally lets go of my chair and I rocket back into one of the large fake plants that are scattered around the office, then bounce back towards my desk.

He moves back a few inches and looks slightly self-conscious. 'Is it me you have a problem with, or the whole sharing thing?'

I sigh. 'It's not you.' It isn't, not really. 'Though I don't trust you not to mess with my stuff!'

A smile teases at the corner of his mouth.

'But you're right, I do love my desk, I do like having my stuff on it, but…' I fold my arms. 'I can't now, can I? So that's that. It's fine, it's not important. We're supposed to be working, after all. It is an office.'

He shrugs. 'You should still be able to add personal touches if you want, if they help you work.'

'Not that *you* want.'

'Well no, but everybody is different. I think it's cool being able to work at home. I mean, what could be better than being paid to work from your own pad half the week?' His half-smile invites a reply. 'Cool, eh?'

I nod.

'I mean, result! I've already worked out how much I'll save on petrol, plus not having to buy crap coffee and sandwiches for lunch when I can get a meal deal from the supermarket or just grab a tin of beans, and, double bonus, all that extra chilling time instead of a boring commute.'

'True.' I bet he doesn't share a place with mad, noisy people.

'Anyway, leave some stuff out if you want, it doesn't bother me.'

'Really?'

'Really! I'm not completely anal about tidying up, it's just I don't see the point. I just have what I need on the desk.'

'You need that, that bobblehead thing?' I think this is the longest conversation I've had with Jamie since we bumped hips in that pub. Maybe it's because he knows he won't have to talk to me ever again.

'Hey, leave Elvis out of this!'

'Elvis?'

'If I tell you this, you have to promise to keep it to yourself.'

I'm intrigued, and, let's face it, I'm not going to turn down the chance to share a confidence with him, am I? I nod.

'Joke from when I was a kid, first time I got my hands on some hair gel I quiffed up my hair. I thought it was cool, my sister thought it was hilarious. She started to call me Elvis and it stuck. She gave me that when she went to uni, so I wouldn't forget her. Some chance of that!'

'Haha, I can just see you with a quiff!' It makes me feel a bit better. Is that why he told me?

'Look, seriously, leave stuff if you want! I'm cool with it. My mum collects cr—' He stops himself. 'Crochet animals.'

'You were going to say crap!'

'No I wasn't!'

'Crochet animals? Really?'

'And stuff I made for her at school or found on holidays when I was a kid; seashells, you know, bits and bobs.'

I can't help it, I smile. Even though I *know* he was about to say *crap*.

'She likes frogs, God knows why, but she collects frogs.'

'Frogs?'

'Not real ones! Glass ones, pottery ones.'

'Crochet ones?' I can't help it. My turn to tease, for once.

He smiles back. The way the corner of his mouth lifts is quite sexy. Oh lord, I promised myself I would not find him sexy.

I would not stare.

But he's never chatted to me like this.

'One crochet one. Though it could be knitted, I'm not exactly an expert.' I could swear there's the hint of a blush on his cheeks. 'I'd better shut up, I'm talking drivel now. But, anyhow, I'm just trying to say feel free to leave a few bits. Your desk is who you are.' There's a pause. I think he must have seen the gleam in my eye and wants to make this less personal. 'But not pink stuff, or that fluffy thing, or, oh my God, what is that?' He's moved closer again. 'Bloody hell, nobody's true self is reflected in a weird blue-legged duck thing with beady eyes.'

'That's Mabel!' I grab her protectively. 'She's a Blue-Footed Booby.' This bit he definitely won't understand. 'I've adopted her.'

'Adopted?' He frowns. 'Sorry, not getting this at all, you've adopted a toy?'

He flinches slightly, I think I might have given him what Lou calls my 'withering look'. I must not sigh, it's not his fault. 'Not the toy, you idiot. I've symbolically adopted the bird. I make a donation to support conservation work and I get this as a kind of thank-you, I guess.'

'And the koala? The one giving the bird the hug of death.' He points at the small koala.

'Yes, and the koala. I like animals, okay? They need protecting.'

'Sure, me too. Just never seen a bird like that before! I've always been more of a puppy and kitten man.'

'A puppy and kitten man?' Must not think of him cuddling cute puppies. Nope. Bad image.

'Well, er, if I was going to buy a cuddly toy that is, for my er, niece or nephew. Not that I'd buy them for me or anything.' He coughs. 'Sorry, why do I sound such a dick all of a sudden?'

'You don't.'

His eyes brighten.

Oops, better be careful here or I will be getting unreal expectations. 'Well, no more than normal. I better get on with packing, it's okay for you to yak on, you've not got any to do!' I look at his desk pointedly, and then drop the blue-legged bird into my box.

'Is that any way to treat an endangered species?'

'Do you really want her on my, our, desk?'

'If she's going to sit quietly behind the plant, then why not?' He shrugs.

'You don't mind me leaving Rodney? But...' I look from him to the plant and back again.

'Rodney?'

'The plant! I can cut some of the babies off if you like, tidy him up?' I lean into the box and pull Mabel out, replace her carefully on the desk.

'Babies?'

'Babies!' I pull the sprouting end of the plant off and hold it out. 'He's yours, to love and protect.'

'I'm not sure I...'

'Not ready for responsibility, eh? Ah, is that why you haven't got any plants on your desk!'

'Sure! But I have got this, and it's staying!' He dips into his pocket. 'My drinks coaster.' He waves the mat. The dreaded Man United emblem flashes before my eyes.

'Now you're pushing your luck.' I can live with his coaster, if he can live with Mabel and Rodney. 'And Elvis?'

'Yep, Elvis stays. Fairs fair, eh?'

'Elvis I can live with.'

'No touching!'

I slide Mabel to the back of the desk with slight reluctance. My fingertips still resting on the feet. 'Okay, I know you were just joking about me not touching Elvis, and I know this, er, might sound a bit childish, but you won't mess with any stuff I leave, will you? You know, throw it away, or, anything.'

'I was not joking! Touch him at your peril.'

I'm not sure if we're joking here or deadly serious.

'Honestly,' he holds his hands up, 'I won't touch yours if you don't touch mine!'

'I'm certainly not touching that!' I point in horror. 'Manchester United? Come on, you can't be serious?'

'Totally. Reds all the way.'

'This is never going to work. We're sworn enemies.' There's a pause, and I look him straight in the eye. 'Though I guess I should feel sorry for you, now your lot have gone down the pan and we are *leagues*,' I stress the word, 'ahead.'

'In your dreams, Dixon!'

Everybody in the office knows I'm a Man City fan, blue through and through.

I shrug. 'In the stats, Lowe.'

'You wait, we'll be back. It looks like we might need some kind of formal agreement here though before I start adding all my Red paraphernalia and my spider collection!'

'Don't you dare!' I would rather have an empty desk than one covered in Manchester United merchandise. I'm not sure if he's kidding or not.

'Hey, you two, setting the rules, are we?' I hadn't heard Lou sneak up, and now she pops up between us, half blocking my view of Jamie.

'We certainly are.' Jamie winks at me from behind her back.

'See you by the lifts in fifteen minutes, for lunch?'

I nod, feeling my face heat up as Jamie wanders back

round to his own desk. He leans forward, as Lou wanders off. 'Seriously, I don't think your stuff is crap, it's part of you and you're the most creative person in this place, Alice in Wonderland.'

I do blush properly then but, luckily, he doesn't see as he's stood up abruptly and headed over to the coffee machine.

Maybe, just maybe, I can trust Jamie enough to share my desk with.

Chapter Eight

'It's going to be odd not doing this on a Thursday, isn't it?' Lou looks at me over her Subway Meatball Marinara, before taking a massive bite of it.

'Very, I thought things were going to go back to normal.' I like normal, I like knowing where I stand.

'Wow, lush, I so needed that. God, I think stress makes me hungry.' She wipes her mouth with a napkin and closes her eyes as she swallows it down. Then opens them and looks me full in the eye. 'Save us some money though, I guess.' She sighs. 'I was so relying on that fucking pay rise we didn't get. No chance now, eh?'

'I wouldn't have thought so.'

'You worked out how you'll manage at home without using Kat's room?'

'I think so, I just need to suss out how to block out Della's sex sessions.'

Lou knows all about my flatmates. She laughs a hearty laugh (luckily, she's swallowed down the last of her lunch) which causes heads to turn. Lou is a head-turner for many reasons. Her laugh, her love of life, her tiny waist and big boobs, her generous smile and sense of humour.

'Bet you'll miss having poster boy Jamie to swoony smile at.' Her eyes are still twinkling. 'He's going to be all mine!'

What's worse, seeing him, or not seeing him?

'Lucky you.'

'Not so lucky for you! I won't miss seeing Sal sitting opposite looking down her nose at me. Honestly, the faces she pulls when I try and eat a biscuit, even though I'm trying not to crunch.'

I smile. I've seen the looks Sal shoots Lou when she's got a bag of crisps or a crunchy apple. Lou just goes into exaggerated slo-mo eating to prolong the agony. 'God, she even told me off for using the stapler noisily once! How the fuck does one *staple* quietly?' Lou is not the press-it-down-gently type, she's the bang-on-it-with-gusto girl. 'So we're both glad we'll be sharing a desk and not a day in.'

This is good stuff. Lou gets to keep an eye on my desk for me, and I get to sit opposite Sal. I've never had any problem with her. She just gets on with her work. It will actually be better seeing her than Jamie. She's not the type of person to lean over my desk or borrow stuff without asking.

'Your desk will look weird, babe. I've got used to not being able to see you behind all the shrubbery!'

'I'm leaving Rodders.' I grin back. 'We agreed. What about you, leaving anything out?'

She shrugs. 'I might have to take my supersonic sex balls

92

that Lurve Toys said would give me an internal workout to beat all others home.'

She only left those on her desk because Sal flinched at the sight of them. 'Gotta display the freebies from clients!' had been her response.

'Sal said she likes a clean-desk policy, and hers is as clean as it gets, just like the rest of her, so I said I was happy with that. She doesn't give a shit what happens when she's not there as long as it looks totally uninhabited when she arrives.'

Uninhabited. That's what makes this so sad. Work is my happy place, and I have to work out how to hang on to that.

At least Jamie has made some kind of effort to find out what I think about all of this. And suggested I leave Rodney and Mabel, it's a start. Now the rest is down to me.

'You'll have to watch your back, sitting opposite Jamie! You'll never guess what he'd hidden on my desk when I got back this morning?'

'Try me.'

'A flipping spider! He knows I hate spiders, the whole office does!'

'I reckon the whole street does.' She chuckles.

'Okay, okay, I don't need reminding.' There's something about the way they move, or dart, and change direction, and go so fast, and you don't know which direction they're looking in. They make my skin crawl. So when one crawled onto my keyboard as I was touch typing, and the first I knew was when it tickled my knuckles, it was no bloody wonder I screamed and literally leap-frogged my chair, is it?

'He's trying to get your attention.'

'Haha, course he is. He's taking the piss, thinking he's funny when he's not at all. Immature.'

'I reckon he fancies you.' Lou rests her head on her hand and studies me. I get even hotter and more flustered, because who doesn't when they're being interrogated about *talking* to somebody?

'Rubbish. He does not.' God, if only she knew what the truth really was – my shame would be complete.

If the kiss had never happened, then we probably would have settled into some kind of jokey work relationship, like the one I have with Lou. Except it did happen, and it spoiled everything. It made me see that I am nothing to him. It made our professional competitiveness more personal. I mean, I can't lose out on that as well, can I?

'And you fancy him. You do, don't you? At least a tiny bit?'

'No, I don't! Have you finished that sandwich then? Time to go back?'

'Yep, I'm done.' We stand up and she links her arm through mine, leaning in. 'A teeny tiny bit?'

'Stop it, Lou! Come on, we'll be late.'

Lou suddenly stops and frowns. 'What happened to your Soph?'

'Oh, she had to cover for somebody at work.' At least we're off the topic of Jamie now.

We saunter back to the office and I feel strangely uneasy. Does he fancy me? No, of course he doesn't. I know that for sure. We're totally different anyway. Nothing in common.

'And he's a Man U fan!' I say, as though that changes

everything. Did I know he supported the other side when I snogged him? Would it have made any difference?

'Sorry?' Lou pauses as she goes to press the button in the elevator. 'You're still thinking about Jamie! Aha! I knew it! You do like him.'

'No I don't.' I lean in and press the button for her. 'I was just wondering if he's going to stick to our rules and not throw away stuff I leave on the desk, that's all.'

'Stop worrying, Alice.' She gives me a big hug, pulling away as the lift doors open on our floor. 'Joking apart, he's a good guy, I'm sure he is. Not everybody is like Dave, trying to make you do things his way.'

Lou never really liked Dave. She used to say that he was bad for me; he wanted to run my life, that I was too good for him, that I let him walk all over me.

When I look back now, at all the little things, I guess I know she's probably right. But he was good for me as well; he was always there when I needed a chat. I could always rely on him to help me make a decision when I was having problems.

I know if I rang him now, he'd help me see how this whole hot desk fiasco could work.

But I don't ring him for help with work decisions normally, do I? If I can be professional and capable here, why can't I be the same with the rest of my life?

'Stop thinking about Dave!' Lou's tone is firm.

'I'm not!'

'You are. I can see that look in your eye. You got this girl; you don't need that jerk.'

'I know I've got it.' I know my tone is cross, but I'm annoyed at myself, not her.

'Good. Right, I better get back to Chris Hemsworth.' She grins, then high-fives me. 'Roll on Monday. See you later, babe.' She's fishing out her mobile as she turns away.

'Sure.'

'Oh wow, have you seen this email from the dragon?' Lou spins round and waves her phone, but doesn't wait for me to answer. 'We can leave as soon as our desks are cleared. Yay! Result! Good luck for Tuesday, hun, have a good weekend.'

Tuesday. Bugger. I have to work at home on Monday.

I packed my box and wiped 'our desk' clean before I went out for lunch, leaving the spider-plant and Mabel balanced on the top of my pedestal. Seeing as Jamie said I could leave them. The surface was bare. Clinically tidy in a way that made me quite sad.

When I moved into my own place, Mum said I had a thwarted nesting instinct. I guess she's right. Being surrounded by things I treasure makes me more than happy, it frees my imagination. I guess some people need a beautiful landscape, some people need the sound of crashing waves, or blue-sky space. I need my happy space.

When I lived at home it was hard. No privacy, nothing felt truly my own. Nothing was just mine – it was all shared, whether I wanted to or not. And then, when I moved, I soon found out it was more of the same.

I felt like I'd been squeezed out. Until I'd made my desk my own. And everything seemed to slot into place; I felt happier, I felt like I finally had space to think and my work kind of took off.

But once I'd cleared the desk, it was no longer mine; it was just furniture. So, going out for lunch with Lou had been the perfect distraction. The perfect break between then and now – time to move on.

I had told myself that when I walked back into the office for the afternoon, it would be to my new start.

But as I look at my desk my stomach hollows. Oh my God, this is for real.

A quick glance round confirms that people are either still out at lunch, or busy packing their boxes and checking for last-minute emails offering a reprieve (or in Jamie's case, more hours at home), or they've already packed up and gone home early.

It already looks strange and empty. Eerie. Is this a sign of things to come? This is so weird. And sad. Like an ending. Except I must not think of it like that. It is a beginning. A new, different beginning that I am sure will have some benefits. Once I dig deep enough to find them.

Not even Jamie is at his desk. Yep, this is the future. I will no longer be able to glance under my eyelashes at him. I won't be able to share a distant eye-roll with Lou.

Shit.

I sling my handbag under the desk and sink down on my seat. Then I see it. The sheet of paper propped up against the monitor, headed 'Hot Desk Contract'.

Fuck. We've even got to sign a contract?

Hang on, there is a Post-it note stuck in the middle. The handwriting is round and precise. I pick it up.

Taken the afternoon off, any probs with the T&C leave me a note! J (p.s. sorry about the spider)

I can't help it, I smile. Jamie! How did he find time to do this?

I'd always imagined he'd have flamboyant writing, to match his personality. But I suppose, now I think about it, he's actually quite quiet – just hard to ignore.

Anyway, my own handwriting isn't precise at all, it's pretty much illegible. Mum always excused it saying that my brain was going too fast for my fingers. I tend to type if I can, it's quicker. It takes me *ages* to write neatly.

I suddenly realize I am stroking the words with the tip of my finger and stop abruptly, with a quick glance round to check nobody has witnessed that, or the stupid grin I think is on my face.

I peel the Post-it note off the 'contract' and flip the title page over.

Contract between Alice Dixon and James S Lowe.

I wonder what the 'S' stands for?

'You can go you know, once you've cleared your desk. As per the email.' I jump guiltily and shove the sheet of paper under the desk. I hadn't heard Diane the dragon lady marching past, obviously keen to get rid of all of us. She must be dying to get in here and wreak havoc, moving stuff and redesigning our space.

'Sure.' I sit down and root through my box, my fingers lingering over the stone with a starfish fossil that I found on a beach with Darcie – our first break away after her 'accident'. I'm on the verge of crying again. It was a happy moment; she'd smiled properly for the first time in ages, and we'd hugged, then blubbed, then bought ice-cream and sat on the windswept beach with our hair whipping around in our faces and the sand sharp against our skin. I'd wanted to take a selfie of us, but it was too soon for her. So I hadn't got a photo to look at, but I had got this.

It's one of the things that Dave carelessly piled to one side when he was helping me 'declutter'. I didn't notice it was missing for an hour or two, then went into a panic when I realized it wasn't in its usual spot.

And it is far more than just a 'pebble', but he couldn't understand that. This fossil is about moving on, about being strong, about regrowth. About love. I blink. Does Dave even understand that bit?

'Al?'

I glance up at Lou, who has noticed what I'm holding. Her smile is gentle and makes it all worse. God, why am I feeling so bloody emotional? It's a desk, it is stuff!

'You okay?'

I nod. 'Sure. Fine. It's just…'

'Weird? But good weird, eh? It'll work out, things will go back to normal before we know it! You want a lift with your stuff? I'm heading home now, but I could drop you off?'

'No, no, it's fine thanks. I've got an email to answer.' She knows it could wait, she also knows I just need time. It's how I deal with things – sitting quietly and thinking. The office is the only place I get that chance, more often than not after most people have gone, just as the cleaners come in. 'Then I'll get the bus.'

'Don't stay too late.'

I shake my head. 'Don't think Dragon Lady will let me!'

'Have a good weekend then.'

'Hey, you too! Don't do anything I wouldn't! Lou,' I stop her on impulse, 'I don't think Dave really knows what love is.'

She glances at my hand, then meets my gaze again. 'Not the way you do.' Then she straightens up. 'Hey come on, keep the emo stuff to pour into your work, you've got a desk to sort!'

'Yes, Mum!'

Lou laughs and waltzes out of the office, shouting out goodbyes to the few people that are still at their desks.

'Well, Rodney,' I swallow down the lump in my throat and move him 3mm to the right, as though my fingers need to claim some ownership, 'you should be fine right here in the corner, shouldn't you?'

I carefully put the stone, which I've been holding tight, at Mabel's feet. Arrange the seashells and fossil in Rodney's pot where they aren't taking up any room at all, prop up the cat card in front of them, and then drop the contract in my bag. As I watch Lou go, and give her a last wave, I feel slightly guilty that I'm glad I put Jamie's contract out of sight. It feels wrong, secretive, we share everything – but I didn't want to share this. I don't want to joke with Lou about it and turn it into something funny.

I'll read it on the bus, where nobody is peering over my shoulder. Well, nobody who knows me.

The rest of the stuff I manage to squeeze into my pedestal. I don't want to overstep the mark here and leave too much on view – I mean, what if Jamie didn't mean what he said?

For a moment I really hated him for putting that spider on my desk, making me feel terrified in the one place I really feel safe. Just thinking about it now makes my heart pound a bit faster again. Git. But he did seem sorry. I have to trust he did. I have to trust that I can leave a part of myself here and it'll be waiting when I come back on Tuesday.

Oh God, I really do have to sort my life. I shouldn't have to hide everything here, I shouldn't be so bloody relieved that I've managed to cram all the best bits of my whole life into a couple of drawers, should I?

I need to be able to take some of my inspiration home with me, so that I'm happy to work there as well. Without feeling I'm risking my housemates, ex, or family pilfering stuff.

I inwardly sigh. I can't be yelling 'don't touch' at people for the rest of my life, can I? There has to be a way I can make my life work, I have to be capable of creating a safe space where I can be me, that I can call my own. And the office isn't that place.

I will sort it. I will. And I won't ring Dave, because he really is part of the problem.

But for now, it's a huge relief that I won't have to carry a bulky box all the way home.

It's time to go.

Chapter Nine

Saturday night

HOT DESK CONTRACT

Section 1 – *This contract is drawn up between Alice Dixon and James S Lowe and will be adhered to by both parties for the duration of their desk share period.*

Section 2 – *Private vs Public*

2.1 Personal belongings – it is agreed that belongings sitting wholly within the personal space on the desk surface will not be touched or tampered with in any way by the other party. To include, but not limited to, strange stuffed toys, weird plants, assorted objet d'art *and* objet de *nature-things, stuff made out of paper and stuff that 'I haven't a clue what to call it, but it has a meaning'.*

It is agreed that the top, locked drawer of the pedestal is 'very personal' and shall not be tampered with, even if the keys have been accidentally left in.

2.2 Public space – it is agreed that the central area of the desk (as per the demarcation) be freely accessible by both parties. Anything left in this area is deemed 'public property' and as such can be abused, borrowed, defiled or otherwise interfered with without penalty. If any party leaves themselves logged into their personal account they may be considered 'fair game' and screen savers and other such personal settings may be altered at will. Essential computer-use items such as keyboard settings, short cuts etc. which may cause a complete breakdown of the party involving screaming and possibly tears if the dragon lady happens to be in the vicinity, are declared out of bounds, and come under the terms for 'personal belongings'.

2.3 'The Grey Area' – remaining pedestal drawers (see above, top drawer) hereby come under the heading of not entirely personal property, and as such should not be looked at, tampered with, drooled over, eaten or interfered with except in hours of need. This has been agreed as a matter of necessity, as essential stationery items and food may be held in these areas. In the case of impending starvation (hereafter referred to as 'the munchies'), or urgent requirement for (not restricted to, but including) hole punches, Post-it notes, rulers and scissors, pedestal drawers will be considered fair game and plundered as

necessary. Leave things unattended in the grey area at
your own risk.

Section 3

3.1 Penalties – excessive entry into the other party's
pedestal (e.g. finishing off a packet of Hobnobs or Pringles
more than once) may be considered 'out of order' and may
lead to a period of being 'locked out'. A second offence will
result in the injured party being allowed to name a forfeit
(extent to be agreed – no forfeit to include sex acts, illegal
substances, keep-fit activities or any other form of total
humiliation without prior agreement. Note 1, it should be
born in mind that 'total' is open to interpretation
according to morals and life experience).

3.2 Forbidden items – neither party to add items to their
personal area that may cause offence or upset to the other
party e.g. spiders. Exceptions – football merchandise.

I fall asleep with the contract on the pillow next to me, and a smile on my face.

Chapter Ten

'I'll have that last Yorkshire pudding if nobody wants it.' Sophie is already leaning in and spearing the fluffy golden blob of yumminess as she speaks.

'Hey! You had the last slice of beef as well, you piggy! Go halves!' Lucy, the oldest of my sisters, is usually quite restrained, but she's preggers again. It makes her hungry, and quite touchy if I'm honest. Her unborn offspring is obviously already the demanding type – following in the footsteps of twins Brad and Leo. I swear she must have been delirious on gas and air, or whatever pain relief they'd pumped into her, when she decided on names for the terrible twosome and sent Dan scurrying off to register them at the hospital. She loves her movies and I reckon she was dreaming about the romance and daring of *Ocean's Eleven*, and *The Wolf of Wall Street*. Instead she was left with *Fight Club* and the sinking of the *Titanic*. I mean, I do love my nephews, they can be cute and funny. But at times just seeing a photo of their cherubic faces reminds me to check my contraception is 99.999 per cent effective.

Luckily Dan has taken them on an adventure for the day, to give Lucy a rest. He's also taken Darcie's new boyfriend Tom with him, for some brother-in-law-ish bonding. I reckon that about scuppers all hope she ever has of him proposing.

'Let her, love, she's eating for two.' Mum's tone is mild, but even Soph the spoiled youngest knows better than to ignore it. You don't drag four girls through their teenage years successfully without an edge of steel.

'More like three or four.' Soph reluctantly cuts the Yorkshire roughly into two, and hands over the distinctly smaller portion to Lucy.

'You sure you can spare that much?' Lucy's pregnancy hormones are very different to the gooey forgiving ones that Darcie has promised will appear post baby birth. Apparently then she will be soft and lovely, nature's way of stopping her from eating her annoying offspring.

'Ooooh! Sarky!'

'Has she told you about feeding that vegan a proper pork sausage?' interrupts Darcie, spooning some veg onto her daughter's plate (not that anybody is going to argue over kale – I mean, who ever thought it was a good idea to eat kale?) and trying to head the conversation off in another direction.

I quietly finish off the gravy and wonder what my desk is going to look like when I next see it again. On Tuesday. After trying to work at home on Monday. I don't know which day I'm dreading most.

'What vegan?' Lucy is eyeing up our plates slightly manically, trying to decide if there is anything worthwhile to nick while we're distracted. She waves her fork optimistically at the roast potato on my plate.

'Sure.' I push the plate closer to her and watch her wolf it down. If she's eating for the baby, I think she needs to seriously reconsider how much she loads on her fork or she's going to have one hell of a job pushing this one out. It is going to be enormous.

'It doesn't matter *what* vegan.' Darcie rolls her eyes. 'He was a vegan, just any vegan, who thought the tofu was the tastiest he'd ever had. Did she tell you, Al?'

I shake my head and forget all ideas about trying to work out how I'm going to cope with hot-desking.

It's hard to concentrate on anything when I'm at Mum and Dad's for Sunday lunch. It was always like this when we were kids. Slightly manic, very competitive, everybody jostling for attention. 'I don't think so.' I suppose I should be thankful the terrible twins, and the two guys aren't here as well. Then it really would be chaos – except once a certain level of disruption is reached, nobody seems to notice if I stay quiet.

'She didn't say anything, she let him eat a whole sausage.' Darcie emphasises the word 'whole' as though a nibble might have been acceptable.

'Isn't that a bit, like, well immoral or something?'

'I did say something,' Soph says, finishing off her dinner and putting her knife and fork down with a clatter and a sigh. 'I said it *was* better than any tofu, ever, anywhere. I didn't lie! Anyway, I did tell you, Al. You were just busy worrying about losing your job.'

'Losing your job?' Dad frowns and everybody stops talking and stares. It's the first time he's spoken for a while. He's like me, he keeps his head down and lets real-life distractions fill his head. I bet you any money that while vegans have been the topic of conversation, he's been working out how to repair the leaking garage roof. He tunes in when important stuff crops up though. 'You never told us you'd lost your job, love.'

'I haven't lost it. I just thought I might, that we all might.'

'Apple crumble?' Mum is spooning out pudding and clearing plates at the same time.

'Please.'

'What do you mean you thought you all might?' Lucy leans back, resting her hands on her bump. Wow, that is one helluva big bump. What if it is all baby, and no water? 'I thought they were still doing okay at your place.'

I shrug. 'Not as okay as they need to be.'

'She's got to desk share!' Sophie announces, commandeering the ice cream. She's barely got a spoonful out when Lucy grabs the tub.

'No way are you hogging that ice cream! Desk share? Wow, that'll be cosy, just like home!' Lucy, as normal, has hit the nail on the head.

'And work at home,' Sophie adds. As though I am incapable of speaking for myself. See, she wants to share absolutely *everything* – including my thoughts.

'Oh.'

I don't think I even need to be here, I can hardly get a word in.

'So, who are you sharing with then? Do you know?'

'Have you got room to work at home, dear?' Mum says before I get chance to answer. She sits down and frowns with concern.

'He's called Jamie Lowe, and no, well yes, I coped before so I'll work something out.' I smile brightly to reassure her. She worries about us, all of us, she doesn't need my concerns on top of everything else.

'You know you can always come here, Alice. Don't you? You could use your old room, couldn't she, dear?' Dad nods.

'Jamie Lowe!' Sophie's shriek stops the discussion about my bedroom dead. Which is good in one way. Much as I love my parents, working here would be harder than in my place. Plus, Soph is here and would either be bothering me more than normal or seeing what she can 'borrow'. But it is hard to say no; Mum means well and misses the chaos of us all being there. I know she does.

The not-good-bit is Soph yelling out Jamie's name at full volume.

'Who's Jamie Lowe? Is he hot?' Lucy has lost interest in picking at leftover food and is all eyes. She's at that stage in pregnancy when she thinks *everybody* else must want to be pregnant. Just mentioning a man's name gives her hope that I might be about to join the club.

'You shouldn't even be thinking about hot men in your state,' Darcie says. 'Is he?'

'No, he's not, he's…' I'm getting all flustered.

'You are kidding? Seriously, you're sharing with the guy who won over the Chocs'n'Cheese lot? *That* Jamie Lowe?' Sophie's eyes are wide, and I can tell she's trying not to laugh. Why on earth did I tell her about that?

I forget my embarrassment and feel myself start to bristle. I'd wanted to work for that client *so* much, and somehow Jamie persuaded our team leader that he'd be the better bet. I am convinced that this is because he flirted with their account manager, then managed to casually drop into the conversation the fact that his father was their main wine supplier.

He got a big budget, cheese and wine hampers, and bubbly and chocolates – I got basic package staplers and paperclips for a stationery start-up. I mean, there's nothing wrong with staplers, but it's hard to make a website for office essentials look sexy, especially when you've got days as opposed to weeks to do it in.

I'd be lying if I didn't admit that, at that moment, I wanted to poke one of my client's super-sharp pencils up his nostril.

Deliriously happy, prestigious clients also mean brownie points; pencil sharpeners don't. And in five months' time we'll both be due our (very delayed) annual review. If he gets promoted and I don't, I will be livid. It would be so unfair.

He can't not even know I exist as a woman *and* get a pay rise better than mine this way.

'Yes, that Jamie Lowe! He cheated; he practically shagged his way to the job!'

'Really?' Soph's eyes are glowing. 'He is hot then?'

'No, he's not hot, he just, just…oh, okay, he might not have shagged her but, well, his dad…'

'Shagged her?' says Lucy with a note of hope in her voice.

'No, he used his dad unfairly.'

'Would you have used our dad if he'd been in the biz?' All eyes are on me.

Luckily, I do not have to answer this question as it is now Darcie's turn to pipe up again.

'Oh, shit no, it's him!' Darcie yells. My heart lurches, as I half expect him to walk into the room. Luckily, I do not spin round and embarrass myself further. 'I know who you mean now! He's the one who completely redecorated her Christmas tree, isn't he, and hung a disco ball above her desk?' She is grinning.

I hate my sisters.

'Cool!' Tilly looks impressed. I am not.

'Well he's a brave man!' chimes in my father. 'Nobody messes with our Alice's baubles unless they know she's either scared of them, or,' he pauses, ruffling my hair, 'likes them an awful lot!'

'I don't like him!' I avoid meeting Dad's gaze and glare at Sophie. 'I knew I shouldn't tell you anything about work!'

Honestly, does everything have to be shared in this family?

'Oh dear, love, have you had to take all your bits and bobs home then?' Mum spoons extra pudding into my bowl. She knows how frustrating I've always found not having a space of my own, but four kids in a house this size had always been tricky, and I'd always tried not to complain. She squeezes my hand. She also knows that it hasn't exactly worked out how I expected in a place of my own.

'I've left some things.'

'So, it's not too bad?' She still looks concerned.

'No, no, not at all.' I am determined to convince myself, as much as Mum. 'And he was quite nice about me leaving things out, and I've put other stuff in my pedestal at work. It'll be fine, honest.' I squeeze back and smile.

'Well that's good.' She pats my hand. 'And you're sure you'll be able to manage working at home?'

'Of course I will!' I cross my fingers under the table.

'I hope you're not going to let Dave interfere with your work; you're doing so well, Alice. We're so proud of you.'

She is looking even more concerned. I know she's never been exactly over the moon about Dave, but she never said much. Apart from when he announced during a family dinner that he thought my home needed a makeover, and didn't they agree.

If he was looking for support, it backfired. Mum was not amused. She told him quite firmly that you are with somebody for who they are, not who you'd like them to be, and without my things I wouldn't be me.

'We've split up,' I say. She frowns. She's heard it before. 'For good, I've not spoken to him for ages.' Better not to mention the flowers. Better to change the subject. 'It will be fine working from home, I just need to be organized.'

As I say the words, I realize they are true.

That's it, isn't it? I have to be organized, but, more importantly, I have to set boundaries. 'And be firm with people.'

I glance over at Sophie, who is looking gorgeous in my jumpsuit. I have to decide what is important in my life, what I don't want to share. Then I have to stand up for myself.

Actually, Jamie's jokey contract has just given me an idea. I need the same kind of thing for home. Maybe not written down, but in my head – for my own benefit.

That thought about making my home, my home? Well I know how to do it. I need a whole life contract.

No visitors during work time (unless I invite them), nobody in my room messing with my stuff (unless I invite them), no borrowing stuff, no making me feel like my space is not my own.

'Is that my necklace? I wondered where that had gone!'

Sophie grins. 'It goes brilliantly with this jumpsuit, you're a genius, big sis!'

And I don't have to cave into flattery.

'I know.' I smile brightly. 'And I need it back, I wanted to wear it today.'

Soph raises her eyebrows.

I hold out a hand. 'Please.' Soph has always been the baby of the family, the one I loved, shared a room with, shared my stuff with to keep her happy and quiet. I've never grown out of the habit, but she's not a baby now. And I need a place of my own, time to call my own, things that are just mine, more than ever.

'What? Now? You're kidding?' She blinks.

I nod. I must stick to my guns. I mean, if I'm going to do this, I have to start now don't I? Step 1 was Jamie and the spider. I must up my game. I *will* have boundaries. I will not be taken advantage of and walked all over.

Not even by my lovely little sister.

'Fine. Have it.' Sophie scowls, unfastens the clasp and drops it with a clatter on the table. 'Why didn't you say so before?' Her tone is cold.

'Because you just took it, I didn't know!'

'You never complained before!'

'You shouldn't just go in my room when I'm not there.' I try and keep my tone mild. But we glare at each other. We both know that she's always gone in there. I felt sorry for her when I moved out and she was still stuck at home, so I wasn't firm enough about what was important to me.

But she's got her own room now, hasn't she? 'I don't borrow your stuff without asking.'

There is an uncomfortable silence. And then she stands up.

'And I guess you want this.' Before anybody can say anything, she unzips the jumpsuit and lets it slither down and pool around her feet. She steps out, spins round and stalks out, slamming the door behind her.

'Oh dear,' says Lucy, leaning over to take her nearly empty bowl. She licks the spoon. 'I can't remember the last time my stomach was as flat as that.'

'That's because you finish her food off,' says Darcie.

Mum and Dad are just staring, open-mouthed. Mum frowns.

Shit. I've spoiled lunch now. I'm the one who is easy-going, who keeps the peace. Who Mum doesn't have to worry about.

Soph does look quite impressive in only undies and high heels though. 'Sorry, Mum, I… I didn't think she'd just, but she…'

Mum looks at me and sighs softly. 'I think we need warning if you're going to stand up for yourself, Alice, Sophie isn't used to you saying no.'

'I do say no,' I say, my cheeks burning.

'But you don't normally mean it.' She rubs the back of her hand down my cheek, then picks up some plates and heads for the kitchen. 'Don't worry, you did the right thing, love. And she'll be fine.'

'I didn't mean…' Bloody hell. I push my chair back noisily, grab the jumpsuit and then rush out after Sophie. How the hell am I going to get this right? I upset Jamie when I shouted at him about the spider, and now I've made my sister strip off over the jam roly-poly.

How do people say no in a way that says they mean it, but don't upset everybody?

My phone pings as I am running up the stairs. It is a message from Dave, asking if I got the flowers. I wondered how long it would take before he got in touch. Lou had suggested I message and tell him to stick his bouquet where the sun don't shine, until I mentioned it could be tricky with something that size. I said I was going to just ignore it. She doesn't know that half of it is my own fault. Whenever we've split up before, I've always been the one to get back in touch. To ask him for help. I've managed not to for absolutely ages this time, but I guess, like Sophie, he thinks I don't mean it.

I scroll down.

Make sure you remove the stamens from the lilies. Right, that does it. FFS, what kind of man gives somebody flowers and feels the need to add instructions? *I know you can be a bit lazy about these things, but a small input on your side will save time in the long run.* Arghh! A bit lazy? Am I really so wet? At work I'm in charge of contracts worth thousands of pounds. I take control of my projects, make decisions. Set boundaries. Why am I so bad at it in my personal life?

And I trust you used the vase my mother gave you, rather than one of those cheap car boot sale style ones you collect?

Sophie pushes past me as I dither about what to text back, nearly knocking me down the stairs. 'Don't worry, I won't come to yours again without a formal invitation,' she says stiffly.

'Sophie, I didn't mean…' My words fall uselessly into thin air; she's already stomped into the lounge, slamming the door behind her. Shit. I'll have to catch her as soon as lunch is finished, as soon as Lucy and Darcie go. Invite her for a drink, a chat.

I glance back down at my mobile. I haven't got time for this. For Dave. Why am I even reading this stupid message?

In for a penny, in for a pound. I've already upset Soph, so I can't make this day any worse, can I?

Please don't send me things at work, or at all. I think it's better if we don't contact each other again. Alice. I hit 'send' with a flourish and grin triumphantly. Wow, I'm on a roll. This feels good, though. Unlike the Soph incident.

Shit. I've just burned my bridges and can't call Dave if I'm feeling rubbish – and I can't even chat to my little sis now either, I don't think.

I take a deep breath. But I have got my other sisters, and Lou, and Mum. There are lots of people. And I'm an independent woman, for heaven's sake. If it's something Dave can help me with, then it's something I can sort myself.

I look at my mobile nervously for a moment, as though expecting it to leap into life with a message. It doesn't. I've got to stop. It doesn't matter what he says, whether he replies or not. I am going to stop wasting my life.

I slip my mobile back in my pocket and head back into the dining room.

'Okay, darling?' Dad speaks softly, and I nod.

'Fine.' I smile and sit down at the table, even though I don't really feel like tucking into what is left of my pudding now. My stomach has hollowed out, and my palms are sweaty. I don't like rocking the boat, I really don't like upsetting my sister. There's the sound of the TV being turned on. Soph has gone in the lounge.

It will be fine, I will be.

'She'll come round.' He winks.

'I know.' I reach across and pick up the necklace, then slip it into my pocket, feeling slightly guilty. But if I'm going to make this work, I have to actually change things. This is down to me.

I will not be caving into flattery, and I also will not be caving into bullying.

It is time I got a grip.

But I also need to get hold of Soph and apologize, no, explain. After she's cooled down.

Chapter Eleven

F uck, don't you hate Monday mornings? I'm only half awake and desperately trying to grab just a bit longer, but big boots Harry is crashing about downstairs making his coffee and sending irresistible bacon aromas up the stairs that are making me feel hungry, and my phone is buzzing like a demented bee.

I reach out blindly and grab my phone and peer through half-closed eyes at the bright screen. Sugar, it's only 5.30am This is not a real time. Humans should only be awake at this time if they have an early morning exciting flight to catch, or a puppy.

But maybe one of the messages is from Sophie? She often texts really late at night, long after I've fallen asleep, because to her the day doesn't end until at least 2am.

Arghhh, I have six missed calls from Dave, and two more messages. Nothing from Soph, though. Bummer.

Dave never sends this many messages. I should have known he wouldn't want me to have the last word on our relationship, wouldn't want me to make the decision. He needs to be in control. Maybe he needs me as much as I need him; as a sounding board, an emotional crutch to hang on to when times are tough. Except 'emotional' is probably the wrong word for him. He only comes to me when he wants his ego boosting, or confirmation that he was right in some dispute.

I went to sleep smiling at Jamie's contract and I've woken up to Dave hassling me. Why is life so unfair? Why does the guy who makes you grin and feel positive see you as a mate and colleague, and the one who wants to spend his life with you is so intense and interfering he makes you feel cornered and sick?

Or is that just me?

He says he is coming round. I can read that bit without actually opening the message properly. OMG. No way can I go back to sleep now.

Shit. How does he even know I'm working at home these days?

I squeeze my eyes shut as tight as I can and try to relax. Tricky when your teeth are gritted, and the anger is building. Why. Can't. He. Leave. Me. Alone?

Chill, Alice, chill.

I sit up. I can't ignore this, and didn't I vow I was going to get a grip and sort things out?

Dave, I gave the flowers away. Please don't send stuff. It's weird and, my fingers still. I delete the 'please' and still hesitate. Is it wrong to lie? Just a little white lie. I have tried being totally honest. Saying it is over, that I'm not the right person for him, that we both need to move on and forget.

That we had a good time, but it is over. Maybe Lou was right, I've been too nice. Not direct enough. Except direct in her way, as in 'sod off and leave me alone you creep' isn't me. Should I? Can I? One little white lie, that might not be a lie for long, who knows? *is making a new relationship awkward.*

I hit send before I can change my mind. I mean, I've not actually lied. I didn't say I *was* in a new relationship, I just hinted. And it would be awkward if I was. Who wants to glance over their girlfriend's shoulder to see a text from her ex?

I'm not sure that will do it though. I need to be more direct, not use somebody else as an excuse, show him this is coming from me. *As I said yesterday, we need a clean break. I'll block your number, it seems sensible.*

There, I've done it.

Right. I can't take it back. I should feel better. I should lie down, close my eyes and make the most of a lie-in. I don't have to get up for at least another two hours. No bus to catch, no Lou to chat with.

Instead I glance over at my clock and see my necklace. Bugger. My stomach twists. I hate not being on good terms with anybody. I can't just leave this, even though she's not messaged. She's my sister. I need to smooth things over. *Hey, Soph, are you still talking to me? Come round for lunch?* I hesitate before hitting send. No, no. Smoothing over is one thing, but I'm working at home today. I need to start as I mean to go on.

I delete *come round* and type *meet up in town tomorrow.* And add kisses.

Sorry can't. Busy and too broke for lunch. Soph.

I hesitate. *After 7pm, here? I'll order a takeaway? Pizza?? A xxx*

Maybe. Will check my diary. S x

I can't help but smile. The offer of a free Domino's was guaranteed to tempt her. This is good, we can talk. I can explain.

Feeling loads better, I jump out of bed and head for the bathroom.

7am

Wow, working at home is going great. The new desk organizers and boxes that all arrived on Saturday are brilliant – well worth the extra cost of next-day delivery. I have room for my laptop, I know exactly where everything else I might need is and can go straight to the right box under my bed or in my wardrobe when I need stuff and I feel totally – well almost – stress-free.

I'm still a bit worried about Soph and burning my bridges with Dave feels a bit strange. But it will be fine.

I wish I'd got this organized when I'd first started working from home; I never quite got round to sorting things out. Which was mega stressful, and why I was dreading this. But I've got my head round it now. This is for ever (or until I change jobs) so I have to do it properly. And who knows, I might get to like it! Plus, lots of other companies might decide that this is the way forward. The new normal.

The flowers on the windowsill that I treated myself to on Saturday, and the few bits and bobs that I've made room for make me smile. This is good. This is my space and I've already started to expand on the new autumnal conker-themed website and made a couple of minor tweaks that somebody else wanted to their contact form.

9am

Zoe's hairdryer has been going full blast for at least a quarter of an hour. I am feeling less zen. I need to concentrate so that I can get this right.

I need next-day delivery. I switch windows, bring up Amazon, sign up for Prime (well worth it in circumstances like this, shame I can't file it as a business expense) and order some noise-cancelling headphones.

Ha. I can do this.

The hairdryer is finally switched off, but now I know I will be ready and prepared when it happens again on Wednesday.

9.30am

I can still smell bacon. This is very distracting, and not even online shopping can cancel smells out. Except, hang on, the little bakery up the road can! I'll just have to order in lots of yummy breakfast things so that next time I won't be hungry.

10.45am

Kat is marching up and down the landing doing her best to make fudge ice-cream sound orgasmic (she does more advertisement voiceovers than she does Shakespeare plays), my God, how many ways are there to say, 'velvety smooth and taste tinglingly good'? She's been doing it for at least ten minutes and has now enlisted Della's help. Della can make everything sound orgasmic.

There's a rap on the door, then it is flung open. Kat does at least knock, one better than Zoe who just barges in.

'Hey, Alice, you've not got any of that ice cream left, have you? I need to get the sensation on my tongue and in my head, and I couldn't find the tub in the freezer.'

This is a joke. It was only working before everybody else started to wake up. I cannot, I will not, get up at the crack of dawn just so that I can get some peace.

'Wow, it looks very professional in here!' Della has followed her in. 'You look busy.'

'I am,' I say, smiling as bright a smile as I can muster. 'Look, I'm sorry. *Don't apologize, Alice! Don't be sorry. This is your room; you are entitled to privacy and being able to work.* 'I am really busy, lots to do, so can we catch up later? When I break for lunch?'

They both stare at me blankly.

'Sure, but if you can just…'

'No,' I say firmly, getting to my feet and advancing towards them. Maybe a bit too firmly as Kat is frowning. 'It's my work time right now. Pretend I'm not here.' I pause. 'But please don't nick my food. I don't take yours.'

'Well, if you're going to be like that.' Della is backing up, but is not amused.

'I need to work. Sorry.'

'I let you use my room,' says Kat.

'I know, it was brilliant, I really appreciate it. Honest. But you weren't here and…'

'I let you share my dips!' Della looks cross.

'You asked if I wanted some, I didn't just root about and take them,' I point out. The fact that they were past their use-by date also seems relevant here.

'Well, if you're going to get picky…'

'Can't you just give me some peace for heaven's sake?'

We glare at each other for a moment. Then they both back out and Della pulls the door shut – not exactly slams, but so forcibly it makes me flinch.

I can hear them muttering as they stomp off.

Fuck. This drawing boundaries lark is hard, no wonder I've not done it before.

It is quiet though.

I sit down in front of my laptop again and look at the email I was typing.

10.55am

It's too quiet.

I can't think, I can't concentrate, because it's too bloody quiet, and I feel bad. I open the door and there is nobody about. I can hear the faint sound of laughter in the kitchen and I feel left out. Isolated. Lonely.

I swallow down the faint feeling of panic. This isn't what I wanted.

This isn't me – I'm used to being surrounded by people. Somehow, I'm going to have to work out how to find a happy medium. How to claim my space without locking everybody else out.

I'll go down and make a coffee. I've earned a break.

The atmosphere is cold in the kitchen. I walk in and Kat walks out, followed by Della.

'Okay, Al?' Zoe takes a mug down for me. 'Coffee?'

I nod. 'Is everybody always home on a Monday?'

'Kat's between jobs, I'm off to do a client in an hour or so, and Della says everybody is too stressed to think about sex now they're back at work. She's expecting an upsurge in a couple of months. Cheer up, it might never happen!'

'I think it already has. I've upset them.' I've not taken into account their lives, how they feel. How can I be so stupid? How can I know so little about them?

'I can't believe that. Not you, you're far too nice!'

'A pushover, you mean?'

She grins. 'A bit but, hey, you stand your ground, girl. They'll get used to it. See you's later!'

1pm

I spent most of my lunch break going down to the bakery and buying cakes as a goodwill gesture. I left them in the kitchen with a note saying sorry and asking if we could chat about my new working conditions. I reckon I haven't really thought this through. I need them onboard. They are my housemates and I like them, and this is about sharing as well as boundaries, isn't it?

The rest of the day goes surprisingly well. Especially when Kat pops in with a coffee for me mid-afternoon and says, 'You should have said.'

Soph texts to cancel because she's got 'a hot date', but suggests tomorrow.

I go to bed feeling positive.

Chapter Twelve

I look out of the bus window and feel nervous, like the first day in a new job. Monday was weird. It was really strange not being on the bus or swapping stories about what people did over the weekend. I messaged Lou, who said it was like starting a new job. Our desks had been rearranged a bit, the giant fake potted plants had been lined up regimentally to mark the boundary of our office area and the other half of the floor was empty.

No furniture, no people yet. She said it made it all echoey and odd. Like moving into a new-build house and not being able to see it as a home.

I suddenly realize it's my stop and hit the bell before making a dash towards the door.

The newly magnified flutter in my stomach isn't because of the smell of bacon today, it's because I am about to go into work and find out what the future at We Got Designs is going to look like.

Oh my God, I put my hand over my mouth and swallow down the sudden lump in my throat.

I don't know whether I should be laughing or crying.

The other side of the office might be a wasteland, but my, *our*, desk isn't. It isn't bare and strange like I'd geared myself up to see.

A strip of yellow and black tape runs down the left-hand side, and along the top, then back down the other side. There are a variety of coloured sticky notes with 'DANGER ZONE!' written on them, then more with arrows pointing to the right-hand side of the desk, 'MAN UNITED FANS ONLY'. Ha, so that is clearly Jamie's side.

In the centre there's just room for the PC, keyboard and mouse and a notepad if I need one.

Rodney is sat in the top left-hand corner, with my booby bird nestled below him. There is a label propped up in front of them – '*Triffids and blue-legged ducks welcome*'. There's a smaller taped-off area down the right-hand side containing Jamie's coaster and 'Elvis'. I try to ignore the Manchester United logo. It's all touching and annoying in equal measures. He's not supposed to be being kind and making me cry!

It's as though he knew how much trepidation I'd come in with this morning.

'Stupid Man U fan!' I mutter in a bid to choke back the emotion, and hope nobody is looking my way.

I was born just south of Manchester, and my dad is a lifelong Manchester City supporter. It's the Blues all the way at home; when we upped and moved further south when I was eleven years old, Dad kept his allegiance – and often took us up for a day trip to watch a game. He had to have been disappointed that he had four daughters and no son, but I suppose in a way I became the substitute boy. I loved football and loved the time I spent in the park with Dad kicking a ball about. It was our time. You know the term 'quality time'? Well this was it. I had Dad to myself. We could talk, or more often not talk, just quietly enjoy each other's company. There wasn't much quiet at home.

The biggest advantage from my point of view after we moved to a new house away from Manchester, was that Dad treated us to match hospitality when we went to a game. We had a posh meal, the best seats and got to see some of the players up close. And I had Dad to myself for *hours*.

I bet Jamie has never set foot in Manchester, he's probably just one of those people who support a team because they're big. Whereas us City fans know all about sticking by them during thick and thin.

I stare at Elvis. Wondering if he means more to Jamie than he's owning up to.

Luckily, I'm in early (yeah, Harry and his bacon sandwiches were of some benefit) and the office is quiet, which makes it easier, because there's a lump in my throat and my eyes are stinging and I don't think I could cope if somebody made some wisecrack right now.

'This is going to work out fine, isn't it, Rodney?' Jamie has marked out the physical boundaries of our new working relationship, now I just have to work out how to get it right with the people in my life. I don't want to hurt anybody's feelings. I just want them to listen to me. I think that bit might be a bit harder to sort than this. I need to be committed though, or it will be like Dave all over again. I must not dither. I must know what I want and stick to my guns.

I power up the computer, and it's then I see the Post-it note half hidden under Mabel's beak.

You left me to starve! Lucky somebody took pity on me, or I'd be extinct by now. There is a pile of what looks suspiciously like biscuit crumbs all over her feet, and a trail of crumbs leading to another note across in Jamie's zone. *Soz, spotted your biscuits and couldn't resist. Only had one, Mabel had the other. J*

I pull open the top drawer of my pedestal. There is one lonely biscuit left and another note, *What were you thinking? Plain Hobnobs, no chocolate?!!! Will restock mine this afternoon and search out a Blue-Footed-Booby-worthy version for you tomorrow! J.*

'Idiot!' I mutter under my breath, then realize I am grinning as I take my stack of sticky notes out, and nibble on the biscuit as I try and decide what I can write back.

Refer you to section 2, para 1 of contract – no touching of other's belongings. Hmm. *Suggest addition of 'or eating'! Refer you to Section 3, para 1 – penalty to be agreed...* I stop for a moment, then grin, and write faster. *I reckon you owe me a packet of my choosing? Alice. PS Booby birds shouldn't eat biscuits, dodgy diets are why animals become extinct!'*

'Morning!' Sal waves breezily as she picks her way over towards her own desk and I slam the pedestal shut guiltily.

My monitor is glowing, I've got no excuse not to start some work while it's quiet. Yesterday was surprisingly productive – in the end.

After a great start, it did hit a bad patch, when my housemates got out of bed. I overdid myself on the assertive front; I think I might have verged on aggressive. And I can't believe how horrible and impossible to concentrate it was when I felt guilty, and it was unnaturally quiet. But once I'd explained, it got better. Definitely. Obviously, it's a work in progress, but it felt good.

As did blocking Dave.

I still don't feel good about Soph. That is going to be trickier.

But just feeling like I'd made some progress, knowing that I should be able to find a new balance in my life, meant before I knew it I was totally absorbed in my work, and humming along to myself as I worked.

I finished off the design of a new website I was really pleased with and sent it to the client. Hopefully they'll get back to me today.

I think my housemates have forgiven me. Zoe will obviously still have her hairdryer blasting away for hours, but Kat promised not to burst in during office hours (and suggested a lock on the door, and a 'Do Not Disturb' sign), and Della gave me a grudging good morning as we passed on the stairs when I was leaving this morning. It's a start.

I type my login details, hit enter and head over to the coffee machine to grab the first coffee of the day while I'm waiting for everything to load up.

There's no email from my new client, which is a bit disappointing. Instead there's an email from Dave.

Flipping hell, that man is impossible!

We need to talk. Please don't make this difficult. As you have blocked my calls, I decided to drop by. I understood you were working from home? I'll wait, your friend has been very accommodating and offered me refreshments.

Oh my God, he is pompous. And I am going to kill whoever let him in. *I won't be home tonight. Please don't wait.* Do we need to talk? No. Do I need to see him? Definitely not. I am going to stand firm. *I said all I needed to yesterday. I'd rather you didn't contact me again or call at the house. We need a clean break. My email at work is for work only, so I will talk to the tech guys and won't be able to read any you send to this account after today.*

Do I say, you better not have bloody messed with my room? Do I end with 'kind regards', or 'best wishes', or just my name?

I need a biscuit with this coffee while I think about it.

I pull open the drawer.

Bugger! I forgot there aren't any left. Bloody Jamie, bloody men.

My fingers are twitching. Is it wrong to check his drawer? Okay, it's his, I wouldn't normally do this – but he did look in mine, didn't he? And he did say he was restocking his own yesterday afternoon, so he must think I might look.

I open the drawer just a smidgen, to peep, totally acceptable. It's not like I've opened it the full way.

Oh my God! Jaffa Cakes!

With a note. Well, a long message spread over several sticky notes.

Knew you wouldn't be able to resist! No more than three – one for Rodders, one for Booby and one for you. For pity's sake, don't add any more to your menagerie or it'll be a packet a day! J

I close the drawer. Trying to resist. But feel strangely boosted. Even if Jamie will never fancy me, reading his notes has lightened my mood.

Which is more than Dave has ever done.

It's almost like Jamie knew what I needed today. A snack and a smile.

It's not all take with Jamie; he wants this to be two-way. We've drawn lines, and we can share!

I look at my email to Dave. Why couldn't he be more like Jamie? I am so over him. I add my name, hit send and send a message to Tech Support.

My inbox flashes. Incoming – from my new client.

Subject: Superb!!

Result!

Chapter Thirteen

Wednesday

I was very tempted to stock up on a 'shared snack tin' for us, as in me and Jamie this morning. Then I told myself I was being stupid.

What's this about 'us'? Arghhh!

For one, he'd think I was being weird. He also might decide we'd be better on a more formal footing to avoid any awkwardness or misinterpretations and remove the tape, and my belongings, from our desk.

Secondly, I don't even know what he likes, biscuit-wise that is. He probably doesn't even like them at all. It's a girl thing. And, thirdly, what the hell am I thinking? I'm getting totally carried away. Who *shares* biscuits? I'm supposed to be taking control, not sharing, claiming my own ground – and he's complicating it by being nice.

And sharing his own stuff. Biscuits.

But if I do that, is he then going to think I've given a green light for him to borrow other stuff as well?

Oh, and yeah, lastly, they have a crap selection of biscuits at my corner shop, and they're four times the price that they are in the supermarket, so when I went in I hovered by the Hobnobs for a while, then settled for a packet of Maltesers and a can of soup. So that is that.

I am *so* rubbish at keeping my distance and looking after number one.

It was a bloody good job that when I got back from work on Tuesday, Dave had gone. It's almost like now I've decided I don't need him he needs to prove that I do. I guess our relationship has always been on his terms before. He's always popped round when it suited him. In fact, it's been about what he wants, not what I want at all. Why the hell has that never occurred to me before?

Okay, he's been at the end of the phone when I need him. But actually available? Emotionally available, as in really listening and thinking about what is best for me?

And, to be honest, I can never *not* answer my phone if it rings – especially if it's him – whereas some days I've had to call several times before he's picked up. I don't know how people can do that, ignore a ringing phone.

All of a sudden though, he's keener than ever. Just like at the start, when he was chatting me up, before I said I'd go out with him.

He'd left a small bunch of flowers were where my laptop normally sits. In a vase his mother gave me.

I know he treated this like a second home. But now

we've split up? That is definitely overstepping every boundary I've been trying to set up.

After a big dose of internal screaming, and a small external outburst that made Zoe stick her head out of her room, I took the flowers downstairs and 'roughly chopped them' chef style (more difficult than it sounds, even with a good knife – but hey, I was determined, and slightly frantic), then put them in the liquidiser, before pouring them over the bedding plants outside the back door. I then plonked the vase in a charity bag that was due for collection the next day.

Anyway, today was fabulously quiet on the Dave front – because he can't reach me via email or phone! And there were no knocks on the door either – maybe I've actually been firm enough and this time he has finally got the message. It meant I could work in peace on the website and was only mildly interrupted by Jack screaming at *Rocket League*, and Della asking if the cucumber in the fridge was mine, as she needed to borrow it for demo purposes.

If I ever do buy a cucumber again, I will be keeping it in my room. Hidden.

She's obviously forgiven me for shouting at her and Kat the other day. And she did ask, not just use it, so I call that a win. I am making progress.

I am making this work; I am making my place somewhere that I can be happy.

Chapter Fourteen

Thursday

I have woken up feeling strangely excited. It is an office day! This is absolutely nothing to do with the fact that Jamie might have left a message. Definitely.

My phone beeps as I get on the bus, and I fish it out of my bag, wondering whether he has left a message, and whether he actually has left biscuits.

Are you sure this is what you want? No chats, nothing?

Fuck, how did I forget to unfriend Dave on Facebook? A week ago, I might not have felt as confident about this, I would have had doubts. But I do know that this is what I want.

I want to block, block, block.

Dave has been a bad habit. I so nearly rang him over the hot-desking thing, but I'm relieved that I didn't. To be honest, Jamie takes me less for granted, and makes me feel better, than Dave ever did.

If I can sort Dave, if I can sort my housemates, then I can sort my life. Make it more like how I always imagined it could be. Even in my cramped room.

I know I should just delete the message without reading it, but I can't help myself. *Do you need a longer break?*

I jab at my mobile phone. *This was never just a break, Dave.* In my heart, I know it's time to draw a line under this. For us both to move on. He's only calling now because he is confused. Dave the decision-maker is suddenly interested; only because I am not. If I cave in now, then within a week he'll have gone lukewarm again *As I've said, I think it would help both of us if we cut off all contact for a while.* I delete the 'for a while' and replace it with 'leave me alone', my fingers shaking as I hit send. But it isn't because I'm scared or unsure, it's because I'm bloody annoyed.

I unfriend him on Facebook (he has never, ever messaged me on there, which is why I forgot), block him, then systematically go through all my social media accounts and check he is blocked on them all.

I'm feeling flustered by the time I storm into the office and stop by the machine to grab a coffee on the way to my desk. Honestly, he's now moved from okay-ex status, to total pest.

Being assertive is easy when it comes to work, but bloody difficult when it comes to breaking ties with a past that at one time I thought would be my future.

I jump at the sound of an incoming text, then realize it is from Lou.

Hey, how's it going? Loving my new desk – Jamie boy is so

much sweeter to look at than Sal to be sure! Hope you're doing okay with old sourface! L x

She's fine! To be honest, I've hardly noticed Sal sitting opposite me. I've been too busy laughing at Jamie's notes, and working.

Hope you've not caved and got in touch with Dave again?! L x

Lou knows my weakness. She also knew I'd find this tough, and when times get tough I either chat to her – or Dave.

No way! Ye of little faith!! A x

Cool!

He did leave flowers in my room on Tuesday.

My phone rings. 'You're fucking joking? In your actual room?'

'In my actual room.'

'That's not like the Dave I know and love! He must be major pissed off that you don't want him anymore. Threaten your flatmates with back-to-back Hugh Grant movies on the TV at full blast for twenty-four hours or something if they let him in again.'

'You just want to be sure I don't see him and change my mind.' There's a pause. It is what she thinks. 'But I'm not going to, Lou. Not this time, I don't need him. And anyway, what's wrong with Hugh? I like him!!'

'So do I, Al. But I bet you anything that the welly-wearer and Joystick Jack will be scared shitless.'

'I think it's Zoe who lets him in, she'd probs be pleased.'

'Shit. Well threaten her with the serious Hughie stuff,

that's enough to stop anybody! Or say you'll cut her hair off while she's sleeping or something.'

'You're evil!'

'I know.' She laughs. 'You need to take a leaf out of my book, Al. Be more evil! Seriously though, you're better not seeing him.'

'I know. I don't need telling, Lou,' I say softly, but firmly.

'Ace, well, have fun in the office today. How's sharing a desk with the big J going?'

'Fine. He's fine.' I pick my coffee cup up and head to my desk, going up on tiptoes as I walk, trying to see if there are any messages. 'Oh shit, I better go, Dragon Lady is heading my way and she is looking grim.'

'Sure. Catch you later.'

'Speak later.' I manage to dodge the dragon – who has spotted somebody else having fun and decided to jump in there and ruin their day – and make it safely to my desk.

I am grinning stupidly as I sit down. There is a note on Mabel's beak!

Dodgy diet? Man, Jamie dude feeds me better than you ever did!

I open the drawer of my pedestal to get a pen and spot another note.

Sorry, I decided that is how a Booby bird should speak! But, really? What about lifestyle, are Booby birds solitary? Are they happy having only a freaky spider plant for company? Thought not!

I frown, not sure what he means and ponder about it while I power up the computer. It is then I notice the tiny penguin nestling under Mabel's wing.

141

It's cute. Incredibly cute.

Don't call Rodney a freak! He has feelings! Alice x

I smile to myself as I write the note, then take a sip of my coffee and open up my emails. This day might have had a shitty start, but it has already improved.

I scan through the notes from my new client, answering some queries I raised yesterday and then get down to work.

The morning speeds by. The atmosphere is actually quite nice, now I've had a couple of days to get used to it. There's still a buzz, but it's quieter, fewer distractions. The nervous glances that everybody was shooting at everybody else have died away and some kind of normality seems to have settled. A new normal.

I don't go out at lunchtime, just grab the sandwich and crisps from my bag and carry on working. For the first time I can remember, I don't even eat all my lunch as I get distracted halfway through when I have a totally brilliant thought. I shove what's left of my sandwich to one side; it can be a late lunch when I get in tomorrow afternoon and will save me messing about in the morning at home when I could be working.

This is the first project I've been *really* interested in for a while – a revamp of the current website for an animal rehoming centre.

I'd had lots of thoughts because I love animals so much, but the tiny penguin and Mabel sitting nestled together actually give me new ideas about theming it around loneliness and needing a pal to cuddle up to. Warmth and friendship. Happiness.

I'll have to thank Jamie. Leave him another note. Even solitary birds need somebody.

The time flies by. I'm actually quite shocked when somebody walks past my desk saying, 'Night, see you tomorrow!'

As I get in the lift, I realize I've not thought about Dave at all.

Chapter Fifteen

Friday

From: Slade, Diane <Diane.Slade @WeGotDesigns.co.uk>
To:
Date: 9 April 2021, 07:30
Subject: OFFICE ATTENDANCE – FRIDAY

Dear all,

After much consideration, it has been decided that office attendance on a Friday will be at the discretion of each individual. Please ensure that if you attend the office, you do so in your allocated time period.

If you work at home on a Friday, mark your progress sheet to indicate this, unless you have had holiday approved.

Regards,
Diane

Wow! My heart had lurched when the email bounced into my inbox with a loud ping, and I'd been crossing my fingers on one hand as I'd clicked it open with the other. I mean, what kind of thing had she cooked up now? But this is good. I think. Well, definitely not bad.

I don't actually want to work at home on my in-office-allocated Friday afternoon. Partly because working at home is still kind of awkward – what with the smell of bacon (makes me feel starving), orgasm noises (very distracting) and general interruptions – even though it's much better than it was.

Not to mention the fact that my mum has said working from bed will lead to a bad back in a few years (how did she guess I do that some of the time?). It is kind of nice to have a bit longer in bed, and although I like getting the bus into work and people watching, I reckon I could get used to doing it less often. After all, it is always the same people, and most of them don't seem to have lives that are any more exciting than mine – so I can skip a day and not have missed much. Apart from the girl with blue hair and the guy who tries to chat her up. He's been trying for weeks, and *that* is interesting. He's working through all different approaches and I reckon he's getting closer to cracking it – or being told to bog off. Either way, I'd be upset if I missed the big turning point.

But, anyway, apart from that. If I don't go in on a Friday

afternoon, I won't know if Jamie has left me a funny note, will I? I'll have to wait until Tuesday!

Oh no, what am I thinking? Since when was a note from Jamie part of my reasoning? Part of my weekend.

Sugar.

Why do I care? I don't care! They're just jokey notes that he would leave for anybody.

The only reason I will be going in this afternoon is that it is easier to work there, and I've got to chat to my client, and the sound of a hairdryer on full blast and Jack shouting 'take that, twat face' is not conducive to a professional image.

Thanks for sandwich, hold the mayo next time? J

WTF? You have to be kidding me? Jamie bloody Lowe is back to his normal, annoying self. He's eaten the leftover sandwich I'd kept for lunch. I didn't bring anything else in and skipped breakfast as well! Bugger.

And what does he mean, hold the mayo? Is he a complete heathen, as well as Man U supporter?

I stare at the neat pile of crumbs at Mabel's feet. Then grab the note and tear it up into tiny bits, with some ferocity, and am just about to drop them into the bin when I have another idea.

Okay, call me petty, but he has EATEN MY SANDWICH! It wasn't just any old sandwich either, it was a special cheese and fancy chutney one, with a use-by date of today. I'd double-checked when I left it last night. I would have taken it home or binned it if I'd thought it would be rank today.

On Wednesday I'd been ultra-organized and bought myself two sandwiches. I'd eaten the salmon and cream cheese one at home, as it was closest to its use-by date, and it's a bit dodgy keeping fish stuff like prawns and salmon, isn't it? It's warm on the bus and I wouldn't trust putting it in our office fridge for even the morning. It's opened and closed (and opened and *not* closed for *ages*) more frequently than a chain smoker lights up. It can't be the proper temperature, so chicken and fish don't go there as far as I'm concerned.

Cheese is fine.

'Everything okay?' Sal is staring at me. I nod, then try and smile, which is pretty hard when your teeth are clamped together, and you want to kill somebody.

I wait until she is looking at her monitor again, then drag open the top drawer of his pedestal. I can't let this go. Ha to you, Mr Neat and Tidy, see what you think about this!

The confetti-sized scraps of paper are falling from my hand when I see it. A second note!

Gotcha!!! It is safe and sound in the fridge! You'd left it on the desk, hope it's still edible? Office is pretty cold overnight, so should be okay J x PS Have a good weekend.

OMG, he knew I'd be straight in there, checking out his drawer! Although if I hadn't, and I'd just seethed and swore about him, I wouldn't have discovered that he was just being nice. Kind.

Shit. Bugger. I scrabble madly to try and gather up the bits of paper. Has being scared about sharing my personal space turned me into a nasty cow? This is not me, retaliating. It really isn't.

This is all my own fault anyway; I should have remembered to put the sandwich in the fridge myself before I went home. Why on earth didn't I?

'Sorry, sorry, sorry.' I stop muttering under my breath and slow my paper-gathering to a steady pace, as Sal peers at me again. Nothing going on here, lady, go about your business.

Shit, shit, shit. I'm going to have to take out all his stationery, and I shouldn't. It's his stuff, what if I put it back in the wrong place? It's one thing to open a drawer and borrow a pen, or biscuit, but to take everything out, tip it upside down, and put everything back?

I'd kill somebody if they did that to me.

What did I say about enjoying coming into the office, and being more productive? Productive, my arse! I've got absolutely nothing done. And now my phone is buzzing.

Shit, it will be my client. Wanting that professional phone call!

I slam the drawer shut, sending paper scraps flying into the air, brush my hair off my face with both hands, take a deep breath and lift up the receiver.

'Hi, Alice Dixon here. How can I help?'

I cannot believe it is nearly time to go home! I've had a lovely chat with Maria, who runs the animal rehoming centre. This project really is ace. And why on earth did I think I couldn't cope without my old desk?

All I need are Mabel, the penguin and supportive notes from Jamie and my imagination works fine.

It's all about having the *right* things at the *right* time. Obviously.

We touched on Blue-Footed Booby birds, conservation, lost dogs and orphan kittens and she sent over adorable photos as we chatted, and we tweaked the colour scheme, improved the font and designed a new fundraising page as we went. It was so exciting, and I got so carried away I hadn't realized the time. I haven't even eaten the flaming leftover sandwich, which basically means I'm starving as I've not eaten all day.

Oh God. I glance down and am quite shocked to see the mess under the desk and remember what I did.

I head to the tiny office kitchen and my sandwich is in the fridge, exactly as Jamie said it would be. Which is lucky. I munch on it as I head back to my desk, and the guilty feeling magnifies. I've been unfair.

Why do I always assume the worse? Just because so many people take advantage of me, doesn't mean he will. He never has. Okay he's been annoying, and introduced spiders into the mix, but he's never crossed the boundaries, invaded my personal space.

Plonking myself down on my chair, I stare at the penguin nestled next to Mabel. It is looking back at me with a shocked expression on its face.

'Stop it!' Gawd, now a penguin is trying to send me on a guilt trip. But I do feel guilty. I deserve it.

What can I do to make up for my nasty reaction? I suppose one good thing is, he doesn't know. Well, not unless I leave any bits of his note around.

I scrabble under the desk, grabbing pieces. Why did I tear the note into such tiny pieces? Why couldn't I be normal and settle for tearing it in half like a normal person would?

My mobile phone pings and I jump and bang my head on the desk, then back out quickly, hoping nobody has seen. I rub my head as I pick up my phone.

It is a text from Soph. *Am in the bar on the corner. Fancy a drink? Have brought a dress of yours that I forgot I had and not got time to take it to your place. Soph x*

She had time to go there when she wanted to borrow it.

It's taken a few days for things to completely thaw between me and Soph, but I think everything is okay again now – and she is actually offering to give me stuff back unprompted. This is positive.

Sure. Where you rushing off to? A x

Got a hot date with the vegan to discuss the morality of sausages!

Do sausages have morals? *You came clean with him?*

Sort of! S x

How can you 'sort of' tell somebody you fed them something they are against eating? *Alice x*

Hurry up! I'm thirsty!! S x

You mean you didn't? A x

I kept it hypothetical. Are you coming or not? S x

I scribble a note to Jamie. *Sorry, had to empty your drawer out, sandwich-related incident.* He won't know what that means; he'll think I dropped some mayo in or something. *Hope I've put everything back in the right place. Hope you had a good weekend. Alice.*

I glance at the second note he left me.

OMG, how did I not see that? Hell, he put a kiss on the note! A kiss!!

My first kiss, well apart from the real one of course, but I'm trying not to think about that. This is a new start! Did he mean it? As in *mean* it.

Shit no, definitely not. It was probably just a habit and he did it by mistake.

I am dithering, I am also being silly. Totally silly. I must ignore the stupid jittery feeling of excitement inside me. It is a friendly note, that just happens to have an X after his name.

I can't leave that in the office, what if the office cleaner plucks it from the bin and tells everybody? Or pins it up on the noticeboard?

It deserves to be kept safe, private. I pick it up, stuff it in my pocket and then grab my handbag. Then hesitate. Should I add a kiss to the note I've left for him?

Too much?

Oi! Hurry up! My phone pings with a message from Sophie. I glance back to check I haven't left anything behind – like incriminating scraps of paper – and make a dash for the lift, just before the doors close.

When I emerge in Reception, she is standing there. Impatiently.

She shoves a bag at me, I have a quick peek – it is my

dress. 'Come on.' She links her arm through mine. 'I need some advice on vegans.'

'But I don't—'

'You're better at finding stuff on Google than me.'

'So you don't just want me to come for a drink because you love me?' I say, slightly hesitant.

'Oh, Alice.' She rolls her eyes at me. 'That's just a given. Now will you fucking hurry up, I'm meeting him in less than an hour.'

'You really like him, don't you?' I grin triumphantly.

Sophie colours up and shrugs as though she doesn't care.

'Oh my God, my burger-munching sister has fallen for somebody who only eats plants!' She's a meat and carbs on the side girl, meat and two veg at a push, definitely not veg and veg.

'I don't think he does, that's what I need to check.' She grabs my arm and practically drags me out of the building.

I wonder what kind of an afternoon Jamie has had?

———

'What's that?' Sophie plucks something off the seat, as I stand up to go and order another round of drinks at the bar.

I half turn. 'Dunno, not mi…' The word dies on my lips as a flash of yellow catches my eye and I realize that it is mine! Oh shit. I lunge at the scrap of paper she's waving in her hand, but she's too quick.

'Oh my God, it's a love note!'

'It is not!'

'There's a kiss!'

I try and swipe it again, but she jumps up and holds it high above her head. There's a flutter of panic in my throat. What did it say? 'Give!'

Soph does not 'give'. She grins. Did I say my little sister can be evil? 'I thought you were going to get some drinks?'

'I thought you were in a rush to meet triple-veg-guy?'

She wiggles a bit in her seat, but doesn't give me the note.

'Haha! I know what you're up to, you're just trying to stop me asking about him. You must really fancy him.'

'He's cute,' she says, avoiding eye contact, which could mean anything.

I wait until she glances up. We look at each other. Like we used when we were kids, and she was deciding whether to push her luck or not.

This time though, we're even. I hold out my hand. I used to do that quite often as well. 'Give.'

She reluctantly puts the crumpled note on the palm of my hand and I form a fist, screwing it up even more, then shove it into my pocket. Properly in this time. I'm going to have to get the iron on it, or my mini flower press which I've had since I was ten years old and kept just in case pressing flowers became a hobby again later in life. See, it might come in handy, it was worth keeping!

'Wine?'

'Gin,' she says. Heck, she must be keen, I've never seen her this nervous about meeting up with a guy before. 'Hey.' She stops me as I turn away. 'That is from Jamie, eh?' I eye her suspiciously, but her look isn't teasing, it's genuine. 'Opposites attract, eh? Like me and Daz.'

So vegan-boy has a name. But Daz? 'He was just being nice, it isn't like that.'

She smiles, sits back. 'So why did you keep the note?'

I don't know how to answer that. So I go and get the drinks.

Chapter Sixteen

Friday, again

I can't believe that it's the end of April and we're several weeks into our new way of working. The days have sped by and even on a Friday I can't wait to go in for the afternoon. Which is slightly crazy. It's always quiet – as it's optional – but I like it.

'You look happy,' Sal says, slightly disapprovingly, as I grab a coffee and waltz past her and round to my side of the desk.

'Sorry.' I suddenly realize I am humming out loud, I'd thought that was still in my head.

'No problem.' She sort-of smiles. 'It's a nice day, isn't it?'

'It is!' I grin back. We're nearly into May and the April showers seem to have finished early, the sun is out and there's a real feel of good things in the air.

I put my coffee down on the desk and sit down. And look expectantly at Mabel. She is not holding the message of the day. Nothing on Rodney's pot either. Or on the mouse. Or monitor. Or under the desk. Or, I get up and look down, under my bum on the chair. I put a hand casually on my bottom, as though I'm smoothing my skirt down (in case anybody is watching) to make sure the Post-it isn't stuck to it.

I'm sticky-note-free.

I am in a note-free zone.

There must be some mistake. I've missed it, or it has fallen off on the floor. I start to move things, I even pick up (yes, I *touch*) the dreaded Man U coaster.

The feel-good factor of the day fades a bit, and I frown.

How can there not be a note? There's always a note! There's a hollow feeling in my stomach and I realize that half the reason I enjoy Fridays (actually look forward to them) is to read the Post-it notes that Jamie leaves for me. Sometimes he is teasing, sometimes just reporting back if something funny has happened in the office, sometimes he's eating my snacks or leaving me new ones, and sometimes he's just plain being nice.

Whatever they say, I look forward to them.

The feeling of disappointment is totally out of proportion.

Oh no, what if he's ill? What if there is something wrong? Has he even been in the office this morning?

Nothing has moved. I double-check. I scrabble around in my pedestal, even lifting my notepad up and rooting about in the pens. I slam it shut. Open his, look under Mabel. I even move Rodney to the side and check under the pot, getting more frantic each second. I must slow down. I must not get worked up.

I prod the soil to see if it is dry. Jamie often waters him on a Friday morning.

It is damp. But is that just damp from another day? Did I water him yesterday? Oh God, I can't remember!

'Are you okay?' Sal's concerned tone snaps me out of my activity.

I blink at her, and nod.

What is wrong with me? Why does this even matter? Since when did the notes become the highlight of my day? Oh bugger, bugger, bugger. Arghhh. I want to scream and bury my head in my hands, but that would bring Sal scurrying round.

Shit, I've been humming as I walk through reception for the first time ever, because I've been excited about heading for my desk.

Now I know why.

This has nothing to do with work. It's to do with Jamie. I've spent the last two years carefully detaching myself from him – well at least making sure he's not aware of my lustful thoughts that are well under control, thank you.

A flutter of panic starts up in my chest and makes me feel all twitchy.

I have also looked forward to leaving notes for him. This is the road to disaster. I have been FLIRTING with him, and he knows nothing about me, apart from the contents of my desk, and now my biscuit preferences.

And I know nothing about him. Well apart from the fact that he like to eat his Jaffa Cakes top to bottom. And I know he hates mayo on his sandwiches, loves beef and mustard, and prawns are a no-no. I warned him not to touch my prawn roll once, because for one I love prawns and, secondly, there was loads of mayo – as far as I am concerned, the two are a marriage made in heaven. Apparently not, according to Jamie. They make him want to vom because it reminds him of the time his mate gave him a maggot sandwich when they went fishing. He never went fishing again. Or ate a prawn sandwich.

I know his mum keeps 'stuff'.

Sugar, I don't know 'nothing' – I know lots of little stuff that I didn't know about Dave by the time we'd progressed to sex. And not even after that.

But I don't know if he has a girlfriend. I don't know if he really is a neat freak, or if he has to have control of everything. I don't know if he forgot our kiss because he was drunk, or because he didn't fancy me, or just kisses lots of girls.

I don't know anything important. I leave kisses on the notes, I save some he's left for me in the bottom of my handbag because they make me smile when I'm on a working-at-home day. I am too involved. This will be more of a disaster than the forgotten kiss and the corridor body bump.

All I know is that I like the side of Jamie I'm meeting through his notes. He's not being annoying, like he was in real life. He's being kind and funny.

Maybe he's just a complete commitment-phobe who can only cope with a message-type relationship.

I check out my biscuits; none are missing.

He must be ill.

Except the note I left him yesterday, stuck to his packet of biscuits, has gone. So he must have been in this morning, but—

A chill runs through me as I remember.

Oh shit.

I bury my face in my hands. The bloody note. I was trying to be funny, but then had seconds thoughts and nearly went back to rip it up, but somebody stopped me at the lifts and was telling me what Lou had been up to the day before. It was funny, I got into the lift with them, totally engrossed, and forgot all about it.

The trouble is our little messages had started to get a bit more personal, a bit more, well, like we were sharing a private joke. And I'd got carried away.

What had I said? Something ridiculous about if we (we!) had children would they be marooned (red and blue, get it?). We'd swapped a string of bad football jokes.

This was the worst yet, but I'd thought it was funny.

And then there was the note about how he'd make a brilliant dad one day – after he had tied a mini balloon to Mabel for her birthday.

He's been in this morning; he has just not responded to my notes.

Oh my God, that was what did it. Shit. It was too much. I'm not funny at all. I've overstepped the mark. What kind of person goes on about kids to a workmate?

I have spoiled this for ever. What did Soph say about opposites attracting? They don't, they scare the fuck out of each other. The last thing a commitment-free guy like Jamie wants is to think about fatherhood.

'Will we be actually working this afternoon?' Dragon Lady has snuck up on me undetected and is looking pointedly at my monitor.

Fuck. I jump guiltily. 'We will!' I say brightly, shuffling the keyboard and mouse into their proper positions, and double-checking there isn't a note hidden underneath. 'Just getting my thoughts in order; the animal rehoming centre said they would be in touch with you later today, they're *thrilled* with the new website. Visitors have already increased, and they've only got the holding version.'

'Good.' She seems slightly mollified as she strides off, then pauses. 'Well done.' Wow, a nice word! She takes a step back and glances down at my desk, 'How amazing, we can see some of the desk surface, it is obviously helping with productivity.'

Why does she have to temper every compliment with criticism? Has nobody told her it is bad for staff morale, and their bloody productivity?

'Splendid,' I chirp out, instead of asking what school of man-management she went to, hammering wildly on my keyboard to try and look super-efficient. 'Silly cow,' I mutter once she's three desks away and annoying somebody else.

I stop typing 'kjfalursljnskanjcbeettfvkjlsfjlsh1t' and open my emails.

From: Lowe, Jamie <JamesS.Lowe @WeGotDesigns.co.uk>
To: Dixon, Alice <Alice.Dixon@WeGotDesigns.co.uk>
Date: 30 April 2021, 11:30

Subject: Hot Desker

Oh my God, an email! He's forgiven me. I duck my head down as I realize that I'm grinning like a loony and might attract unwanted attention.

Hey desk buddy!

Say hi to the menagerie for me! Wasn't in this morning and I know they'll be missing me. Rodders has been watered and rotated; he was getting lopsided leaning towards the light.

Have a good weekend.

He doesn't mention my note, or our children, thank goodness. He really will make a good dad one day, though. I'm pretty erratic about watering and rotating. Rodney is the only houseplant I have ever had that has survived more than a year, because spider plants are pretty indestructible. They survive. Jamie is disciplined. Logical.

I close the email feeling slightly sad and open up the website I've been working on.

We can move on from this; he has forgotten it already. Like he forgot the kiss that I have obsessed about for the last two years. One day, when I'm an old granny, or old spinster, I will be obsessing about the summer of notes.

An emails pings in and I open it automatically, my mind still occupied with the moving banner I've decided to put on the website. Is it too twee if a little dog is pulling it across? Yes definitely, this is serious, we don't want too cute. We want the people driven to adopt to have love, desire, commitment for life. Not be lured in by gimmicks.

I'm still thinking hard and don't focus on the email straightaway. Then it sharpens up.

Sorry, forgot to say. Our children will need my discipline and order, as well as your generosity, chaos and creativity! Will they be mixed up, or just plain all-round amazing?

Wow, the relief that he's still talking to me, properly, is so massive I actually laugh out loud. Then hide behind my monitor when Sal perks up. I'm still smiling though.

Amazing! I type back. *How can they be anything else?*

I know he's only messing about, teasing, but I don't care. I am not going to over analyse this. I am going to go with the flow.

Should I have lasagne from the freezer tonight or go mad and order a pizza? Delivered? I rather feel like I have triumphed today – on the work front, and on the Jamie front, and should treat myself. I deserve it! In fact, I am feeling rather smug as I stride into the house. Shouting hi to Jack, who grunts and waves briefly before shouting, 'Hell yeah, take that, you suckers' at the TV. I don't think his lifestyle is healthy. He needs to get out more. But what the hell, who am I to judge? He is happy.

'You look happy!' Zoe says, moving Harry's wellies from the middle of the passageway to the side, holding them with the tips of her manicured nails. 'Good day at the office?'

'Fab!' I am definitely having pizza. The works. A meal deal with garlic bread, and possibly cookies. Or should I raid my snack cupboard, if nobody else has, that is? Although I have to say, apart from one time when a packet of biscuits had gone – but money had been left in their place along with a note saying 'desperate circumstances, sorry' – my belongings have been left untouched.

'Oh, Al, that guy came by looking for you?'

I look at her, I am puzzled. 'Jamie?' How does he know where I live?

It's her turn to frown. 'Dave? Who's Jamie? A new one?'

'Dave?' It takes a moment for the name to sink in. Why would Dave be here? I've not heard from him for ages. Well, like three weeks. Since I told him we had to break all contact, since the sandwich incident with Jamie.

Jamie. I feel the smile twitch at the corner of my mouth. I've not missed Dave at all, not had the slightest urge to call him.

Dave must either be very bored, or there must be something really wrong. But that's not my problem, is it? He must have somebody else, somebody close who can help.

'I thought it was over between you two,' says Zoe.

'It is,' I say firmly. See, I am feeling firm as well as happy. I have a positive outlook. 'I've told him not to come here, please don't let him in if he does.'

Why on earth didn't I tell my housemates not to let him

in? Except it hadn't really occurred to me. He'd listened. He'd moved on. No need.

'Oh.' The tone of her voice stops me in my tracks. 'Er, sorry, Al, I didn't realize. I thought you guys were back together again after he brought those flowers round?'

'We aren't, he was just trying. Was it you who let him in?'

She shrugs and looks guilty and I feel sorry. Bugger. Things had been going so well at work, and here that this had never occurred to me. Since my outburst things had improved no end, and I was slowly working out how my room needs to be organized.

'He said you were expecting him, and he, er, well he went to drop something in your room. Is that a prob?'

She looks so upset that I give her an impromptu hug. Shit, I'm going to mess up again and make her hate me. 'Don't worry, no harm done! But please don't let him in again.' All my housemates have been great lately, and I'm being OTT again. This doesn't have to be a big deal, I'm over-reacting.

'Sure thing, you should have said!' I should. 'He's very persuasive, though.'

He is. I know what he's like. He's one of those smooth-talkers that has the confidence to barge his way in anywhere, and he's so totally convincing it's really hard to close the door in his face. 'I know, sorry.' Shit, I have to get out of the habit of keeping saying sorry.

'Isn't it a bit weird, the way he won't listen?' I nod. 'If it was me, I'd threaten him with the police or something.'

I head up the stairs. She might have a point. I am not

going to let him ruin my good mood, though. He's done enough of running my life, or should that be ruining my life. Enough.

I throw my bedroom door open, a small swirl of dread in my stomach and my heart thumping, expecting a room full of flowers or something gross.

OMG, he has tidied up. I realize my hand is over my mouth. My ex, who I have not spoken to for weeks has made my bed.

I feel sick. This is so, so wrong.

He used to make the bed when we were together. I'd do it quickly, then he'd adjust everything. Straighten the sheet, adjust the pillows an inch or two.

At first it seemed sweet, his attention to detail, then it started to annoy me. I didn't want somebody correcting everything I did, suggesting it wasn't good enough.

Now he's still doing it and anger bubbles up inside me. He's also straightened up things on my workspace. I can tell. Minor adjustments so that things are more uniform.

I'd forgotten he was quite this bad.

I'm just about to cave into the impulse and jump on the bed and mess up all the sheets when I see it. The note.

I love reading the notes from Jamie. Jamie is light, teasing, fun. But getting one from Dave is totally different. I don't want him back in my life. It's too complicated – it would make it too easy to fall back into my old ways, to start to rely on him again. Then he'd let me down or start telling me what I should and shouldn't do.

Like the way I should make the bloody bed.

Sorry I missed you. Thought I'd pop in for a catch-up, see if you wanted to come to Joe's wedding with me?

Ha! He wants a plus one, that was what this is about. Dave can't be seen as single, can he? I thought it was a bit weird, even for him, to suddenly appear again after so long. Stalkerish, which he isn't.

Had a bit of a tidy-up while I waited – thought it might make it easier for you to work. See, this is what I saw as good about Dave at the start. I thought he did these things for me. Other people thought he was wonderful as well (so helpful, you make such a good team, a keeper!). The perfect, caring boyfriend. It took a while for me to work it out, but it wasn't about loving me, it was about shaping me into the person he really wanted. He wasn't just rearranging my stuff, he was rearranging my life.

Maybe relocate some things to give you more space? I could take some to my place?

And re-bloody-locate? Where the fuck does he think I can move stuff to, even if I wanted? And 'take them to his place' means chuck them out. I know him too well.

If he has thrown a single thing out, I will kill him.

Arghhh, I hate the man! And he honestly thinks I will go to his mate's wedding with him? He's mad.

It would be so much bloody easier to just ditch this place for now. Do what Mum suggested and move back home – at least until Dave has decided to leave me alone. Or, oh my God, what an amazing thought, move in with Jamie. Jamie doesn't mess with my stuff, he's just thoughtful and sweet. He gives me space, I can trust him…maybe he has a spare room? I actually feel lighter inside just thinking about that.

Bloody hell, pull yourself together, girl. Move in with Jamie?

I reach for my mobile. I need to ring Lou. I can't talk to Soph when I'm this wound up. I know she's my sister, but I don't want her rushing round to help (I know she will) and telling the whole family (I know she'll do that as well). I know they mean well, but I need to have a rant and I need to make my own decisions. Mum would definitely suggest I move back. But that would be so wrong.

This is my room, the space I've fought to make my own – and I have to sort it out myself.

I don't want to worry them. I do need to let off steam though.

Or do I?

I slowly put the phone back in my pocket. I don't need Lou, or anybody to help me through this. There's a much better way to let off steam! I'll re-sort my room, unmake my bed. I need to erase Dave and push on. This *was* going well.

Maybe I've been a bit wishy-washy with Dave, maybe I've unconsciously hung back a bit because he's always been my safety-net, my security blanket? This time I will do it properly. I don't need his shoulder to cry on. I've got this.

What am I waiting for? I need to get this done and earn my pizza.

Chapter Seventeen

Saturday

I have not slept well, which is bloody annoying. I like my sleep at the weekends. I like to go to bed late after a good movie or book and climb into bed knowing that there is no alarm going off in the morning. That I have *hours* in bed.

Instead I am wide awake, and it is 5.30am The birds are tweeting, but not even Harry is up cooking bacon.

You'd have thought that after my frenzy last night, putting my room back to normal, I would have been exhausted, that I would have collapsed and slept solidly.

Nope.

I lay on the bed, fully clothed, thinking about Dave. I crawled under the duvet an hour later hating Dave, and I have woken up thinking about fucking Dave. He is doing my head in. I need a better plan.

I lie flat on my back and try not to scream.

We split up ages ago, why does Dave still think he can use me when it suits him? He is still treating me like his girlfriend. No, it is worse than that. There's a rush of hot and cold through my body as I realize. I blink. He is treating me like I belong to him. Like a possession.

He's not decided it should be over, so in his head it isn't.

Honestly, this being firm in my private life is a minefield compared to work. I upset Soph when I said no, sent my housemates into a tizzy and felt like I'd been sent to Coventry (which was horrible) when I asked them to leave me alone, but blocked and ranted at Dave and not made the slightest impression.

He thinks he is in control. And, in a way, he is. I'm allowing him to be. I'm thinking about him, which is exactly what he wants.

My whole frigging time with him was about compromise – but all one-sided. I took my stuff to work, because he didn't like it here. I let him rearrange my stuff. I snuck stuff back out of the trash, rather than playing hell with him for putting it there.

I let him make the bed the way he wanted to, dip my light because it was too bright in his eyes – which meant I couldn't see to read in bed, so stopped trying.

Why the hell did I do that? Was I scared that I'd be lonely without the noise, chaos and constant interruptions of my family home, and then student living? Had I been frightened that my own company wouldn't be enough, that I needed to hang on to somebody who I knew (haha) would be there for me?

Or maybe it's just been easier to let Dave get away with

walking all over me, than risk him going – even though I've known for a while he isn't the one for me.

I did really hate it when I upset Soph and she wasn't talking to me, and when my housemates gave me a wide berth, were super quiet and stopped knocking on my door. It was nearly as bad as the constant interruptions and invasions of my privacy. Nearly.

So, I obviously do like, need, some background buzz, to know people are there. I'd never make it as a hermit. But some things I can do without.

So much of my stuff was at work because Dave didn't approve of it (and everybody else who liked to 'borrow'). It's no way to live, is it?

I am not going to mope; I am going to put this right. I am getting out of bed. While I was putting my room back in order, I was plotting.

Step one is to throw out everything connected to him. Why on earth didn't I do that when I was rearranging my room ready for working at home? Step two is to make sure everybody is crystal clear about not letting him in, and I'll work out the rest later.

An ASBO would be nice, but I don't think you can get those for annoying exes who you haven't told to piss off clearly enough.

The only person who can change this, who can make things happen, is me.

I stand in the shower and let hot water bounce off my already warm skin, force myself to relax. The sound of heavy footsteps on the stairs stops me dead, my entire body stutters. I stop soaping myself and strain to hear who it is, where they are going.

Oh God, I wish Jamie was here. I feel kind of chilled when I'm around him.

Safe.

Bugger, why am I thinking such stupid thoughts? I think I need to turn the shower on to cold setting. And it isn't that I'm not safe. I'm just angry, and frustrated.

Anyway, logically it is somebody going down, not up. So it definitely isn't him. I force myself to take deep, steadying breaths. But I still feel on edge. Since when am I the type of person who is constantly listening out for trouble?

There's the distant sound of the kettle being filled, the clatter of plates and then the smell of bacon drifts up.

Harry. See? Nothing to worry about.

I get out of the shower more pent up than I went in. Harry even offers me a bacon sandwich (that's a first), so I must look like I need help – and that is his currency. Nothing wrong with a man who wants to feed you, but keeps himself to himself.

He pushes the sandwich in my direction when I sit down at the breakfast bar with my coffee. 'Alright?'

I nod. 'Thanks.'

He puts together one for himself and picks it up, mug of coffee in his other hand. 'Better go plant some pansies.'

'Really?'

'Kiddin'' He winks. 'It's a digging day, body under the patio and all that.'

'Wow, you've just given me an idea!'

'Well I'm your man if you need a shovel.'

I'm not sure if he is being serious or not. I don't know him. This is the closest we've ever come to a conversation.

'Laters.' He strides out of the kitchen, munching and humming to himself.

I wish life was as simple as a shovel and big hole.

I swallow down the last bite of my bacon and head back upstairs, coffee in hand. Then I roll up my sleeves and get cracking again. Boy this has been a busy weekend so far. I will start to the left of the door and work my way round the room.

By 11.30am, all trace of Dave is in boxes and binbags. I reckon a forensics team could sweep the place and not turn up a single strand (or whatever unit it comes in) of Dave DNA.

I have also realized there is a step three. I grab my laptop, open my emails and type.

Dave

Don't come round again, I've told my housemates not to let you in. Sorry, but I don't love you. So NO I don't want to go to Joe's wedding with you. It would be weird. Whatever we had has gone. I have asked you to leave me alone. If you contact me again, I'm going to take legal advice.

Alice

The last bit seems a bit OTT, but so is Dave. I hit send and collapse back on the bed, exhausted and frazzled.

Sunday

I realize my job here is not done. I have things to fix before the working week starts again.

I have spent the last few years discarding (or relocating) my own stuff – first for my family, and then I repeated the pattern all over again with Dave. How stupid is that?

My room is my space, and I am reclaiming it.

'What are you up to?'

I need a break from my room, so have brought my laptop down into the kitchen and I'm scrolling through the photos of Dave that I've got backed up on it.

'Is it back on again then?' Kat smiles.

'Definitely not.' I find one of him staring straight at the camera, unsmiling. 'I want to make sure nobody lets him in again, he's being a pain. I'm going to print a couple of these out at work tomorrow then stick them up.' I hesitate. 'That's not been over the top, is it? I won't upset anybody?'

'No way, it's cool. We all know where we stand if you do. I mean it's tricky, isn't it, if somebody turns up and swears they're welcome? You just kind of take their word.' I nod. 'Look, you can borrow my printer if you like?'

'Wow, you've got a printer?'

'Sure, that's partly why I put a lock on my room, cos there's stuff in there that I don't want messing with or nicking if somebody forgets to shut the front door. We can do them now?'

'Brilliant!' I grin at her, and she squeezes in next to me at the table, to help me blow up and print out a couple of photos of Dave. Then she whizzes off to her room to get them.

We stick one on the pinboard. 'Why not turn it into a WANTED poster?' asks Zoe.

'Because he is unwanted,' I reply. 'Like the dog that was bought only for Christmas. He needs rehoming.'

She giggles, 'Or euthanising?'

'Rehoming,' I say firmly, grinning at her and Kat. 'Although Harry has said he's got a big shovel!' I'm beginning to realize how much I like my housemates. All along, all I needed was a few ground rules to set my own boundaries.

'Aww, hun, I wish I'd known he was being a pain in the arse,' says Zoe, suddenly serious. 'He seemed so sweet and like he really loved you.'

'My mum always said to look out for the quiet polite ones, they are the worst.' Kat shakes her head. 'At least you know where you stand with a gobby git who oversteps the mark on purpose.'

'True. I never thought Dave would be like this, but it's just like my opinion doesn't matter, he doesn't hear it.' I sigh. 'I mean, what kind of person just assumes their ex will be happy to be their plus one at a wedding?'

'Does Della know not to let him in?'

'Not sure, but I'm going to tell her, tell everybody.'

I then go round and explicitly state to everybody else

that they must not let Dave in, I also stick a reminder note and another photo of him on the back of the front door. Which Zoe thinks is hilarious. But I don't want him getting in, whether I am here or out.

Harry said 'fair enough' and stomped off in his wellies, Jack said 'cool' and went back to his Xbox warfare, Della suggested he might be sexually challenged and was looking for a way of asserting his male identity.

Anyhow, they all seem to have got the message. I feel a sense of achievement. So, rather smug about my new assertiveness (get round that one, Dave!), and all warm and fuzzy about my lovely housemates – who all of a sudden seem to have become friends and a real benefit in my life, not obstacles and unwelcome presences in my home – I decide I need an afternoon of chilling. I will go for a long walk.

Chapter Eighteen

Monday

Monday morning comes, and I don't feel like I can work here, in my room. Even though I've achieved loads, it's been a bit stressful and I need a break from the place. I don't want somebody to accidentally gatecrash my peace and quiet and spoil it all. I want to hang on to the feeling that it's finally all starting to fall into place.

My home can be my happy place.

I will work at one of the hot desks set aside for people who urgently need to be in the office on a stay-at-home day. I'll tell the dragon I've got workmen in, or no internet, or no electricity, or something.

I slap on the minimum acceptable amount of make-up, swap my sloppy wear for slightly smarter (and less coffee-stained) work wear and pull the door of my room decisively behind me.

I'm tempted to put a hair or something above the door

handle, like they do in movies, so I will know if anybody has been there. Which is ridiculous. I have to trust that what I've done will work. Or how can I ever move forward, without looking over my shoulder?

Jamie is whistling and carrying a cup of coffee as he strides past me. He's got particularly nice bum-hugging chinos on so that you can almost see the strong lines of his muscles through as he strides along, and…

He stops abruptly. Backs up a couple of paces until he's level with me and does a double-take. 'What's up?'

'Thought it would be easier to work in the office, my internet is a bit…' The lie I had prepared for the dragon dies on my lips. 'I just fancied it.'

It is odd, sitting at one of the 'hot desks' that are lined up along the wall of the office for anybody who has to come in on a day that isn't officially 'office' for them. It's a bit like working in a coffee shop window, but without the view. Or the decent coffee.

Okay, it's not like working in a cafe, it's more like being in a school exam hall, or at one of those working areas at the airport, where the shelf is only just wide enough for your laptop, you're right next to the queue for beer and you don't want to look at a blank wall because you're scared you'll miss out on something exciting. Like a strip search, or your gate being called.

But anyway, right now it is better than being at home. I don't really expect Dave to come round again, he's not stupid, but if he did it would cause upset and friction.

He is *so* going to hate what I've done. Which is fine, I don't want his approval. But I do hate conflict. I guess I've always been the people-pleaser of the family, taking after Dad. I was the peacekeeper when my sisters were yelling at each other. I was the one who appeased little sister Sophie when one of our older sisters said she was too young to join in with what they were doing. And I got to be even more that way after the attack on Darcie. Life's too short.

I feel all twitchy. The sooner I can get my head into work the better, I need something to distract me.

'Well you can't sit there.' Jamie grabs the pad and laptop off my desk and puts a hand on my elbow so that I'm forced to grab my handbag and follow him – or else create a big scene and attract attention. I reckon he knows I won't do that.

'Why? What? It's a hot desk, I'm allow—'

'Nonsense. No way am I letting you sit there. You can't kid me that you prefer that to sitting in your own room at home.'

'Well actually…' I am about to tell him he is talking rubbish, and doesn't know anything about what I'd prefer, when I realize that he is steering me towards my, sorry, our, desk.

'Oh no, no! Stop, Jamie!' It's hard to be indignant quietly and dig my heels in too obviously. People will notice if he's dragging me, sliding across the office floor. Won't they? 'I can't, it's your day in. I'm fine at,' I wave towards the hot desks, 'one of the spare—'

'You need it more than me, Alice, I know what it means to you to be with your own stuff around you.'

I am getting used to the office not being like a home to me, not having as much of 'me' on display. I realize that I've actually been feeling a lot more confident about not needing so much 'stuff', and it's getting easier every day – now I'm starting to feel confident that my private property will be there for me, untouched, where I left it, when I get home.

But Jamie is right, this is a bit of a step too far right now. At least I can see my Rodney and Mabel from the hot desks though. If I crane my neck or sit up meercat style.

'I'm fine, honest. I won't be here all day, I —'

'Here we go.' He puts my notepad down and points to the chair.

Oh my God, I am going to sit down on his still-warm chair.

'Lucky I've not even had chance to sit and settle in for the day. Eh?' He grins.

Oh bugger, yes, he was on his way in. What am I thinking? Our chair is un-sat on, not yet warmed up. Shit, I hope he doesn't know what's going through my mind, he'll think I'm a right weirdo.

I plonk myself down and sit bolt upright, a bit stiffly, then he wheels me in closer to the desk as though he's my mum. He leans down, his warm breath fanning my neck. Not at all like my mum. 'On one condition though.' His voice is soft, deep, sending a shiver down my spine and goosebumps along my arms. Gulp. 'You come for a coffee at lunchtime?'

I nod, not daring to speak because my throat is dry and

I'm trying not to lean into him or turn my head and gaze into those gorgeous eyes.

Oh my God he smells nice. I don't know about 'cedar notes' or 'woody' or 'spice undertones' or any of that crap. It's a bit like with wine; I don't analyse it, I drink it. And with this, I just want to sniff him. Oh boy. It's just male, and sexy, and clean in a just-washed, not worked-myself-into-a-sweat-at-the-gym kind of smell.

Although I'm sure even his sweat smells nice, not like that OTT teenage testosterone smell that made me nearly puke when I accidentally wandered into the boys changing room at school after athletics practice. Never again.

Why are my eyes closed? Why am I leaning like the tower of Pisa?

I probably should move away. Quickly. Now. Now, Alice.

I stare ahead stiffly, and his head suddenly appears in my vision as he ducks down in front of me making me jump.

'You sure you're alright?' There's a quizzical but caring look on his face.

My nodding dog impression kicks in.

He reaches over to pick his pen up off the desk, his warm bicep brushing against my arm. Then he stands up straight. Phew.

'Half past twelve?'

'Sure,' I squeak, recovering slightly now there's a small distance between us. 'And thanks, for…' I indicate the desk.

'No probs.' He smiles. A proper smile that reaches his eyes.

'Alice!' Everybody looks up as Lou yells across the office before bouncing over, splashing people with hot coffee as she goes. It's a good job it is early and there are not many people in yet. 'Oh shit, you're in! Why didn't you tell me?' She goes in for a hug and I flinch away as her coffee cup goes whizzing in the air. 'Sorry.' She giggles and puts it down. 'Come here, girl.'

I'd forgotten just how impulsive, how crazy, how loud, how wonderful Lou is. Wrapped in her arms, I remember and my eyes sting. She releases me, so I sniff and blink rapidly. 'Shit, it's nice to see you, we've got to do a catch-up. Oh my God, we could have done lunch, but I've got a meeting with the poo puffs.' I chuckle. This is not a non-PC comment, Lou has been working with a small company who are going to revolutionize lives all over. Whether you pass wind in the bathroom, the living room or, heaven forbid, the bed, the poo-puff will detect it and puff a special neutralising smell that you will barely notice. Ha, yes. I'm not sure if these guys are for real. We used to have a dog that had the power to make the gassiest after-curry offering from a human fade into non-existence. So good luck with that, poo-puffs. 'You should have let me know and I'd have rearranged. We could do one evening? Why haven't we done that yet?'

We have swapped messages, but seeing her in real life is different.

I've got on with Lou since the day I started working at We Got Designs, but it's always been a work hours type of friendship. We've done lunch once a fortnight or so and gone to the bar across from the office after work sometimes, but we've never actually had a proper night out, away from work, thing. I guess with me living west of the office, and her far north we've just kept our socializing office-based.

'I don't know! We've got to, I've missed you.'

'I'll head over to the wasteland.' Jamie gives me a thumbs up.

'Thanks, honestly, you didn't have to—'

'I know, I want to. Look forward to seeing you at lunchtime.' He winks cheekily, throws his rucksack on his shoulder and strides back across the office.

Lou opens her eyes wide. 'Wow, he gave up the desk for you, must be love.'

'Shut up, Lou.' I try and shake my head dismissively, but, from the way my face feels, I suspect I am the colour of a beetroot.

'And you've got a lunch date! Won't be as good as me, mind you.'

'Never!'

She grins. 'Better get to it!' She picks up her coffee and waltzes round to the other side, sits down at her own desk and chuckles. It's infectious, I grin back. It's going to be funny working opposite each other!

I settle down. It's weird being in on a different day, seeing people I haven't seen for ages. Seeing Lou. It's amazing how quickly we've adjusted to the new normal and come to accept the way things are.

I spend the rest of the morning getting to grips with a particularly boring change request to a website, which means peeping under my eyelashes at Jamie is far more interesting an activity. Gawd, I wish I had something mind-blowing and exciting, or just plain tricky to do this morning – which would mean I have to concentrate.

It gets even worse when Lou catches me do it. There's a big grin on her face.

'Are you okay?' Jamie is looking straight into my eyes, the hint of a smile on his face.

I bite into my baguette as a delaying tactic.

'What?' I try and act as though I don't know what he means.

'You're in? I mean I know it must be hell for you, not seeing me, but…' The smile is encouraging, his words only gently teasing.

The man gave up his desk. He's been nice. He's bought me lunch. I owe him at least some kind of explanation, I guess.

'Reading your notes just isn't enough!' I say jokingly, and he chuckles.

'Mabel misses you.'

I wish he did.

'But?'

I sigh, put my lunch down and wipe my hands briskly on the paper napkin as though being brisk will make this easier. 'It's my ex.'

'Flower man?'

'Yeah, Dave.' Wow, how does he even remember about Dave sending the bouquet? I try and get my thoughts in order, decide what to say. Jamie waits. Not eating or drinking, just patiently waiting. But, strangely enough, it doesn't feel like pressure.

'You don't have to tell me, it's none of my business.' He cracks first. 'But you just don't look happy.' His tone is soft.

'He went round to my place when I was out and messed with my stuff,' I splurt out, look at him in astonishment, then instantly feel better. 'He just thinks he can step in when he wants and just carry on where we left off.'

Jamie nods, looking thoughtful.

'Sorry, he just wound me up. It made me cross that it doesn't seem to matter to him what I think, he can just carry on as though we never split up.' I guess though what has really got to me is that he could do it again, and, if he does, we'll have to have it out. Properly. I'll have no choice if he's ignoring what I've said in my emails. God, I hate confrontation. It just seems so stressful, and so unnecessary. 'It's nothing, it's my fault for not being clearer with him.'

'He doesn't want to let you go.'

'Well, I wouldn't say—'

There's the hint of a smile curling the corners of his kissable mouth. 'I get that.'

I feel the heat spreading over my cheekbones, but try to look casual, as though I'm not totally embarrassed.

'I don't think I'd want to let you go, Alice.' His gaze makes me heat up even more; I'm holding my breath. This is unreal. Then he glances down, stirs his coffee. 'But if you said it was over, then I might of course have to double-check and not give up too easily, but then I'd back off. If I knew it was what you wanted.'

'He thought I'd go to a wedding with him.'

'Not yours?' Jamie has a gentle smile on his face.

'Shit, no! His mate's,' I say slightly breathlessly, then sigh as the reality of Dave hits me again. 'I mean, what kind of thick skin do you need to do that? He didn't make the decision to split up, so he thinks it's fine. I'm just available, on tap, to be used. I can't believe he sat in my actual room waiting, though, and went rooting about.' Maybe he thought I wouldn't make a scene with all my housemates about.

'That's a bit freaky.'

'He was bored. It's a typical Dave thing to do, he even made my bed!'

Jamie's eyes are open wide. 'Wow, most people don't even make their own.'

'Exactly. We're not compatible at all.' He blinks. 'Not about bed-making, I do make my bed,' I add hastily. 'I mean with everything else. He tried to change me, make me what he wants, and it took me ages to realize.' I need to get this all off my chest now I've started, I don't really know why I'm trying to justify our splitting up to Jamie though. 'He used to throw out the bits of my stuff he didn't like, which was most of it,' I say wryly.

'Ahh, so that's why,' he says softly, his eyes never leaving mine, 'you keep stuff in the office? Where it won't get touched?'

This is why I'm telling him, because subconsciously I know he'll understand.

'Sure, the home for my crap.' I laugh awkwardly. It's either that or I'll be tempted to kiss him again.

'It's not crap! It's cute, very you.' There's just the hint of a smile now, I don't think he's teasing. I think he means it. I'm cute. Me. I can't breathe. I really do want to kiss him. 'You Blue-Footed Booby girl!'

Oh. Not sure how to take that.

I stare down at my napkin.

'But it is stuff he might have binned, or touched or…' The teasing note has gone.

'Yeah, partly. Well, mainly, but there's never been much privacy in my life, seeing as I've got three sisters who like to borrow stuff. And housemates who eat my food, and desk sharers who eat my sandwiches.' I raise an eyebrow and give him a look, and he laughs. A proper deep-throated, sexy laugh that makes me grin back. It lifts the intensity for a moment, makes it easier to carry on.

'I didn't actually eat it!'

'I know. You're forgiven.'

'But your sisters don't throw your stuff away?'

'Nope.' I circle the crumbs on my plate with a finger, then pull them together into a neat pile. 'Just borrow stuff, especially Soph. Dave's the only one that does that. It's my own fault for not being clearer with him, but I've got it sorted now.'

'Normally just saying you want to split—'

'But we've split up before, then got back together and I guess he thought it was just that.' I look him in the eye. 'I'm a bit of a pushover.'

He grins. 'Oh my God, I wouldn't say that! Alice the killer negotiator!'

'That's at work. I'm easier going at home,' I say, grinning back. Far too easy-going. 'To be fair, it's not just Dave, I'm just not much good at laying down the law with anybody which is why it was such a nightmare working at home last time and why I was dreading doing it again. But I think I've got it sorted now, I've got my room how I want and an understanding with my housemates—'

'No more nicking your sarnies?' His eyes are twinkling.

'Exactly. Though I might need to be a bit firmer with my desk-sharer.'

'Ouch, I guess I asked for that!' His eyes really are gorgeous. Crack on, Alice, ignore how sexy he is.

'And I don't want Dave barging in and spoiling it, it feels like he's invading my private space just as I'm starting to like it.'

'He is.' Jamie nods as he speaks. 'It's not on if you aren't there.'

'That's why I wanted to come in today really.' He must think I'm a right drip. 'I just didn't want to start the week on the wrong foot. And…' Time to be totally honest. 'I didn't know what he'd say if he did come round, I don't know what I'd say.'

To be totally honest, I don't want to fall out. It's not that I've ever thought Dave would be violent, he's not like that. It's just me. After what happened to Darcie, the acid attack, confrontation of any kind makes me nervous. She'd had the smallest of tiffs with that guy's girlfriend, then refused to fight. She'd walked away. And look what happened to her. I spent lots of time with Darcie in those days, I was the natural choice – the quietest sister, the one who'd listen, the one who wasn't mad about going out and wouldn't nag her to have fun. I love all my sisters, but I loved Darcie so much back then. My heart hurt for her. I learned so much from her – about self-esteem, about bravery – about how it can be better to just walk away rather than argue.

But I'm not saying that to Jamie.

'You're worried?'

'I just didn't want to be there if he came. It would turn into an argument and it would spoil things. I'm not going to let him spoil anything,' I say firmly. 'And my housemates have got my back, they know not to let him in now. I should have made it clearer at the start, but I honestly never thought he'd do that.'

He squeezes my hand, and I suddenly realize he still has his over mine. He pulls back.

'The worst bit was on Friday. I went mad. I trashed my bed,' I say, to break the silence. There are better ways though; it is embarrassing remembering what a fury I was in.

Jamie chuckles. 'I'd have liked to have seen that!'

'You wouldn't, believe me! Then,' I take a breath, he'll think I'm mad, 'I went through everything in the house that was his, or that he'd bought me, and I trashed the lot.'

The grin on Jamie's face makes me want to laugh. His eyes are shining and his whole face seems to light up, to be animated.

'And then I made posters of him and made sure everybody knew he wasn't allowed in.'

This time he laughs, a proper belly laugh. 'That's the Alice I know and love! Every option covered. You're amazing.'

'You don't think I'm terrible?' He said I was amazing!

He also said he knows and loves me. Though he just means in a work-mate way. It's just a turn of phrase, not a flaming proposition. I still feel all hot and bothered and over-pleased with myself though.

I think I am glowing.

'No way. Crystal clear is the way to go with a guy like that. A girl's gotta do what a girl's gotta do.'

'Even if it's nasty?'

'Oh, Alice, you're not at all nasty.' The grin fades, but he looks even more gorgeous now. Not at all judgemental. 'Look, don't take this the wrong way, I don't want to interfere, but if you're still worried that he'll come back…'

I nod. I really don't want to get into a shouting match with anybody. And if I got home and found him in my room, what if I couldn't help myself? What would the consequences be?

'So how did you manage before?' The change in direction throws me for a moment.

'Well partly 'cos one of the girls was away and let me use her room.' I smile. 'Her room with a lock!'

Jamie leans forward, rests his strong forearms on the table, his fingers knitted together. 'Ahh. Well that's what we need to do then.' His smile is soft. He really is attractive when he's in a gentle mood like this. Instead of teasing me.

We? I didn't know we were in this together. That I had backup. 'What?'

'You need a lock on your door.'

'Well I did think it might be an idea, but I trust my housemates, they won't go in now, and they won't let…'

'Call it an insurance policy. Just in case somebody

doesn't lock the front door properly. And hey, it'll stop your sisters from popping by and borrowing stuff, won't it?'

This is true. And I had thought a lock could be a good option.

My housemates would let Soph in, no question. This sets a very firm, non-confrontational boundary. I just have to explain why I've done it, without upsetting anybody.

'It'll give you some privacy?'

I nod, still a little bit doubtful about how everybody will take it. 'You can say it's something you need for work, as you'll have sensitive material there?'

Ahh, now that sounds more promising. I can go with that, and there are rules about data privacy and client confidentiality, and the risk of copying, aren't there?

And I mean, if somebody accidentally left the front door open, and somebody walked in, and took my laptop... It doesn't bear thinking about.

This time I nod firmly and smile. He smiles in response. We seem to be doing a lot of smiling at each other. 'I'll come around later and do it for you then. Okay?'

'But, I can...'

'You've got a lock? Screwdriver?'

I shake my head. I'm not the type of girl who keeps a toolbox.

'Well then, stop arguing. Right, drink up or the dragon will be after us!'

I knock back the rest of my coffee and realize I'm smiling, and I feel relieved. Wow, do I feel relieved. It is like somebody has got hold of the tight knot in my stomach and unfurled it.

I can't believe I've told Jamie all of this. I can't believe he's offered to come round and put a lock on my door.

I open the front door cautiously, which is stupid. Nobody would let Dave in.

There's no sign of anybody else as I walk slowly upstairs and push my door open. The air comes out of my lungs in a massive whoosh of relief when I see that everything is just as I left it. I hadn't realized quite how tense I was.

I sink onto my back on my bed and stare at the ceiling. Wow. I feel all floppy and pathetic.

Dave has not been round to the house today. This is excellent – I don't want him here, and I was frightened that if he saw what I have done with his stuff it would cause MASSIVE conflict.

But I don't need to explain myself, do I? This is my space, my life.

And shit, is that the time? I need to get changed.

I try not to overthink it as I pull a clean T-shirt over my head. Was it really a good idea to agree to Jamie coming here? Our chat this lunchtime has left me feeling even more conflicted. He's a nice guy, he's being kind, but he hasn't a clue that I have the complete hots for him. Letting him in my bedroom isn't exactly keeping him at arm's length, is it? Even if he stays the other side of the door, and I'm by the bed, it is still barely an actual arm's length. And he will have seen my bed, and my clothes, and…oh bloody hell!

Look at the state of the place! There are knickers on the floor.

'There's a guy for you, Al!' yells Zoe and my knees tremble. Oh shit, shit, shit. Dave is back. He must not come in here; I can't handle that at the moment. I'm not ready for a showdown. And I've got Jamie coming.

Heavy footsteps come up the stairs. My heart is hammering as I shoot out of my bedroom door, pull it shut behind me and try and compose myself.

My hands are shaking, as well as my knees.

This is bloody ridiculous. Zoe would have said if it was Dave.

'Hey! Do your mates always let strange men in?' Jamie grins, and my heart starts pounding hard for a totally different reason. Relief floods through me, leaving me feeling all weak and hysterical.

'You're the strangest yet, haha!' How can I be so jumpy? I'm losing the plot. 'You're early!'

'Keen! This is it, then?' Jamie motions at the door. Bugger, better let him get on with it. He's here to do a job and get out quick. He must have lots of more interesting things he needs to do on a Monday evening.

'Sorry, yeah.' I fling the door open with a flourish. Shit, black knickers on the floor! I do a kind of weird dance, trying to kick them under the bed casually. Oh hell, they're hooked over my heel, I need to flick them, casually, backwards, behind me.

He doesn't say anything as I prance around like some mad Spanish dancer. He doesn't seem to notice; the door is more interesting apparently. He waves a bolt in the air. 'This isn't that strong, it's not like one for an external door, but I reckon it's more of a deterrent than anything?'

'Definitely.'

'Great.' He takes a screwdriver out of his bag.

'More visitors on the way up! You're popular tonight, Alice!' chuckles Zoe, waltzing past.

Oh shit. Jamie and I look at each other. This is not good. Unless I throw myself at him, which would really send out a strong message to Dave.

I could apologize profusely to Jamie later. He'll understand, it is in a good cause. It might even bring back memories of Reading Festival, of me, of kissing…

Except she didn't say it was Dave, and everybody knows that Dave isn't allowed in here. She definitely wouldn't be laughing if it was him.

'Well, well, well, big sis, what is going on here then?' Sophie bounds up the last two steps and looks from me to Jamie and back again, then grins at me and opens her eyes wide mischievously and mouths 'ooh sexy' at me. I send back a 'don't you dare say a thing' message with equally wide eyes. Which has never ever worked. 'Hi, I'm Sophie!' She looks back at Jamie, head tipped on one side.

'Jamie,' he says, smiling.

'Oh my God,' why does she have to be so dramatic? 'Not *the* Jamie Lowe?'

'Sophie!'

'I have heard *so* much about you.'

Don't you hate having sisters sometimes?

'Really?' He raises an eyebrow.

I glare at Soph, sending silent death threats. 'She'd be lost without you; you've been so kind. Al deserves kind.'

'She certainly does.' He goes back to turning screws. I wish I could turn the screws on Soph. Or superglue her mouth shut.

'What's the lock for?'

'Dave,' I say, at the same time as Jamie says 'work'.

'Dave came round and made my bed and moved some stuff round.' Soph will understand the 'Dave' reason, she hates him. She won't be so hot on my need for privacy though, I still need to do some work with her on that one. 'As if we never split.'

'No shit? And you don't want to shout at him?' Sophie bowls past me into the room and sits on the bed, effortlessly going into the type of cross-legged pose that would send me toppling over if I tried it.

I'm not going to try it, and definitely not with Jamie and Soph in attendance. I did go to a yoga class once. I could cope with the lying on your back and breathing part, but when she started to talk about dying dogs and trees, she lost me. She moved on to a plank-like thing that had my whole body vibrating in a not good way; it was like I was on a train that was permanently in shuddering-to-a-stop mode. Then she demonstrated this heels-over-your-head weird handstand that looked seriously dangerous and I was out of there. If that was the end-game, I'd rather play Scrabble.

'Not really. I haven't seen him though,' I admit. 'But I did send him a message, and I did tell everybody that they shouldn't let him in. But we think a lock is a good idea, not just for Dave.'

'We did, did we?' She grins. 'So you and Dave are deffo over?'

'Deffo. It made me so mad the way he just *assumed* he could waltz in here. I chucked all his stuff.'

'Wow, you chucked his stuff? All of it? Oh please tell me you smashed that man shitting himself on a rock thing?' She clasps her hands together as though she's begging.

'That was Rodin's *The Thinker*.' I shake my head.

'It was Dave being a dick. What kind of woman wants something like that on their bedside cabinet? Eurgh, gave me the creeps.'

'Well you shouldn't be in my room looking at it.' She colours up, which makes me feel slightly guilty but also pleased. Progress! 'No, I didn't smash it or anything, but I did box it up.'

'Awesome! He will be fucking furious. Ace!'

'Soph!' She never was very keen on him. 'I'm not trying to make him angry; I just needed a clear-out.'

'You've never got rid of any of his stuff before, not even the gross things.'

'Exactly. I've never really meant it before,' I say softly. I've been guilty of muddying the waters, of being selfish and using him as some kind of emotional crutch. I don't need him now, but he's not to know that, is he?

'Well thank God you've come to your senses, you can do way better than him. What do you think, Jamie?'

'I think it's better to be safe than sorry,' he says, tightening the last screw and jiggling the lock to check it's firm. He winks at me, raising his eyebrows. I guess now he appreciates the irresistible force that is my sister. And why a lock is probably a good thing where she's concerned. 'There we go. I'd better be off, lovely to meet you, Sophie.'

'And you! Hey, why don't you come over to our barbecue on Sunday?' She turns to me. 'He should! Daz is invited, it'll be ace. And then Daz won't get all the attention and be interrogated.'

I sigh. 'You just don't want them to notice your boyfriend is vegan! You can't use Jamie like that!'

'It's fine, I don't feel used.' Jamie is grinning, hands on hips, looking very manly. And sexy. He has a big screwdriver in his hand. That is sexy, believe me.

'Nobody gets all the attention in our house anyway!'

'Oh shush.' Sophie chuckles. 'Me thinks you doth protest too much!' She grins at Jamie. 'It'll be fun! Sun shining, beer, we can boogie around the barbecue—'

'Sounds cool. Purple hair, glowsticks and beer round the fire until the sun rises…' His voice tails off as our eyes meet. I stare at him. Purple hair and glowsticks. Reading.

'Not sure about staying till the sun rises, but I'm loving the glowsticks, aren't you, Al? Ace!' Jamie breaks eye contact before I do, messing around picking up an imaginary screw off the floor. Soph bashes on, not noticing the hitch. 'Right, see you Sunday then, Alice will text you the time and address. She owes you for doing this anyway, I reckon a burger and a beer is a good trade-off!'

'Can't say no to an offer like that,' Jamie says. I must have imagined that brief look; he could have been talking about any gig where the girls had purple hair and we all drank beer. I'm being daft. This isn't about Reading. He doesn't remember. Or he doesn't remember the bit that features me. 'But Alice hasn't got my number.'

'Well here you go.' Sophie chants out my phone number. 'You can message her, then she will!' And high-fives him.

'Do I need to bring anything?'

'Just your gorgeous self,' says Sophie.

'Sorry,' I mouth at him.

He's not even out of the front door when my phone pings.

See you Sunday, look forward to it! J x

'Oh my God, this is so exciting!' Soph reads it over my shoulder. 'I knew that sticky note that fell out of your pocket was important!'

'Shush!' I shove my mobile out of sight. 'That's rubbish.' She doesn't know how forgettable he finds me. How he forgot a kiss, how he didn't even remember me when we were crushed together in a corridor. 'You can't just go inviting random people to our barbecue though, it's weird. What will Mum say?'

She shrugs. 'It's cool, and he's not random, and it's not weird, you owed him for doing this.' She points to the lock.

She does have a point. But I still feel uneasy, so I cover it up by changing tack. 'Anyway, what are you doing here? I thought you worked on a Monday evening?'

'They let me go.' She rolls her eyes. '*Apparently*,' this is said in a very sarcastic tone which tells me it actually hurts more than she wants to let on, 'it's not company policy to invite people in off the street and give them the mis-shapes for free.'

I sit down next to her and give her a quick hug. This is what she's come for, even though she's not into lengthy signs of affection. 'Is there such a thing as mis-shaped burgers?'

'Well no, not unless somebody has accidentally squished them as they put them on the tray.' She grins. 'The manager was a tosser, what can I say? He's got nasal hair and said I shouldn't let dogs in!' I'm not sure about the connection here. 'Eurghh. Anyway, the pizza place said I can do some deliveries for them.'

'You? Deliver? You've not got a car.'

She chuckles. 'They've got a scooter! It's ace, I bet I can make it do wheelies!'

I shake my head. They're definitely going to have mis-shapen pizzas if they let Sophie deliver them.

'Anyway, stop changing the subject.' She lies back on the bed, propped up on one elbow as though she's settled in for a while. 'Give me the goss! Are you going to shag him?'

I don't answer.

She sits bolt upright. 'Have you already shagged him?'

'No, I haven't,' I say it firmly, but the regret claws at my stomach.

'I would!'

Yeah, so would I, Soph. So would I, if he had the slightest interest in me. Instead, the bloody man has fallen for my Blue-Footed Booby bird.

I wait until she has gone, then message Jamie back. *Thanks for doing the lock, I owe you one. Don't feel you have to come to the BBQ. I know Soph put you on the spot a bit. A x*

Don't you want me to? J x

Do I? Of course I do. I think. Isn't it a bit odd inviting a guy I hardly know to a family BBQ? Well, to be fair, I didn't invite him. Soph took that decision out of my hands, and she was honestly a bit out of order.

But now she's asked him, and he said yes, un-asking him would seem mean, wouldn't it?

And, well, I want him to come, but how will I handle it? Soph is being bad enough, but can I cope, can I not give away the fact that I'm lusting after him? My humiliation will be massive if the whole family knows I've got a crush, and Jamie is totally oblivious, or, oh my God, what if he realizes and doesn't know how to politely tell me to sod off? Shit, I hadn't thought about that. We've only sat desk-width apart and traded insults, or shared messages when the other person hasn't been there. This evening was the first time we'd been together for any length of time, and in my personal space. And Soph was here being a pain, so it wasn't awkward. But I can't tell him he is uninvited. And I do want to see him. *Gah.* My yes/no switch has gone into overdrive. My hand is shaking as I type. *Of course, but I didn't want you to feel pressured into saying yes, if you didn't want to. A x* There, I've done it.

Should I ask him why he mentioned purple hair though?

No pressure. Have a good day at the office tomorrow. J x

Chapter Nineteen

Tuesday

I notice it before I've even sat down. Mabel has a necklace made out of paperclips. I grin and shuffle around in my chair, then lean forward and pick her up.

How on earth did he find time to do that? We were both in the office yesterday, and I was sitting at our desk. He must have waited until I'd gone.

There is a note at her feet. *You don't show her she is special often enough! Endangered species deserve extra love and attention. J x PS These blue feet worry me, I think you're kidding me when you say it's natural, does she need slippers? Can birds get chilblains?*

I chuckle then duck down behind the monitor as Sal glances up.

The now-familiar flutter of need fills my stomach as I touch the paperclip chain. It's not fair, the effect Jamie has on me. But I don't want him to stop. Coming into the office is the best part of my day.

It's funny. When it was the old-normal, all of us working here five days a week, he was a pain. I guess his teasing, and total lack of any sign that he actually liked me (or, let's face it, fancied me) got to me more than it should have. It was all magnified because the more I tried to not like him, the more I ended up wishing we'd be thrown together in a small space again. I know. Ridiculous.

But it has happened twice, so how can I really in my heart (however much my head tells me I was being daft) believe it couldn't happen again? That one day we will be thrown together – and this time there will be no crowd to drag us apart. This time we'll kiss, and this time he'll look into my eyes properly and he *will* remember. And even if he doesn't, it won't matter, because this time he will enjoy it as much as me.

Since we've moved over to the new-normal though, it just feels different. He's not teasing me like he'd tease a sister, he's not taking the mickey. It feels like we're working together. Like we're supporting each other. Like we've got our own private jokes. And it makes me feel like I'm being hugged inside.

It's weird as well that I'm sharing more with him than I am with anybody else in my life, but it feels fine. I don't feel threatened. I trust him. I like sharing a desk. Biscuits. Notes.

And, however much I try and tell myself, that this note-leaving, gently funny stuff is enough, I know I'm kidding myself. I do want more. A tiny part of my heart still believes that this was meant to be. And so does most of my body. Let's face it, whatever happens, I fancy the pants off him.

It's going to take bloody ages to undo all these paperclips though and put them back in their pot. I shake my head and place Mabel back in her spot, then power up the computer.

After Jamie went yesterday, it was a bit weird, Soph and I had the best chat we've had for ages. I didn't want her to feel I was locking her out of my life as well as my room, but she seemed totally chilled.

Even when I pointed out that the lock was to stop *everybody* getting in.

This morning I woke up feeling lighter. Splitting up with Dave in the first place had been sad, but finally burning my bridges and being totally certain about this has taken me far too long.

A clean break, even if it meant mess and confrontation along the way. I had to do it. He wasn't going to throw disfiguring acid at me, it might just be unpleasant. Fine.

I'm sure that other people have told me that my boyfriend was over-bearing, bossy and running my life – but Jamie turning round and asking if that was why I had turned the office into my home had made me realize how bad I'd let things get.

I'd let things drift on because it was the easy thing to do. I'd compromised and let him boss me around because I don't like confronting people in my personal life. I'd let him mess with my stuff because I'd been able to create another safe space for it somewhere else. I'd carried on because I thought I needed him, I thought he was supporting me, I thought it meant I had somebody to turn to when I had a problem.

I hadn't realized how desperate I'd been for a place of my own, how much I'd retreated into my tiny space at work. My desk. Until it had been taken away from me.

All the compromise has always been on my side. I had lost all my independence and was turning into a faithful collie that buried its bones in the back garden so that they couldn't be thrown away. But now I have dug them up. Metaphorically speaking, of course. And I have rediscovered some of my bounce.

It's like clearing all the two years past its use-by date stuff out of the cupboards, or painting over the mould in the corner of the room. Okay, maybe not quite that. Mould comes back if you cover it up, and I don't want Dave back. I've put bleach on that spot. But you get what I mean, right? I've discovered that feeling of freedom from a problem that's been nagging at me, depressing me, at the back of my mind, for ages. Part of me has been freed, emptied.

And now Jamie has made me a necklace out of stationery items.

Result.

Who knew my mind would ever think that?

I grab my Post-it notes and tap the end of the pen against my chin as I think.

Loving Mabel's necklace, it's nearly as rare and precious as she is. Loving my lock as well – thank you! Alice xx PS Blue feet aren't always cold feet. Sometimes blue things are just blue.

Just like sometimes nice people are just nice.

I half stand to stick the note under Elvis so it isn't too obvious.

'Some people have got plenty of time on their hands.'

The dry tone makes me jump guiltily and screw the note up in my hand out of sight.

The dragon gives me her look of intense disapproval as I sink back onto the chair. She looks disapproving around 99 per cent of the time, but it varies in intensity. There's the resting-face version (mild) all the way up to the killer-look (shut up and say yes to everything she says).

How does she know I've been swapping notes with Jamie? Shit!

I suddenly realize she is not looking me in the eye, she is staring at Mabel. The necklace! I cackle – relieved and embarrassed at the same time.

'I, er, it helped me think. I was thinking, I was planning…'

'Of course you were.' She shakes her head slowly. 'Well think about this.' She sticks a note firmly in the middle of my monitor. 'Get a feel for their business, I'd like us to win this contract.' This time she does look at me directly. She gives me a piercing look. 'Okay?' I think this means that if we don't, I am to blame.

'Sure. I'll make it priority, er, this can wait.' I sweep my notepad to one side and pick up the note. But she's already gone, off to terrorize somebody else.

Phew.

I slowly uncrumple the note I'd written to Jamie, and smooth it out with my hand. I hadn't thought about it before, but what if anybody else does read our notes?

What if the office cleaner does and wonders what the hell we're up to? Sugar. My heart beats a bit faster, but it's a kind of excited panic, not an 'oh shit something terrible is about to happen' panic.

Oh my God, we could be misinterpreted (well he could) and she could decide to write a book. *Memoirs of Mrs Mop the Charlady – Love, Lust and Office Supplies.*

But she can't know about the love and lust, can she? *Can* she? I close my eyes (it helps) and try to remember exactly what we've written. And how many kisses there have been. There has definitely been an escalation – from zero, to one, to two. Oh bugger, what if she's reading things into these notes.

Maybe in future I should hide them out of view. Today was a close call. The dragon does not approve of flirting in work time – even via scraps of paper.

I mean I know Elvis is half-covering this note, but if I was an office cleaner, I'd be tempted to have a quick peep and check out what it says.

Chapter Twenty

Friday

I feel all fidgety. Wednesday at home was non-eventful.
As in totally.

I had some very boring changes to put into one
website, some weird bugs to sort out in another, and
research on the possible new client to do for the dragon
lady (a company so boring I will lose the will to live if I
have to work for them). Three biscuits and a handful of
dry granola for lunch because I need to go shopping, and
a cheese toastie for tea because I still needed to go
shopping.

Dave has not been seen since he invaded my room, I am
hopeful that this will be the end of it. It feels like a victory.

Yesterday, Thursday, Jamie had not responded to my
note about Mabel's jewellery, or the last-minute one I'd
written about the Mrs Mop memoirs. I'm not sure if he
thinks I'm being serious (or don't want him to write notes),

or he's worried I'm actually expecting lust and love off him, or he's just got fed up of leaving notes.

It left me a bit antsy. And worried. I want us to be friends.

I'm scared I've over-stepped some mark and messed this up. I still seem to be pretty rubbish at making it clear who I want to share what with.

Worrying about him completely shot my concentration. I nearly messaged Lou or Soph to ask what they thought. But that would have been ridiculous – 'the guy I share a desk with didn't respond to my jokey message'. 'So what?' would be anybody else's response. It would have been mine as well before now. In the past, if Dave hadn't replied to me, I'd have just presumed he was busy. I wouldn't have worried I'd upset him. Although, with Dave he'd have soon let me know if I had. He made it easy to know when I'd overstepped the mark.

I'm overreacting. Jamie was probably busy, or just didn't know what to say.

Anyway, I was packing up on Thursday afternoon, ready for home, when I realized he *had* left a note – under my biscuits, where no Dragon Lady or office cleaner would ever notice it.

I grabbed it, all excited and relieved, then was stopped short by what it said.

Can we have coffee Friday lunch before you start work? If you've got time. I need to clear the air before the BBQ. J

No kiss. Short and terse, not funny at all. I have upset him. I must have.

Oh God.

He needs to clear the air by spelling out that he has not been flirting, there will be no memoirs, he's worried I've taken him the wrong way.

He wants to share a desk with somebody else.

I feel queasy, my stomach is all hollow.

So, it's Friday. Luckily I had a shitload of work to do this morning so I couldn't sit there wondering what Jamie meant by 'clear the air' – though I did have the eight hours from 11pm last night when I got in bed, until 7am when I got up this morning.

I have arrived at the cafe thirty-five minutes early, and Jamie is already there. He looks on edge. This is not good.

Be normal, Alice. 'Hi! Another coffee?'

'No, I'm fine.' He glances up. 'Thanks,' he adds as an afterthought, and smiles. It's a bit strained, he's trying to soften the blow.

'I'll just go and get…' I croak out.

My throat is dry, and it feels blocked, like it does when I'm trying not to cry.

Okay, I think I'm trying not to cry.

I'm standing stiffly, all awkward.

It's fine, I'm going to be fine. This is not even an office romance, it's a swapping of a few bits of meaningless paper. As long as he is not going to insist that we wipe our desk clean, as well as the slate, it will be fine.

Fine.

Don't you hate the word fine?

My hand is trembling as I pick my coffee up and slowly walk back over to him. Delaying the inevitable. Working up courage to face this.

'Look I hope you didn't think—' Rashly, on my long walk over I have decided that the best way to deal with this is head on. Deny everything.

But he stops me with a raised hand.

'Please.' There's a look bordering on pleading in his eye. He's not telling me, like Dave would have done, he's asking me. 'Can I say my piece first? If I don't get it out of my system quick, I might chicken out.' He looks apologetic.

'Sure.' I sit down, shuffle about. Move the little menu to one side, then back again.

I really, really want to tell him I haven't read anything daft into his intentions, I don't fancy him, the Mrs Mop was a joke. I'm cool, we're cool. Instead I do my best to zip it. It is difficult, the words are bubbling up inside me, trying to break out of my mouth.

I don't want to lose what we've got.

We look at each other.

Oh my God, Jamie. Speak, quickly, say something. Tell me, put me out of my misery.

He's playing around with the teaspoon in his saucer, which isn't like him at all. 'Okay, here we go. I've got a confession.' He takes a deep breath. Stops fidgeting and puts the spoon down carefully so that it doesn't even make the tiniest of clinks. He looks directly at me. 'I've felt guilty about this for ages but didn't know what to say. I kind of missed the first chance, then I couldn't find the right time to say something, and I felt like a git for pretending, but I couldn't exactly turn the clock back so,' he takes a deep breath, 'I just thought I'd leave it.'

Confession? Turn the clock back? What is he talking about?

'I'm sorry.' Oh hell, here we go, I hate those words. I want to close my eyes, because for some strange reason my brain thinks not seeing him say it will soften the blow. I don't. I am manning up these days. Facing my issues head on. 'I've been a shit.'

Leading me on? Oh, fucking just say it, put me out of my misery! My teeth are gritted, it is starting to set up a throbbing in my temple. I can't just sit here quietly any longer. I'll explode if this goes on much longer. 'Look, whatever, it's not a problem, forget it. I get it, you're not—' What am I about to say? Into me?

'I remember you,' he blurts out.

We stare at each other in shocked silence. The hum of the cafe carries on, but I feel removed. We're not part of it.

'You…' My hands are clammy, the back of my neck is all prickly. It's excitement, I think, and anticipation. And disbelief. Does he mean what I think he does?

'I remember kissing you.' He takes a deep breath, but he looks relieved, as though he's needed to say the words. 'At Reading Festival.' He adds the qualifier, but he doesn't need to. No need at all.

'Reading Festival,' I echo, closing my eyes as it all floods back. Then, ping, all the loveliness vanishes and my eyelids spring open. The relief and excitement is replaced by a hurt that floods through me with shocking intensity.

This man I've grown to really like, this man I've trusted, shared with, joked with, has been lying to me.

He remembered. He pretended he didn't. I suddenly realize his hands are over mine, and pull away. 'Don't touch me.' My voice is shaky. All this time when I've been agonizing about whether to say something. *How* to say something.

All the embarrassment I've felt and tried to hide as the lust was obviously totally one- sided. The awkwardness that has only gone when we've been swapping notes and not having to see each other face to face. When I've been able to relax and not feel daft, when it's felt like a new flirty relationship. A fresh start.

He knew he'd kissed me *and* still frigging walked away in that bar. Then totally blanked me.

'Purple hair and glowsticks,' I say quietly as the words he said in my room to Sophie slip into place.

'It slipped out.' His cheekbones are red-tinged.

'And that's why you decided to say something,' I snap.

'Not just that, I—'

'You've ignored me,' I whisper, the bitterness sharp to my own ears. 'You pretended for two fucking years that it didn't happen.'

'Fuck, Alice. I'm sorry.' He buries his head in his hands, then runs his fingers through his hair before looking up at me again. I've never heard him swear before. I'm not sure if that, or the fact he remembers, is more shocking. 'I knew you'd recognized me; I saw it in your eyes.'

'And you still walked away.' My voice is flat. I can't quite believe this. I have spent the last few years dreaming of the boy I'd kissed, crushed against him in the middle of a crowd, wondering if I'd ever meet him again, wondering if he was just a figment of my imagination. And then, when we did, he let me think it was too insignificant, I was too insignificant for him to remember. I'm angry.

'It was shitty to pretend I didn't recognize you. I get it if you hate me.'

His words, the genuine tone of his voice, the way he is looking at me, so sincere, dissipates some of the hurt. I'm not a naturally angry person, I don't hate. Well, not often.

It ebbs away, leaving confusion. 'But why? Why?' I want to shake him. 'Was it so bad?' I try and get my thoughts in order and stop the words just falling out of my mouth in a jumble. Too many questions, too much hurt, too much lust. 'You… I thought you must have been so drunk you didn't remember.'

'It wasn't bad at all.' He smiles a small rueful smile, and I don't know whether to love him or hate him. 'I was wasted, but I couldn't forget something like that.' He stares straight into my eyes. His blue-grey ones studying me intently and even though I'm angry, I think I've lost the power to breathe. This is the bit in the movies where they grab each other and kiss passionately, make up for all the lost time.

It isn't a movie, it doesn't happen. The air between us is full of static though. That tension, when you're waiting for something to happen.

'I couldn't get you out of my head for months,' his soft voice breaks the silence.

'I couldn't either.' My mouth is dry. I couldn't get him

out of my head for years, I want to add. Ever since. But I don't.

'You were the crazy, gorgeous girl that I couldn't find again.'

'You looked?' I swallow to moisten my throat. I can't be angry, it's like I'm looking at that guy again.

'Yep.' He nods, smiles, his dimples deepen. 'I also drank a lot, danced a lot, sang a lot and generally had a wild time. But I did look in the in-between times.'

'Me too,' I admit. Why pretend? 'There were a lot of people there.'

'Mayhem.'

I want to say it, I need to say it, I need to ask about the bar. It wasn't mayhem in there.

'I didn't recognize you straight away, when you started at We Got Designs.' He smiles. 'Your hair was a different colour, and your clothes, well…' He chuckles.

'I hope you're not dissing my plum hair and denim shorts.'

'Not one bit, they were so sexy, along with the wild make-up and all those leather bracelets and rings.' Wow, he took in more of me than I did of him. The feel of his lips on mine, his hot mouth, are my main memory. 'Well, what I saw of it all, before you were swept away.' He tips his head to one side. 'You had a fringe, and a ponytail, it made your eyes look so big.' He grins. 'You were like a punk Audrey Hepburn.'

'Ah, the elfin face thing, I've put weight on since then!'

'It suits you, it's just different, it confused me. I'm easily confused.' He grins. 'I really didn't recognize you straight away, I guess I couldn't believe it could be you. But there was just something familiar about you, that I couldn't put my finger on.'

'I was the same. At first I thought you were festival guy's double.'

'Festival guy.' He grins.

We stare at each other. Remembering. I wonder if our memories are the same? I can't help but smile. 'Your hair was longer, shaggy.' I'd fantasized about running my fingers through that tousled hair as we snogged.

'In the bar, when I bumped into you in the corridor it all came flooding back.' The corners of his generous mouth lift. 'It must have been because we were crushed together again! I realized it really was you, I wasn't going mad, you were my festival girl.' The smile broadens. 'Different hair colour, different make-up, different clothes, but it was the same you.' He nods his head, remembering. His voice is so soft, I can't help but lean in towards him. 'Same scent, same lips, same soft skin.'

I try to swallow the lump in my throat away. I hadn't been wrong; I hadn't been kidding myself. We'd had that moment of *knowing* at exactly the same time. I've been waiting for this for so long, and now it's happened it isn't how I imagined at all. 'I should be so mad at you right now.'

'You should,' he says softly. 'I thought my mind was playing tricks at first, that I just *wanted* it to be you. But when our bodies touched, I knew it was you.' He breaks eye contact. Stares at his coffee. 'I was going to kiss you again, and then that silly twat barged into us.'

Oh my God, so near and yet so far.

'I felt such an idiot for not saying something the day we started work, asking if we'd met before. but I couldn't. I just couldn't. What if I'd got it wrong, what if you weren't that amazing festival girl? Then the fact it nearly happened again, it felt like maybe it was meant to be. I was going to come and say something, until...'

'Until?'

The chatter in the cafe, the clatter of cups on saucers, the laughter has all receded, barely noticeable. There's just him and me and it feels like this moment is important. Our fingertips are touching, even though I've tried to keep a distance. It's as though he has some magnetic hold over me. Only his teasing, and the distance between our desks, and being so sure he didn't remember me, has forced me to resist. To keep my distance.

'I realized it would be a mistake. It would ruin everything.' His voice is flat.

Boom, just like that the lovely feeling is popped.

'A mistake?'

'It seemed stupid to even mention I recognized you. That kiss was so fucking amazing,' he is staring into my eyes, 'why mess it up with real life?'

I stare at him. 'Mess it up?'

'Okay, you're going to think I'm crazy, but I'd been remembering, fantasizing about that moment at the festival for so long I almost didn't want to meet you again. It was perfect.' He stares into my eyes. 'But I reckoned it had to be my imagination, it was all in my head. A kiss couldn't be that good, real life could never live up to that.'

'What? You're saying I'm not good enough? Thanks, that's great. Great.' Heads turn. I lower my voice, and my head. I scowl at him and start to push my chair back. I need to get out of here.

He reaches out a hand, but stops short of actually grabbing me. 'Alice, no, it's not that at all. I didn't mean that. Please don't go, wait. Jack, the guy who bumped into us?' I nod. 'He said something in the bogs about how you had a steady boyfriend. I mean…' He shrugs.

'That's just an excuse! You could have told me that you remembered.' I sink back down onto my seat, but perch on the edge – ready to go.

'I'm doing a shit job of explaining; I don't even know what I'm trying to say. Hell.' He rubs the palms of his hands over his eyes. 'Okay. Right, I thought it would have been wrong, wrecked how I'd imagined it might be. How it was supposed to be. I couldn't even think about kissing you again when I knew you had somebody else.'

'But you could have said something. Not chickened out.'

He folds his hands together and stares down at them, then glances up. He keeps glancing up, catching my eye, it's as though he can't help it. 'I didn't want to kill the dream completely,' he finally says. 'That would have been the end of it, wouldn't it? If I'd said something, and you'd laughed it off.'

'I get that.' I know that feeling.

'Look, I've had relationships, girlfriends, we've got on fine, liked the same things, respected each other, fancied each other and I've been happy. It was normal, great and I thought that was it, what it was all about,' he pauses, 'and then I met you.' He stares at me. 'When we kissed, I was completely blown away, it felt totally different. It was only a few seconds, but wow! That was all it took. I couldn't forget you; I was totally obsessed. I couldn't stop thinking about you, about us. It was unreal, Alice, it wasn't me. I'm not that kind of person. I'm sane, sensible, steady. Normal guy, normal life. I was scared, Alice. Nothing could really be that good, I told myself it was just the high of the night at first, the booze, the atmosphere. But when I got home, and my hangover had gone, I still couldn't stop thinking about you. It was crazy. And then when I saw you again...' He shakes his head. 'When I saw you in the office, I felt the same.' He looks at me intently. 'I panicked, I was an idiot, a coward. I decided I couldn't risk it. Nothing could be that good, could it?'

'How do you know, if you don't try it?' If he'd said all this a few months ago, I might have just nodded and said I got it. But it's not just about him, is it?

This is as bad as me yelling at my housemates and throwing them out of my room, this is taking it too far to protect yourself. Not taking other people's feelings – mine – into account. 'You didn't trust me enough to tell me, risk it.'

'I didn't know you at all.' He leans back away from me a bit. 'But I do now, so that's why I wanted to try and explain. I do trust you, Alice.' He flattens his hands on the table, only inches from mine. 'If I could turn the clock back, I would.' He stares through me, into the past. 'I went out with this girl, in the sixth form, not long before that gig. I thought we were brilliant together. She was pretty, clever, funny, we had a good time. Then she said it wasn't working, that we weren't mad enough about each other. I didn't get it at all, back then.' He shakes his head. 'I was devastated, shook up because I'd really thought we were right for each other. Then I kissed you and I got what she was saying. Kissing her had never been like that. I've never been with anybody and felt like it was *everything* until...' There's a long pause. Our gazes meet, lock. 'I kissed you. You were everything, Alice.' He shakes his head slowly from side to side. 'I did want to find you, at first, honest, then I got scared that it was just a one-off. One kiss that I'd built up in my head as something more than it was. I thought if I saw you again, I'd find out you were just human, like any other girl, that if we got together it would just turn out to be normal and flawed and we'd row, get it wrong, get it right. It kind of confirmed it when we nearly kissed again, and I found out you were going steady.'

'Not so perfect,' I say softly. 'I was the girl who'd two-time.'

'I didn't say that. I just wanted to keep that magic moment. Remember what being mad about somebody, being sure they're the one, felt like.' He taps the side of his cup, not looking at me. 'I didn't want to lose it because I might never feel it again. It's the closest I've ever got to thinking having something that good could exist for me.' His blue-grey eyes stare directly into mine. 'It felt like it wasn't meant to be, Alice.' His voice is soft.

'You could have at least said hi, haven't we met before!' I could have done that as well, I'm just as guilty, but he'd been completely stonewalling me. I'd been too embarrassed. He obviously didn't remember me, or fancy me, so I'd decided to keep quiet.

My God, can you imagine if I'd brought it up and he'd denied even being at the festival?

He looks embarrassed. 'I'm sorry. I know, I should have done. But, well, I thought I'd be better keeping my distance and forgetting about it. And things got a bit complicated, you had your guy and I got chatting to this girl and...' Didn't he just. I think I am scowling. 'It didn't mean anything. She was just somebody who was funny, and no expectations, just normal.' He looks uncomfortable for a moment. 'I thought.'

'I'm sure she'd be delighted to hear you sum her up like that!' I say, my voice dry.

'It was supposed to be just a bit of fun, she wasn't serious, or I wouldn't...' He still seems really on edge, then sits up straighter as though he needs to move things on. 'Anyway, that doesn't matter, I felt a total git for pretending and I didn't know how to put it right, how to explain. I kind of thought you'd just think I was a massive dick if I suddenly turned round months later.'

I raise an eyebrow.

The corner of his mouth lifts in the start of a smile. 'Okay, okay you think I'm a dick now, but hey I had to come clean now we've been...well, with the notes and, well, we've kind of got to be friends.' Eurgh, I hate that word. Friends. 'It felt wrong not being upfront.' He looks at me, studies every feature of my face as though he's trying to look into my head.

'And you cocked up by mentioning purple hair?'

He looks bashful, shifts in his seat. 'Yeah, and that. We can still be friends?'

We had other people to consider back then. But what about now? I can't help the little flutter inside of anticipation. Of hope. Does this mean... Or when he says friends, does he really mean that. End of.

'To be honest I was a bit pissed off when I found out you had a boyfriend, because I was so close to saying to hell with it and grabbing you. One minute I thought you wanted to try another kiss as much as I did,' oh my God he did, he wanted to try another kiss! 'then,' he shrugs, 'I reckoned I must have misread the signs, and maybe you regretted snogging me. Maybe you didn't want reminding, and I reckoned it would make it really awkward at work for both of us.'

'I wasn't seeing Dave when we were at Reading, I was single.' I need to make that clear. His memory of that kiss seems to match mine. Perfect. I don't want him thinking I'm a two-timing tart. I swallow to clear the blockage in my throat, the huskiness from my voice.

Jamie nods slowly. 'Same here.' Our gazes meet again. 'I was single, not looking for anybody. Just single.'

'I wish you had told me,' I say softly, feeling sad. Jamie wants to just hold on to that memory of a fabulous kiss, skip the relationship bit because I could never live up to the promise.

I wish he'd told me when we were in that corridor, I wish he had kissed me that second time. I wish I'd been single. I wish Jamie hadn't got chatting to some other girl instead.

'So do I.' His voice is soft, his smile is lopsided. Sad. 'I wish we'd talked. But...' He shrugs.

'Things happen?' I can't help myself. I have to fish. I have to know. Is he telling me this so he can draw a line under the whole thing? What happened between him and that girl? Claire. Are they still together?

He nods. 'Things happen. Life gets in the way. Good, bad.' There's the hint of a frown between his eyebrows that he shakes away. 'Well not bad, unexpected.'

'Unexpected?'

'It's just I found out...' He hesitates, as though he's going to add something else, then stops himself. 'You know, just life.'

I'm not sure I do know. I feel like he's skipping something, brushing over things still. I feel like I'm losing him all over again.

'It was good though, wasn't it?' The sadness in his face lifts, there's a glimmer in his eye. 'That kiss.'

'Amazing.' Oh God, this is awful. There's a lump in my throat. This is how my fantasy ends. Our moment confined to history.

'It did scare the shit out of me though, and the fact I've never been able to get you out of my head!' His mobile beeps and he doesn't look at it, but it seems to snap us back to the present. 'Hey, you're going to be late for work. You should get to the office, I suppose?'

'Yeah, guess so or the dragon will be after me.'

'I just wanted you to know, you know that I remembered.' He grins, a more normal cheeky grin. 'You were pretty unforgettable you know.'

'Not sure if that's good or bad!' I try to joke, laugh it off, but inside I want to cry.

'Good! Look, I know we've moved on, things have changed, I've got all kinds of crap going on in my life right now and we work together, and all that shit so it wouldn't happen. But I still think you are.'

'Are?'

'Unforgettable.' He touches the back of my hand. The lightest of touches, that sends a shiver through my body. I want to grab his hand. I want to say, 'Hey maybe we're not so different, maybe we should try it again, take a chance, just so we know.' But I don't. 'Now go on, you better get moving!' I stand up. 'Hey, we're cool? Clean slate? We can be friends?' There's a small worry frown between his eyebrows.

I nod. What else can I do?

I get moving. I go into the office and sit down at my, our, desk and stare out of the window. So that is that, he does remember the kiss. It was unforgettable. But now it is over, the dream I've been hanging on to – the hope that one day he would remember and want to do it again.

Things have moved on, he said. Things have changed. He's got crap going on.

What type of crap?

I don't have Dave, he knows that, but he must have somebody in his life. Or else he just isn't interested in anything with me.

Or else he's just more sensible than me and knows an office romance would be a big mistake.

I don't know quite how I feel. I just know how he feels.

He wanted to clear the air, tell me, so that he could move on guilt free.

Great.

Bugger. Soph is going to kill me when I tell her he's not coming to the barbecue. Because he won't now, will he?

I open the pedestal drawer, and there is a note.

See you Sunday, unless you've just blown me out in disgust, in which case I won't. J x PS My mum is making Mabel some socks, we worry. Blue isn't always just blue. Things aren't always as straightforward as we'd like them to be!

What on earth does his note mean? Apart from the socks bit, I understand that. I think. Gawd, his mum must think he shares a desk with a complete weirdo. But what does the 'straightforward' bit mean? And why does he want to come to the barbecue if he's moved on? Although if he is still seeing Claire, or whatever her name was, I'm pretty sure he wouldn't be coming to a barbecue with me.

I'm not sure I'm cut out to be his buddy, or, worse still, his confidant, if that is all he wants. I don't want to hear about his woman problems!

I want to kiss him again. More than ever now. Just to find out if it really was as good as I remember. So that he knows it wasn't a one-off.

Shit, I'm screwed.

Chapter Twenty-One

Sunday

I have spent most of the morning trying to decide what to wear for the barbecue. This is not usually an issue – after all it's family, it's in the garden, it's casual.

But this is not 'usually', this is 'Jamie is coming'.

I've got this stupid, overwhelming urge to bring back memories of Reading. To be the girl he met there. Goodness knows why, I mean he's made it more than clear that he just wants to be friends. We've missed that magic moment when it could have all been different. Where something could have happened.

But I can't help myself.

The weather is really hot and sunny for May as well, so it isn't like I should wear jeans and a sweater. Nobody will.

But a summer dress seems a bit OTT.

I kneel in front of my chest of drawers, dig out the T-shirt I'd worn that day, and can't help but smile. It's one of those T-shirts that you wear to death and love, and then can't bring yourself to throw out even though it's faded.

It holds memories, it's cool. It is Reading.

Oh my God. It still smells faintly of beer and cigarette. Very faintly, if you sniff hard, I'm not in the habit of putting stinky gross clothes in my drawers. Or wearing them.

I pull it over my head and stare at myself in the mirror. Then drag my hair back off my face. Trying to see that younger, hopeful me. The one with plum streaks in her hair, eyes kohled to the limit, plastic beer cup and feet that can dance until dawn.

He's remembered the hair; does he remember the clothes?

'Loving the T-shirt, cool!' says Zoe from the doorway. She's slouched, leaning against the door jamb, drink in hand.

'Retro,' I say, smiling as I let my hand fall to my side. My hair falls loose. A sudden thought comes to me. 'Are you busy?'

She shrugs. 'Nothing happening round here, babe.'

'You couldn't…' I hesitate. Glance back at my reflection. 'Cut my fringe, you know Audrey Hepburn style, like you said. I mean, just a quick dry cut, nothing fancy and…' I gabble on, only stopping when she claps her hands and does a little jump in the air.

'Yay, the girl has seen sense at last! Come on, come on, come to Zoe and let her work her magic!' I'd been on the verge of changing my mind and backing out. But I don't have a choice, she's grabbed my arm and is ushering me down towards her room.

Zoe does indeed have magic.

'Wow, it looks ace!' I turn my head from side to side, swish my hair. It's all sleek, and even now – several pounds heavier than when I was a student – it seems to make my eyes look bigger. 'Thank you, what do I—'

'Nothing!' She puts her hands on my shoulders and our gazes meet in the mirror. 'You've helped me out so many times Al, but you've never let me help you! You look gorgeous.'

She's put in the caramel highlights that she wanted to as well.

Not plum, caramel. I'm not that carefree festival girl, I'm the older, wiser version.

'Are you going out?'

'Just a family barbecue.' I shrug. 'Nothing important.' Ha. Who am I kidding?

'Out is out, it's always important! Right, come on, sit down again. I'm going to do your make-up as well!'

'But, I...'

'No buts, babe.' She leans in closer. 'Your Soph told me she's taking her new boyfriend, and you're taking that hot guy that put the lock on your door!'

'Soph?' I groan. 'When did you talk to Sophie?'

'She popped in yesterday so I could do her hair, she didn't come anywhere near your room,' she adds hastily. I smile, she relaxes again. 'She is mega keen on this guy of hers, isn't she? She was so nervous; I've never seen your sis like that about a man! Ser-i-ous! Close your eyes.'

I close my eyes. Surrender.

Well if Soph has had her hair done, and made an effort – it would be stupid of me not to, wouldn't it?

I arranged to meet Jamie at the train station up the road from my parents' house, but I do a double-take when I spot him. Just to make sure.

Some guys can't really carry off shorts. But Jamie can. He looks indescribably sexy in his casual gear. The T-shirt just tight enough to show off his toned chest. For a moment I have to just stand on the spot and ogle.

Then he sees me and waves. I wave back and walk across the road. He is carrying a bag. He holds it a bit higher. 'Beer and wine! I couldn't come to a barbie empty-handed; it didn't feel right!'

As I reach him, he goes to kiss my cheek, then suddenly stops and moves back to arms' length.

'Wow, if you'd turned up at work dressed like this, I'd have recognized you instantly! You look amazing, Alice.' He does kiss my cheek then, which is lucky as it means he is too close to see that my cheeks are flaming.

I'm suddenly pleased I made an effort. Well okay, I was worried I'd gone a bit overboard, but I think I've done the right thing. I'm also glad I put my shorts on, instead of a summer dress. It is now sweltering hot, and I don't want to melt, so I've got a good excuse.

We stand for a moment, me feeling awkward, but I'm

not sure about him. He seems quite chilled. 'We better get going, don't want to be late.'

'Lead the way!' We fall into step. Yep, he is totally relaxed. This is good. He chats, jokes as we walk, and I soon find myself relaxing again and joking back. He's back on form, now he's guilt-free and he's cleared the air. Trouble is, I still think he's cute and very kissable. Blocking those feelings out, compartmentalizing them, was easier when he was treating me like his annoying sister.

'On best behaviour for the parents!' I say jokingly as we walk up the driveway. Jamie comes to a halt.

'Woah! Your parents are here?'

'Er, yes. It's their house!' I frown. 'Family barbecue. Wasn't that what Soph said?' It was, wasn't it? I screw up my eyes and try to remember.

'Er, no, not exactly. I thought she just said barbecue, that's why I said about drinking all night! Unless I wasn't listening, I thought it was just a, well, mate's or something. Shit, I've got shorts on, and beer.' He looks down at his knees slightly despairingly.

'I've got shorts on as well!' I put a hand on his elbow, suddenly worried he's going to do a runner. I've scared him off forever now. 'It's nothing formal, just you know a normal barbecue in the garden.' Oh shit, he thinks I've trapped him into some weird 'meet the parents' situation. 'That's why Soph wanted you to come, cos it's my family, and she's got a new boyfriend, and…'

'Doesn't want all the attention.'

'If you don't want to come, I quite—'

'No problem, really. It's cool, I just...' He grins. 'It just wasn't what I was expecting.'

'But it's not like you have to impress them with...' I wave in the general direction of his legs.

'My knees?' His grin has broadened.

'I didn't mean that! Not that they aren't impressive.' I try not to stare at his legs. Stop, Alice, stop before this gets worse. 'I mean...' He is still grinning at me, bemused. I think I need to change tack.

'I want to show you something.' I grab my mobile and scroll through until I find what I'm after. A photo of Darcie.

She's gorgeous, my sister. I wish I had half her looks – but she still has this scar on her face. When she's working or out for the night, she covers it up – expertly, but quite often at home she doesn't bother.

I don't want Jamie reacting to it. It's not that I think he will, or say anything he shouldn't but... Well, I don't know what it is. I'm not protecting my sister; I think I'm protecting him. I want them to like him. I know it's stupid, but I do.

'My sister, Darcie. She had this accident, acid, and...'

'The starfish fossil,' he says.

'How did you know about...?'

'Lou warned me off touching it, and well, it's not her fault, I kind of pressed her about why and she said it was from a holiday with your sister, and then I asked why you didn't have any photos and...' He shrugs, looking embarrassed. 'I didn't mean to pry, she just said your sister didn't like having her photo taken round that time because of some accident.'

'Oh.' I don't know what I'm more shocked about, Lou telling him about the fossil, or him remembering. 'This jealous girl picked a fight with her, she thought Darcie was after her boyfriend. Which she wasn't, it was just she was gorgeous and, well, she didn't think she was gorgeous anymore after the bastard came back and attacked her without warning.'

'Shit. That's terrible, it must have been so scary for her, for all of you.' He searches my face, but all I can do is nod. It's still hard to talk about. 'That's why,' his voice is so soft I can barely hear him, 'you hate confrontation, isn't it? At work you can be assertive, fight your corner, but when it's personal... Oh, Alice.' For a moment I think he's going to hug me, but he doesn't, he pulls back a bit, takes my mobile from my hand. 'She is gorgeous,' he says, matter-of-factly as he studies the photo, then he glances up at me, 'like you.'

I've never really thought much about why I don't stick to my guns, protect my corner, tell people to eff off when they're overstepping the boundaries. But I guess Darcie's accident scarred us all in some way or another.

But she's moved on, and now, finally, I think I have as well.

'Alice!' Sophie's yell makes me jump. Which is good, very good. This is getting embarrassing, and intense.

'Shit. Look,' I mock-whisper behind my hand jokingly, trying to lighten the mood, 'it's fine if you want to run.'

'Anybody would think you didn't want me here?' There's a question in the lift of his voice.

'Of course I do!' The blush comes about a nanosecond after the words fall out of my mouth. He smiles in response.

'Then it's sorted then.' He opens his elbow towards me, and I slip my hand through without thinking.

'Will you two stop whispering like you're up to something.' Soph grabs my other hand. 'You're late.'

'No, we're not, we're on time.' I double-check.

'Fashionably on time,' adds Jamie, winking at Sophie.

We are late. I'm pretty sure that we got here on time, but we've been standing outside for longer than I realized.

'Hey, everybody, meet Jamie!' shouts Sophie as we walk into the back garden.

'You said he wasn't hot!' Lucy looks at me accusingly as she hauls herself out of her chair.

'Excuse her, she's preggers,' Darcie points out the obvious, you really can't miss the bump. 'It's making her randy.' At least if Jamie is worrying about my sister's sexual urges, he's not wondering about me telling them all he wasn't hot. Or wondering about the fact that I've been talking to my family about him full stop.

'Wow, congrats!' Jamie smiles. I think the wow refers to the pregnancy, not the randy-ness. 'Wow!' He says it again. I think he is close to speechless, he is overcome by the size of her belly, and possibly worried he might have to help deliver the baby before the end of the day.

'It's okay, she's not due yet, just fat,' Sophie reassures him.

'I think WTF, not congrats, is the correct expression.' Darcie waves towards Leo and Brad, who are having a hot dog battle. 'I mean, why would anybody want more when they've got those two angels?'

'Would you like me to relieve you of those, young man?'

Dad wades into the rescue, taking the beer off Jamie and ushering him towards the kitchen. 'Let's get you both a drink before you get character assassinated by my lovely daughters. They're a shock to the system at first, but you'll get used to them I'm sure.'

'Are you the man with the disco ball?' Darcie's daughter Tilly was impressed by this fact and hasn't forgotten it.

'Oh my God, Disco Ball Boy! I forgot about that!' Darcie laughs.

'Sorry,' I mouth. He winks, looking totally chilled about the whole situation.

'Oh, my goodness, why have you brought them into the kitchen? It's a mess, and so am I!' My mother appears to be blushing as Jamie turns on his full-power grin, but when it fades, she recovers. 'You're not vegan as well, are you? Hello, darling.' Her attention switches from Jamie back to me before he has chance to answer, but I'm sure she is still looking at him out of the corner of her eye as she kisses my cheek. Holding her hands away from me. 'Mayo fingers! Sorry darling, been mixing the coleslaw.'

'No, not vegan.' Jamie raises his eyebrows. Why on earth did I let Sophie invite him here?

'Oh, thank heavens! Not that I have anything against vegans,' she adds hastily, reaching for a cloth to wipe her fingers. 'Or vegemites, or those pesky ones.'

'Pesky?' Jamie mouths at me. I shrug.

'Pescatarians, Gran.' Tilly tugs at her sleeve.

'I did buy extra veg, but there's so much meat we don't want it to go to waste.'

'We don't,' agrees Jamie. 'I will do my best to make sure I eat my share.'

'Wonderful. Lucy, will you please control your boys? Dan popped out to get shopping.'

'Shopping?' My father frowns.

'Bread rolls, dear, I forgot them. Remember? I was thinking about the gin and tonic, and all the fancy bits, and I forgot the bread! Do you want a G&T, Alice? It's a special one. Make her a G&T, dear.'

'Well, yes.'

'Your young man can have beer, or wine? Or you can have gin if you want? Put a raspberry in it,' she directs my father.

'He's not—' As normal, I don't get to finish a sentence, let alone a denial.

'Beer is fine, I brought...'

'Here you go, James, Jim, Jimmy, Jamie? What will it be?' Dad holds a can out. 'What do you mean, raspberry?'

'In Alice's gin. Lucy!' Mum has her commanding voice on. 'Those children always run amok when their father isn't here. Honestly!'

The children are still sword-fighting with sausages and are wading through the bedding plants shouting, 'Watch out for the jungle monsters!' Lucy doesn't budge; she sometimes takes quite a laid-back approach to parenting.

'Hey up!' The deep voice rumbles from somewhere behind us and we spin round. 'How's it going, Soph? Thought I'd lost you.'

The first impression I get is startlingly blue eyes, as in *really* blue. The second is slightly too long and very tousled surfer-dude hair. The third is muscles. He has shoulders and biceps that make my jaw drop. Some men can carry off the sleeveless T-shirt look – this guy is one of them. He can also carry off the knee-length cargo shorts.

I can also imagine him carrying off my little sister, by the look of adoration on her face.

'Daz!' She squeals and looks like she wants to jump on him.

So this is Daz. I'd got a hazy picture of him in my head that included dreadlocks and dirty toes peeping out from worn leather sandals. Not quite this.

Not that I'm guilty of stereotyping or anything.

'No chance, Daz. You're never going to lose me!' That's a sentence I never thought I'd hear my sister say to a man. They fist bump and Sophie smiles. 'Meet my sis Alice, and Jamie.' I've never seen her looking quite as shy and smitten, I reckon Sophie has finally met her 'one'. She's had loads of boyfriends over the years, more than the other three of us put together, despite being the youngest sister. Although, to be fair, Lucy married Dan about three seconds after she left school, and Darcie swore off men for quite a while after she had Tilly.

Daz waves a hand in our direction then slips his hand round Sophie's waist and she gazes up at him in the adoring way I haven't seen since she was about three years old.

Mum catches my eye and smiles. She's seen it as well. 'Lucy! Boys!' She shouts a final warning before heading inside to get the salad.

'Auntie Alice! Alice Palace!' Leo (or is it Brad?)

screams and launches himself at my midriff, splattering my stomach with sausage. 'Oh, buggering hell, my banger!'

'Brad!' Dan's voice booms across the garden. 'Who on earth says that?'

'Mummy, when she gets stuff wrong, she's always getting stuff wrong,' Brad announces, then look at me and whispers confidentially.

'Or when the fear-tus kicks her in the fu—'

'Leo!' This time Lucy decides to assert some parental authority, before we're treated to a full run-down of her unsuitable-for-children vocabulary. 'And don't call it a foetus, it's your little sister, I told you!'

'A girl!' shrieks Sophie. 'You never told us!'

'Oh goodness, how wonderful.' Mum puts her hand over her mouth and looks like she might cry. I don't blame her, she adores Tilly, and another granddaughter to cuddle and dress in cute dresses is all she wants. Boys in the family were a novelty, until the terrible twins learned to walk and talk – now their nana loves them but in very small doses. And only if she can give them back. 'Oh, let's have another G&T!'

'Oh shit,' Lucy whispers and grimaces at Dan. 'I said we'd keep it as a surprise, didn't I?' He shakes his head and smiles.

'I'm getting another buggering banger,' mutters Brad quietly to my stomach. 'See you in a bit, Auntie Alice.' He turns away, then pauses. 'Did you bring any sweets?' There's hope in his voice. I shake my head.

'No, I—' He's halfway across the lawn, dodging his

father, and Leo's rugby tackle as he tries to grab a sausage off the table by the barbecue.

'Watch the barbecue, it's hot!' yells Mum.

'I don't bring him sweets, honest,' I say to Jamie, who isn't looking as shell-shocked as I expected him to. He just looks slightly bemused. 'Well not often, they don't need a sugar rush. Best advertisement for contraception that I know of.'

'Love the shorts, big sis!' Sophie grins at me. 'I couldn't borrow them next weekend, could I?'

'No!' Jamie and I shout in unison, then look at each other and laugh.

'Oh God.' Soph rolls her eyes. 'This one is going to be a real pain; you need to get rid of him.'

'He looks good to me.' Darcie holds out a plate. 'Burger? I think we need to get eating before Mum serves us any more triple gins.'

Things calm down a bit as we get stuck into the food. The twins are quiet for at least ten minutes before dashing off to help Mum decorate the trifle.

'Jamie?' Tilly has spent quite a lot of time gazing adoringly at Jamie and has now plucked up courage to ask another question. 'Do you keep the disco ball on your desk?'

'Nope.' He grins back. 'I've not got much stuff at all.'

'Not enough room with all of Alice's stuff,' interjects Sophie, but Tilly ignores her. She is fascinated, it seems, by a man who owns a disco ball.

'What have you got?'

'Not a lot.' He shrugs. 'A mug, Man U coaster, a—'

'Man U?' shrieks Lucy, who has been too busy eating to talk up until now.

'Language!' Dad walks over, with a plate full of sausages.

'Jamie's a Man U supporter, Grandad!' Tilly no longer looks awestruck, she looks shocked.

Everybody is shocked. They are all staring at him. It is the first time my entire family has been silenced for ages, well, for ever.

'Well, I suppose everybody has their faults,' Dad finally says. Then the corner of his mouth quirks up. 'I'm sure if you hang around we'll be able to convert you, or we'll have a bloody good try.' He winks at me. 'Burger? Beer?' He shakes his head in disbelief. 'Honestly, Alice, there I was thinking you'd brought a half-decent one home, and he turns out to be a Red!'

I warm up inside. Dad thinks Jamie is half decent. Okay, he is not impressed about his football allegiance, but he thinks he's half decent.

The afternoon drifts on; the last of the salad and meat is eaten up. Lucy and Darcie settle into a competitive discussion about whose contractions were worse last time round, and Soph and Daz are sitting cross-legged on the lawn gazing at each other adoringly.

Dad has turned down all offers of help in tidying things away and so Jamie and I sit at the table swapping jokes about people at work.

The sun is blazing down and it's one of those moments I'd be happy to live with for a while. Until Sophie comes to collect the bottle opener and spots that I've still got some trifle left in my bowl.

'Not eating that?' She giggles and has grabbed my spoon and shoved it in her mouth before I have time to retaliate.

'That's the bit Leo decorated after he'd been to the toilet,' I say. 'On his own.'

'What?' She puts her hand over her mouth. Gagging. We both know that our nephew's toilets habits haven't been refined. 'You're kidding, right?'

'I might be.'

Jamie chuckles as she dashes off saying she's going to gargle just in case.

'She's always been the same. What's mine is hers,' I say, smiling at him.

He's got a quiet and gentle side that I've never seen in the office. Okay, he's still teasing, but it's nice. Affectionate. 'But what's hers is her own?'

I've never felt this chilled with anybody, never felt so totally accepted just as I am. Dave was always on edge. He didn't like it when my sisters had hot debates, he didn't like the whirlwind of activity as the twins lobbed balls past his head. He disapproved of the untidy rows of bright bedding plants, and the clutter in the house. I could tell he was always itching to tidy up the pile of shoes by the door, to straighten the cushions. But Jamie just seems to have accepted it. Accepted us as we are.

I don't feel on trial, as though I need to be somebody I'm not or make excuses for my family. I've not felt this relaxed when I've brought a guy round for, well forever.

'All quiet on the Western Front?' Dad wanders over, still

wearing his striped apron and carrying two beers. He passes one to Jamie.

'Great barbecue, thanks,' says Jamie.

'Bet you're ready for some peace and quiet now, eh?' He chuckles, then checks his watch. 'I reckon I'm off duty just in time, staying to watch the match?'

He glances from me to Jamie, and back again. My stomach does a little lurch. 'Er, we need to get back, Jamie's train is in…' My voice tails off. I'd been so wrapped up in deciding what to wear, and what Jamie would think, and whether my family would like him, and a hundred other things – I'd completely forgotten City were playing. And I always stay and watch the game with Dad if I'm here. It is still *our* time. Bugger. 'I could come back and…'

'You stay,' says Jamie. 'It's no problem, I can…'

Dad smiles. 'We're going to have to convert you, lad.' He pats his arm, then kisses me on the cheek. 'Nice to meet you, don't forget to say bye before you go, Alice. We can chat when the highlights are on later.' He pauses, raises an eyebrow at me. 'If you're not too busy.' And with a wave he sets off inside, not willing to miss a minute of the game – and I turn the colour of a beetroot.

'He's nice, your dad.'

'He is. He won't let it drop, you know, next time you come he'll give you a full run-down of the match and highlight all the reasons through history that make City better than United.' Oops, did I say, next time you come? Jamie doesn't seem to have noticed. 'Coffee before we go?'

He shakes his head. 'I'm fine, unless you want one?'

I check my watch. 'I think it's time we went actually, if

that's okay with you? I need a lie down and I bet you do too!' I say jokingly, then blush again as Jamie's warm gaze meets mine. 'I mean, I need to get home, for a rest.' My cheeks burn. 'Too many G&Ts, and too much laughing and competition, you know.'

'I do.' He grins. 'I get why you like your own space at work now.'

'Exactly! It's always been like that, total chaos, everybody competing for attention.'

'And food!' He grins. 'You're the quiet one?'

'I guess.' I shrug. 'I love my family—'

'They're fantastic.'

'They are.'

'But?'

'But—'

'Nothing is ever your own?'

'Yeah, it was hard to feel that anything was mine as a kid. There was never much privacy, I shared a room with Soph.' I think my smile is what you'd call 'wry'.

He chuckles. 'And everything else?'

'Pretty much. She's always borrowed my clothes and stuff, I mean she doesn't mean anything, she just doesn't think.'

'And then you moved into your own place and nothing really changed?'

'You got it! I had plans to have my own little place but,' I shrug.

'We Got Designs isn't exactly the highest payer.'

'Exactly.'

It takes about ten minutes to extricate ourselves from the

bosom of my family, and, as we head for the gate, Leo is still hanging onto Jamie's leg – and only lets go when Jamie agrees to helping him build 'awesome stuff' on Minecraft.

'You don't have to,' I say as we head up the street, waving to the twins – who are now hanging off the gate, Mum will pay hell if she sees them – as we go.

'Not a problem. Though he'll have forgotten all about me by bedtime.'

'I doubt it,' I say softly.

It was once kissed never forgotten for me, but I think even if only our gazes – and not our lips – had met, I'd still have remembered him. Those kind, caring eyes, his grin, the unruly hair, the soft, sincere tone that emerges between the jokes and one-liners.

I don't know whether he heard me, but our pace has slowed.

'You had quite a challenge on trying to fit all the stuff that you don't want messing with on your desk,' he says ever so softly, and it feels like we're in our own little space here. Me and Jamie. Jamie and me.

He's got me. Just like that. 'Yep.' We swap a smile. I try not to stare. He understands. 'It's not that I'm mean and don't want to share…'

'I know.' Our gazes lock. 'But sometimes you need to keep some bits for yourself.'

'Yes.' We're walking in step; my hand accidentally brushes against his and my body fizzes in response. 'It's not just Soph,' I blurt out, wanting him to understand. He raises an eyebrow. 'It was okay really, until Dave. He didn't like my tat—'

'It's not tat!'

'Not to me.' I shrug. 'But he wanted to buy me the stuff he thought I should have.'

'Arrogant.'

'Or confident? I'm not making excuses for him,' I add quickly. 'He thought he knew best,' I say softly, remembering the delicate jewellery he'd wanted me to replace my heavy pendants with, the silver he'd thought was better than beads, the tasteful mug that was better than my jokey one.

'Or he needed to make his mark?'

'Suffocate mine, more like. It was a bit claustrophobic.' I sigh, but I don't want to spoil the day, spoil this moment. I've had more fun today than I have for ages. I've felt, well, carefree. 'It was my own fault though, I let him. I should have stood up for myself, but it didn't seem important enough to make a scene.' And I didn't want to lose him – not completely. He wasn't bad, *we* weren't bad as a couple. We just weren't that good. But hanging on had stopped me from being forced to make my own decisions, stand on my own two feet, stand up for myself. Be my best me. I get that now. 'But that's all over now.' I realize my voice is steady, my smile isn't brittle or too bright like it was for months after we'd split up. I really have got a handle on this. 'I've got rid of his stuff, and he can't get in now you've put the lock on, and my housemates know how I feel. Why the hell I didn't have it out with them earlier I don't know.' Sometimes solutions are easier than you think, aren't they? Sometimes in your head you make problems bigger, tougher, than they are. You just have to stop, think, keep it simple and say what you want. 'So, anyway, my stuff is safe! Thank you.'

'No probs.' Our hands make contact again, and this time he links his little finger with mine. 'It's not the lock that's made the difference though, it's you. And I didn't do it so that you'd move your stuff off the desk.'

'You better not have done!'

'I like it. It reminds me of you.'

We walk on in silence. Did he really just say that he likes to be reminded of me? 'Not that I've got blue feet.'

'I'll have to check that out one day!' He chuckles. The tiny bubble of anticipation grows inside me. It's not just the sound of his deep laugh, or the warmth of his body next to mine. It's the words, the promise. The intimacy that I've never felt in a bed before, let alone a street.

Does this mean he's prepared to take a risk? Find out that our kisses don't have to be perfect every time?

A crowd of teenagers push past and tease the moment apart, break the mounting tension and the stillness that had been growing between us.

'They're fun, your family. We never had barbecues like that!'

'I don't think many people do.' I grin at him as we walk on, move very slightly further apart, but even though his words are lighter, it is still there. That closeness. That feeling that there is only the two of us.

'You're lucky. When I was growing up it was just my parents, who are pretty quiet and studious and more into each other than anything else, and my annoying older sister who hated me.'

'Hated?'

'You know, proper sister–brother love–hate relationship.' He smiles, it reaches his eyes. 'We get on a bit better now, now we live miles apart and only see each other a few times a year.' He grins, then pauses, our pace slows. 'I tried to think of you like I do her.' We've stopped. He's gazing at me, his eyes darker than I've seen before, and the smiles fades.

'Miles away?' I say, the words croak in my dry throat.

'A sister,' he says, his look intent.

'You tried to think of me as somebody you don't get on with?' My voice has a tremor, my laugh is nervous. I can't help myself from staring at his generous mouth, the deep dimples, the white, even teeth.

'I did. To stop me wanting to kiss you again.'

'Oh.'

'It hasn't worked.' There is a husky edge to his words. 'The moment I saw you again, I wanted you, Alice. It scared me.'

The gin, laughter and sunshine whirl together in my body leaving me breathless.

'I could never get that first kiss out of my head, and then you were there again. Standing in front of me.' His fingers are at the nape of my neck, tangled in my hair. 'The real you, not some fantasy. It would have been easier if you'd just been a dream.' His voice is husky, sexy, stirring up all the want that I've tried to ignore for so long. 'Pushing you away felt so wrong.'

'You shouldn't have,' I say breathlessly. 'Hanging on to it as a dream stops you from opening your eyes to the good stuff.' I don't want to be some ideal on a pedestal. Untouchable.

I want to be touched. I want to be touched so much.

'I know.' His warm hand rests on my arm and a tingle runs through my body, leaving goosebumps inside and out. I shiver. 'You're cold?'

'I'm hot right now.' I've taken a step in closer without even realizing, until my body bumps against his. Boy am I hot, and he can take that any way he wants.

'Alice.' His hands are cradling my face. His forehead rests against mine. Our gazes lock. This isn't like that drunken moment at the festival. That was exhilaration, a mad moment. This is so much more. So real. 'You've always been hot.'

My heart pounds faster, my lips part. Oh my God, I want to kiss him.

'You looked so wild and free, and happy and beautiful.' His thumb brushes my cheek. 'And sexy.' I lean into the touch of his slightly roughened skin, wanting more. 'I thought I'd never see you again. I thought you weren't real.'

'I am,' I whisper.

I can't close my eyes as he tilts his head slightly. I want to see him, see his face, his eyes. I slide my hand along his back.

His muscles move below my fingertips as his lips meet mine.

He tastes of beer, of burgers, of ketchup. I clutch him tighter, my body sinking into his and I can't help it now, I close my eyes as I drink in the smell of him, the taste of him. The taste of lust and sex. He nibbles my lower lip and a shiver runs through my body as I reach one hand up to run my fingers through his hair.

'Oi! Get a room!' There's the honking of a car horn, and laughter and as the car speeds past we leap away from each other. Shocked.

I blink in the bright sunlight.

His hands are resting on my upper arms, he's holding me at arm's length. We stare at each other wordlessly. Then it's as though reality hits. His hands drop to his sides, leaving me cold. Abandoned.

'Oh hell, I'm sorry. I shouldn't have done that.'

I can't speak. My head is still spinning. I'm still in the kiss, wanting it to go on longer. I can still feel the firmness of his lips against mine, the warmth of his breath, the heat of his touch.

And he's saying we shouldn't have!

'What do you mean?' I say stiffly. My voice not sounding like my own.

'Shit, I didn't mean.' There's a look of panic in his eyes as he runs his fingers through his hair and it's like being slapped. 'Oh my God, sorry, I didn't mean…' He reaches out to touch me, the tips of his fingers no longer scorching.

I take a step away. It hurts that he *so* dislikes the thought of anything happening between us. Is he going to blame the beer, the heat, my bloody shorts that made him think we were back in Reading? 'Alice, it's not you.' He stops himself short.

'What do mean, it's not bloody me? It is me! Hello, I'm here, in the flesh. Real! You kissed me again and it wasn't a frigging dream.'

'Shit.' He moves back in closer. Rests his forehead against mine. I try and step away, but his hands are on my shoulders, holding me still. 'I wanted to do that, but I shouldn't.' His voice is soft as he gives a little shake of his head. 'I promised myself I wouldn't. It's not fair on you, Alice. I want to, but it's not... I can't. I just can't.' He kisses my forehead, then steps back properly this time. 'You're gorgeous, lovely, but it's...'

'Complicated?' I want to spit the word out, but I can't. It comes out soft, sad. Small. 'Oh, Jamie.' I've waited for this moment for so long, and now he's behaving like some jerk.

'More than complicated. Alice, it isn't just about you and me, things are fucked up enough, without... Shit, I need to shut up.'

'You do.'

'Look I didn't mean...it's not, I'm not saying you'd fuck things up. Arghh.' He puts his hand to his head. 'My life is a mess right now. I wouldn't want to drag you into it.' He shakes his head. 'I wish I could explain, but I...'

'Well, why don't you?' I fold my arms defensively.

He ignores me. 'Look, I should go.'

'You probably should if you can't even talk to me. What is it with you and not being able to explain stuff?'

We stand awkwardly for a moment. His hands clenched into fists at his sides. Strangely formal. 'I can't right now, I will do though, I promise.'

'Life isn't frigging perfect preserved moments, Jamie. It's about being real! You're supposed to make mistakes, do things your own way.' I'm yelling at him now. I want to stop, but I can't. 'Hanging on to a bloody memory rather than risk spoiling it is no better than me hanging on to fucking Dave because it meant I had somebody there when I needed them, is it?' As I spit out the words, I realize they're true. Was it so bad hanging on to a boyfriend who wasn't 'the one'? No worse than preserving a kiss in your head and heart like a fossil – never to be spoiled, but never to be lived or enjoyed either. 'You lied to me and now you're still not being honest!' The person I never thought would take advantage of me. 'I've had enough of this, Jamie. Enough of your excuses.' The temper has died out of me, I'm all shouted-out. I just feel sad and tired. The new, assertive me, should have bawled Jamie out the other day when he admitted he'd been pretending, not waited until now. Waited until we'd kissed again, until he'd made my toes curl and my heart lift with the promise of things to come, and then shot it all down again.

This is going to hurt so much, but I can't let him take advantage of me like this. Not even him. If I do, I'm letting myself down. Falling back into my old habits.

'I can't do this. I'm not going to be walked all over, I'm not going to be taken for granted.'

'I'm sorry.' He looks sorry. He looks lost, and I regret blowing up at him. 'Alice—'

I glare at him.

'Stop. Don't say another word.'

He hesitates, as though he wants to say more. 'Thank you for a lovely afternoon. It was great.'

'Lovely,' I say woodenly. 'The weather was perfect.' How on earth did we switch from lust to weather forecasts?

'Couldn't have been better.'

And then I turn on my heel and walk away from him – before he has the chance to do it to me.

I should feel positive, but I feel confused, hurt. Upset.

The birds aren't singing any more. It's not a beautiful spring day, it's too hot. I'm sweaty on the outside and churned up and cold on the inside.

My phone beeps, and I'm tempted to ignore it. I don't want to read any funny messages from my sisters saying how cute Jamie is. But I'm rubbish at ignoring my mobile. What if it's something important? Urgent.

I'm a shit. Sorry. You're right that life should be real, and you're right about making mistakes. Except I have something in my life I have to sort out. I made one mistake lying to you, I can't turn the clock back and make that right, but I can try and sort out the other mess in my life. I'd never take you for granted J x

Chapter Twenty-Two

Tuesday, again

'Are you going to be long?'

'I'm on the bus.' I hold my mobile phone to my ear and gaze out of the rain-spattered window. The early promise that May showed has not lasted. 'Another fifteen minutes probably?'

Sophie's sigh carries clearly. 'It's a bit shit not being able to get in your room when you're out. Can't you give me a key or something?'

'Well no, not really.'

'I won't forget to lock it or anything.'

'It's not that, Soph.' I try not to sigh. 'I didn't get a lock just because of Dave, I got it because I need my own space. I can't share everything all the time.' There is silence on the line. 'You do get that? I can't live in my office, Soph. I want to live in my home. I want somewhere of my own for once.'

'S'pose so,' she finally says, grudgingly. 'It's just we always shared.'

'I know,' I say gently.

I have discovered the backbone that my sister said I needed, and I don't think she likes it. I am standing firm on this one though. I need my privacy; I need my own space. I also need somewhere I can mope without fear of interruption.

Why can't my life be more straightforward?

It's been a week and two days (not that I'm counting, much) since the barbecue, and the kiss, and now Jamie has gone MIA.

No sign of him at all. No notes, nothing moved on the desk. No new socks for Mabel.

I don't think he's been in the office.

'You've not heard from him, have you?'

'No, Soph,' I reply glumly. I've not heard from him at all and it's surprising how much it hurts – even though I yelled at him and said enough was enough.

I close my eyes and I can feel his touch, taste his kiss and I have to scrunch up my eyes to stop the tears. This is ten times worse than the first time.

Worse than thinking he didn't recognize me.

Last week was bad enough, but I'd hung on to the thought that he'd be in the office yesterday, that he would leave me a note, that we'd be back to normal.

'That's good news then?'

It dawns on me just in time that she's talking about Dave. Not Jamie. She doesn't know about our snog; she doesn't know I feel like I've now been ghosted.

'So?' she prompts because I haven't immediately answered her.

'Yes, brilliant,' I add hastily. 'I think he's got the message at last.'

'Cool. Hurry up, eh? I've got something I'm dying to tell you!'

'Great, can't wait!' I smile, despite my grumpy mood. 'See you in a bit!' In the past week the subject of Jamie hasn't arisen with Soph because she has been too full of what is going on in her own life. Sophie has gone from a little bit in love, to falling headlong into the whirlwind emotions of passion and hope. I've read about them, these over-the-top emotions that leave you giddy and unable to think about anything or anybody else. I've seen them on the movies, but the closest I've got is fantasizing about fleeting snogs that were blurred by the beer in my veins and pounding music in my ears.

And now I can add to that. A never to be repeated heartachingly perfect, lingering kiss on a pavement around the corner from my parents' house.

I close my eyes and try to push the memory away. Then realizing the ache in my fingers is because I have my mobile phone in a death grip, I slip it back into my pocket. It beeps again just as I get off the bus and I make a grab for it.

I can't help myself. How pathetic is that?

It's not Jamie, it is a message from Lou. In response to my casual: *Office was flaming quiet last week. How's it been on your days? Has everybody resigned, and I'm the last to know?! Hope you've not abandoned me as well! Al xx*

Lou is not daft. She reads between the lines. She knows what I mean by 'everybody'.

Can't get rid of me, babe! Your desk mate has been missing though, working at home my sources tell me. I'll let you know if he surfaces tomorrow, bet Rodders is dry and barren without him. Fancy a crossover lunch on Friday? Lou x

You're on! Normal place, 12.30ish? Missing you. Al x

I check the time, then push the phone deep into my pocket, and start power-walking towards home. Maybe I need to think about ways to raise my heart rate that don't involve snogging Jamie. More exercise would do me good, and if I'm shagged from running, I will be worrying about dying and won't have the spare brain capacity to think about the might-have-been, will I? Or I could get a cat or dog; a daily dose of cat yoga would calm my mind. Or I could just try a bit of everything.

'Guess what?' Sophie is sitting cross-legged on my bed, grinning like a Cheshire cat. I have never seen her so happy. I want to hug her.

'You've found a new brilliant hairdresser?' I say, teasingly. She shakes her head. 'Got the sack?'

'We're going travelling!' she blurts out, unable to play the game a second longer. 'Daz was planning on it anyway and he's asked me to go as well! Travelling, going places.'

'I know what travelling means.' I laugh, and I do hug her then. She's as excited as a little kid. She bounces about in my arms; she can't sit still.

'He's borrowing this old VW campervan from his mate, and it's really hippy style, but it's got a kitchen and this cute stove, and this bed that pulls out and has got fairy lights round it.' She stops talking as fast and the grin on her face is replaced with a dreamy look. 'It's so cool, Al. You've got to see it! Do you think Mum and Dad liked him? We're telling them tomorrow about going and I don't want them to lose their shit, you know how they went ape the last time I said I was going away with a guy.'

'You were sixteen and still at school.' I say. 'And the guy was twenty-two and a useless wanker. I think this might be a bit different.'

'But I'd like them to like him. I really would.'

Soph is cute when she gets all sincere and is desperate for approval. It doesn't happen often. She generally does her own thing and doesn't really care if anybody else has given their blessing. Well at least that's how she is on the outside, but inside she is bothered.

'I'm sure they like him.' Our parents have always been pretty cool about our life choices. They say they've done their bit, hope they've taught us about right and wrong, about hopes and expectations, about value and aspirations. They're happy to guide and advise if we ask, but basically once we passed eighteen, they reckoned it was up to us. It explains in part why Soph is such a free spirit, I think that part of her came from Mum. I think Darcie's determination and bounce-back came mainly from Dad.

'Really?'

'Really!'

'Cool.' She grins. 'Are you okay?' Sophie asks, as an afterthought.

'Fine. Work is great, I got two new clients last week!'

'Ace, clever big sister. At least one of us has a brain!' She high-fives me. 'And how's Jamie dude?'

'Not heard from him.' I shrug, as though it doesn't matter. 'I think he's been working at home. Stop looking at me like that!' She is regarding me closely. She used to do that sometimes when we were kids and I was pretending to be asleep, but worried about something. I'd open one eye, and she'd be watching me intently and accuse me of 'not breathing right'.

'You like him!'

'He's okay!'

'There's something you're not telling me! Tell, you know I can't stand secrets.'

'There's nothing.'

Sophie is like a terrier; she hates thinking she is missing out on something and won't let up until she gets the truth. 'Oh, come on, Al, you can't kid me. I know you.' She leans forward, takes my hands in hers. 'What is it with this guy?'

I pull my hands free, then crash down on my back on the bed, and Soph lies down beside me.

'Do you think love at first sight is actually a thing?'

'Normally takes three pizzas, a few snogs and a couple of shags for me.' She grins. 'But who knows?'

'If I tell you this, you promise you won't tell?'

'Promise!' Soph has good intentions, but her willpower isn't that hot. She likes to share. She *has* to share. 'Oh my

God, stop teasing, come on, TELL ME! You can't say it was love at first sight then clam up.'

'Swear on Daz's life?' She purses her lips. 'I'll tell about your tats,' she wavers, 'and you letting Sparks out.' When she was six, Soph opened the garden gate because she thought our dog wanted to explore. He ran off. He was missing for two weeks after (we presume) spooking at the traffic. Mum blamed herself for not closing the gate properly when her hands were full and Soph never 'fessed up. She also got a tattoo on her back that she had done after too many tequilas when she was seventeen. This would not have been important, except Dad had said he would give us £100 on our eighteenth birthday if we resisted. He wanted to be sure we were old enough to make the decision he said – alongside the fact that it would also have been illegal to have one done earlier, and Dad doesn't do illegal. Not even a tiny bit illegal.

Soph took the money and only showed off the tattoo a month later.

I only know these things because she read my diary and recited bits from memory during Sunday lunch one day, so I nicked hers in retaliation when I was home from uni in the holidays. She'd kind of 'spread out' into my half of the room when I was away, and so it wasn't my fault I found it in my wardrobe, was it?

'And I'll tell Daz you fed him a sausage that wasn't remotely vegan and had never come into contact with any trace of a vegetable.'

'Oh fine, for fuck's sake, just bloody tell me!'

I take a deep breath. 'I met him at Reading Festival you

know, when I was at uni?' She nods. 'And we snogged just before the headline act came on, then I never saw him again.'

'Wow!' Sophie's eyes have widened.

'We didn't say a word. Just snogged.'

'Fuck! You.' She grins. 'You of all people kissed somebody you didn't know! Wow!' She flops back on the bed. I think I am slightly pissed off that she finds this such a surprise, me kissing somebody on impulse. 'And?'

'It was amazing.' I put my hands over my face, but she springs up, leans over me and peels my fingers away.

'That's awesome! Shit, love at first kiss! It usually takes me swapping more fluids than just saliva before I think I've got it made!'

'Sophie!'

'Shit, we are talking about Jamie here?' I nod. 'That is something amazing to tell your kids.'

'Then he pretended he didn't remember.'

'Fuck, you're kidding?'

'For two years.'

'Wow.'

'Then admitted he did remember just before the barbecue.'

'And?'

'And kissed me on the way home.'

'Ace!' She sees the look on my face and hesitates. 'That's good, isn't it?'

'He's not interested, he started making excuses, so I blew him out.'

'You? Bloody hell, Al! Go big sis, you rock!'

I don't feel like I rock. 'He's avoided me ever since.'

'Which is what he should do if you yelled at him like you yelled at me, except you didn't really want to blow him out?' I nod, sad. 'Oh. Here, you need chocolate.'

I take the piece she offers. It's nice, very nice and... 'Where did you get this?'

She shrugs, the picture of innocence.

'It's mine, isn't it? You nicked it while I was in the bathroom!'

'Whatever. Did he actually say he wasn't interested?' See? Terrier!

'He said it was complicated, and some other crap. He said we shouldn't have kissed.'

'Well there you go then.' There is a note of triumph in her voice.

'What do you mean, *there you go*? He's ignoring me!'

'Don't give me your evil look! Complicated can be sorted. Simple. It's just code for I'm fucking scared, not the same at all as I-wish-you'd-fuck-off.'

'No it isn't simple, Soph.' I hold out my hand for another piece of *my* chocolate.

'Was it a good kiss?'

'Amazing,' I say, a hint of wistful in my voice. 'Even better than Reading.' I munch sadly on chocolate.

'Then he must have been up for it, mediocre kisses are one-sided. Amazing kisses defo take two.'

'If you say so.' I think he was up for it. Then he wasn't. 'He was probably just hysterically relieved to get away from the twins and got carried away.'

'Haha, you're so funny. Can I borrow those denim shorts to go away with?'

I am taken aback by the change of subject, but not that taken aback. I know how Soph works. The Jamie talk was just a distraction. 'No!'

'They'd remind me of you.'

'Soph, you're not going to forget me. I'm your bloody sister! Buy your own shorts.'

'But they're proper vintage.'

'You cheeky cow!' I bash her with a pillow. 'I'm not that old, I've not had them that long.'

She giggles and bats me back with the other pillow.

It's like we're kids again, back at home, sharing a room, sharing hopes and dreams, sharing the crap, hating each other, loving each other. We're soon standing on the bed, launching at each other with squishy pillows until we both find our legs have gone wobbly and sink down in a heap. We collapse back, giggling. Both tilt our heads at the same time and our gazes meet.

She reaches out and touches the back of my hand.

'It'll work out, Sis. There'll be a reason. He seems a nice guy and he has been honest.'

We both stare at the ceiling for a moment. She doesn't know him.

'Ask him. Go on, track him down and ask him. Then you'll know.'

I nod.

'You need to know.'

I nod again. She's right. I do.

'Another thing you need to know is that there's a fucking big spider by that light fitting!' She screams and jumps up, and I jump in surprise and fall off the bed the other side.

She peeks at me under the bed from the other side.

'I'll just get these and be off then.' She's on her feet and scampering out, and I don't realize until she's heading through the doorway that she's got something denim in her hand.

I look up at the ceiling. There is no spider.

'Give those back!' I hurtle after her but know there is only one way. I'm on the bannisters before I give myself time to change my mind, and I land practically on top of her on the bottom stair.

'Ouch!'

'You deserve it! Now give me those.' I prise my shorts out of her hand and hold them up triumphantly.

'You are such a spoilsport sometimes. At least I got this!' She holds the rest of my chocolate in the air, then sprints for the front door.

I let her. Laughing and shaking my head as she turns to wave. 'Wish me luck, Daz is coming round in a couple of hours' time, so we can tell the oldies about our trip!'

'Good luck, Soph! Though you don't deserve it,' I wag my finger at her, 'that was my nicest chocolate, I was saving it!'

I watch the door long after she's gone through it.

Family is the best, the real thing. Even if it's chaotic, annoying, interfering. You can rely on your family.

But a tiny part of me won't stop saying that I need more.

Chapter Twenty-Three

Thursday

S ugar. The breath catches in my throat as I put my handbag down under the desk.

Mabel might not have new socks, but she does have a note wedged between her feet. My heart is pounding as I stare at it. I want to read it, but I don't want to read it.

Is he telling me that it is over, he has moved on – to another desk? Has he found a new job, is that why he isn't in the office? He's really moving on and I will never ever see him again.

I hesitate, trying to build up my courage. Then I snatch it up. If this is bad, I can sprint over to the ladies and be there and locked into the privacy of a cubicle before it hits.

Hope you're okay? Shit, this is strangely formal. Formal means bad. I plonk myself down heavily onto the seat. *Sorry for fucking up. You're right, I should be able to talk to you, not avoid it. Can we talk? I need to explain myself. This is way awkward, I hate awkward, I liked being friends. I miss you. J*

No-kiss Jamie.

I gulp. He misses me, but not in that way. More like he misses the sister he sometimes hates. And friends? Friends! I don't want to be friends. I don't think I can do that any longer. I don't want to be friends with somebody I fancy the pants off. It's too hard. There will always be that glimmer of hope.

I screw the note up angrily.

I need to be calm. This is stupid.

We can talk, he can talk, say what he wants to. I will say I can't do this. I cannot be friends.

We can be colleagues. Keep a professional distance. Go back to how we were. I didn't go to all this trouble of making sure my life, my belongings, were my own to throw it away again like this and pretend to be somebody I'm not.

Except can we go back to the way we were before we shared a desk? Does that ever work?

I power up my computer to distract myself, open my emails.

'Somebody to see you, Alice.' I glance up at the sound of my name.

'Alice.' Dave's voice is loud and echoing in the half-empty office.

Shit.

'How the hell did you get in?' I have enough trouble getting in myself.

'Jack signed me in, I told him I wanted to surprise you!'

Shit, I forgot he's met Jack a few times. 'Well he

shouldn't have!' Grrr, I should have put posters of him everywhere.

'Not a very nice welcome, though, I thought you'd be pleased to see me?' He raises an eyebrow, sounding reproachful.

I swallow my nerves down. 'Why would I be pleased to see you?' I can do this. 'What are you doing here? I thought I'd made it quite clear that I didn't want to see you?' I am aware that although people have their heads down and are hammering away at their keyboards, they are listening in. I can't blame them. I'd be the same. But I don't want to take this into the meeting room. That will give out the wrong signals; he'll think he's important, that I want to speak to him. This has to be in the open, it needs to be brief. Impersonal.

I'm also a bit scared about being locked in a room having a row with anybody. Which is stupid when he's an ex, not some random stranger. But just the thought makes my heart hammer.

'Oh Alice.' He sighs, shakes his head. 'I know we needed a break.' He leans forward, touches the back of my hand and I snatch it away, repulsed by the touch. I don't want him to touch me, it makes my skin crawl.

'Not a break, Dave. The end.'

'Oh come on, you've said that before and then wanted to make up! You know you need me; you know you can't cope without knowing I'm there for you. Come on, admit it.'

This is the problem; this is where I've got it wrong in the past. I have turned to him. Always. Hung on to him, like an old, thin, faded tea towel that no longer dries the dishes properly but you're comfortable with. Dave has been my comfort blanket.

But I don't need him any longer. Not even now I'm upset with Jamie. Life without Dave has been better than life with him ever was. And now I've had the briefest glimpse of what being with somebody like Jamie could be like, I know I could never go back.

I realize what I really want, need, out of a relationship. I know what I couldn't accept with Jamie, I know what was so wrong with what I had with Dave.

If you're going to stick with somebody, if you love them, then you trust them, don't you? You share your space, your life, the good bits and bad, you can show your vulnerabilities and you respect each other's boundaries. Where you can go, where you can't. You can be one good couple, but also two good individuals.

'I'll admit no such thing. I don't need you, Dave.'

'It's been long enough, Alice. I'm sure you've done some thinking. I have and I've made a decision. I know this is what you want, what will make you feel happy and valued.'

'Dave, I am happy,' I say softly. I don't need to shout. This time I'm confident in who I am. 'I'm happy without you.'

He ignores me; he clearly has a prepared speech. 'I've realized that we are meant for each other. I might have taken you for granted a bit.' He laughs as though he doesn't really believe it. 'We belong together.'

The old Alice would have backed down, it is what he assumes I will do. But I know this is one confrontation I'm happy to face, and I know I don't need him in my life, not even for another second. I don't need an emotional crutch like I have in the past.

I also don't deserve to be spoken over and ignored. I stand up.

'You need to go.' I could call the dragon lady over, she'd soon chase him off. No, I can do this on my own. And if I make a stand, he'll know I mean it.

It would be better if I do this myself. Better for me, and for Dave.

If I hadn't had my mind on Jamie, I'd have been more on the ball when he walked into the office. I'd have turned him round before he got to my desk.

'Not until I've said what I came for...' Shit, he is down on one knee. I can see Sal's face out of the corner of my eye. She is wide-eyed. Lots of people are looking our way. If anybody takes a photograph, they are so fucking dead. 'Marry me.' He's smiling, he's confident.

'Haven't you heard a word I've said? Get up, you're embarrassing me.'

'I don't care. You don't care.'

'I bloody do!' I hiss. 'This is my job!'

'You won't have to come back after the wedding, you can forget this place, forget your little job—'

'It's not a little job, it's my career. And I'm embarrassed for you, not me, you idiot!'

'You don't have to worry about what these people think. I've even shortlisted some wonderful houses for us to look at,' he says with satisfaction.

'Are you joking?' He is unbelievable.

'No, I'm not. All you have to do is find the perfect dress, and Mother will of course be on hand to help.'

'Your mother?' I laugh. I can't help it. 'I'm sure she bloody well would be. I'd be buttoned up to the neck, covered down to my toes and unable to eat or even bloody breathe in a boned and tied corset her great-great-grandmother had handed down because "they knew how to be ladies back then".'

'Alice!'

I've finally done it. 'Sorry, I don't mean to be disrespectful to her, but you need to get up on your feet and get out, Dave.'

'We're the perfect couple, Alice. Say yes and I'll get up.'

'And you realized this when? When I wasn't the one chasing you anymore? Okay, if you won't go I'll tell you what I think. I'll marry you over my dead body. If you were the last man on earth, I wouldn't say yes, Dave. How can I marry somebody that I don't trust?'

'You do—'

'No, listen for once in your bloody life! I don't. I can't share my life with a man who I have to hide things from, who doesn't respect my stuff, doesn't listen to what I want. I can't share things with you, Dave, because you just take advantage of me, it's all about you and what you want and what you think I should want. You don't give me a say in my own life! And you've never really been there for me, supporting me. We just used each other, not loved each other.'

'Rubbish. How can you say that?'

'Because I love somebody else!'

'No you don't,' he says flatly. Totally disbelieving.

'I do.'

'You haven't had time to meet anybody, and I know you Alice, you are measured, careful.' He is still being patronising.

'Well I haven't been this time, I've been impulsive, and I have known him for a while, ages actually.'

'What's his name?'

'Jamie!' I answer without thinking. Because it's true. 'And I first met him years ago, and then we bumped into each other again.' Oh shit, who heard that? This is going to be all over the office.

'You're such a romantic girl, but this is real life not one of those films. It's a silly fling, it won't work out, Alice, but you and I will.'

'I'm not wasting my breath even answering that. I've got a lot of work to do. I'll show you to the lift, or would you like me to call Security to help you?'

He slowly gets to his feet. Rests his hand on the desk, and I instinctively move mine back.

'I can find the lift myself, I think.' His tone has an edge of sarcasm.

'Good.' I turn back to my desk. I am trembling as I move stuff round on my desk waiting for my nerves to settle, for the adrenalin rush to seep away. Waiting to hear the ping of the lift so that I know he's gone.

'Here.' Sal very gently places a cup of coffee on the shelf between us, and a bar of chocolate. 'You look like you need this.' Then she stands up and heads over to the printer before I even have time to thank her.

Marry me? Two little words that are supposed to be magical. Desired. Not the effect I thought they would have on me at all. I've dreamed of hearing them since I was a teenager. I've lived my reaction over and over again.

In my head those words make me feel dizzy with excitement, so happy I can barely speak. I cover my mouth with my hands, leap about like Tigger.

Hearing them wasn't like that at all. Instead I feel like I want to scream with frustration. And I am really fucking annoyed that Dave has spoiled it by doing this. Just how dense is he?

I head off to the toilets to splash my face with water in private and take some calming breaths. It is always cooler in there than in the office. And I can pace. And scream.

My mobile rings as I'm leaning over the basin staring at my flushed reflection.

'Hey.'

'Are you okay, Al? You sound a bit…'

'I'm furious! Dave managed to worm his way into the office, then bloody asked me to marry him in front of the whole office! What planet is he on?' I yell down the phone at Lou, then start to pace up and down. Which means I take three steps in one direction and bang my knees on the bin, then three steps back and stub my toe on the door. Which I am tempted to kick. I am literally hopping mad. That question, 'marry me?', was supposed to be a good one.

'Really?' Lou suddenly giggles. 'Did he gallop up on a white horse?'

'No, he came up in the lift! Stop laughing, it's not funny, it's bloody embarrassing.' It is funny though, I can't help it, I start to smile. 'He's totally lost the plot.' I realize I am running my fingers through my hair, then look at myself in the mirror and try and smooth it down quickly, before somebody comes in and labels me Crazy Woman. It's very funny. I start to laugh, and she joins in. 'Oh shit, why do these things happen to me?'

'Because you're so lovely.'

'Soft, you mean.' I sober up a bit. 'It's my fault, I guess. I should have told him to sling his hook months ago.' He'd been my go-to, my crutch. But I've outgrown him.

'True, but lots of people do that, they hang on way past the sell-by date of a relationship.'

'He's only interested now 'cos he thinks I'm playing hard to get. He was like that when we first met. But he was always a bit distant, a bit...'

'Emotionally unavailable?'

I nod my head, even though she can't see me. 'Yeah.' Emotionally unavailable; I was drawn to him like catnip when I needed support, reassurance – but I never really got either from him. Not really. But I just couldn't help myself.

Oh shit, is that what I'm repeating with Jamie? The man who keeps pushing me away. I've been turning to him more and more lately, relying on his notes. He made me feel safe, I felt I could trust him, share, he helped me stand up for myself, never took advantage, but now—

'Al? You still there?'

'Yeah. Sorry, Lou, I just needed a shout!'

'I'm not fucking surprised! Anything you want as an

engagement pressie?'

'Sod off!' She laughs. I run the water, splash my face.

'Bugger, I can't even remember why I called you now! I'll call you later when I remember, yes?'

'Sure, speak later.'

'Er, you did say no?'

'Lou!'

'Just checking!' She starts to laugh again. I press the end call button deliberately slowly. Then I smooth my top down, tuck my hair between my ears and march out of the ladies, wondering what kind of looks I am going to get. Shit, how many people heard me declare my love for Jamie? I'm going to have to pretend it's a different Jamie. Yeah, they won't know it's this Jamie.

But nobody seems bothered. Sal is the only one who shows any sign, and she's standing by the coffee machine.

'Hey, thanks for the coffee earlier. You were right, I did need it!'

She smiles. 'It looked a bit heavy.' There's no question in her tone; she's not fishing.

'My ex, who doesn't seem to have accepted that he is my ex.'

She takes her drink out of the machine and looks me straight in the eye.

'I'm not prying, but I thought you did great. You told him.' There's a hint of a smile on her normally straight face.

'Not that he was listening.'

'They don't. It was he who sent the flowers, wasn't it?'

I nod.

'Look, it's none of my business, but stick to your guns if

he pesters.' She turns the cup in her hands, as though trying to decide whether to say anything else. Then it comes out in a rush. 'I had an abusive husband; it started with subtle control I hardly noticed and then I found I couldn't get away. I'm not saying your ex...' She frowns. 'File a report with the police if you feel at all threatened. Yes? They're clever.' She pats my hand.

'It's okay.' I squeeze her arm back. 'He's harmless, just got a big ego.' I smile. 'Thanks though, I appreciate it, and I'm sorry about your ex.'

'So am I. My fault for being such a doormat, I guess.'

'No!' I say firmly. Even though I've just had similar thoughts about myself. But Dave is different, Dave is just a stupid twat – Sal obviously had to cope with something far worse. 'It's never your fault, never.'

'I wish I was assertive as you, Alice. You're always so confident, you know where to draw the line.'

'I'm a work in progress,' I say, smiling as it hits me just how much progress I have made with my line-drawing. 'But getting better.'

'Me too.' She smiles, a full-on smile that transforms her serious features. Then she turns away and walks back to her desk, her back straight.

I watch her go as the coffee swirls out of the machine into my cup.

Judgy Sal as Lou calls her, the quiet one who likes order and doesn't like noise and disruption. The girl who has observed quietly and actually been quite kind, but not judgemental at all, since the hot desking started. And I've never really responded.

A pang of guilt hits me as I realize that I've never made any effort to chat or find out anything about her.

You never really know people, do you? The hurt they carry, why they are like they are? I should be kinder, I should listen more to what people are really saying, not just the words I hear. We all should.

I sit down at my desk. Look at all the things on my side. I know what I must do. I need to clear everything personal off this desk, make this one hundred per cent professional. I can at least do that. Then when, if, Jamie and I talk I can explain that we can have a fresh start.

Dave's proposal was a bit of a shock, but it proves that sometimes you have to draw a strong line under the past, however much you don't want to. I've been as guilty as Dave in not doing that. I've hung on to my past fantasies about bumping into the boy I kissed – just as Dave has held on to his idea of him and me.

Jamie and I can't go back to how we were. I know that. I no longer have that hope I'd hung on to for two years that one day he'll remember me and fancy me as much as I fancy him. The day he admitted he remembered was the day it all changed. The day he got carried away and kissed me again was the day it all ended. Once and for all.

Whatever is going on in his life, he doesn't want me to be a part of it.

And that is fine.

Next time I'm in I will bring a bag and pack everything

away, and it will be quite safe in my newly locked room. From now on the office will be just the office. Not some substitute home. End of.

I click on the website I'm working on and get my head down.

I'm turning my computer off for the day, when the note Jamie left catches my eye again. I peel it off the desk. Run my finger over the indents the pen made. It makes me sad.

Jamie asked how I am, which is more than Dave ever did. Jamie said sorry, which is more than Dave did.

Jamie just wants us to be friends.

Dave doesn't.

Why, just when you think you're doing the right thing, when you think you're starting to get your life how you want it, does it all have to come and punch you in the stomach?

I slip the note in my handbag. Push my chair in. Wave goodnight to Sal and make my way to the lift.

As I leave the building I stop and take my phone out on impulse. I text Jamie.

Yes, it would be good to talk. Alice x

I mean, I have announced to Dave in particular and the whole office in general, that we're an item, so it's not just him that might need to explain themselves.

What if next time he comes into the office there's a barrage of congratulations?

Tricky.

Chapter Twenty-Four

Friday

I stare at the black door nervously. Double-checking I've got the right house number, playing for time while I compose myself and rehearse what I'm going to say in my head.

I've been doing that since I left work. I haven't come up with anything witty and original. Isn't it a bugger how when there's no pressure you can be hilarious, full of witty one-liners? Standing on a doorstep, the witticisms just don't come. *Hey, long time no see* (lame) and *Rodney and Mabel miss you* (needy – he'll know I mean me; plants and stuffed toys don't have feelings or thoughts) have come out top. Well, they're the only lines.

I decided to dismiss my first ideas *Where have you been? I've been worried* (even though I have) and *I can't stand not hearing from you* (even though I can't), *I'll be friends, anything, just name it* immediately. On the grounds that a. they might terrify him, and he'll run for the hills, and b. they might lead to images of me lying prostrate at his feet, hanging on to his trouser legs like the twins did. Not becoming. Or professional. Or sexy. Well, maybe sexy, done in the right way – but I'm pretty confident that it won't turn out that way.

I am worried about him though. I've been doing some thinking and, I mean, he's not going to not come into the office because of our hot snog, is he? Particularly as I'm not in when he is. It doesn't make sense.

He said his life was a mess, has he done something terrible? My head can't get round that idea at all. Maybe he's helped out some relative or friend who's done something illegal.

But why couldn't he have explained to me why we shouldn't have kissed?

It must be something terrible.

He must be married, or an illegal immigrant, or in a witness protection programme so he has to lie low.

I'm being ludicrous now. And why would he ask me here, to his home, if any of that was true?

Unless it isn't actually his home.

Oh hell.

Now I'm here, staring at the door, none of my opening lines seem right. It's quite an imposing front door. In fact, it's quite a grown-up house, not like my shared one.

Although Jamie might share a house. I don't know, do I? I don't know much about him at all. I feel more jittery than ever. I could just go home.

No. I can't.

Right, let's do this! I raise my hand to knock, and the door swings open. I narrowly miss hitting him on the nose and instead almost topple into his arms, then stagger about like I'm on the rush hour train with standing room only.

'Hey.' He puts out a hand to my elbow to steady me, then drops it as though I'm red hot. 'Er, thanks for coming round, I wasn't sure you would.' He sticks his hands in his pockets awkwardly.

How could I not? Even before Dave crashing in, and I announced my undying love to the whole office, I guess I'd known in my heart that I couldn't ignore his note.

Couldn't ignore him.

I don't want him out of my life. I'm not going to let him take advantage, but I've missed him like hell; the funny notes, the teasing. And I do want to check there's nothing wrong. I mean, it's a bit extreme not going into the office because of me, isn't it? I'm not even there in person!

His reply to my text was totally unexpected though. An invitation to pop in to his after work one day.

He looks as gorgeous as ever, but tired. His eyes aren't sparkling, the lines on his face don't look like smiley lines; they look like exhaustion. Mum would say he looks drained.

'How could I resist? I needed to chase up Mabel's socks!' I try and add a spark of humour to cover up the fact that I feel nervous as hell. And confused.

He doesn't laugh, he shifts uneasily, then leads the way into his home. 'Come in. Drink? Wine?'

'Wine?' I check my watch. 'Am I going to need it?' I ask, half serious.

'I think I do, and it is Friday after all.'

'True. Any excuse will do me, make it a big one, haha.' Shit. I've gone over the top now. It's because I'm wound up, I know it is. I need to wind it in, slow down, stop bloody flapping and be cool. He's just a friend.

Hell, he has got a seriously sexy bum.

I stare around at my surroundings to try and take my gaze, and dirty mind, off his body.

As entrance halls go it's pretty normal. As in, boring and not much to look at. I'm still thinking about his body. Coat hooks, stair bannisters, mirror. Bugger, why didn't I slap some more lipstick on, on my way over?

'Your wish is my command!'

I wish! His words immediately switch my attention from the not-at-all mesmerising magnolia walls.

In the kitchen, he reaches for a bottle of already opened wine. I'd never really noticed before how lightly his forearms are brushed over with fine hairs. 'Red okay, or I can open white?' Or how strong-looking his fingers are.

'Pink?'

'Now you're pushing it, unless you want me to mix them!'

This enforced jollity is not good. It's not us. What happened to feeling comfortable together? That not-needing-to-talk thing? Now we're blabbing away to fill every crack of silence and it is horrible. It is making my stomach all hollow and empty, because I'm dreading what will happen when we stop talking drivel. When we get to the meaningful stuff like 'I've got a new job', 'I'm moving' (could be why he gave me his address, haha), 'I've asked for a desk transfer'.

'Good job the weather's warming up, or Mabel would need her socks!'

He hands me a glass of wine. A *very* large glass. 'Wow, planning on getting me tipsy?' Shut up, Alice. You're flirting, you're making it worse.

'Sorry, I didn't mean... I can pour some out.'

'Don't be daft, I was kidding.' I hang on to my glass. I might need it.

'Here.' He signals away from the kitchen area into the open-plan lounge. 'Shall we sit down?'

Oh God, this is so bad he thinks I need to sit down. He's planning on telling me he's married or something and he feels like he's being stalked. Why did I come here? Why did Soph ask him to the barbecue? Why did I kiss him again? Why, oh why?

I swallow down all the horrible thoughts and follow him over, slide onto the leather couch and look everywhere but straight at him.

I must look like some nervous virgin, knees pressed hard together, clutching my glass of vino, gaze fluttering round the room wildly. I'm even making myself feel more on edge and nervous.

It is actually quite nice in here though. My shoulders relax down a fraction.

Not cluttered, but homely. The seats are squishy, not the slide-off type. It's all a bit muted but the cushions are a splash of colour, there are crowded bookcases and... Oh my

God. I lean forward before I can stop myself and nearly slip off the non-slip chair.

My shoulders are hunched back up, practically cradling my ears.

There's something, I swear, there is a green and red plastic toy sticking out from under a book on the bottom shelf!

'Everything okay?'

'Yes, er sure. Sure.' I turn back to him, bright smile on my face. 'Why shouldn't it be?' It must be a dog toy. He's got a dog. A very quiet dog. 'Impressive place you've got, bit bigger than my hobbit hole,' I say to distract myself. But seriously, how come he can afford a place like this when I've got a box room in a house share? He's got to have either inherited it, or somebody has chipped in to help him out. 'You never said your parents were millionaires! Not that it's any of my business,' I add hastily. He's going to think I'm a gold digger now.

'You never knew I was one of those bitcoin billionaires?'

'You're not?' My jaw drops.

'No.' He grins, chuckles, and some of the old jokey relationship between us seeps back. 'I'm housesitting for my uncle while he's working in Saudi. Five-year contract. Gives me chance to save up a deposit for a place.'

'Oh.' Oh shit, there's something else nestled in the books. It is much too small, even for the smallest dog. Choking hazard.

It is a dinosaur.

I am familiar with plastic dinosaurs; my nephews have many.

Why is there a dinosaur on his bookcase?

I introduced him to my family, I told him about Dave, I very possibly totally overshared. But he never told me he had a house full of children's toys?

Okay. Slight exaggeration. Take a deep breath, Alice. One toy, well two, okay there's a tractor down next to *Pub Walks on the Coastal Path* as well.

I glance along the bookshelves distractedly, wondering what other prehistoric creatures are going to jump out. T-Rex doesn't. Something else does. On the table next to where I am sitting.

'Oh wow, is that your nephew? You never said! He's so cute!' The picture of the gorgeous chubby-cheeked laughing toddler catches my eye, and I grab it for something to do. Phew, that explains it. It's not even Jamie's house, of course they're not his toys!

He can't actually have a toddler like that living here. There are no sticky fingerprints. Sticky blobs of solidified Calpol on the carpet.

There's something about the baby's smile, the shape of his mouth, his eyes that makes me sure he must be related to Jamie. He's like a mini version, but with blond hair. And, hey, why else would he have a picture of a toddler in his place? And his toys. The sister he loves to hate must have children, or at least a child. Or his uncle has grandchildren. 'He looks so like you, I bet he's better behaved than my nephews, the terrible twins! Isn't it great when they're not yours and you can have fun, then hand them back? That's what Mum always says!' I am blabbing on, relief making me a bit loopy. All explained! A few stray toys, that's all! I suddenly realize he is staring at me in a way that's a bit unnerving.

I put the photo down guiltily. 'Sorry.' He must be one of those people that doesn't like you moving stuff. I check it is in the same spot I got it from, tricky 'cos he hasn't got dust on the tabletop like I have on mine, so there's no mark. Don't get me wrong, I'm not a complete housework slut, I just don't always pick stuff up to dust under it. Sometimes, not always. I always thought lots of people did that to save time, you know they say 'a quick dust round', don't they? Round being the important word there.

I started to have doubts though when I said it to Lucy (who, let's face it does only have time to do things quickly – maybe that's why she acts sex-starved, maybe it is not baby hormones, maybe it's because she has to do everything at super-fast speed and has to settle for a tremor not an earthquake down there?) and anyway, she gave me a very funny look with raised eyebrows and said, 'Haha, you are kidding, right?' I never mentioned housework to her again.

Jamie still hasn't said anything.

There is no jokey comeback. In fact, the silence is a bit strange. Unnerving. I glance up. He isn't looking at me though, he's staring at the photo. I have definitely put it back in the wrong place. I shift it a couple of millimetres.

The corner of his mouth lifts in a twisted smile. Not the normal Jamie at all. And no smile. No laughter in his eyes.

The silence lengthens, and I am *so* tempted to fill it – because that is what happens in my family. There is never any room for silence, even though I often wish there was. Which is why I now keep it buttoned.

I stop my twitching fingers from touching the photo again, feeling slightly guilty.

'He does, doesn't he?' There's a catch in his voice. He coughs to clear his throat, and then his gaze meets mine. He's looking directly at me, in me, if you know what I mean. His face totally serious.

I nod, swallowing to moisten my dry mouth.

'You might even think I could be his dad.' Now it is his turn to lean over and pick up the photo. His turn to smile, but the smile isn't a full-on happy smile. It's soft, sad.

The way he says it, the expression on his face. It hits me so hard that I feel like I've been whacked in the stomach and all my breath has come out in a rush. It can't be...he can't. I look at the photo, back at him, then back at the photo. The impossible truth dawns. The blond curls, happy grin, eyes that sparkle with mischief. His and the baby's.

Then I sneak a sidelong peek towards the dinosaur crew.

'You could,' I finally squeak out, unable to bear the wait any longer. My throat is sandpaper-dry, my voice scratchy. I force two more words out. 'Are you?' I'm holding my breath. Thoughts swirling about randomly in my head. This isn't what I expected at all.

He nods towards the photo. One short nod, then looks back at me and the tiny nods of his head get stronger, slower as though he's making sure I understand, as though he's almost convincing himself. 'He's called Alfie.'

Oh my God, he's not only married, he has got a child. Maybe children! I glance round wildly as though I'm expecting them to crawl out from under the furniture, from behind the curtains. From between the books.

There I was, joking at work that he isn't even up to taking responsibility for a mini spider plant, and he's got a real living, moving, breathing noise-making mini-me.

He said complicated. Bloody hell, he's telling me. My mind is boggled. Him? A baby? An actual bloody baby. He's a dad.

Shit. I kissed him. I made him kiss me. My heart is thumping, and there's a painful lump in my throat as I stare at him. Then my gaze flickers round nervously.

I can't help it; I realize I'm searching for more signs of family life here. There are no high heels under the sofa, or spare lippy on the mantelpiece (or is that just me?). There is no baby paraphernalia around, no sign of a child apart from this picture.

That's impossible. I know that from Lucy, from Darcie. Babies come with stuff, lots of stuff. Not just a handful of toys.

It all spreads to all corners of every room, impossible to tidy away.

Jamie's home doesn't even say serious relationship, let alone 'dad'.

'He lives in Cornwall.'

I stop glancing round guiltily. 'Oh.' I am well confused now.

'My life is a fucking car crash right now, believe me, you really don't want anything to do with me,' he says wryly.

Believe me, I would. If he wasn't already part of a happy family with somebody else. Except he can't be, can he, if his son lives miles away?

He puts the photograph down slowly.

'If you want to talk about it...' What am I saying? He doesn't want to talk about it, he wants to tell me to stop flirting, stop hoping. Step out of his life. I don't bloody want to talk about! Do I? Oh God, I hate my nosiness sometimes. 'Does your er, wife, ex...' The word sounds strangled as it is forced from my lips.

He suddenly sighs, then sinks down onto the sofa, puts his head in his hands. Rubs his eyes with the palms of his hands, and then he sweeps his hair back and leans back onto the cushions.

He looks knackered. I want to hug him. Instead I sit on my hands.

'This is what I had to explain to you. But it's not how it looks.'

'How does it look?' I know what he's getting at. I'm still sneaking looks. In a minute I'm going to have to 'drop something' so I can sneak a peek under the sofa.

He nearly grins, as though he's read my mind. 'Like a bachelor pad?'

I smile, the totally awkward moment broken, but still a bit hard to get my head round. 'A very homely bachelor pad.' It is. It might not have many hints of a kid showing, but it isn't really what I imagined at all. I suppose I'd thought his home would be an extension of his desk; he's Mr Neat and Tidy. Clean, everything there for a reason, no excess. But this is warm and soft at the edges. Okay, it is tidy, but it's also lived in. Loved. Welcoming.

I could imagine curling up on this couch with a drink. And Jamie.

It's cosy but perfect. Bugger, this would be so much better if I hated it.

'There is no wife, or ex.' His gaze is direct. 'His mother didn't want me to even know he existed, let alone see him.'

'Oh.'

'It was a one-night stand.' He glances at me as though he's expecting judgement. 'I'm not proud of it, but it was. I had no idea…' He shrugs, looking uncomfortable. 'The first I knew about Alfie was when a mate of mine bumped into Claire, the day I came over to fit that lock for you?' I nod. 'He mentioned she had a kid the spitting image of me. He thought it was hilarious; it was all nudge, nudge, wink, wink because he had no idea.' His smile is wry.

But it isn't that niggling at me, it's something else he's said. Something I can't quite pin down, because I need time to concentrate. Think about it. I know I'm frowning, repeating his words in my head, then I realize he's talking, and I need to listen. 'At first, I laughed it off, then I kind of panicked a bit. It seemed unlikely, impossible, but you know when you get something in your head, and you can't shake it off? When you have to check it out?' I nod. I know exactly what he means.

'So I decided I needed to accidentally bump into her myself. See with my own eyes. I felt a bit of an idiot, like I was being ridiculous. But I couldn't help myself. I couldn't stop thinking that what if he was mine, what if I had a kid out there who I knew nothing about and who didn't even know I existed? It seemed wrong.'

This isn't the office Jamie at all, it's not even the caring, quieter, more considerate Jamie I've come to know since we started to share a desk. This is a worn and emotional Jamie who is trying to hide how he feels. Who feels daft, but who feels he has to explain. Which stirs up the conflicts inside me. He's going to all this trouble, dragging a story out into the open that's private. Just for me.

But why not just come out with it? I mean, it's not a reason to not date is it? And lots of people have kids outside marriage.

'I've not been in the office because it's been easier to work from here.' He pauses. 'I've needed some space to try and get my head round the idea. When I met you for a coffee, I meant to tell you, I really did. But I wasn't even sure I quite believed it myself, and by the time I'd offloaded about pretending I didn't recognize you,' he gives me a guilty look, 'it seemed too much to drop this on you as well, and the phone went and you had to get into work, there wasn't enough time and…' He shrugs. 'Then after your barbecue when we, er, kissed, my mind was totally kind of blown because I never saw that coming. Baby, you, everything kind of hit me at once. I didn't know whether I was coming or going. I couldn't do that to you, I couldn't start something when I'm in this mess.'

'Isn't that my decision as well, Jamie?' I say softly. 'Don't I have a say?'

'Well yes, but… I shouldn't have done that – kissed you, led you on. I don't even know if I'll be able to see him, or anything. I wanted to wait, I wanted to be sure who I was, what I was offering you before I said anything, because…' He takes a deep breath, looks me straight in the eye.

'Because kissing you was like the first time all over again, but better.'

I frown. I stare at him, then at the photograph, trying not to think about what he's just said. 'So you didn't know about him until then? You've only just found out?'

'No. Hadn't got a clue.'

'The day you did my lock?'

'Yup. That's why I needed a couple of days off.' He hadn't been ignoring me, or my notes, he'd been at home. In shock. 'It made me realize as well that I had to be straight with you before I came to the barbecue. I felt a shit, I couldn't go out for the evening with you and deceive you.'

'Like she did to you?'

He nods. 'Sorry. Does that make it even worse? The fact I did it right after I found out she had hidden Alfie from me?' I shake my head. 'It didn't really hit me that it was true until I saw him the next day.' He shrugs. 'She went white as a ghost when I popped out of the bushes in the park, so I knew...' His voice tails off, and it is like he's remembering. 'She said I was never meant to find out, she'd moved away, she was just visiting a friend here for a few days. It was this massive coincidence that I saw her. If I'd gone looking two days later, she wouldn't have been there. She'd be back at her new place. She brought him round here and once I'd held him, made him laugh...' He stares into the distance. 'He was real, Alice. A real baby, part of me.'

I look at the plastic toys again. 'Wow.' Getting my head round this takes some effort. He's got a kid. He's not supposed to know he's got a kid. He's got a kid with Claire.

Kissing me the second time was as good as the first.

Better. But that isn't what I should be thinking about right now.

Claire, Claire, Claire, that name is niggling at me.

'Then she went back home with him, all the way to bloody Cornwall, as though none of it mattered. I didn't matter.' He looks me directly in the eye. 'She doesn't want me to see him, but I think I should. Every kid should know their dad, shouldn't they? She was really cold about it, dead direct and the more I thought about it after they'd gone, the more wrong it felt. She blew me out when I tried to call her, told me to stop fucking with other people's lives. But what has she done, what is she doing?' The upset shows on his face and it makes me feel hurt for him. 'I don't know what I want, I've never even thought about having kids, I don't know what kind of relationship I should have with him. But I want to get to know him, so I went and talked to a solicitor.' He takes a deep breath. 'Then I went down to Cornwall to try and talk her round. I booked a couple of days annual leave and worked remotely the other days.'

'Hang on,' I need to back step a minute here, 'you said she doesn't want you to see him? Not at all?'

'Nope.' He shakes his head but is looking at me directly. 'I'm not supposed to be part of his life.'

'What?' I lean back, a bit flabbergasted.

'She said she was actually quite pleased when she found out she was pregnant, she loves kids.' He leans back, looking like he feels battered. He's trying to make light of it, but I can tell it hurts.

It is then, as I stare at him, that it hits me. My throat is dry. What he said has finally registered. I look at the photo again, then at him. 'How, er, old is Alfie?' Time seems to have stopped. I'm holding my breath.

'Nearly eighteen months.'

Claire. Eighteen months, nine months of being pregnant. Oh my God, just over two years ago. I get it. I feel a bit dizzy. I don't want to, but I have to ask. He can tell me I'm being ridiculous; he can laugh it off. 'Claire. You said his mother was called Claire, she's not—'

He nods before I can say another word and sinks back into the couch. 'Yep, that Claire. Claire from work. That's partly why I didn't come clean with you straight away.'

'What?' That's why he was so edgy about Claire when we were chatting over coffee! Claire had been more than just a girl he'd kissed in the bar that night, when he should have been kissing me. *She* was the complication! Now I come to think of it, he'd said his time with her was *supposed* to be fun. Supposed to be! Bloody hell, why didn't I notice it more then, why didn't I push it, grill him? I was too busy thinking about him pretending he'd forgotten me.

'Well you knew her, and it didn't seem fair on her. At least until I was totally positive it was true, he was mine.'

I'm not quite sure why he's so keen on being fair to her, she's not exactly being fair to him, is she?

'It looked like she didn't want people to know, and if it got round the office, the gossip...' His voice tails off. Then he starts to talk again. 'She'd already handed her notice in and told me she was leaving, said how about a quick fling, the evening I...' He gazes into my eyes. We stare at each other. That evening, that after-work drink when I was so sure he'd recognized me – before he'd wandered off and spent the rest of the evening with somebody else. Claire. A bit of fun, ha! 'The evening I recognized you properly. It was mad, I'd been so close to kissing you. I wanted you so much, then I was scared shitless of fucking it all up. It had been so amazing at Reading, I'd thought about it, about you so much every bloody day after, and then there you were and I ducked out. I wasn't ready to meet the one, I wasn't ready to risk losing you if you were. I daren't do it. I was drunk, Claire was all over me.' She was ALL over him. 'I was so fucking stupid. I took the easy way out in case you didn't remember some quick snog, or it wasn't as good as I'd remembered…and look where it got me. I fucked up big time, didn't I?'

'I was interested,' I say softly. 'I'd never forgotten that kiss. But,' it's my turn to feel in the wrong, 'I did have a boyfriend, and still really wanted you to kiss me again.' My face heats up, but I have to admit to how I felt. I have to be honest.

'I used the fact you had a boyfriend as an excuse to avoid facing up to how I felt. I should have at least told you I remembered. And,' he pauses, 'I guess I was scared that if you were in love with another guy, then the last thing you probably wanted was being reminded about that night when some drunken twat lurched at you.'

'It wasn't like that. It was perfect.'

'But I didn't know that Alice.' He touches my hand briefly. 'I know none of it is an excuse for behaving like I did with Claire but… Shit, I was just so stupid, except.' He looks up at the ceiling, blinks, then looks back at me. 'Except I can't regret Alfie.' A hint of a smile plays on his lips. 'He's so cute, so funny. Look, I'm sorry. I feel like I'm offloading on you, it's not fair.'

'You're not. Honest, it's fine. Carry on, I'd like to know.' I need to know. And I want to know that he fancied me as much as I fancied him. That there were reasons for him acting like he did. I want to watch him talk about his toddler son; he looks so caring, so gorgeous when he does. You can see the love in his expression, his eyes.

And you know, so what he's got a baby? I can do babies. This doesn't have to be the end of us before we've really begun. Now I know why he's been keeping me at arm's length, I can handle it. I can deal with it. I can persuade him it needn't be an issue.

'But we can't …' He hesitates. 'Alice, I can't see you, or anything right now.'

'But you can, I mean, it doesn't matter,' I say softly. 'I won't say anything to anybody who knows her. I don't mind about Alfie, honest.'

'It's not that.' He looks down at his hands for a moment, then back up as though working out how to say the next bit. 'I just feel like I've got to be squeaky clean or it might mess up my chances of seeing him. ' Uh-oh. 'The solicitor said I have rights whatever, but I want to come across the best I can. Do you get that? Clean living,' he waves a hand to take in the room.

'Very clean!' I force myself to grin, and he finally grins back. It's nice as the tension rolls away. It makes me feel good. 'It won't stay that way for long when he comes visiting!'

'If we'd already been seeing each other it would be

different, but I can't be seen to be starting something up, or casually dating, or—'

'I get it.' I do. I can't be selfish.

'Just until we've sorted something.'

'Really, I get it. Getting access to Alfie is the most important thing in the world. Putting your life on hold for a few months will be well worth it.'

'I'd ask you if you'd put yours on hold as well, but it wouldn't be fair.'

'I—'

He holds a hand up to stop me talking. 'I don't know how long all this will take; it could be weeks, months, years. I haven't got a clue. I just know I've got to fight for him.'

'I waited years after that first kiss,' I say. 'And then nearly two years after I found you.'

'But this is different,' he says softly. 'I've no idea what's going to happen. I might end up moving to Cornwall if I can talk her round, I can't ask you to do that. Not when I don't know what direction my life might go in, Alice. I'm sure I could get a job down there, or even work remotely with this one and just come up to the office once a week or something. Or, who knows, she might come back here. I reckon from what she said she's a bit lonely down there and she misses her friends from round here. But she wanted a clean break; she wanted to go where nobody knew her and there wouldn't be any gossip.'

'I wish you'd told me sooner.'

'I felt such a dick over pretending I didn't remember you, and I wanted to tell you about Alfie so much, but what if...' He pauses, his eyes searching my face. 'What if you'd told me that was it, no chance, you'd already got too much chaos in your life and you needed some quiet, your own space, not some baby. That would have totally been it.'

I think back to all those gestures of Claire's that had made my stomach feel hollow, the way they'd put their heads together in a confidential huddle. The giggles. Yuk. I'd been jealous, I am jealous. So if I'm truly honest with myself, how would I have reacted if I'd known about Alfie earlier? *Their* baby?

'I didn't want to find you, then lose you again before we even had a chance…'

'You didn't trust me enough to tell me though.' My default setting has always been to trust people, and then they've taken advantage of me. But, well, if I ever had thoughts of a relationship with Jamie that is well and truly out of the window if he doesn't trust me at all. I've trusted Jamie with my stuff, with my problems, but it wasn't two-way at all it seems.

'I do trust you,' he says softly. 'That's why I'm telling you now. I haven't told another soul, but I had to tell you. The other day, I didn't trust myself not to mess it up, say it all wrong. I didn't trust myself to get it right, but then I knew why I felt so shitty. I knew I should have explained, I couldn't not tell you. But,' he pauses, 'I know it's not fair to expect you to want to share my life now I'm a guy with a baby. You wouldn't want to.'

'Don't tell me what I would and wouldn't want to do!' I shout out, exasperated. 'I'll decide.' Wow, I am getting assertive.

'But you've always had to share, you've never had your

own space, Alice. You have now, you're getting it sorted. I can't take that away from you.'

I lower my voice. 'I've never been able to *choose*. It's about choosing when to share, who to share with, isn't it? You can't take it away from me, I can decide if you can have it. I trusted you, Jamie.' I realize as I'm speaking that I've never thought about it before, but I have trusted Jamie. I have been happy to share with him, because I've instinctively felt he wouldn't take advantage. He wants what is right for me, as well as for himself. And I'm not going to be afraid to tell him when he's got it wrong.

'I know. I told you I knew I'd mess things up.'

'We all mess up, make mistakes. That's life. Nothing is perfect for ever.'

'That kiss was.'

'No, it wasn't. It was a promise of something that could be good. It was the starting point, not the whole thing.'

He is studying me steadily, but when he speaks there is a shaky edge to his voice. 'Actually, I don't think I asked you here because I felt I had to own up, explain this to you, I think it's because I do trust you. I wanted to tell you, I wanted to share this with somebody and you were the right person. It had to be you.'

'Good,' I say quietly, not quite sure what else to say.

'I didn't want to burden you with my problems though, you don't deserve…'

'Hey, stop. I want to know.' I pause. I want to share the good and the bad. 'So, she definitely knew she was leaving?'

'Yep.' He follows my lead. 'She told me that in the bar.

She didn't tell me she was going to frigging Cornwall though! Not that it would have made any difference at the time, but it meant that if I had found out later that she was pregnant, I wouldn't have been able to find her even if I'd wanted to. And...' His smile is wry. 'I guess after he was born, Covid helped her disappear. There was practically no chance of anybody from around here that knew her bumping into her.' He sighs.

'But he's yours as well!'

'I know. I think she's scared it will complicate things though, change things for her. She told me she just wanted to be left alone with Alfie, to bring him up how she wants. She said her dad ruined her life and she doesn't want to risk a repeat.'

'But you're not her dad!'

'I know, but it's easy to say stuff like that, when you don't know what went on, isn't it? I'm trying to give her the benefit of the doubt here. She thought she'd got it all planned out; I'd never know anything about it, and she was nearly right. It was pure chance I found out. It would never have occurred to me, even if I'd bumped into them myself, if he didn't look the spit of me at the same age in all my baby photos. Hell.' He put his head in his hands again, then peers up at me. 'My mum is going to kill me when she finds out.'

'She'll be cross she's only knitting bootees for Booby birds, and not babies!'

'Fuming. Oh God, how did I get myself into this mess?'

'You want the scientific answer.'

'Nope. More wine?'

We sit in companionable silence, only sipping at the wine. Both immersed in our own thoughts.

'Is everything okay with you?' He finally breaks the silence. 'Sorry, I never asked.'

'Fine, fine. It's pretty quiet in the office and I miss your notes.' We swap a look. Even now he's thinking about me, when he's got major worries of his own. He's a nice guy. He gives more than he takes, nothing like Dave at all. A long, lingering look that should turn into a kiss, but doesn't. It turns into an awkward wriggle as I desperately try and think of something to say. 'And Mabel misses you.' I clear the lump in my throat.

'I miss your notes. I miss you,' he says simply.

'I miss you too,' I admit. Glad to actually say the words aloud.

'I'm glad you came, and I could explain everything. Thank you.' His fingers linger by mine. Our little fingers touching, just the lightest of contacts that tells me he's there for me. We're there for each other.

Reminds me that there's something I should tell him.

'Dave came in the office.'

'You're kidding? You're not …' His piercing eyes rake over my face.

'He thinks we should get married.' I can't help it, I grin.

'So it's not over?' There's a sudden flash of doubt in his eyes that I want to chase away.

'Oh it is. I told him I'd found somebody else, I had somebody.' I look him straight in the eye. 'You.'

I'm not sure how I expect him to react. I don't expect him to grin back, like he is doing.

'Sorry, I had to say something.'

'I'm glad I could be useful!' He chuckles and we're almost back to where we were before. Flirty, comfortable.

'Er, there is one problem, other people might have heard. They might think…'

He shrugs. 'So what? Let them think. Hey,' his gaze is soft, 'don't worry about that.'

His tenderness makes me shiver inside. I talk just so I don't have to think, to feel. 'I was just fuming at the time. And I feel a bit sorry for him, I was always an easy option.'

'You're not responsible for his life, Alice.' He puts his hand gently over mine, then lifts it away almost straightaway, but not so quickly that it feels like he wishes he hadn't. 'His happiness isn't down to you, it's down to him.'

'I know,' I say softly. Glancing round again, biting my tongue – or more accurately –my lower lip. Trying to think of something I can say. 'I've, er, tidied our desk a bit.'

'Why?' He raises an eyebrow.

'I thought you might not—'

'Get it put back, or I'm moving out!' He leans forward, kisses my cheek. The slight stubble brushes against my face. 'I am sorry, you know. For everything, for not owning up, for fucking up, for not being that guy who you could carry on sharing amazing kisses with.'

So am I. But I don't say it.

'If I could turn the clock back and be your festival guy and start again, I would. If I could pick anybody in the world to share with, Alice, it would be you. It would always be you.'

I don't have an answer. If I look back at him, I'm going to want to kiss him.

I swill the last of my wine round in the glass. Reluctant to finish it. To end the evening. But all good things come to an end as they say.

'Better be off, I guess. Can't have strange women exiting your home after dark, can you!' I say it jokily, trying to lift the atmosphere, and he chuckles back, but we both know there is an element of truth. An undercurrent we can't escape. 'Thanks for the wine.'

'You're welcome. You can get home okay?'

'Number 27 bus, door to door.'

'Handy to know.' We stand up at the same time. 'In case I need to rush over to put another lock on the door or anything.'

I smile, then he surprises me again by resting his hand on my forearm.

'I am here if you need me, you know. Persistent exes, nosey housemates.'

'I think I've got it covered,' I say softly. 'I can be assertive if I need to, you know.'

How did I go out with somebody like Dave for so long? He always decided where we went on dates, liked to order for me in restaurants. At first it seemed romantic, then after a bit slightly annoying. Now it feels like he was controlling me from the start.

'I know. Well, ring me if you need me, yes?' I nod. 'Any time.'

'And you ring me if you need a chat, or, you know, advice on handling toddlers. I'm ace at funny faces and balloon dogs!' We share a tentative smile. It feels sad. It feels like he is standing on the edge of something, but I'm not invited. I want to hug him, I want to tell him how I feel, how much I've really missed him. Instead I land the smallest of kisses on his lips. 'I hope you get it sorted. Keep me updated, eh?'

'I will. I'll be back in the office soon.'

'Thank God for that, I was getting worried I'd never have Hobnobs again!'

We both stand up, hover awkwardly. 'Right, well.' I head for the door, stop and turn before opening it. He's right behind me.

'Oh, Alice.' He leans his forehead against mine, then cradles my face in his hands. 'I'm sorry.'

'Don't.' I pull back. I don't want our one perfect kiss to become a string of nearly kisses, of regretted kisses, of broken promises. 'Let's wait and see what happens, eh?' I'd so much like to be irrational, stupid, impulsive. I really want to say, let's snog, don't stop, can I stay the night. Can I stay here for the rest of my life?

No, I don't mean that bit. That is just my weird fantasy.

He kisses the tip of my nose. Then his lips brush over mine. The lightest of touches, but it still sends a shiver through me. 'Thanks, Alice. For understanding, for everything. If this is meant to happen it will, won't it?' He shakes his head gently. 'I thought you and me... I thought that night, that you'd be the rest of my life. You'd be everything.'

I smile gently. Let myself touch his cheek, then I turn

and walk down the path. Walk back towards the life, the space I've started to carve out for myself.

And all I can think is that I want to share that space. I want to share my stuff, my thoughts, my hopes, my life. With him.

Chapter Twenty-Five

'Some old woman came round to see you,' Jack says as I walk through the lounge, not taking his eyes off the TV screen, or his thumbs off the game controller.

'Old woman?'

'Think she said she was creepy guy's mum or something.'

'Dave's mum? Here?' I stop, all nice 'maybe one day' thoughts being shot out of my head instantly. Although she'd have a fit if she knew she's been called 'old woman'; she's Botoxed and root-refreshed to an unnatural degree.

'That's the one. Get out of my fucking shot, you moron!' Luckily, I know he is talking to another player, not me.

'You didn't let her in?' Did my 'no-entry' rule extend to friends and family?

'Yes! Got you, you bastard.'

'You did?'

'No, sorry, not yes to her. It was Harry answered the door not me, he had one of – Oh piss off, you have to be joking! – his big boots at the ready, no way was anybody who mentioned Dave's name getting past him.'

I am touched that my housemates are taking my request seriously. I nearly kiss him. But don't.

'Oh, for fuck's sake. Shit.' He drops the controller on the table in disgust, then turns his head to peer at me over the top of the couch. 'You're late, been out on the razz after work?' He grins.

I'm surprised he has ever noticed what time I come in and out, he is always glued to his game and barely grunts. Maybe I've underestimated the people I live with, as well as the people I work with.

They're quite nice, very nice actually. Occasionally annoying, but isn't everybody?

'Just a quick drink with a friend after work.' I can't help but smile back at him. It was so nice to see Jamie again, to know he is alright. It wasn't me that scared him off. I haven't majorly cocked up. It's nothing I've said or done. Or my batty family.

'Cool.' Jack turns back to the TV, picks up the controller again. 'Oh, the douchebag's mum left something for you, it's on the kitchen table I think.'

'Thanks.' He is already twiddling knobs; I don't think he heard me.

There is a bag on the table, quite a big bag. Oh shit, what the hell is it? The last thing I want is some romantic gesture. I'm tempted to just throw it away without looking.

But I'm not that person. I need to know. I'd be climbing in the wheelie bin at midnight trying to retrieve it. And anyway, if I don't check what is inside, I won't know which recycling bin to put it in, will I? And I do try and recycle efficiently.

It could also be my stuff. Yes, that's it! I bet he's had a clear-out of his place, packed up everything I own that I left there and then sent her round with it because he's finally got the message and is too ashamed of his behaviour to show his face.

Haha, a likely story. I can't remember Dave ever thinking he needs an excuse for the way he behaves.

I look at it dubiously. I don't think he ever let me leave more than a small carrier bag's worth of stuff in his tidy place.

The bag is quite heavy, but not heavy enough to be an incendiary device. His mum was always very protective of her fabulous son, who could never do any wrong. She could be lurking in the bushes and planning on blowing me up. Although with my limited, Netflix-acquired, knowledge of bombs – that would take quite a big one.

I unlock the door of my room and put the parcel on the bed. Watching it as I walk around the room getting changed into something comfortable.

It doesn't move. It is just there. Unavoidable.

I go downstairs and grab a glass and bottle of wine, put a pizza in the oven and go back upstairs. The bag is impossible to ignore.

Inside is a box, a big flattish one, like the type you'd get long boots in. I slide it out, carefully lift the lid.

White tissue paper.

A note. *David told me he was going to propose. How exciting for you!* The *you* is a bit pointed – it isn't exciting for her, as she was always hoping he'd marry somebody slimmer, prettier, more like her. *I look forward to seeing you wear this, although you are a bit sturdier than I was at your age so may need to lose a few inches. Sincerely, Stella.*

I frown as I rip open the flimsy covering.

White satin.

There's only one item of clothing comes in white satin. Shit.

Masses of beads, no doubt carefully handsewn on. No wonder it's bloody heavy.

I feel queasy. It is a wedding dress. His mother's wedding dress.

Oh fuck! I can't help myself. I start to laugh. He hasn't told her yet!

'Fucking hell, Alice! That was quick work!' Sophie's unexpected chuckle from behind me nearly sends me sprawling on top of the dress. 'When I invited him to meet the parents, I didn't think this would happen. And you, in white? What's so funny?'

I can't breathe, I can't speak, I think I'm hysterical. I point. She leans over and picks up the note.

'Stella? Oh fucking hell, Dave's mum, and she says sincerely? Who says sincerely? She is so up herself. The big mummy's boy hasn't told her, has he?'

I shake my head.

'I'll go and get a wine glass, shall I?'

'Yeah and grab my pizza out of the oven while you're there, it should be ready.'

'He is such a loser, who tells their mum they're proposing when they've already been dumped?' Soph pulls a funny face with raised eyebrows and it creases me up again. I lie back on the bed, trying to calm down.

Soph comes back into the room a few minutes later, armed with pizza and plates.

I have managed to stop laughing. I can breathe again.

I look at Sophie. She has brought two plates as well as a glass for herself.

'Bloody hell, Soph, it's only a small pizza, it's hardly big enough for one person! Me!'

'Share and share alike, and, well, you have got to lose a few extra pounds if you're going to fit in that dress.' She sniggers and it nearly sets me off again.

'Stop it!' I lob a cushion at her – after she's put my dinner down.

'What are you going to do with it?' She motions at the box with a slice of pizza. 'Chuck it?'

'Oh shit, I can't do that. I mean look at it, it's—'

'Ancient?'

'I was going to say beautiful and possibly worth a fortune.' I say trying to be serious. 'It wouldn't be fair to throw it away, I can't.'

'The snotty cow would have a duck fit.'

'She's not a snotty cow.' I sigh. Dave's mum is very upright, very contained and controlled. Now I come to think of it, I don't think I've ever seen her laugh or do something silly or unpredictable.

Which must be where Dave got it from. How come I have never seen him quite so clearly until now?

'She looks down her nose at me. Oh, Alice, I'm so pleased you're not marrying him.' She wraps an arm round me and rubs her sticky cheek against mine – smearing me with tomato sauce.

'So am I.' I've been thinking while she's been downstairs. 'I'm going to drop it back at his mum's and seeing as he hasn't got the guts, I'll tell her myself that it's over.' She is going to take it personally, she is going to be affronted, but I'm sure she will believe me. I'm also going to tell her the same lie I told Dave, that there is somebody else, to soften the blow. I don't want to make Dave look bad in her eyes, a disappointment, it wouldn't be fair. But I am not going to tell Sophie that, or she'll get carried away and make a big thing of it. 'He's had plenty of time, and if he hasn't got the backbone she still needs to know.'

'When?'

'When, what?' I take a bite out of my own pizza, before it is completely demolished by my sister.

'When are you taking it?'

'Tomorrow. I need to get rid of it, but it's too late now, and I've had a few drinks.'

'Great. Oh,' she goes to grab another slice of pizza and I slap her hand away, 'only came to tell you that the parents are excited about me and Daz! No shit! They said something about broadening my horizons.'

I think they meant they'd be glad for her to move out, but I don't say that. 'Ace.'

'We're taking the camper round on Sunday so you can all see it. Shit, is that the time, Daz is waiting outside. We're going to this open mic thing and he's got his guitar with him. I told him I'd only be a sec, but it's like breaking into Fort Knox getting in here.'

'Really?'

'Yeah, that Zoe answered the door, then she had to ask the guys if you were in. I thought she was going to frisk me or something.'

'That's on the way out!' I say with a dark look. 'To check you've not borrowed anything.'

'Haha, you're funny! Anyway, see ya, Sis!' She leans in again and gives me a sticky kiss, honestly it is like having a five-year-old sister sometimes, then she drains her glass of wine and slides off the bed. 'Can't wait for you to see it!'

I give her a thumbs up, and hear her clattering down the stairs, shouting out 'hi's' and 'bye's' to my housemates.

There is one tiny slice of pizza left. I do not intend to lose weight, or get married, and I am famished. I need more food. Comfort food. I pick up my mobile. 'Crispy duck, please, and prawn crackers. Yeah, fifteen minutes is fine. Great, thanks.'

That will give me just enough time to jog down to the in-convenience-store and grab some snacks.

There's not much of the evening left, but what there is I am going to spend eating and watching TV. I am not going to give that silly dress a second thought.

Or the fact that Jamie and Claire were at it hammer and tongs after our close encounter in the pub. As I suspected.

Or the fact that he has a child and doesn't want, or can't have, a girlfriend.

The dress is so heavy, so tight. I can't breathe, so tired and hot and sweaty as Dave whisks me around the dance floor. My family are standing in a line, horrified, staring at the cobwebs that hang from my dress. I'm a modern-day Miss Havisham and I can't escape. He's holding me tight. The dress is musty, yellowing, strangling me. His mother is holding us both. Firmly, so firmly so we can't run away, I can't get away from him. 'You're too fat, too fat,' she whispers in my ear. 'It's your own fault.' The band is playing louder, louder, faster and I'm spinning. 'Ladies don't eat pizza. Pizza, pizza…'

I wake up in a sweat, panting and thrashing about wildly. Except I am pinned down.

I am alone, but I can't move. Panic hits again.

And so does the band.

I groan, stop struggling and flop on my bed. It's my mobile, and I'm all tangled up in my sheets. I wrestle an arm free and take a few deep breaths before reaching for my phone.

It lights up the dark room. Sugar, it's not even midnight. How can it only be that time, and why is somebody ringing me this late? Something has happened to Soph! I start to panic again, then realize it is Jamie.

'Hey.'

'Are you okay?' I can imagine the frown on his face. 'You sound a bit strange.'

'Er, yes, hang on.' Getting one arm out was relatively easy, but I feel like the rest of me is trussed up like a mummy. I need unrolling, I can hardly move my legs and have to drag myself up to a semi-sitting position. 'Fine, fine, carry on.' I think this is how a butterfly must feel trying to yank itself free of its chrysalis case. It's no wonder they don't live long, they're knackered before they start.

'It's okay, it's late, I shouldn't have called, sorry, I…'

'Jamie!' I yell. Then wish I hadn't shouted so loud. But he must not ring off. I don't want him to go.

'I just wanted to talk to somebody who'd understand and…'

I feel a rush of feel-good warmth. We still have something, a connection, trust. We can work on the rest.

'You weren't asleep? I didn't wake you?'

'Oh goodness no, me, on a Friday night haha.' Then I remember who I am talking to. 'I might have dozed off, with all the wine.' Dozed off? What am I talking about, I've been tossing about deliriously. 'Has something happened?'

'Claire messaged me not long after you went.' He sighs and I can picture him running his hands through his hair. 'She's going to Spain.'

'Oh. That's nice.' He's woken me up from my nightmare to tell me about the mother-of-his-child's holiday plans. Really? I'm already struggling with the friends concept, but I definitely need more than 'friends' for this kind of thing. Snog buddies and shag buddies have far more privileges than plain old buddy-buddies.

'No it's not! How can I see Alfie if he's in bloody Spain?'

'Well it's only for a week or two—' As the words come out of my mouth, something twigs in my drowsy brain. 'What, you mean—'

'She's going to stay out there, live there, with Alfie. Soon, like as soon as she can get flights sorted.'

'What?' He has my full attention now. I push all the bedclothes aside and sit upright.

'Fuck.' There's the sound of him banging his hand against something. 'Who the hell does she think she is?'

I want to say calm down, but when did saying that ever help?

I'm worried about him. And I can hear strange background noises. 'Where are you?'

'What? Well, er, I'm not really sure. Near Tesco? I'm driving round, it helps me think. I needed to get my head round it and I can't ring the solicitor at this time of night.'

They do on TV cop shows. Although that's probably if they've been arrested, or somebody has died.

I make a snap decision; he needs to talk and I can't go to his place. I've been drinking, and he has to be Mr Squeaky Clean. Even though she's not here, she might have spies watching his place to keep notes about all the late-night female comings and goings. If there were to be any. 'Come over here.'

'What?'

'Please, you need to talk to somebody and you're halfway here already. Unless you're actually near Waitrose, which is way over the other side of town.'

'No, it's Tesco.' I can hear the smile in his voice. 'Want me to bring anything?'

'Just you.' I say, casual on the outside, but churning up on the inside.

Shit, I need to tidy my room. Tidy myself.

Chapter Twenty-Six

I s it very wrong that there's a big worry he could lose Alfie, and I'm wondering if I have a chance to wash and dry my hair before he gets here?

It's just I'm a rank, sweaty mess with total bed hair and it will make him feel worse sitting with somebody who smells, won't it? It would be like offloading your innermost secrets to a bag lady who hasn't washed for months. Not that there is anything wrong with a bag lady, and not everybody has personal hygiene options – but I do and so I owe it to him to tidy up and present my best side. In his moment of need I don't want him to remember me as somebody he couldn't wait to get away from.

I've showered and kicked all my rubbish under the bed, and my hair is damp but clean, when I hear Harry's bellow. I give the room a quick onceover, pull the duvet cover straight and bomb out onto the landing.

'There's another guy at the door for you, Al! Do we let

this one in or put him in the body-bag in the shed with the other one?'

'I'm glad you're taking me seriously!' I say primly to Harry who has one wellington-clad foot wedged firmly behind the door. He has a can of beer in his hand. I've never seen him holding anything but a bacon sandwich, coffee, or gardening implement. This is new. It makes him seem more human.

'That's the new one, you daft twat,' says Zoe, who has appeared on the stairs behind me and is leaning over the bannister. I think they might be taking my demands a tad too seriously. 'Let him in. Unless you've changed your mind, Al? I don't mind entertaining him.'

I shake my head. 'Hands off, he's got enough problems.'

'I like solving problems.' She grins.

'So is it a yes or no?' asks Harry, still acting as door stopper. He's very effective.

'Yes!' I shout, worried that Jamie will have given up and wandered off by now.

Harry relents and throws the door open wide. 'Enter! Beer?'

Jamie looks slightly confused, but at least he's still there.

'Really glad you let me do your hair, chick. That must be why you're so popular, and this one is way sexier than the last one! It looks cool, doesn't it?' Zoe directs the second comment down the stairs, and Jamie and Harry both nod. 'Super! My job here is done. See you lot tomorrow, I'm off to find somebody shaggable. Unless?' She looks from Jamie to Harry. Harry gulps and dives into the kitchen.

Jamie shakes his head. 'Like she says, I'm in enough trouble already.'

'Come up.' I motion up the stairs, and he bounds up.

'Is it chaos everywhere you go?'

'Pretty much.' I smile. 'I'm not quite sure how I managed to swap home for this place.'

'It suits you, maybe you'd miss all the noise and borrowing if you were somewhere quieter?'

'I wouldn't mind trying it.' He raises an eyebrow. 'Okay, okay, you're right. It was horrible when I flew off the handle and nobody was speaking to me. I think I'm working out how to get some kind of balance though.'

'Good.' He smiles. 'You'd be welcome round at my place if you needed to escape, but...' That hangs in the air for a moment. 'Except it won't bloody matter soon anyway. I'm screwed.'

'She can't just go out to live in Spain, she can't stop you seeing him, can she?'

'Well I didn't think so, but I wanted to keep this friendly.'

'You can object and, she's not got a house, or school for Alfie, or...' I'm floundering. Then it hits me! I've got it. We've been overreacting. 'Ha! Visas! She needs a visa, she's not got a visa or whatever, or a job, and...' I feel I have to add even more obstacles on top, even though the visa is a gamechanger. Thank God for Brexit. Well, there are four words I never thought I'd say. 'And she can't even speak Spanish, I bet!'

'She can,' he says glumly.

'How can she? I mean, not properly.' She doesn't look

like she speaks Spanish. Not that I jump to instant conclusions about people or anything.

I used to tell people I could speak French, because I had a grade A at GCSE. But that is holiday French, it isn't French-French, is it?

'Fluently. She's got Spanish citizenship.'

'Really? She doesn't look it!' I am dubious. I'm not going to get into stereotypes here, but she doesn't. Put it this way, she looks nothing like Carmen, or the topless Spanish beach babes Dad couldn't take his eyes off when we went to Mallorca the first time.

He sounds a bit defeated as he sinks down onto the bed. Not like Jamie at all. Jamie doesn't panic, or flap, or give up. So, I stop trying to imagine slim blonde orange-tanned (yes, I can be bitchy) Claire cooking paella or dancing the salsa for a moment and concentrate on him. 'She is. She's got family out there; they've got a villa practically on the beach. She told me when…well, you know.'

I bet she did. She tried every trick in the books including a skirt so short I could see that she *was* wearing knickers. They were pink. Bright, tarty pink, not just any pink.

'And she says it's what she always planned on doing eventually, moving over permanently.'

I sit down next to him. Try to stop babbling, try to stop thinking about Claire, and talk in more measured, helpful tones. One of us needs to be logical here, to be calm. It has to be me.

She is such a total cow though.

'I still don't think she can just go, can she? I mean, not now you *know*.'

'I honestly haven't a clue, Alice. But it makes it harder, doesn't it, if she's there and I'm here?'

'But you've met him, she knows you want to see him grow up.'

'But it could take months to sort out; he'll have forgotten who I am. I don't even know if she has to take any notice of the law here if she's there. She won't answer my calls, Alice, she doesn't want to talk. It was never supposed to be complicated, she said.'

'Yeah, but babies are,' I point out.

'She says I know about him; I've met him now and isn't that enough?' He looks at me, his blue-grey eyes clear. 'But it isn't.' His voice has an edge. His despair has given way to obstinacy. Much better.

'No, it isn't enough. I'm sure the law has to be on your side,' I say with all the confidence of somebody who hasn't a clue. I mean, you hear these horror stories where the parents are different nationalities, and they divorce, and the bitter father takes his kids to outer Mongolia or somewhere and the mother never sees them again until she sells everything so she can change her appearance, her name and her residency status and hitchhike over on a camel. And she's penniless and the kids don't care about her anymore.

Happens, doesn't it? All this is going through my head, but I don't say any of it.

'You'd hope so,' he says.

I nearly shriek 'what', because I'm still thinking about camels, then I realize we're both hanging on to the hope that the law is on his side.

Jamie sighs. 'I've emailed my solicitor, so as soon as

she's in the office on Monday she'll get back to me hopefully.'

'I'm sure she will. Maybe Claire's just threatening to go to get you to back off?'

'I don't think so.' He groans. 'Sorry for offloading on you.'

'I don't mind at all. You've helped me, with the desk, and the lock. That's what friends are for, eh?' Although friends don't feel like this. Friends don't want to kiss the other person's face off and drag them into bed.

He nods, his gaze intent, not saying anything for a moment.

Any minute now and he's going to say he'll go. I don't want him to go, I want to spend a bit more time together. Talk. I resist the urge to grab his hand, or his leg Leo-style.

Instead I reach for the bottle of wine.

'You don't fancy a glass of wine, do you? Shame to waste it, and I dozed off before you rang, so didn't get far.'

'Shit sorry, you had company?' The features of his face tighten, and he glances round as though he half expects somebody to pop out from under the bed.

'It was Soph, she popped in and had a glass, then shot off to meet Daz.'

'Ahh. Did the guys let her in?' He grins. 'They're very protective.'

I smile. 'Nice, aren't they? They wouldn't let Dave's mum in either!'

'Dave's mum?'

'She came with a special delivery.' I nudge the box with my foot.

'Big box.'

'Yeah.'

'Sorry, I'm being nosy, none of my business.'

'It's a wedding dress.'

He raises an eyebrow. 'In case you didn't mean it when you told him to bog off?'

'I don't think he's owned up to her yet.'

'Poor Dave,' he says unexpectedly as we both stare at the box. 'Nobody wants to look bad in their parent's eyes, do they?'

'No, but he probably shouldn't have told her we were going to get married, should he? He shouldn't have assumed I'd say yes.'

'He shouldn't.'

'He just thought I'd be a pushover, go along with it for an easy life.'

He smiles. 'But you're no pushover, Alice. You never really have been, have you?'

I push the box under the bed, out of sight.

'I shouldn't drink any more wine, I'm driving, and I had a glass earlier.' He stands up.

'Sure.' Shit, he is going to go. But I can't try and persuade him to drink-drive, can I?

'Do you fancy some fresh air? A walk?' he says abruptly.

I'm putting my shoes on before he can change his mind.

I've never been for a middle of the night walk before, apart from when I've been staggering back from the pub and the only thought on my mind is whether I can manage to stay on the pavement.

We turn away from the town and head up the lane where there are no streetlights, just the moon and stars, and soft ambient light that you can't escape from the distant houses – and then take the footpath that tracks across common land. The silence, the dark, makes it feel strangely intimate. As though we're the only two people on the planet.

I might not live in the middle of the countryside, but I'm right on the edge. Straddling the two worlds.

It's a warm evening, the sky clear and dark.

We fall into step effortlessly. Our hands brush together, like they did when we were walking home after the barbecue, and this time it isn't just his little finger that catches mine. It's his whole hand.

It's warm. Comfortable. It feels the most natural thing in the world – holding hands. Our sides bump as we walk across the uneven land and his grip tightens on mine.

I take a deep breath of the night air and then glance up at him, and all of a sudden it feels as though anything is possible. As though we're back at that festival and it's a new start. It's as if just here, now, in this moment the rest doesn't matter.

This time there are no jostling crowds, nobody to drag us apart, to sweep us along.

'Cold?' His voice is soft, the back of his hand strokes along my cheek.

'No.' I shiver as I lean into his touch.

His hand drops and our fingers tangle together, and

then our lips meet, and there is no grasping or touching, just the pureness of the kiss. It only lasts a few seconds, but the dryness of his lips and the heat of his body is imprinted in mine.

'Shall we go back?'

I nod, and we retrace our steps. Not talking, not hurrying.

The house is quiet when we enter. The lounge and kitchen deserted, but we tiptoe up the stairs as though we're doing something we shouldn't, and that illicit feeling heightens my senses – my heart is pounding, my legs are trembling and my lips quiver when his mouth comes down over mine as he pushes my bedroom door shut behind us.

He pulls my top over my head, barely breaking the kiss, his touch on my bare skin startling even though I am expecting it. My scalp tingles as his fingers run through my hair, my muscles tense and tremble with each touch.

Foreplay has never been like this before. With every nerve ending on high alert, with the anticipation bubbling up inside so that it's unbearable.

I want him to hurry, but I want him to go slow. I want it to happen, but I want to hold on to this moment for as long as possible. This perfect nearly there moment.

We don't say a word. It's not fumbling, clashing, clothes-ripping, but we've both got a slightly desperate edge, a desperate need, as though nothing could divert us from this. Nothing can stand in our way.

It feels like it was inevitable. That this was always meant to happen.

'Alice?' He gazes into my eyes, his breathing heavy and

I'm glad he hasn't said 'this is wrong', or 'it's not fair on you', or 'should we?', or 'are you sure?' because I don't want it spelling out, or questioning. He knows. The way he says my name asks everything.

'It's okay,' I say softly, 'I know this doesn't change anything, I just want this now. Us.'

Then I wrap my legs around him, cup his face with my hands, lift slightly so my lips meet his and it is better than the promise all those years ago.

It's like riding a horse into the sea, one minute grounded and steady, the next faltering and uncertain, until with that final step the beach disappears and it's effortless with a rhythm all of its own that we can't hold back, we can't control.

I gaze into his eyes. He's holding my hands pinned either side of my head, and he leans down and plants the lightest of kisses on my swollen lips.

I blink back up at him, slightly dazed. Wow, that was unexpected. So was the feeling of galloping horses. The last time I experienced that I was on a runaway pony and was screaming my head off. At least I wasn't screaming this time, well I hope I wasn't. Our resident sexpert will have something to say about it tomorrow if I was.

'Okay?' he says softly. I'm pretty sure he hadn't planned it, I'm pretty sure it was impulsive on both sides, but at least he doesn't look like he regrets it either.

I smile. He rolls to one side.

We lie side by side, holding hands, staring into each other's eyes. And then he pulls me into his arms, against his body, and I rest my head against his chest, his chin resting on my head. And I can't help it, my eyelids are so heavy. It's late, my whole body is tired. I feel drained in a happy way. I close my eyes, feel his steady breathing filtering through my body.

When I wake, weak daylight is edging its way through the window. We haven't moved.

I tilt my head slightly to look at him and he's watching me.

'How long have you been awake?'

'Shhh.' He twirls a strand of my hair around his finger, drawing me closer, closer…then his lips are on mine in the gentlest, warmest touch, that still manages to fizzle its way right to my core.

'Is it wrong that I still want you?' His voice is husky. 'You're irresistible, you know.' He nibbles my ear, bathing my skin with his warm breath, sending a shiver of goosebumps down my neck.

'I know what I've got to do.'

'Ugh?' I open one eye. Jamie is sitting on the edge of the bed. Fully dressed.

How come I blink in my sleep, and he's awake, whereas

he can get up walk round and get dressed and I sleep through it?

'If she goes to Spain, then I'm going out there as well.'

'What?' Both my eyes are wide open. I've been lying here wallowing in that after-sex feeling, and he's been planning on going to Spain?

'I stand more chance of persuading her to come back, and it will look better in the courts I reckon?'

'Well…'

'And, well…' He shrugs his shoulders. 'Living in Spain for a bit has its benefits eh? Sun, beaches, cheap beer.'

But no *me*, I want to scream. Instead I say, 'But you can't just *live* in Spain.'

'What's the difference? Cornwall, Spain?'

I would like to chip in and point out the many differences – like the Atlantic Ocean will be between us for one. Instead, I settle for saying 'Visa?'

'I can go for up to three months, then decide what to do next. I'm not talking about for ever. I just need to get this sorted, then if it means I have to go out for a few weeks every year to see him, I will.' He shrugs.

'Maybe you need to chat to your solicitor first, I mean, try and work it out, let's not rush into anything.' I sound in a panic even to my own ears. Cornwall is one thing, but Spain? He can't go to Spain, it is too far, too hot, too different. They eat paella and talk Spanish. I'll never see him again. I'll never have sex with him again. Or at least not for months. 'She might say they can prevent her going?'

Or I could go as well. Learn Spanish. Babies manage it so I'm sure I can if I have to.

'I won't do anything daft. But if I've got to, then I've got to. You get it, don't you?' He holds my hands in his. 'I know you of all people get it.'

I don't want to get it at all, if getting it means losing him.

'Of course I do. I know you need to see him, he's your son.'

'It's only a tiny bit out of our lives. Look, I better get off, I'm sure you've got lots to do.'

'No rush, have a coffee if you like?' I don't want him to go. I want to hold on to this moment as long as I can. Who know when I'll see him, touch him, again. He'll be sending e-postcards not leaving Post-its. Rodney will frazzle up and die and Mabel will have cold feet for the rest of her life. 'The only thing I've got to do today is take the dress to Dave's mum's house.'

'I can give you a lift if you want?'

'Well—'

'It might help your case if he's there; you've got proof that you're with somebody else.'

I smile. We both know it's not necessary. But it's nice. 'I'm just going to give it to her straight, nobody can force me into something I don't want to do. Not even with emotional blackmail.'

'Good.' He kisses the tip of my nose.

'Though I wouldn't say no to a bit of company, and it's a heavy box for little old me to carry.' I grin at him. I just want to keep him here, with me, for as long as I can.

'Thanks for listening to me, thanks for understanding.'

I shower slowly while he Googles 'how long can you stay in Spain', 'can you leave the country during a custody battle' and stuff like that. Then we have a cup of coffee, and I pick up the box. I need to close off the old bit of my life before I start worrying about what comes next, don't I?

And I've got to get my happy face on before I see Soph and Daz's campervan tomorrow.

How the hell am I going to do that when all I can think about is that I've just had the most stupendous sex of my life, and the guy responsible is about to bugger off to Spain? If I'd thought the kiss had been an issue, I've just made it a hundred times more difficult.

Chapter Twenty-Seven

'Come in, come in, Alice. Oh, I was so pleased to hear you'd got back together again and—'

'We haven't.' I feel terrible as the smile on Dave's mum's face is replaced with confusion. But that's not my problem, is it? I can be kind, but I am not going to be weak and wishy-washy. 'I won't come in, if that's okay with you. I'm not stopping,' I say as firmly as I can.

'But...' She looks at the bag I am holding out. But doesn't take it. 'But why are you getting married if...'

'We're not getting married.' I feel like the worst nearly-daughter-in-law ever.

The smile returns. 'Ahh! I understand. Oh such a shame you don't want to, you modern girls are so independent these days, but I suppose there's nothing wrong with living together.'

'We're not living together. We've not got back together,' I add to make it clear.

'But the house? He showed me the house, it's got a

conservatory, and en suite.' I shake my head, and her smile fades. 'But it's on a lovely estate and—'

'I'm sorry. I'm sorry he didn't tell you,' I add, as it's his fault not mine that this is happening.

There is a long silence, then she folds her arms. 'He got carried away again, didn't he?' she says flatly.

Again?

'Oh dear, that boy is so impulsive.' Impulsive is not the word I'd use. Obsessive maybe, but not impulsive. 'This happened a couple of years ago.'

'It did?' I am interested, despite myself, and my best intentions to hand the dress over and leave rapidly.

'She was a lovely girl, but she said he was just too intense, he wouldn't listen, and they were too young.' She shakes her head. Now she's got over the shock she's gone on the defensive. 'You girls today want it all, don't you? You'll regret it when you're older. You'll have missed the boat.'

I stop feeling sorry for her. She won't listen. It's obviously a family trait.

'He is very fond of you. Exceedingly.'

I hold the dress out again.

'You could think it over.'

I shake my head. Honestly, I can see where he gets it from. 'We're not in love with each other.'

'Love isn't everything.'

'It's the start though.' I put the bag down on the step, seeing as she still isn't making any effort to take it.

'We split up ages ago—'

'You had a break.'

'No, we split up. I've found somebody new.' I gesture towards the car, and Jamie waves. 'I'm sorry it's been a shock for you, he really should have told you.'

As I walk back to the car my step is lighter – and not just because I'm not carrying that wedding dress, which weighed a ton.

Jamie raises a questioning eyebrow as I get in the car and I give him a discreet thumbs up, and smile.

Being with Jamie, even if we aren't dating, is totally different to being with somebody like Dave – whose whole world revolves round himself. I feel like I actually am with somebody who has my back. Who listens. Who will be there for me.

Except he won't.

The light feeling that I felt moments before fades slightly.

I mustn't let it though. This isn't about not having Jamie – this isn't even really about finally escaping from Dave. It's about me.

I don't look back as we drive away. 'Thanks for bringing me over.'

'No problem.'

I feel a twinge of pity for Dave, but it's only a tiny, tiny twinge. His mum didn't exactly slam the door, but it was closed pretty forcibly.

I'm not going to be walked all over or made to feel guilty or apologetic any more though. If I don't even trust a person enough to share my belongings, my private space, with – how can I even contemplate sharing my life with them?

We come up to the junction where Jamie will be turning right towards his home, and I will go left towards mine. 'Drop me here, it's fine, I can walk.'

'Sure? I can take you, it's no problem.'

'I'm positive,' I say firmly. 'It's the opposite direction for you.'

He slows the car, pulls to a halt and we look at each other awkwardly.

'Alice, about last night.'

'It was good,' I say primly, my hands in my lap.

'It was amazing.' He covers my hands with one of his and squeezes, so I have to look up and meet his gaze. 'Well it was for me.'

'Me too.'

'But—'

I look down at our hands. 'Sort your life out, Jamie. Sort your son out, then,' I shrug, and force the words out in as casual manner as I can, 'who knows.'

'I'm sorry, Alice, I'd give anything to be able—'

'Jamie.' I do look him in the eye then. His clear, gorgeous eyes, and know that I trust him. And I know that whatever happens between us, I don't need him as a crutch like I thought I needed Dave. I can stand on my own two feet. 'I've realized that it's not good obsessing over the things I can't change, I've got to focus on the things I can. I used to worry about Dave chucking my stuff, but it's not about him doing that, is it? I was desperately hanging on to everything I valued, to stop it disappearing. But it wasn't losing my things that really worried me deep down, it was the fact he was replacing mine with his. He was trying to change me into some other girl. It was about me, and I can change what I let people do to me, even if I can't stop them wanting to do it. If that makes sense?' It did in my head; I'm not sure now it's poured out of my mouth. 'And I can't change the fact that we can't date, but what I can do is be a good friend and help you sort things out. If you want me to?'

'Oh, Alice.' He hugs me, his words muffled in my hair, 'we must be mad wanting to keep torturing ourselves.'

'Yep.' I disentangle myself, because it's far too nice being held by him, and I'm trying my hardest to be objective about all this. Even if, deep down, I know I'm just kidding myself. It was hard enough being near him every day and fancying him like mad, when I thought he was just an annoying co-worker. Now I've had that glimmer that we could have been good together, now I know that in real life he really is the gorgeous guy I thought he might be all those years ago, I don't know if I can settle for the role of supportive friend. But I can try. 'I better get back.'

He lets me move away, puts his hand back on the steering wheel. 'See you round then?'

'I'll be expecting sticky notes to resume soon!' I smile, but it feels strained.

'You got it!' His grin is hesitant, as though he wants to say more. But I don't want him to.

I open the car door. 'Good luck with the solicitor on Monday, let me know how it goes?'

He nods, and then leans over and plants the lightest of kisses on my mouth. 'I will, my gorgeous festival girl. I will.'

Chapter Twenty-Eight

Sunday

It is really strange, but I've come back from lunch at my parents' house feeling liberated. Feeling like I know exactly what I need to do with my life – with or without Jamie.

The camper van was dinky, but cool. As I'd known it would be – why else would Sophie agree to the trip? Well apart from the obvious addition of Daz, of course.

Soph had bounced around like an excited child, opening drawers and cupboards so that we could see everything (not that there was that much).

There was a dinky fridge, already stocked with beer, and a double burner which she put pans on to demonstrate exactly what it was for. She even jiggled the frying pan to simulate frying eggs – though I'm pretty sure she's never fried an egg in her life.

Her enthusiasm brought a lump to my throat. What had

happened to my own zest for life? When did I stop having fun and taking pleasure in the little things – like a shell I'd found on the beach – rather than just collecting them as memories?

She made Daz pull down the rock and roll bed so that she could scatter it with pillows, cushions and rugs, then throw open the back door so we could imagine what it would be like lying on the bed looking out at the rolling waves crashing on the shore. Okay, we were actually looking at cars driving past the house, but we got the vision.

There were stickers all over the table, the places the camper had already visited without them – and I knew Soph would add to it in her own way.

She showed us the cupboard where they'd already stashed their rucksacks, the basket she'd got for her undies, the tray for her make-up and toiletries.

The toilet which… Well, enough said about that.

'You've not got much room for your things,' Mum had said.

'I don't have much!' Sophie laughingly replied.

'Because you borrow mine!' I'd hugged her as I'd said it, and she'd grinned. Then I did a double-take. 'Bloody hell, Soph, you've nicked my denim shorts!' How the hell did she smuggle those out of my room?

'You were distracted.' She giggled.

'No.' I shook my head and wagged a finger at her. 'It's not on, Sophie.'

'Please? Pretty please?' She clutched her hands together, pleading.

I folded my arms. In the past, I'd have backed down at this point. Not wanted to spoil the moment, cause a scene. After all, they're only shorts, and I'd get them back one day. But it isn't the past. It is now. 'You ask, Soph. Not just help yourself to stuff. It's selfish, and it's disrespectful, and how am I supposed to trust even letting you into my room if you just help yourself to things after I've said no?'

She stared at me, open-mouthed. There was silence.

A silence I wasn't going to break.

'Oh. Sorry.' She reached over, grabbed the shorts and held them out. This time she didn't have a tantrum, she didn't say it was me, that I was selfish and mean. She just handed them back. 'I am sorry, Al. I shouldn't have. It's cool, honest. You're right.'

Lucy laughed. 'Good move, Alice. They'd be unwearable by the time she gets home; she'd wear them in the sea, in crappy hole-in-the-ground toilets.'

'I won't actually go in a hole in the ground,' Soph said sensibly. 'You stand at the side and take your knickers down first.'

Lucy glared. 'Have you never heard of splashback! Anyway, you know what I mean. Alice has kept these for a reason.'

'Jamie!' Soph's eyes glinted.

I heated up like a chestnut in the embers. My cheeks were positively crackling. And I glared at Soph in a 'don't you dare say another word' way. She did a zipped mouth gesture, grinning all the time.

'Actually,' I slipped my hand through the crook of Lucy's arm. 'It's fine.' And it is. I don't need the shorts to remember Reading Festival. Maybe they need a new adventure. I hold the shorts out.

'Really?' Sophie hesitated, looked surprised.

'Really.' I nod decisively. I don't need the shorts, I just needed to be asked, not taken for granted.

'If you're really sure?'

'Honestly, am I going to have to force them on you now?' I shake my head, exasperated.

'I don't want to take advantage; I know I should have asked.'

'You should.' She took the shorts, we hugged, and I tried to stop the hot prickling of tears. 'They might bring you luck!'

Soph pulled back and winked in a very dirty way. 'Now that kind of luck I won't turn down.'

'Sophie!' chorused my mum and sisters, but we were all laughing.

I had my adventure, I fell for a gorgeous guy – our eyes didn't meet across a crowded room, our lips met in a crowded space, and I'm glad. But I think I'm learning how to let go. Some stuff needs hanging on to, some stuff doesn't.

We'd popped the top of the camper, switched on the fairy lights, spun the captain's seat, and then we'd all sat in the garden eating, drinking and swapping holiday stories.

I'd given Soph a big hug as I left. 'You're crazy you know, leaving everything behind!'

She'd hugged me harder back.

'And brave,' I whispered in her ear.

'I'm not leaving much, apart from you. I've got shit jobs,

still live at home, wear my sister's clothes.' She'd grinned. 'I'm a complete dead loss at a dead end. Nothing's ever going to change if I carry on doing the same thing, is it?'

I shook my head. 'Nope, if you carry on doing the same thing you carry on getting the same result, as they say.'

'Some things I can't do anything about, so I'm ditching them. I'm in a rut, Al, and Daz has made me see that I can do stuff. I can explore the world if I want. Anything is possible! He's so bloody positive you know, he always looks at what he can do, where he can go, not where he can't.'

'You're made for each other.' I held her tight. Whatever she thinks, she's never been in a rut, never been a dead loss. And she has always managed to look on the bright side despite the fact that holding down a decent job isn't one of her skills. Soph just needs a different type of life, and I know she'll find it. She's brave, like Darcie.

And when I headed home, I felt strangely happy, as well as sad.

I'll be sad not to have Soph around borrowing stuff, and lending stuff. Because she would always offer – I just didn't take her up on it. I guess I was scared of taking, because I'd got scared of becoming somebody else. A person someone else wanted me to be.

But now I'm not.

It's not what you've got, is it? It's who you are inside – and not letting anybody change that.

Sophie hasn't got room for much, but the look of happiness on her face today says it all. She's being her; she's doing what she wants. She is with who she wants to be with.

I've hung on to all my stuff so fiercely because I was trying to gain back control. But I have got it now. And so none of it really matters. Well, some of it does, obviously. Some of my stuff means a lot, it's about my life, memories. It is important. But I think I need to think in camper van terms. I need to decide what is important, what adds to my life, what helps me be creative at work – and I need to store away the stuff that doesn't. I don't have to chuck it. I just need to move it to one side. Because my bedroom really isn't big enough for things that don't really matter, and I've just realized that hanging on to it so tightly has actually been making me more stressed. Not less.

Like Sophie said, if you carry on doing the same thing, nothing is ever going to change. I need to start doing things differently.

I've hung on to absolutely everything, because it has connected me to the times when I felt really happy. The pre-Dave times. And now I need to start finding room for new memories. For the things that matter to me today.

In the camper van it felt freeing, in Jamie's house it felt relaxing and safe. And you know what? Neither of those places are crammed with 'stuff'.

Yeah, I do know that I need to surround myself with beautiful, meaningful things if I want to be able to do my job properly. But I don't need *everything*.

I can't blame Dave for driving me out of my home, squeezing me out of my own life – because I let him. I'd been so desperate for my own space, a space I didn't have to share with my sisters, but then I let people take it away from me.

I wasn't with Dave for that long, but in that short time he threw my life out of balance, and I didn't object; I didn't leave because it was predictable, it was familiar. It seemed safe because I felt like I had somebody to run to, but it was actually wrong, he was bad for me.

I'd felt threatened, I can see that now, because he didn't just smudge the personal boundaries like my sisters and housemates sometimes did. He tried to demolish them, rebuild them to suit himself. And I let him. And I'd over-reacted. I'd hung on to everything. Hoarded stuff in my cupboards, hoarded stuff at work.

Life is about sharing, isn't it? I'm a natural sharer, I want to give – but you have to share with the right people, you have to know when to say no, don't you? Or there's nothing left of you, nothing to call your own. You have to guard the bits that needs guarding, so that you can feel totally chilled about sharing the rest.

Saying no has never come easily to me, it's not something I've had enough practise at. If I'd learned to say no to Soph earlier then maybe I wouldn't have had to lose my rag and upset her. And if I'd learned to say no to Dave we probably wouldn't have lasted more than a couple of weeks. He would never have had chance to drive me out, and I would have made my place my home earlier.

And if Darcie hasn't been hurt, maybe I would have stood up for myself more.

And if I'd told Jamie I thought I recognized him the first day we started work at We Got Designs, who knows…

But none of that really matters, does it? What matters is

what I'm doing with those experiences, what I've learned. What matters is the way I live my life today, tomorrow.

What matters is who I let in, who I share with, where I draw the lines.

I think it's time I do to my things what I did to Dave's. Have a proper sort out.

Jamie had told me to put the things I'd tidied away back on our desk, but I've just realized; it doesn't matter.

I make myself a coffee, go up to my room then stand by the door and look around. This job needs doing systematically. I am going to work my way round the entire room and sort everything into piles. I've read enough 'declutter your life' articles to know that I need to work out which stuff can be thrown out, which things I use (or want to look at) regularly, and the things that I don't want to get rid of, but are just taking up space. The space-taking-uppers are just like Christmas decorations, aren't they? They need to be put in a box and stashed in the wardrobe – to be taken out on special occasions.

I look into my make-up box and shut it again quickly. How can I have so much? I can sort it another day, can't I? No, I can't! I've said I'm doing this today, and I am going to. Yesterday I cleared out my emotional baggage (apart from Jamie), today I am clearing out the rest.

My make-up box is a bit of a nightmare. I don't actually wear that much for work or at home, so who knew that I had three mascaras, had hung on to some midnight-blue eyeshadow that hasn't been opened since my uni days, and a glittery lipstick that probably should have a health and safety warning slapped on it.

Oh God, but if I'm going to do this, I'm going to do it properly.

I tip the contents out onto a towel on the bed and start to sort through.

Since when did I like brown lipstick?

———————

I'm exhausted by the time I drop the last half-filled notepad into a box. It's getting dark and I'm starving and feel pretty grimy. Shoving the last of the boxes into the wardrobe, I push the door closed and head for a shower.

Now there's just my feelings for Jamie that I need to deal with. I'm not sure I can shut those away quite so easily.

Chapter Twenty-Nine

Tuesday

There is no note from Jamie when I get into work on Tuesday, which hits me harder than I thought it would.

It's all well and good thinking you can sleep with a guy one day and be casual buddies the next, but doing it is different, isn't it? I guess I have the type of expectations you'd have of a boyfriend, not of a colleague.

Before the weekend, I guess I had started to rely more and more on his little notes; we had moved on from work mates to flirting. The days when I didn't hear from him had been bad enough then. But now?

He'd said he'd be back in on Monday; he'd messaged me saying he was having the morning off to talk to his solicitor.

I expected a note. Or a text. Or something.

The desk looks bare – even though when I cleared some of my stuff off, I still left the important things.

I power up the computer, tell myself to get a grip and pop out to get a proper strong coffee and a sugar-laden pastry.

I get back to find that I have several urgent emails in my inbox, and a cuddly St Bernard dog in my pending tray. How the hell am I supposed to declutter if clients keep sending adorable stuff like that?

'If that's a gift, declare it and put it in the meeting room,' snaps the dragon lady. Well that solves that problem. I apologize to the dog and relocate it, before sending a thank-you message to the lady at the dog rescue place and put her request for a couple of website tweaks to the top of my to-do list for the day.

'Alice?'

'Shit!' I've been so engrossed in work that I've managed to shut everybody else off altogether, and when somebody taps me on the shoulder, I nearly jump off my seat. 'Jamie!'

'Sorry.' His trademark grin is back. 'Thought I'd surprise you!'

'Ten out of ten for that.' I wriggle back into a safer position on my chair, then glance at the time. Wow, I hadn't realized it was nearly 1pm! I frown at him. 'What are you doing in, I thought—'

'I messaged to ask if you had time to grab a sandwich, but you didn't reply and…' He looks a bit sheepish. 'I was worried something had happened, or you were pissed at me.'

'Just busy. Some of us have to work for a living you know!' Now he's here I'm buzzing inside and the world is a wonderful place again.

'Can you drag yourself away from,' he leans in and looks at what I'm working on, 'Dippy Deb's Designer Dolls?'

'Well,' I draw the word out, 'tricky one, but, seeing as it's you.' And I grab my handbag before he has a chance to change his mind.

'So, Spain,' I say as soon as we sit down, determined to get the worst bit over first.

'Not happening.' He takes a big bite of his panini and munches silently for a few minutes. Then he wipes his mouth. 'Well not imminently. Sorry, starving. I seem to have got my appetite back!'

I grin at him. Now I know it is not imminent, I can relax and eat my own lunch. Surprisingly, I find I suddenly have an appetite as well, so we eat and drink, then he pushes his plate to one side and reaches across the table to touch the back of my hand.

'Right. I saw the solicitor.' He takes my fingers in his, and then draws back as though he's overstepped the mark.

My stomach dips. I can't help it. Being with Jamie is like being in the middle of a suspense movie. The anticipation grows and grows, then just as you get to that moment … everything stops. You're left hanging. Not sure.

I put my hands in my lap, under the table so I can feel in control. I'm the one moving them, so he can't touch them, so I can't be disappointed.

It doesn't help. I want to put them back. I want him to touch me.

'So?' I say, trying to keep my voice steady – which is easy if I keep to single syllables.

'Well first, she said that regardless of how Claire sees it, in a legal sense I'm not just some random sperm donor, I'm a parent.' He glances at me, so I nod. 'It doesn't matter what her intentions were when she found out she was preggers, things need to be done officially with all the paperwork or whatever.'

'Right.'

'So, I can make an application to court for contact, and it's Alfie's right, not hers or mine, to be able to see both his parents.'

'That's good then,' I say encouragingly. Wondering how a toddler makes a decision like that.

'She said it would be best if we can reach some kind of agreement between us, but if there's a child arrangements order then Claire can only take him out of the country for up to a month on holiday, not for ever. If she tries to take him out there without my permission permanently, then it's abduction.'

'Wow.'

'And I might be able to get a parental responsibility order

which would give me a say in all kinds of things about his upbringing. I mean,' he shrugs, 'I'm not sure how far I want to take all this, I just know I need to see him growing up. I need to be around him at least until he's old enough to know me, to remember me, then it's up to him. If he doesn't want me in his life…' His words tail off, and he stirs his empty cup.

'I'm sure he will.' I bring my hands from under the table, put one over his.

'I'd hope so, but who knows?'

'But one step at a time; at least you know she can't leave the country.'

'Not unless she's already gone. And I'm pretty sure she hasn't.' He stops stirring, relaxes a bit. 'The solicitor said that it's not as easy as it used to be to relocate, even for a mother, as it's all about the child's welfare. She said if Claire did apply then she'd have to be very careful how she does it. It could be seen by the courts as a ploy to stop me seeing him.'

'Especially if she does it now so soon after you've found out?'

'Exactly! They could think it was that, rather than a genuine intention to move because she really want to.'

'Even though she's got family out there?'

'Yep. She'd need to say it was because all her support was out there, or she'd been offered some fabulous job she couldn't get here, or something like that really. And the fact she's lived in the UK quite happily for years would definitely make it harder for her to justify it.'

'That's so positive!' I squeeze his hands. I'm so happy

for him, and a lot of the stress has already lifted from his face. He's almost back to the old teasing Jamie.

'It is.' He rubs his thumb over the back of my hand. His voice is soft. 'I need to talk to her, have a good chat and try and get her to understand that I'm not a threat, it's for Alfie.'

'You do.'

'And I have to do it before she firms up her plans. So I need to go down to Cornwall.' His gaze is direct. 'Tomorrow.'

'Sure.' It will be strange not having him around, and for a second the wild thought of booking time off work and going with him lodges itself in my brain, and then common-sense hits and tells me that I'm being ridiculous. He might want my support; he definitely doesn't want me in Cornwall with him.

'I'm so glad I've got you to talk to.' He squeezes my hand. 'Guess I'm going to have to tell my parents when I get back and have some idea how this is going to go.'

I nod. 'You probably should.'

'Not sure they'll be able to believe I'm a dad.'

We sit in silence, holding hands across the table, oblivious to the comings and goings around us as I look into the now familiar eyes.

'I'm not sure I can believe it, to be honest. I've been so totally wrapped up in being indignant, and fighting to see him, but, well…being a dad? An actual dad. What does a dad do? I haven't a clue what happens if she says I can see him.'

There's a faint look of alarm in his eyes. I don't think

he's had time to actually think about the implications of this, about what it really means for him. Let alone for us, if there ever is a chance of 'us'. But I'm starting to think there might be; I'm starting to think that this is a two-way thing between us – we rely on each other, we want to talk, share our problems. And that's something, isn't it? Really something.

'You'll be a good dad,' I say softly, and hope with all my heart that he's going to get what he wants. I don't want his heart to be broken.

Chapter Thirty

From Cornwall, with love

I hoard digital things, as well as actual, physical things. I hardly ever delete emails, just in case they are going to come in useful. I hate deleting photos – even if they're a bit crap, slightly out of focus, or I've got two more identical ones. I keep my messages because I like to flick back through them. I keep every 'ah' moment I can.

I have made a start in tidying them up though. I have gone through and unsubscribed from every website where I haven't opened the last twenty emails from them. It is just so stressful knowing you've got 1,283 unread messages.

I've deleted all the emails with offers that have passed, and all the Dave ones.

I've backed up all my photos then started to go through and delete ones that really are rubbish – though that bit is taking a LOT of time, because I get caught up looking at them and remembering.

I've not deleted any of the messages from Jamie though. Or the many photos he has sent while he's been in Cornwall.

Hey Festival Girl, how's it going? A bit weird being here and knowing you're at our desk without me. Seems to be going okay. When I got here, Alfie was a bit quiet, weighing me up. I don't blame him, I'm nervous as hell myself and I'm supposed to be the grown-up! Mum used to say I did that, just watched people quietly as though I was working out whether I liked them or not. I wish I knew what he was thinking. J x

I know I'm biased, but Alfie is a little belter. When I tell Mum she'll either kill me for not telling her sooner or be so totally in love she'll forget all about me. J xx

OMG, Alice, I can see why you looked round my place with that look on your face after I told you I had a child. Tidy and kids don't naturally go together, do they? Unless you spend half your life putting things away. Every surface is covered with beakers, bibs and Lego blocks. Miss seeing your bits and bobs, and you J xx

Claire said her mum came over to see her last week. She couldn't believe that she'd not told me about Alfie earlier, she'd just kind of assumed that his dad must have been a one-night stand with a total stranger, or a tosser who'd run for the hills as soon as she told him I was preggers. She read her the riot act. Miss you J xxx

I'd forgotten how much I used to love Lego. x

Some of the messages made me laugh, some I smiled at because in my head I could see him sitting on the floor sticking building blocks together like a big kid, and some melted my heart. I got to discover a new Jamie through his messages when he was down in Cornwall. A different Jamie to the one I'd got to know through Post-it notes.

I watched him playing quietly today and it really hit me, Alice. He's mine, part of me. My son. It's already too late to walk away, he's in my heart, part of me. I could never give up on him. I need to know him. I need to watch him grow up. I want to buy him a train set, play football with him, take him to matches. Teach him to drive.

I told Claire that the solicitor said we should try and sort this out ourselves and she said that's what her mum had said. But she's not heading back here. She said this place means a lot to her, that she'd always dreamed of moving there to bring her kids up. It's one of the few places she remembers her mum being really happy after her dad walked out on them. She said she misses the gang, which is why she came back for a few days, but she reckons this is a better place to bring Alfie up. I reckon she's right, it's ace. Jxx

I had to reply to that one. *Sounds like you're having fun! You won't want to come back.* I was fishing, definitely fishing. But what if he doesn't?

*Oh I will. I'll be back, you can't get rid of me that easily. I
know you can't cope with Mabel and Rodders on
your own!*

Cheeky!

*I'll be back soon. But if my son is going to grow up largely
without me, then I guess here is the right choice. Oh my
god, he's drawing on the wall, what is that he's got? Oh
bugger. Got to go.*

It could be worse!

*It has been worse. Yesterday he threw up on my laptop, it
was so gross. Who knew a child this size could harbour
stomach contents that vast? And with bits. I will be
forever finding bits between the keys.*

And there were the days when he found out what being
a dad could mean.

*Shit, she wants me to look after him. On my own. How do
I do that? She obviously doesn't realize that the only thing
I've ever been responsible for is a plant. I've not even had
a goldfish. But hey, men do it all the time, don't they?
How hard can it be to stop a toddler from screaming?
J xxx*

*Apparently, it is quite hard to stop a toddler screaming
second time round. First time, the funny faces I pulled*

worked a treat. He wasn't falling for it a second time. You knew, didn't you? J xx

Soz, Alice, I know it's only 7.30pm, but I need to sleep. Looking after toddlers is exhausting.

Then there were the ones that made me sure he would come back.

Claire asked about you. I told her I'd always had you at the back of my mind since that very first kiss. I've measured every other kiss against it. She remembered you, said she knew I'd fancied you from the first day she started work. How did she work that one out? Why am I such a dickhead? J xxx

Some of his calls I wish I could save, some of the time I wished I was closer so that I could hug him.

'He said Dada today! I could have cried, I could feel the tears welling up at the back of my eyes, my throat constricting. She said she'd told him, he knew, 'cos he needed to. But it's not enough, is it, Alice? I don't know if I can forgive her or not. I feel a little bit sad, no actually I'm gutted that I've missed out on so much of Alfie's life already to be honest. I can never get that back, can I?'

The next day he was more upbeat when he rang.

'I don't want to count my chickens as my mum would say, but I've got a good feeling about this. I think we can work it out. Claire does love Alfie to bits, which is what's really important. We're going to draw something legal up, like my solicitor recommended. But it looks like we agree we don't want to go to court if we can avoid it.'

'That's brilliant.'

'God, I feel so far away from you. I wish you were here, and I could share this moment with you properly. I can't wait to get home and talk to you properly.'

He wants to share the moment with me. A moment that's really important in his life. That's the type of sharing I need in my life.

Then there was the message I'd been waiting for.

I wish I could capture Alfie's chuckle, it's amazing. Nothing like the pure joy of a happy child, is there? I've told Claire I don't want her to move. This is an amazing place to bring him up and I'll still get to see him. We've drafted an agreement out with the help of a local solicitor, and it's been emailed over to mine. I'm heading home, Alice! Can't wait to see you J xxx

And the email I've kept and backed up. Never to be deleted.

I miss you, Alice. Wish you were here with me. I miss your notes if you don't leave them on the desk, I missed you the moment you left me after dropping off that wedding dress, I missed you the moment we finished lunch after I told you I was coming to Cornwall.

I guess I've been consumed with Alfie ever since I found out about him. Partly because I'd been deceived, partly because it seemed unfair, partly because I hated the thought of him never knowing me – of me never knowing him. But I've not been fair to you. I've trampled over your feelings. The girl I've spent years dreaming about.

The girl I fell in love with as I watched her dance towards me – only seeing me at the last moment. As I'd seen the look in your eyes when you did, the taste of your lips beneath mine I swore you were the one for me.

I've done a good job the last couple of years pretending I wasn't bothered. How could I treat you like that? I hope you can forgive me, cos I'm not sure I ever want to let you go again. I want you in my life.

From Cornwall, with love.
Jamie xxx

Chapter Thirty-One

Friday

The two weeks Jamie has been down in Cornwall seems like years – even though he's rung me most days and sent me all those photos of Alfie crying, Alfie laughing and Alfie covered in ice cream. There have also been photos of seagulls, cliffs, beaches and giant Cornish pasties. But the Alfie pictures are the sweetest.

Even with the calls and messages though it has seemed weird going into work and there never being a message from him. He has seemed so far away.

Those Post-it notes had been the highlight of the day for a while; reading them, and even trying to come up with a witty response had meant I'd rushed in each morning to give myself extra time before the office filled up and it all got too chaotic.

Since he's been away there's been no sense of urgency, no real need.

Today though it is Friday, and Jamie messaged last night to say he was home. Knackered, but back.

He might not have made it in this morning, but it doesn't matter. He is back! The day he went I'd felt different. I'd felt sad, I'd felt that any moment he could leave my life for ever but gradually, over the last fortnight, things have changed.

Our chats have gotten longer, our messages more intimate, things have shifted. I've realized I'm missing him so much not because I'm half afraid it could be over for good any moment before it's properly started, but because I know he'll come back. To me. To us.

Okay, there's no knowing exactly what that means, but I know it means something. I'm sure of it. And if it goes, as Soph would say, tits up, then at least I'll know we gave it a go, this thing between us. This spark that was there the very first moment we saw each other and has never quite gone away.

It is 1pm when I waltz in the office, humming to myself. I am practically skipping –wondering if I'll cross paths with Jamie – when the dragon lady leaps out of her office and bars my way.

'I need to talk to you about dildos. Now! In my office!' She practically drags me through the doorway while I'm still trying to work out what she's talking about. '*This* is not funny. I'm all for complimentary products, but whatever you have said to them, they have got the wrong idea.' She glares at me. If she was actually a dragon, I would be on fire, severely frazzled. As it is, just the strength of the stare is making me feel a bit queasy.

'I'm sorry, I—'

'Look!' she hisses.

Her whole desk is covered with multicoloured dildos and vibrators, and every sex aid you can think of – and some I have never, ever imagined. And some of them are enormous. They make me clench my thighs together.

'It's nothing to do with—'

'What the fuck did you tell them, Alice? We wanted to road test the whole range?'

I'm also clenching my teeth, trying not to laugh. 'I'm not sure road test is the right—' I stop talking. Her gaze is withering.

'You will have to move them, get rid of them, take them home, I don't care!'

Take them home? Is she mad?

'But we aren't allowed to take…' I'm sure she is growling. 'This is nothing to do with me.'

'You're designing the website!'

'No, I'm not!' Haha, I realize what is going on now. 'I swapped accounts with Tina. This is hers, I've got Doggie Bites.'

'Oh.' She folds her arms. 'Right, well, if you see her tell her I want to see her. Immediately.'

I glance at the time as I stomp out of her office, head held high as I am not responsible for the surfeit of sex aids. Though I was tempted by the gold 'bullet' which did look rather tasteful. And cool.

It's late. Even if Jamie was here this morning, he will have left by now. He'll think I'm working from home. I feel a bit deflated.

There's no sign of Tina, which is lucky for her. Or unlucky. It might be just what she wants on a Friday afternoon.

My desk looks odd even from a distance, and as I get closer I realize it is because there are additions. There are sticky notes of all colours, and... Oh my god.

Mabel is wearing a bikini. A bright-blue one. She has a note stuck to her foot. I peel it off and read. *It's a no socks time of year. Thought she should be colour coordinated with her feet.*

Grinning, I sling my handbag under the desk and sit down. Oh my, it is so good to have Jamie back, even if he's not actually here.

I've missed him so much.

I open my emails, just so I look like I'm working if the dragon lady comes by, and then pick up the nearest note.

Top drawer of your pedestal

I open the drawer tentatively – the Jamie of old would have put something in there that launched itself out at me. Nothing springs out. I open it wider. Next to my notepad is a pebble, washed smooth by the sea, with a large 'A' painted unevenly on it. I pick it up and uncover a note. *A present from Alfie, from one A to another. J x*

My throat constricts as I run my finger over the smooth stone. Oh my god, does this mean he's actually told his son about me? I carefully place it in my bag. I don't want to leave this here; I want it at home where I can look at it whenever I want.

In Rodder's pot! says the next note. In the pot, next to my fossil there's a little jar, full of coloured sand with a tag that says, 'Love from Cornwall'. On the back he's written: *Another memento from Cornwall, thought our desk was looking a bit bare. J xx*

Check your emails, look like you're working! is the last note. So I do.

The email from him is brief and to the point.

After-work drink? Missed you J x

I feel so giddy; my hands are trembling and I can hardly type but I manage to message him back, then, still smiling, start to work my way through my other emails.

I must concentrate, I must, I must, I must. If I don't get cracking, I'll be here all night, and no way am I going to miss seeing him this evening and finding out how it went.

And I'm not going to miss touching him, smelling him, hugging him.

My mobile beeps and I pick it up, expecting a message from Jamie, but it's from Soph.

How did it go? Is he back? Is he going to Spain? Speak to me!!!! S xx

I grin. She's always been impatient and demanding. She's also always been lovely, and she knows I've missed him.

Not seen him yet, but he's back, he left notes. A x

And?

From the notes it sounds good! Seeing him later A x

The notes are good, they're happy. He sounds happy.

Keep me informed! We've just come off Le Shuttle! Oo la la!! Epic! S xx

It's accompanied by a selfie of her and Daz driving along in the camper van, grinning broadly. Then a shot out of the window of them following the other vehicles off the train onto French soil.

So, after a week or so of trying out camper van life in the UK, my little sis has crossed the border, the sea, off on her big adventure.

But Jamie has come back to me from his. I think. I realize my fingers are crossed as I type a reply to my sister.

Awesome, bring back lots of wine and send photos! Need to work, will update you later. Love you A x

I go and get a fresh cup of coffee from the machine, then get my head down.

'Somebody looks happy!' says Sal as she passes by, and I realize I'm smiling as I type away.

I've been clock-watching ever since I read Jamie's email and, with ten minutes to go, I'm feeling so fidgety I can't sit still and, rather than working, I'm pretending to tidy things up. Office supplies have never been so tidy. Our pen pot is looking particularly well organized, with our pens and pencils alternating – instead of his on one side, and mine on the other, and I'm just about to turn my monitor off when an email lands.

Disaster. So sorry, Alice, my parents have just arrived on my doorstep. They never come here, and they never, ever turn up anywhere unannounced. Unless they've just discovered they've got a grandson. Made the mistake of breaking the news to them on my drive back up from Cornwall. I could sneak over to yours later? Am sure they won't stay too late. J xx

Is it mean and inconsiderate to hate his parents right now?

Sure. I'm yours whenever! A x

I realize about ten seconds after I hit send that that wasn't exactly subtle. But I don't care!

There's an instant ping on my mobile and I grab it. It isn't a message from Jamie, it's from Lucy.

HELP!! My waters just broke. Can you come over and watch the twins? I'll pay you in as much gin and chocolate as you want. I'll take you for a spa weekend (once I can walk again).

She couldn't walk properly for quite a while after the twins arrived.

I'm desperate! Mum and Dad aren't answering, and Darcie won't. PLEASE!!

To be fair to Darcie, last time she babysat the twins they painted her handbag and filled it with worms. It was a very expensive designer handbag that she'd been waiting for *for evah* and had owned for literally four hours. She'd left it on display on the kitchen table, so that it could be admired. A bit rash really, knowing Leo and Brad.

Of course I can. Be there in fifteen, can you hang on that long?? Xx

What else can I say? 'Jamie has just got back, and I've got to see him before I explode with need'? Yeah, right.

Can she hang on that long, though? When your waters break does it mean the baby could pop out any minute, second time around? Second babies come quicker, don't they? Bugger, bugger, I better hurry up.

You're amazing. Dan's getting my stuff, Dee said she'll wait in for you as long as it isn't going to be more than 30 minutes as she's got an appointment. Love you!!

Well she can still text, that's promising. She can't be having contractions from hell if she can type. Dee, Lucy's neighbour, probably hasn't got anything of the sort though –nobody likes looking after the twins for more than thirty minutes.

Love you too! Can't wait to meet the new addition!! Alice x

Sugar, sugar, sugar, hope I'm not going to meet it landing on the living room floor just as I walk in. I try not to panic, but I'm multi-tasking and turning off my computer as I message.

At least her timing as far as my office hours goes is impeccable. Total rubbish timing as far as my potential love life is concerned.

Shit, shit, shit. I can't believe it! How can this happen when I am *so* close to getting my eyes, my hands, on him again?

I message Jamie as I wait for the lift.

Bugger, Luce just messaged. Got to babysit the twins, her waters have broken! Can you believe it??? I was so looking forward to a catch-up. A x PS Are your parents over the moon, or on the warpath?

I hit 'send' and wonder how Lucy would feel about me bribing Dee to stay a bit longer? Nope, let's face it, Dee has known the twins since they were born. She's never going to fall for that – no amount of money (not that I can afford much) is going to work. Or inviting Jamie along? Hmm not sure on that one. I'd been looking forward to being reunited under slightly more intimate conditions than the twins throwing chicken nuggets over our heads.

You're kidding? Wow – hope it goes okay.

I wonder if he means for me, or for Lucy?

Keep me updated. Sorry, can't apologize enough about the

parents though. I can't believe they're here! Over the moon is an understatement – they've brought toys, bubbly, clothes, the works. Not sure when they'll leave. How about we catch up on the phone when they do?

That is a lovely thought, but unless Leo and Brad are asleep, they won't give me a minute's peace. He'll be chatting to them not me; it will be as romantic as meeting up in the baboon enclosure at a zoo.

Then meet tomorrow? Picnic?? Looks like it's going to be a nice day J x

It *is* going to be a nice day, whatever the weather. I'm sure it is. Even eating stale sausage rolls under an umbrella with a gale force wind blowing my hair in my face would be nice. Though I don't mean for one moment that I can imagine him bringing stale pastry items.

Picnic sounds great! Sorry, got to dash, will message you later A xx

Chapter Thirty-Two

Saturday

'Door for you!' bellows Harry. I was already on my way down, but he beat me to it. 'It's the okay one.'

Haha, the okay one. I just realize that I have not thought about (or seen) the not-okay one since I returned his mother's bridal wear. 'On my way.' I'm already breathless and all I've done is dive out of my room.

Oh boy. It's the more-than-okay one. Jamie is standing at the bottom of the stairs when I hurtle down and, wow, does he look good. Would it be wrong to jump on him? Cornwall must have suited him. Or maybe it was Alfie as well.

'Thanks, Harry,' I pant out, trying to sound casual and failing miserably. He waves in acknowledgement. He's got a bacon butty in his other hand, and his wellies on, so he must be heading out to do some work. Though I hardly notice, I can't take my eyes off Jamie.

I've seen him in work gear, when he's always looked

good but a bit of an everyday guy, I've seen him in shorts, sexy and chilled, I've seen him in all kinds. But today, in tight jeans, chunky leather belt and white T-shirt, his hair just flicking over his ears, the hint of a kiss curl on his forehead, he looks as hot as hell.

He could carry off a cowboy hat and boots right now, and not look a prat or a poser. He'd just look perfect.

'Hey,' he says, and for a moment I feel shy, standing there drinking him in.

'Hi!' I squeak back. Still staring, hesitating.

He's always looked good to my eyes, but it takes me a moment to work out why he looks even better than normal. He looks, as Mum would say, 'well'.

The tan suits him, but he looks brighter, less stressed. He looks totally chilled, at ease. And he's got the biggest grin on his face I've ever seen. I think he's pleased to see me.

'Come here, stranger!' Then he opens his arms, and every bit of hesitation goes. I'm in there. No invite necessary.

I expect him to give me a quick hug, but this is more than that, this is one major, hang-on bear hug, and he plants a smacker straight on my mouth. 'Too much?'

'Never.' I look up at him and grin back.

'You ready to go?' I nod, and he finally releases his grip on me, takes my hand in his. 'Come on then.'

'Where?' I can't stop smiling. It is just so good to see him, I didn't realize how much I'd missed him until now. If he's only here for a day, a week, a month and then he's heading off to Cornwall, or Spain, or wherever, I don't care. I decided while he was away that I was going to make the most of every moment of my life if I can. I'm going to take things as they come. We can work this out.

'Up the bridlepath to that bench on the hill?'

I nod again. We went up there just before he left. It's a sunny spot, with views over the farms, the village below.

We don't speak as we walk. We hold hands and the warmth of his in mine is reassuring, each time our shoulders bump we glance at each other and smile.

———

Jamie shrugs the rucksack off his shoulders, pulls out a rug and lays it down on the grass a few yards in front of the bench, and pulls me down beside him.

His lips are firm and dry as they meet mine, and I close my eyes so that I can drink him in. The taste of him, the feel of him as I cling on. The warmth of his breath, the heat of his touch.

'I missed you,' he says softly, when he finally lifts his mouth from mine. His hand still cradling my face.

'I missed you too,' I whisper back.

For a moment we sit on the rug, our thighs lightly touching, my heart rate gradually dropping to near-normal.

'Thanks for the presents,' I say, and our gazes meet again. I feel like a teenager again, on a first date.

He smiles, a soft smile not his boyish grin. 'I thought the desk was starting to look a bit bare, after your tidy-up.'

'Mabel is very excited about her bikini.' I hesitate, and then decide I have to say what's been on my mind. 'Jamie, are you sure you should have told Claire about me? She's not, well,' I don't want to sound mean, if she is being genuine, 'tricking you and then when it goes to court—' I mean, Jamie is normally quite savvy, he's not daft. But he's so desperate to see Alfie, that maybe he's not seeing things straight.

'I wondered the same at first, but she's not. She wants Alfie to be happy, she wants me to be happy, and she knows you're nice not some screwball.' I raise an eyebrow. 'We drafted an agreement. She's not going to go to Spain, not yet anyway, her mum gave her a bollocking for even thinking about it.'

'Really, her mum did?'

'Yeah, total. She told her she wasn't being fair on me.'

'Wow. And you don't think she'll come back here?'

'Nope.' He shakes his head, his gaze soft as he squeezes my hand. 'She loves it in Cornwall, and I don't blame her, it's a fantastic place. So, I mean, well, how do you feel about spending summers down there?'

I stare at him, trying to get this straight in my head. Be sure I'm not getting over excited about nothing. My pulse is racing, and there's a fluttering in my stomach, but I don't know if I dare believe what I'm thinking.

'What exactly—'

'I've missed you, Alice.' He puts his hand over mine. 'Really missed you. I've had loads of time to think. It was easier to ignore how I felt when I was seeing you every day in the office. Is that totally odd, or does it make sense?'

I nod. I do know what he means. When we were in the office every day, I fancied him like mad, but managed to tell myself it meant nothing. I could somehow keep my feelings under wraps. We were just colleagues. He teased; I shook my head at his rubbish jokes and pretended he was a prat.

It changed when we weren't seeing each other.

'I know how odd it sounds, it's weird, but once we were swapping notes things changed.' He is studying my face intently.

'I know.' It was more intimate somehow.

Notes are easier – notes you say things, notes you're more you. You drop your defences.

'Alice, I know I've cocked up, I know I just pushed you away because of Alfie, but—'

'Alfie's important.' I turn my hand over, curl my fingers into his. 'The most important thing. You need to be part of his life.'

'I'd like you to be part of his life as well, Alice, if you'd like to. But, well,' he lets go of my hands and runs his fingers through his hair. 'Look, the reason I've not said this, apart from not knowing if I can see him, is, well…'

'What?' I prompt, because he's floundering, and I'm scared of what he's going to say.

He looks me straight in the eye. 'I nearly said something on the phone, but I know you need space, I know you've always had to share, and your life's been crowded, and the last thing you need is a kid. Somebody else's kid.' He pauses. 'Picking everything up, your stuff.'

'Sometimes I need space,' I say carefully. 'But you were right when you said the chaos suits me. I do like to be surrounded by people, by things going on, even if I don't say much sometimes. When you and Soph left it kind of hit me how much.' I look straight at him. 'I don't mind sharing;

I don't want to put my stuff under lock and key that isn't how I want to live at all. I don't need to; I just need to stand up for myself.' He nods. 'I'm working out what my boundaries are,' I say softly. 'I want you to be inside them though.'

'I want to be there too,' he says, his voice so low and intimate it's like pillow talk. 'I want you to be part of Alfie's life and mine.'

'I'd like that too,' I say simply. 'Except I do need to know something.' He raises an eyebrow. 'What does the S stand for, your middle name?' It's been niggling me since he wrote that contract. I'm a saddo, I've got to admit I've dug it out and stared at it, and held it, on a regular basis while he's been away.

He chuckles. 'Nosey! You'll take the piss if I tell you, everybody does!'

'I had to put up with you taking the piss out of me in the office for ages, so I think it's fair!'

'I didn't!' he says, then relents. 'Sorry, I wasn't really taking the piss, I just liked to tease you. It was my way of getting your attention without me having to admit to myself that I couldn't stop fancying you.'

'So?'

He raises his eyebrows, purses his lips and shakes his head. 'Silas.'

'Silas?'

'Stop it!'

I'm trying not to smile, but it's difficult. 'Where's that come from?'

'Well,' he draws out the word, 'it means someone who

belongs in the forest because…' There's a hint of pink along his cheekbones.

'Your parents, they, you…'

He nods. 'I was the longed-for son and so my sane and sensible parents got so carried away they needed to have a constant reminder of where it happened.'

I'm trying really, really hard to keep the laughter in and I'm managing it. Until unexpectedly he grins, then chuckles. I can't hold it in any longer. It's not really that funny, but I guess all the heightened emotions, all the anticipation, all the worry bubbles over and for a moment we both laugh helplessly.

Jamie sobers up first and shakes his head at me. 'Unbelievable, I trust you with my deepest, darkest secrets and this is what I get. I need a drink!'

Then he reaches into his rucksack and pulls out plastic glasses and a bottle of rosé. 'Pink!' He grins. We silently toast each other, still smiling, and then he pulls out the rest of the picnic.

Not a stale sausage roll in sight.

'So it did go okay then with Claire?'

'It did. I guess things could change, but for now I think it's going to work.' He munches for a while. 'She's a good mum. Whatever I thought of her, she really loves him. Oh hey, I nearly forgot.' He delves into the pocket of his rucksack and pulls something out, holds his hand over mine and lets it fall.

It's a conker. I frown.

'You said you were going to bring one into work to keep the spiders away,' he says softly.

I'm still confused. And then he opens his hand so that I can see he's still holding another one.

'I found a shell with two in just after Reading Festival. They fell early that year, and,' he smiles at me shyly, 'they were nestled perfectly together, meant to be, and it just made me think of you.'

I blink at him.

'So I kept them, because I thought maybe one day…'

Wow, this is an eye-opener. 'And then the time never seemed right?'

'No, the time never seemed right. Until now.'

'Thank you.' I close my fingers around it. Not sure what else to say. Jamie never ceases to amaze me. Surprise me.

He puts his arm around me, and I rest my head on his shoulder. Staring down the valley, the sun warming my skin.

'Are you sure you can stand my mess as well as Alfie's?' I ask, glancing up at him. Wanting to be sure.

'Of course, you're my gorgeous clutter bug.' he says and leans forward to kiss the tip of my nose.

'But I thought you weren't that keen on clutter.'

'I never said that! And anyway, you wouldn't be you without your stuff.'

'It's not a deal-breaker?'

He chuckles. 'No, but your Manchester City obsession might be!'

'Ah, I need to talk to you about that. Dad isn't impressed about having an enemy in our midst, he'll be determined to convert you.'

'No chance.' He kisses the top of my head. 'Some things

are non-negotiable.' He sighs dramatically, and I wonder what's coming next. 'I suppose I better confess now, rather than later.'

'What, another confession?'

'A terrible one! My sister is married to one of the players.'

'No shit?'

'No shit,' he says solemnly. 'Think it will be a problem?'

'Could be,' I say, looking down to hide my smile. 'Might not be able to get past something that major. It makes you winning the Chocs'n'Cheese account by sneaky means fade into significance, so we'll have to see how it goes.'

'What do you mean, sneaky means?' he says, pretending to be affronted.

'Playing the "my dad knows your dad" line!'

He chuckles, then rolls me onto my back and leans over me. His eyes glinting, dimples at the side of his mouth.

'He did!' he says. 'Sometimes the end justifies the means, the freebies were un-be-lievable! Cheese, wine, chocolates to die for.'

I try and punch him in the ribs, but he's too quick for me. His hands grab my wrists and he's kissing my neck and then his mouth is on mine and I can't fight any longer. I crane up, hungry for more kisses, deeper kisses, hungry for him.

When we stop kissing, we're breathless. I want him so much my voice is shaky when I speak. 'You can't get out of it like that.'

'Oh no? I'll have to try harder then.' He kisses my neck again, and this times it is gentle, sensuous, not passionate and demanding. Then he pauses and looks down into my eyes. 'We can make this work, can't we?'

I smile. 'I think so.' I've never felt more sure in my life of anybody, anything.

'When did you know?' He asks, sitting up and pulling me beside him. 'That first kiss?'

'That first kiss.'

He reaches into his back pocket, pulls out a crumpled note. 'This is when I really knew there was no way I could fight it.' He smooths it out. It is the sticky note I left saying he'd make a brilliant dad one day. 'I took it home and stuck it on my mirror to remind me. It helped keep me going.'

'I thought I'd upset you with that one,' I admit.

'Upset me? Why?'

'You know, talking about kids, getting too personal.'

'No way. You weren't going to get rid of me that easily.' He chuckles. 'How's this for personal?' Then brings up a photo on his phone. It is a plant. 'My sister sent this over with my parents. Said something about me needing the practice looking after something and not killing it, cheeky mare. I told you we had a love–hate relationship.' He puts his mobile down. Then puts his arm around me again. 'Our first plant – what do you think we should call it?'

'I think you'll find it's our second,' I say primly. 'You'll be upsetting Rodney.'

'And we don't want that, do we?' he says. 'I think I feel faint with all this responsibility. Come here, I need a lie down.' He topples over and pulls me back onto the rug with him, and slips his warm hands under my T-shirt, sending a tingle down my spine. 'You did say it's always quiet up here, absolutely nobody comes this way, didn't you?' His voice is husky, a rough edge that makes me want him more than ever.

'Very,' I say, shivering as his thumb brushes over my nipple. 'I've never ever seen anybody else here.' And I let him pull me down until I can feel the length of his body beneath mine. 'I always wondered why somebody put a bench here.' And then I can't say anything else because his hands are stroking my body, his legs are wrapped around mine and he's kissing me.

Acknowledgments

It has been a very strange eighteen months or so, and harder than ever for most of us to concentrate, find inspiration, and plough on. I guess I've come to appreciate more than ever all the acts (large and small) of love, courage, and kindness.

Awesomeness comes in many forms, and I feel incredibly lucky to be surrounded by, loved, and supported by, so many wonderful people. I can't thank you all individually here, but I hope you know who you are.

When I submitted my first novel to the fabulous Charlotte Ledger – a lovely person, inspiring publisher, and brilliant editor – I never in my wildest dreams thought that a few years on more than half a million copies of my books would have been sold. I am so incredibly lucky to have found you, Charlotte, thank you so much for taking a chance on me and for everything you have done (and continue to do) for me!

To the awesome Amanda Preston. The best thing I ever

did was hound you until you caved in and agreed to be my agent! Thank you!

Special thanks to all the lovely people (and fellow clutter bugs) on Facebook who helped me shape Alice's desk, and her character. All your suggestions inspired me, but particular mention goes to Christine Davis, Suzie Tullett, Kathryn Coules, Jennifer Gordon, Ashleigh Scott, Clare Wall, Sarah Bennett, Tanya Jayne Phillips, and last but not least Sonia Bradley.

To my writing buddies, in particular Mandy Baggott and Jane Linfoot, who are always there for me with a supportive word – thank you! And to my family, who have had their own individual struggles over the past months, I love you all and couldn't do this without you.

And finally, thank *you* for picking up this book – I hope you enjoy the story!

Zara x